Three Rode The Trail

Richard Lear

DEDICATION

This book is dedicated to four special women: my wife Debbie who was there at the beginning and never let me quit; Sheryl Wilson whose friendship, belief and tough love remain with me in spirit; and Amber Moyer and Sheryil Griffin for reading early drafts of the book when I needed objective eyes and opinions

PART I

BEFORE

CHAPTER 1

San Luis Valley, Colorado, 1878

He was going to shoot that dog. It had no business barking and howling right under his window every goddamn morning. OK, it wasn't right under his window, but it was loud enough to be right under his window. It didn't matter that was the mayor's dog. Filled with self-importance, it had appointed itself town watchdog, and duty started at 3:30 A.M. every goddamn morning. Christ, not even roosters were up this early.

Sheriff Yulin Temple remained in bed. He had every intention of shooting that dog for disturbing the peace—*his* peace. A .45 Smith & Wesson Schofield nestled in his hand, which rested on top of his chest whenever he slept. But the loud report of the gunshot inside the small room would set his ears to ringing something fierce. It would be worse than the barking and howling of that dog outside the window. Tomorrow he'd give Mayor Chet Carson the word that it would be that goddamn dog's last day on earth. Tomorrow? That didn't sound right but it was still dark outside, so it had to still be last night. He'd have to think on it.

The sheriff's house was right next door to the mayor's house. The mayor's front porch might as well have been right under his window for how loud the dog's barking was rattling the insides of his ears. And then, after barking and howling all night, the dog slept throughout the day.

Mayor Chet Carson had bought the dog before the election five months ago. He said walking a dog made him look "mayorly"—meaning respectable. It was typical of the mayor's lack of original thought that he named the dog Rex. He actually hated dogs but felt obligated to keep this one after it helped win him the election. Carson kept the dog chained to the front porch of his house except for the exceedingly rare occasions when he took it for a walk. In fact, the dog left the porch only four times a year: to accompany the mayor in the parades for New Year's Day, Independence Day, Thanksgiving Day, and Christmas Day. At his Inauguration Day swearing-in ceremony, the dog stood on the platform between the mayor and Mrs. Carson.

The earlier actions of Sheriff Yulin Temple had conformed to his established routine. Starting at 9:30 P.M., he began his nightly rounds at the north end of town, finishing up inside the Silver Strike Saloon within fifteen minutes. After the saloon closed at 2 A.M., he made sure there was less liquor to put away for the coming business day. Finally collapsing into bed thirty minutes later, he was awakened after an hour of unsettled sleep by the barking and howling of his canine next-door neighbor.

Hell, he thought, I might as well get up since I sure won't be getting back to sleep again. Several times now, he had ordered Carson to keep the dog indoors, but the mayor insisted the dog's presence helped keep the town quiet. Quiet my ass, he thought. Not in the part of town where I live. He considered sleeping in an empty jail cell in his office. He had slept there once, but the backache he woke up with was far worse than the sleep he lost to the vociferous dog.

"Hell, I might as well get up since I sure won't be getting back to sleep-- again!" he said, shouting aloud. With the Schofield in hand, he got out of bed and walked over to the wash basin, still filled with dirty soapy water from yesterday morning. Well, it would just get dirtier and soapier today. He laid the revolver on the wooden stand upon which the basin rested and grabbed a bar of soap. As he washed his face, he looked in the mirror. A pair of baggy tired dark-rimmed eyes looked back. Eyes of deep blue, at one time sharp and clear—and described by some as cold—marred now by broken red tendrils in the corners.

Yulin Temple was fifty years old but looked older. His thick mane of hair, once jet-black, was now white streaked with black, matching his untrimmed, drooping moustache and long sideburns. Only his eyebrows remained black, which accentuated the whiteness of the hair. Reva usually cut his hair every spring, summer and fall. This past winter, his hair had grown to the length where he liked it. Because of this, he was putting off the haircut, even though spring had arrived almost a month ago.

Yulin let Reva trim his hair because he didn't trust barbers—at least not the one in town. Macdonald "Mac" Sampson, besides being the barber in town, was also its occasional surgeon. Yulin worried Sampson might get confused, performing the wrong service with him trapped in the chair.

There was one other "barber" in town. Luann, who kept a room on the second floor of the Silver Strike Saloon, sold her favors outright to single men, and sold "haircuts" to the married ones. The married men, including Mayor Carson, would claim to their wives they had been to Sampson's barbershop when they had actually partaken of Luann's unadvertised two-for-one deal.

Yulin's darkly tanned face had more creases in it than the leather wallet he carried in the back pocket of his pants. He wasn't proud of that face. When he'd been a young man, his hard, chiseled features had gotten him quite a few free nights in brothels. After he had married Lillian, she would tell him that she hadn't deserved such a good-looking man. Now, the years of riding the range had aged him, helped by the cigarettes he rolled throughout the day. Reva told him that he was still a good-looking man. "Still," she had said. That was like saying Gramps was old but could still get around.

He left enough soap on his face to shave with. When he finished, he looked for a towel, but remembered he still hadn't found the towel he'd lost the previous week. He lifted his shirttails to wipe the last remnants of soap from his face, then tucked the shirttails back in and combed his hair. Taking a last look at his face in the mirror, he picked up the gun, walked back to his bed and flopped down. To hell with the goddamn dog, he thought, and went back to sleep.

CHAPTER 2

It was ten o'clock in the morning when he opened his eyes. Carson's dog had stopped barking, and the quiet had woken him up. He sat up, swung his legs over the side of the bed, and placed his stocking feet on the floor. He shoved the Schofield into the holster on the small bedside table. Once again, he had fallen asleep wearing his pants, still belted around his waist. Looking down, he didn't see any noticeable dirt or stains so he decided they would do for another day.

His boots hung upside down on the bedposts at the foot of the bed. No matter how drunk he was before he fell into bed, he always made sure the boots hung upside down. Even though he had been sleeping indoors for the past four years, he still followed the open range safeguard of keeping boots upside down. This ensured no rattlesnake had sought refuge inside one of them during the night. He lifted each boot up from its bedpost perch, shaking it to satisfy himself that no nocturnal squatters had taken up residence while he had slept. Sitting on the bed, he pulled the boots on, lowering the cuffs of his black pants down over them.

Looking down again, he decided he should change his shirt and unpinned the tin star. Throwing the old one in the laundry pile he planned to take to Reva, he found a clean, light blue one in a dresser drawer. After donning the shirt and buttoning it he pinned the star on the right side of his chest. No sense in making his heart an easy target. He picked up a black ribbon tie from the dresser, wrapped it around his collar and tied the knot.

Reaching over to a small table next to the bed, he picked up a half-empty bottle of bourbon he had carried home from the saloon. He uncorked the bottle, took a swig, and pounded the cork back in with the open palm of his hand. Standing the bottle back on the bedside table, he picked up the holster and buckled the gun belt around his waist. Also from the table, he picked up a silver star and pinned it to his shirt just above his heart. He lifted his black Stetson hat—he still wore one with a Cattleman crease—and his black frock coat from the mahogany coat rack. He donned the coat and standing in front of a mahogany oval stand mirror, placed the hat squarely on his head. Fully dressed, he gave a final check of his image in the mirror. Satisfied with what he saw, he walked out the front door and stood on the porch. Sheriff Yulin Temple was ready to meet the day.

The sheriff's house, along with the mayor's, was built at the northern entrance to the town where the street was lined by a row of trees. It was the only section in the entire town where a paved sidewalk ran in front of houses: those of the mayor and the sheriff. From his front window, Yulin could see between the trees all the way to the far end of town.

Next door, the mayor was rocking lazily in a wide, wooden rocking chair on the front porch, smoking one of his fat Cuban cigars. Chet Carson was a large man in his mid-forties. His rapidly graying, thinning hair was parted on the side in waves of heavily pomaded tresses. His bushy moustache extended out to both sides, joining his sideburns to form bushy muttonchops. Whether it was a sweltering, hot day or one where snow blanketed the town, Carson always wore a three-piece suit. Tucked into a vest pocket was a 14-karat gold-plated watch fob. He had chosen 14-karat gold because it *looked* more expensive than 18-karat gold. The watch hung from a chain with the other end of the chain fastened around a vest button. Stretched across the mayor's ever-expanding girth, the chain was fighting a losing battle to remain in one piece.

"Mornin' Mayor," said Yulin Temple, without actually looking at Carson. Standing at the edge of the porch, he took the makin's out of his shirt pocket and began to roll his first cigarette of the day.

The mayor took the cigar out of his mouth and tilted his head back, exhaling a long stream of thick, white smoke. After the last wisp of smoke had cleared his mouth, Carson lowered his head to return the greeting. "Mornin' Sheriff."

Yulin placed the rolled cigarette in his mouth and stuffed the makin's back in his shirt pocket. He struck a match against a white-painted wood post and lit the cigarette. Taking a drag, he blew a perfect smoke ring. His eyes fixed on the street, he said, "I'm going to shoot your dog."

Carson smiled as he continued to rock. "Shoot my dog and you'll lose your job," he said calmly, placing the cigar in the corner of his mouth.

"Nothing like sweetening the deal," said Yulin, stepping down from the porch steps onto the pavement. He strode off down the middle of the dusty street toward his office.

The entire town of Stovepipe was about two blocks long, with a small residential section on the east side of the main road through town. Downtown was comprised of false-front buildings made of wood and brick. The only real two-story buildings were the hotel where the stagecoach made its stop each week, Reva's Café, and the Silver Strike Saloon. There were a number of small businesses downtown, most notably a mercantile store and a livery stable. Since it was Sunday morning, half the small town was still in church. Others were still sleeping off the night before, while some folks were already working at their jobs or businesses.

Yulin Temple liked to walk. Unlike many Western lawmen, he didn't keep a horse tied to a hitching post unless he planned to go out riding. Having never been a cowboy, he felt no disgrace when going afoot. Even on warm, dry mornings like this one, with dust rising up and swirling about, Yulin enjoyed walking down the middle of the street. Forcing riders on horseback and wagon drivers to steer around him were the perks of being sheriff. On his nightly rounds, he'd walk down Main Street while looking through windows of buildings on both sides of the street.

When he'd first come to Stovepipe, Yulin had just been passing through on his way to no particular destination when he walked into the Silver Strike Saloon for a cold beer. It was his unfortunate lot in life to be born with a face other men liked to challenge to a fight. One such man was Jake Blanchett, a local tough and self-styled gunman. Blanchett made the challenge with his gun, Yulin answered it, and the town's population was reduced by one. Since Blanchett had been the one who killed the last sheriff, Mayor Carson offered the still-vacant job to Yulin. The town council, already gathered inside the saloon, quickly approved the appointment. After years of wandering through the West, Yulin decided a job paying $125 a month—with a free house thrown in—sounded pretty good. That had been four years ago.

Yulin Temple had had many lives. He joined the Texas Rangers in 1858, serving under Capt. John S. "Rip" Ford, fighting Indians and Juan Cortina. He was married to Lillian then. Yulin, Jr., or "Weed", was born three years later. During the Civil War, Yulin managed to avoid conscription into the Confederate Army. With the war ended, he mustered out of the Rangers just before spring in 1866.

Yearning to own land, he took advantage of the 1862 Homestead Act and started a cattle ranch on one hundred sixty acres located northwest of La Grange. To help run the ranch he hired as foreman a Civil War veteran named Emmett Johnson, who had served with the Colored Troops. Abigail, Johnson's wife, hired on as housekeeper and nursemaid, helping Lillian with Weed.

The ranch grew fast. The range was full of longhorn cattle and mustangs free for the taking, the descendants of livestock set loose by Mexican and Texan ranchers after abandoning their own ranches years ago. The only price Yulin paid for building his herds, was the long hours of backbreaking work flushing longhorns out of brush and briar and chasing down and roping mustangs.

Additional land was easily obtainable as well. With no one updating records on the status of the old land grants, Yulin took possession of hundreds of acres by running his herds of branded cattle and horses on vacated grasslands.

Within the year, the ranch had grown to well over a thousand acres, while Yulin and Emmett amassed close to nine hundred head of Texas Longhorn cattle. To help with the expansion of the ranch, he hired on men who had fought on both sides in the Civil War, as well as some vaqueros who had ridden with Cortina. Emmett recruited men from his old unit in the First North Carolina Colored Volunteers, and freemen emancipated by President Lincoln and the War.

Yulin Temple was now rich in land and cattle but badly in need of capital to pay expenses and payroll. In June of 1867, he hired a team of drovers to drive his first herd of cattle to the new railhead and stockyards in Abilene, Kansas. To save himself a hundred dollars, he took on the job of trail boss rather than hire someone more experienced to head the drive. But for insurance, he appointed one of the drovers with leadership skills foreman, agreeing to pay him a bonus after the cattle were sold.

Leaving Emmett in charge of the ranch, set out to drive his first herd of cattle to the new railhead and stockyards in Abilene, Kansas. The first leg of the cattle drive ended in Austin, Texas, where Yulin's herd would join up with one belonging to a cattle rancher named O.W. Wheeler. The combined herd would be the first to travel this new northern route to Abilene, following what would soon be known as the Chisholm Trail.

Losing just over one-third of his cattle on the drive, the combined herds arrived at the Abilene stockyards in August. Assisted by Wheeler, he negotiated a very good price for his cattle, netting a profit of $19,000 after paying all expenses.

Yulin wasted no time in heading back. Visions of Lillian and Weed beckoning him home with smiles and open arms sped him onward. He arrived at the ranch two weeks later. But, during his months-long absence, a yellow fever epidemic had devastated southern Texas. Just days before Yulin's return in mid-September, the epidemic had taken the lives of Lillian and Weed.

Waiting until Yulin had dismounted from his horse, Emmett gave him the news at the front porch. A very pregnant Abigail was standing inside the doorway.

"Ain't no other way to tell it, so I'll just say it outright," said Emmett. His face looked somber, his eyes welling up with tears.

Yulin, a moment before in high spirits after returning home, had already suspected something was wrong. Lillian and Weed weren't standing on the front porch to greet him. He steeled himself for whatever Emmett was going to tell him next.

"Yulin, Lillian and Weed are dead. Yellow fever—took 'em both less than a week ago."

Yulin stood there, numb with disbelief. His bright, expanded world had just turned to bleak and utter darkness.

"I buried them under that ol' live oak tree that Lillian loved so much. It was her wish, Yulin." Emmett stood and waited for Yulin to react, to say something.

Yulin did neither of those things. He turned around and strode out to the gravesite under the live oak. Emmett had built a white picket fence around the graves. Yulin opened the gate, walked over to stand between the two graves, and collapsed onto his knees. He remained sitting at the gravesite late into the following afternoon, refusing to leave. Abigail would come up to him a few times during the day, also refusing to leave until he drank the cup of water she brought him.

On the evening of that second day, Yulin surprised Emmett by walking into the dining room where he and Abigail were eating a quiet dinner. He took a roll of cash out of his pocket and placed it on the table in front of Emmett.

"Emmett, I've given it a lot of thought. Here's the money I made off the cattle. $19,000. I'm giving it all to you."

Emmett began to rise from his chair in protest.

"You ain't got no say in this, goddamn it," said Yulin.

The forcefulness in his voice sat Emmett back in his chair.

"And I ain't finished." Yulin paused, setting his jaw firmly. "I'm signing the ranch over to you."

Now Abigail began rise to protest, but Emmett put a hand over her arm. She remained seated.

"Think about it," said Yulin. "You're going to need land of your own to raise a family. Emmet, you built this ranch as much as I did. I'm quick deeding it over to you and you're going to accept it."

Emmett was stunned. "This wasn't part of our deal, Yulin." A gasp escaped Abigail's lips.

Fighting back tears, Yulin said, "There ain't nothing here anymore for me. Nothing." He pushed on, the stern conviction in his voice hiding his anguish. "Tomorrow you and I are going down to the bank. We'll sign all the paperwork, and have it legally witnessed and recorded. You're already on the business bank account. I'll have my name taken off it and you can deposit the money from the cattle sale. I'll ride out after it's all done."

Yulin was good to his word. He signed the ranch over to Emmett, making sure the land transaction was legal and binding. At the bank, he had his name removed from the ranch account. In the coming years, Emmett would grow the ranch into one of the largest and most successful cattle operations in the state of Texas.

Yulin left that same day. He never returned to the ranch nor saw the Johnsons again.

He drifted northward to Kansas, working stints as a deputy marshal in Ellsworth, Wichita, and Newton. In each town he involved himself in more shootouts than any other deputy on the force. Every job ended the same way: Yulin asked none-too-politely to leave town—immediately and permanently. His reputation as a loose cannon with a death wish preceded him, closing all doors to future employment in law enforcement in the state of Kansas.

After Newton, he switched to bounty hunting, manipulating his human prey into shooting confrontations, hoping each one would result in his own death. Surviving nine shootouts, Yulin Temple faced the realization that he'd been inflicted at birth with an inextinguishable will to live.

This realization led to a second one: he was tired of the wholesale killing. Besides, if he was cursed to survive shootouts beyond all reasonable expectation, he might as well prepare for a future he never wanted.

Making his way into Colorado, Yulin deposited his bounty earnings in a Denver bank. With telegraph lines running throughout the West, he could wire money to himself from any town with a Western Union office.

He continued to drift, not planning beyond the present day. This vague, meandering trail led him to Stovepipe where he had the gunfight with Jake Blanchett and was immediately appointed county sheriff via a unanimous town council voice vote.

Yulin hadn't planned on this career change. He decided to keep the job until he tired of it or was gunned down. It didn't matter either way. Still, all in all, being county sheriff became a lucrative enterprise for him. Besides the benefits of the salary and the free house, he charged all prisoners for their jailing and for escorting them to court. Either the prisoners paid him willingly, or after they were knocked unconscious by Yulin's fist or the barrel of his gun. He also charged a fee to the federal government for handing territorial prison-bound convicts over to US marshals. If payment for those fees was slow in coming, a few federal prisoners somehow made successful escapes from his custody.

In his first couple of years as sheriff, Yulin had done too good a job of eradicating crime in both the town and county. He wasn't making much off the jail anymore, but then he didn't need to. There were other sources of income. Burt Owens, owner of the Silver Strike Saloon, paid him a percentage of the monthly take from the gambling tables. Yulin's mere presence in the saloon was enough to prevent gunplay from disgruntled, losing gamblers.

He negotiated with Mayor Carson, who doubled as county manager, to keep forty percent of the taxes he collected in town and around the county. . Carson had been forced to agree to the deal. He might have had a personal dislike for the man but Yulin Temple was the most effective sheriff the county had ever had.

Despite his excessive drinking, Yulin honored his grudging commitment to stay alive. To this end, he regularly practiced his fast draw and shooting accuracy. Setting up cans and glass bottles on a wooden rail fence he had built near the road leading to town, he positioned himself fifty feet away from the targets. With each bullet he shattered a glass bottle or sent a can flying upward, dancing and zigzagging in the air before it fell back down to earth.

Yulin did not stage his target practice for an audience but it was a bonus if there were witnesses. The wondrous delineations of his shooting exhibitions had their desired effect: outlaws gave Stovepipe a wide berth.

County sheriff was an elected position but Yulin never had to run for reelection. During his first year in office he handily dispatched another gunfighter of some renown named Brink Jeffords. With nine notches carved into the walnut handle of his gun, Jeffords had ridden into town with the aim of making Sheriff Yulin Temple the tenth notch.

Yulin was standing at his customary spot at the corner of the L-shaped bar in the Silver Strike Saloon. From there he could see the entire room, including the batwing doors and windows. He held a shot glass full of whiskey in one hand, an empty bottle stood on the bar in front of him.

Jeffords walked in, glanced around the saloon, and saw Yulin. Wearing a smirk on his face, he sauntered over to the bar and ordered a beer. Lifting the glass mug to his mouth, he gave a sideways glance at Yulin standing to his left. That was perfect. Jeffords was lefthanded and could quickly pull his gun.

His eyes also took in the empty whiskey bottle. The gunfighter had heard stories that while this sheriff was fast, the vast amounts of whiskey he consumed had slowed his hand down considerable. It was possible to beat him to the draw if you timed it right. Anyway, this sheriff was so drunk he'd never be able to find his own gun, let alone fire it.

Jeffords watched Yulin. Were those beads of sweat on his forehead? Was the hand that held the shot glass shaking just a bit? How long had it taken to finish that bottle? Judging by the unfocused look in the bloodshot eyes, not that long at all. Those stories seemed true enough. In just a few moments, Brink Jeffords would be known forever as the man who gunned down Sheriff Yulin Temple.

Jeffords set his glass down on the bar and waited. Yulin threw his head back as he drank from the shot glass. Jeffords turned, called out, "Sheriff!" and went for his gun.

What he failed to notice was Yulin holding the glass in his left hand. What he further failed to notice was Yulin never taking his eyes off him.

Jefford's revolver had barely cleared leather when a bullet from Yulin's .45 Schofield buried itself deep into his chest. The gunfighter fell backwards to the floor, lying face up as he drew his final breaths.

Yulin stood over him, looking down. "That was just my first bottle. You should've waited till I finished a second one." Jeffords eyes became lifeless, and his breathing stilled.

After that, there were no more challengers to Sheriff Yulin Temple's fast draw, and no competitors for his job.

CHAPTER 3

Reva's Café was a relatively short walk from Yulin's house. It had the best food in town—and it had Reva. Now in her mid-thirties, Reva Delgado was born Eula Mae Sundstrom in Marion, Illinois. The third of nine children of a Baptist minister, at sixteen she left what she felt was her father's suffocatingly restrictive home. Arriving in St. Louis, she quickly found her uncommon beauty and curvaceous figure prompted many men to open doors for her—figuratively and literally.

Over time, her intelligent planning enabled her to amass a small fortune from her wealthy clientele. But the more successful Eula became, the more she worried that word of her thriving profession would filter back to her family in Marion. She decided to reinvent herself. One afternoon she bought a bottle of hair dye and by the next morning, the Swedish honey-blonde, green-eyed Eula Mae Sundstrom was transformed into the red-headed, green-eyed courtesan from France, Francoise "Frenchie" Dubois.

Frenchie, yearning to experience adventure in the growing West, left the next day by train for Kansas City, Kansas. Hearing of all the money to be made in the Kansas cattle towns, she followed the same circuit that Yulin Temple had traveled a few years before. Working in saloons and in brothels, Frenchie's immense popularity enabled her to work independently, declaring the percentage of her earnings she would pay to a saloon owner or madam, something unheard of at that time. In Dodge City, both the mayor and the town marshal gave her their unofficial imprimatur as they battled each other for her luscious favors, attempting to outspend and out gift each other.

But there came a time when she'd had enough of the smell and violence of the Dodge City cattle herds and cowboys. With tens of thousands of dollars saved up in the bank, Frenchie Dubois felt it was time for a career change. She was tired of the courtesan business, but what to do next?

She'd always had a talent for cooking. Often, she had been in the kitchen of a saloon after whipping up meals for the other working girls. The praise for her cooking was always the same: she was in the wrong business and should open a restaurant. Well, thought Frenchie, it was time to prove them right.

Hearing stories of opportunities abounding in a mile-high city prospering in the foothills of the Rocky Mountains, she decided to try her luck in Denver. With this new plan came the need for a new identity. Back in St. Louis, she had known a high-priced escort from Argentina who had been wildly popular—partly because of her naturally blonde hair and blue eyes. With this in mind, the green-eyed Frenchie stopped seeing clients and stopped dying her hair, keeping it wrapped inside a colorful turban. Within a couple of months, her natural honey-blonde hair had grown long enough to be set free from its silk prison. She packed up her most important possessions and boarded the stage for Fort Hays. There, she bought a ticket on the Kansas Pacific Railway to Denver. By the time the train pulled into the station, Francoise "Frenchie" Dubois from France had disappeared, and Reva Delgado from Argentina stepped onto the railway platform.

After arriving in town, Reva artfully negotiated a low rate on a long-term lease for a hotel room. Now with her base of operations in place, she started to hunt for a suitable place of employment where she could learn the restaurant business.

It was a short hunt. On the first day she found an Italian restaurant in Larimer Square. She charmed the middle-aged male owner into believing she was the disowned daughter of a wealthy Argentinian cattle rancher, recently arrived in America to seek her own fortune. He had her cook a dish, sampled it, and after a wide smile crossed his face, hired her as his assistant cook. Over the following months, Reva proceeded to wheedle from him all he knew about cooking and running a restaurant. As the owner was married, Reva spent almost as much time fending off his advances as she spent learning to cook his Italian dishes. Back in the cattle towns she had learned to cook steak. Upon her request, her steak was added to the menu and the little Italian place became a very popular Italian steakhouse.

Within a year she was confident she had learned all she needed to run her own place. Adding most of the restaurant earnings to her savings, she began looking for a restaurant opportunity of her own. She found an ad in the Rocky Mountain News: a restaurant with living quarters above it for sale. It was in a small, south-central Colorado town called Stovepipe.

The owner had suddenly abandoned shop to seek his fortune in Virginia City, Nevada. Chet Carson, as part owner of the town bank, had taken possession of the property. He had planned to demand a lease with a large deposit from the next prospective new owner. However, Reva surprised him by offering cash to buy the place outright. Awestruck by her beauty, brains and seductiveness, he readily agreed.

When Reva took inventory of her new business, she found that the previous owner had indeed left in a hurry. In the kitchen was a handsomely made five-door oak icebox. When she opened the top ice compartment doors, a veritable waterfall poured onto the floor. The block of ice inside had thawed weeks ago, also filling the water pan below.

Since she had to clean out the icebox anyway, she opened the other three doors. An overwhelming stench assaulted her sinuses like an uppercut to the nose. Inside one compartment there were aged fruit and vegetables so wilted and black with mold it was impossible to tell what they had been in their former lives. The meats in another compartment had colors and odors she had never experienced before. Cleaning up the mess took several hours, a mop and two buckets full of hot soapy water, eight towels, and a push broom. The back doors and all windows remained open into the early evening, allowing the hot summer air to dry out the kitchen. During this time, she paid her first visit to Phipp's Mercantile to purchase supplies that hadn't been bequeathed to her by the recently and quickly departed restaurant owner.

But Reva also discovered buried treasure inside the icebox—buried treasure in the form of a clay jar with the words "Boudin French Bakery, San Francisco" embossed on the front. Inside the jar, she found a dormant sourdough starter. She knew exactly how to revive it. The owner of the Italian restaurant in Denver had prided himself on his Italian sourdough bread and had taught her all his breadmaking secrets.

With a new block of ice resting in the icebox, and the compartments filled with fresh food and beverages, she sat down to plan her daily menus from the recipes she had brought with her. She was ready to cook.

First, she set about bringing the sourdough starter back to life. Three days later, she began creating what would be her signature French sourdough bread. After all, she thought, a French-style sourdough bread should be made from French sourdough starter. Following a week of baking test baguettes, she had it perfected. The local airborne yeast had done its job.

Reva had just placed a test sourdough round loaf on a cooling rack when she heard a knock at the back door. She hated being disturbed when she was at work on a project. She glanced at the door and saw Mayor Chet Carson standing behind the window, holding a bouquet of roses and wearing a broad, hopeful smile on his face.

"Damn," Reva muttered. But she screwed a smile on her own face and opened the door.

"Good afternoon, Miss Delgado," said Carson, unctuously. "I hope I'm not disturbing you."

Yes, you most certainly are, Reva wanted to respond. But she knew that men like Carson made better friends than enemies. Besides, he was so obvious in his intentions he was easy to handle.

"Not at all," she answered. "In fact, you're just in time. I've been working on perfecting my French sourdough bread. Would you care for a little nibble?"

Carson's eyes grew wide, and his smile nervous. He gulped, noticeably. If he could just maneuver himself into a position of trust with this woman...

"Eh, I'd be happy to, Miss Delgado. I'm sure it will be as delicious as *you* undoubtedly are," he said, in what he thought passed for witty, flirtatious banter. "And, er, these are for you. Welcome to our town." He held the bouquet out to her.

"Oh, they look and smell lovely," Reva said. "But could you hold onto them for me, please? I'm right in the middle of something. In fact, you can help me with it, if you don't mind."

She tore off a small piece from the end of the loaf, and then tore it into two chunks. Holding one of them between her thumb and forefinger, she moved to stand opposite Carson. Almost his same height, she brought her face close to his and slowly pushed the bread into his open mouth.

"Here, Mayor Carson, give me your honest opinion."

Carson stood there, wide eyed. The roses were shaking in his still-outstretched hand. "Please," he said in a trembling voice, his mouth full of bread. "Call me Chet."

Reva smiled. She had him. "Don't forget to chew. I wouldn't want you to choke to death in my own kitchen…Chet."

Carson chewed as instructed; his yearning eyes fixed on Reva.

Her lips were just a few inches away from his. "How do you like the way it tastes, how it feels in your mouth?"

Carson was visibly sweating as he swallowed. But now that she had asked, he realized the sourdough bread was good—very, very good. "This is delicious," he exclaimed. "You sure know how to bake, Miss Delgado."

Reva was genuinely gratified. "It makes me so happy to hear you say that. But let's try one more, just to make sure. Alright…Chet?"

He slowly nodded, mumbling weakly, "Uh huh."

Reva slowly inserted the other bit of bread into his mouth. Carson chewed the bread very slowly, wanting to extend this ephemeral moment for as long as he could.

"Well?" A luscious smile danced seductively across her lips.

Carson was a beaten man, swallowing his self-confidence with that last bite of bread. He stood there awestruck in her presence. "This is the best bread I ever ate in my whole life, Miss Delgado," he whimpered.

Reva clapped her hands together as she stepped away from Carson. "Oh, I am so glad. Then I can look forward to both you and Mrs. Carson having dinner at my café on opening night?"

Carson was visibly deflated by Reva's question. Talking about his wife always provoked that reaction. "Well, uh, yes, Rev—I mean, Miss Delgado. Yes, you can."

"That's wonderful! *Wait* until you taste the rest of my food." Reva smiled, slipping an arm through Carson's while smoothly leading him to the door. As she swung it open, she said, "I'll put an ad in the town newspaper announcing my grand opening. There will be a big sign in the front window next to the front door where you'll enter my café from now on, with or without your lovely wife."

She closed the door with her back. She remained there; arms crossed. A lock of hair had fallen over her brow. She exhaled sharply, trying to blow the hair away from her eye, only to have it flop back down again.

Carson stood there, confused and not knowing exactly what had just happened. Just that he was standing outside the kitchen, still holding the bouquet of roses, and there would be no more knocking on that back door.

On the night of August 12, 1876, Reva's Café opened for business, serving both western fare and Italian specialties. Sheriff Yulin Temple was her first customer. Stunned by her loveliness when she greeted him at the entrance, he unconsciously removed his hat and followed as she led him to his table.

Fifteen years of living out West had aged Reva's beauty but had not diminished it. In fact, maturity had endowed her with a beauty far richer than it had been during her youth. Afterwards, Yulin couldn't remember what he had ordered, but the café owner was unforgettable.

When Reva first saw Yulin standing just inside the doorway of her café, she held her breath. She gazed upon a tall man dressed in black with a handsome, weathered face. White hair, badly in need of a trim, spilled out from beneath a black Stetson hat. He stood in a confident manner, his hands on his hips, his open coat revealing a silver sheriff's star pinned to his shirt. Although she knew nothing about him, from that day forward there could be no other man for her.

After a time, Yulin's excessive drinking bothered her, but she knew there was nothing she could do about it. Liquor couldn't touch whatever he was trying to drown. He just needed an inducement to stop making the attempt. Someday—if she played her cards right—it would be her.

Despite his infatuation, Yulin Temple was not looking for a close relationship. After Lillian had died that was no longer possible. However, he was open to exploring other options.

This morning when Yulin had walked in the front door of the café, he didn't see Reva, but heard her rattling and cursing from the kitchen in the back. He pushed through the swinging kitchen door and saw her bent in front of a coal-fired cook stove. She had her hair pinned up and was wearing an apron. He watched as she lowered the oven door, sliding a large baking pan with small, individual meatloaves into the main cooking chamber. The meatloaves— as far as she knew—were her own creation. Starting with a custom mix of ground beef and pork, she filled the center with mozzarella cheese. The meatloaf was topped with marinara sauce and baked in the stove.

Yulin never believed for a moment that Reva was from Argentina, and he didn't care. Out West, anyone could reinvent themselves and people would accept them at face value. But he did admire the shape of her backside and smiled, knowing the rest of her was just as voluptuous. He gave Reva's rump a slap that was just a mite sharper than he had intended.

"Damn it all, Yulin!" She straightened up and whirled around to face him, green eyes flashing with anger. "Keep your hands off me when I've got my head near that stove! It's a good thing Luke ain't here setting tables for

breakfast or he would've seen it! Besides, I'm running behind enough as it is."
Reva had hired a widow and her son to help with the café. Luke worked before
and after school, and his mother worked evenings.

Yulin smiled at her choice of word. "It's your *behind* that's making me
hungry, Reva."

That riled her up even more. "Wipe that smirk off your face right now,
mister!" She turned back to the oven. "I should've had these little Italian
meatloaves in the oven thirty minutes ago right after the rolls were taken out.
They're stuffed with mozzarella cheese in the middle and marinara sauce on
top so they take extra-long to cook. They're so popular I need to make two
batches ahead of time. Anything I don't sell I put in the icebox for the next
day. It's a lot of work, Yulin."

"Reva," Yulin said, "enough about the meatloaves." Although he loved
her cooking, this Italian stuff with the sauces and funny flavors still took some
getting used to. He turned her around to face him and gently brushed away an
errant lock of hair nestled against her floured brow. He kissed her.

Reva collapsed against his chest. "Oh, Yulin," she said in a soft, breathy
voice, "where we going with this?"

"Well, first you're going to make me breakfast."

Reva looked exasperated and slapped him sharply on the chest. "You
know that's not what I meant. Where we going with *this*? Whatever this is
between you and me?"

Yulin hated when the topic came around to *this*. After almost two years he
wasn't yet sure what *this* was and where he wanted it to go. "Let's just get to
breakfast and see where it goes from there."

"Damn you, Yulin Temple!" she said as she turned and closed the stove
door. She wiped her hands on the apron that covered her dress.

"Did you make me any breakfast?" asked Yulin.

"It's two hours old if you want to risk certain death," Reva said as she
nodded toward a cast iron skillet on the stovetop.

Yulin picked up a plate and walked over to the stove. "In my job, I'm
always risking certain death. At least with your food I know when it's coming."
He picked up a spatula and, dipping it into the cast iron skillet on the stovetop,
filled his plate with scrambled eggs.

Reva slapped him between his shoulders. "You can't talk about my food
that way! It was perfectly good when I made it fresh this morning." She walked
over to a cutting board table and started to mash boiled potatoes for the lunch
menu.

"Then start making it two hours later. I like to sleep in." Yulin grabbed
some sausage links and bacon with his hand and dropped them onto his plate.
He picked up a clean fork from silverware set aside for place settings.

"I know how you like to sleep in," Reva said mockingly. "We were
supposed to have "breakfast" this morning at five-thirty." Breakfast was what
they called their frequent early morning trysts. Reva liked to fit them in before

she had to start preparing the actual breakfast she would serve to customers later. "Where the hell were you?"

Yulin forked some scrambled eggs into his mouth. "Well, there's this goddamn dog— "

"That goddamn dog! I know all about that dog! I've been hearing for six months about how you're going to shoot that goddamn dog. Well, you haven't shot it yet! Next excuse!"

"I'll shoot the goddamn dog when I'm good and ready. he said. "Besides, I've lost so much sleep if I shot that mutt point blank I'd most likely miss." He made a shooting gesture with his gun hand.

Reva's face and voice both softened. "You—you could sleep over here. I can't hardly hear the dog barking with my windows and curtains closed."

Yulin held a strip of bacon in front of his mouth. "I just may do that," he smiled, biting off and chewing some of the bacon.

Reva fingered the long hair at the base of his neck. "You're overdue for a haircut, Sheriff. And I don't mean one of Luann's."

"Let's have "breakfast" and you can cut it afterward," Yulin said, setting the plate of food down on the cutting board table.

CHAPTER 4

"Breakfast" and the haircut led to Yulin moving his few belongings into Reva's two-room apartment above the restaurant that night. The next morning Yulin was surprised to discover he had slept through the entire night. Reva's alarm clock on her nightstand said 5:28 A.M. There was no goddamn dog to be heard.

Lying on his back, he ran a hand through his freshly trimmed hair and smiled. He turned his head to see Reva sleeping beside him. She was lying on her side, her hand on his chest. She drew comfort from the rise and fall of his breathing. He watched the slow rise and fall of her large, full breasts as she slept. The sight was giving him much more than just comfort. But the sexual stirrings of desire were offset by more serious considerations. It had been a long time since he had spent the entire night with a woman who loved him. He asked himself if he loved her, if he *could* love her. Hell, could he love *any* woman again after Lillian? Just asking this question started a tiny ball of guilt eating away at his stomach. He decided that he had time to find the answer to that question but now wasn't the time. The tiny ball of guilt took a rest.

He took his hand and caressed her hair. She gently awoke, stretched her arms, and smiled at him. She moved her feet to rest against his legs, another type of physical contact she enjoyed and needed with him. The 5:30 A.M. alarm bell rang. Reva turned to silence it and then turned back to lie on her side facing him, her head supported by her hand.

"How about some breakfast in bed?" he asked her.

Reva smiled. She lifted the top sheet and looked underneath at Yulin's growing pleasure at her being awake. "Um hmm," she said.

Yulin drew her nearer to him so that their bodies were aligned, touching each other. His eyes drank in the loveliness of her face. She was so goddamn beautiful. He knew how lucky he was. Many men would pay—literally *had* paid—to be where he was now. He knew that she was in love with him. Inside his stomach that little ball of guilt began to gnaw away again. He told himself that the fact that they were now living together didn't change anything. "Just stick with the now," he said softly, not meaning to have spoken out loud.

"What was that?" Reva asked, a slightly confused smile on her face.

Yulin, a bit embarrassed, thought quickly. "I want you now, I said."

Reva gave him a wickedly sexy smile. "Then stop talking," she said breathily, and pressed her parted lips to his. Any feeling of guilt inside him melted away as he gave in to the now.

Later, after he had finished his actual breakfast in the café dining room, Yulin walked out the door with a little spring in his step. As he headed down the boardwalk past D. Phipps Mercantile, he spied Reverend Heady standing to the side. The reverend tipped his hat. "Mornin', Sheriff. Missed you at church yesterday."

"And you'll miss me again next Sunday, Reverend," Yulin said, and kept walking.

*****

Stovepipe was located in the eastern half of Rio Grande County. Not only was it the county seat, it was the only town in the entire county. The bulk of the county population lived within the Stovepipe town limits. Outside of town, the ranching families employed roughly three dozen cowboys. The farms were family affairs, birthing homegrown farmhands as needed.

Located near the western edge of the San Luis Valley, at over 7500 feet in elevation, Stovepipe was a mountain valley town. The Rio Grande River flowed past on its journey southward. The lush valley grasslands, with a handful of cattle ranches and a few farms scattered about, were irrigated by a vast underground aquifer.

To the south lay the desert leading down to the state border and into the Territory of New Mexico. Winter came early and summer came late to this area. But with the onset of an early heat wave, the year was apparently not going to follow the weather patterns of previous years. This boded to be the hottest spring on record in southern Colorado.

To the west were the San Juan Mountains. Here, mining speculators had taken over land that had been Ute territory for anywhere from hundreds to thousands of years (depending on which historical records were used). Near the mines was a shantytown built by groups of gold miners flocking to the first gold rush some twenty years before. Between one hundred and two hundred wage-earning mineworkers now lived in those shacks and lean-tos, the original inhabitants having sold or pulled out long ago.

Stovepipe was literally the end of the line. The telegraph line that connected it to the rest of the country went no further. The railroad hadn't yet made it this far, but Stovepipe would logically be its western terminus if the Denver & Rio Grande Railway could only be sold on extending its track to the town. Mayor Chet Carson had set himself up as the salesman but could find no buyers among the managing partners and board of directors of the D&RG.

All the great gold and silver strikes that had spread through Colorado like wildfire had somehow circumvented the nearby San Juan Mountains. Only the long-established mining companies were doing very well, and they took care of their own transportation needs. None of the independent miners were getting rich. They sold the ores of their labor in town.

Thus, the town was caught in a vicious circle. In order to grow it needed the railroad, but the railroad saw no justifiable economic reason to go to the expense of laying track to such an inconsequential small town as Stovepipe.

And Mayor Chet Carson was forced to agree with the D&RG.

Carson was eager to see Stovepipe quickly grow, but not so eager to watch it slowly die. Something had to be done—and fast. And he had developed a plan that he would unveil at the next town council meeting.

In contrast, Sheriff Yulin Temple was very happy with the way things were in Stovepipe and the rest of Rio Grande County. Quiet. Peaceful. Predictable. During his bounty hunter days, he'd been in boomtowns that hadn't existed a few months' earlier and would be ghost towns in two years' time. He knew all about the violent crime that moved into those towns. Gamblers, prostitutes, con artists, thieves, robbers, and murderers descended like plagues of locusts, leaving only after the mines were played out and there was no money left to be made or taken.

Yulin's small jail with its two cells was the perfect size for the existing amount of crime within the county, which was practically nil. More people flooding into the county would mean more crime, necessitating a bigger jail. A bigger jail would mean more income to him but would take a lot more work to earn it. He was doing just fine with his current income.

And he had to admit he had grown tired of gunfights. He didn't want to go back to killing men. At this point in his life he no longer looked forward to being killed.

Mayor Chet Carson was fully aware that Sheriff Yulin Temple opposed his plans to grow the town. And the mayor knew there was not one thing he could do about it. The sheriff, despite being an incorrigible drunk, was the most popular man in Stovepipe. In fact, Carson suspected that it wasn't the dog that had gotten him reelected mayor. No, it was the great sport the voters enjoyed in watching their sheriff humble and irritate Carson at every turn. Carson, not being well-liked among the citizenry, would suffer periodic but suspicious bouts of damage to his various downtown properties.

When Yulin was upset with the mayor, it seemed like those crimes of vandalism never seemed to get solved. Well, Carson often thought, that's where the dog came in handy, waking Yulin up in the middle of the night with its non-stop barking. Why else was he keeping that ugly, smelly, flea-bitten mutt chained to his porch just outside the sheriff's bedroom window?

The object of Mayor Chet Carson's ongoing frustration and displeasure, Sheriff Yulin Temple, also collected property taxes and other fees countywide. He kept a hefty percentage of the collections as hazard pay since some ranchers and mining companies needed persuading as to their legal obligation to pay said taxes and fees. When he chose to employ them, the threat of jail, his menacing persona and reputation with a gun made Yulin very persuasive.

Taxes and fees were collected every six months, and today was collection day. Although his wandering days were over—at least he hoped they were—he enjoyed getting out of town when the opportunity presented itself.

Yulin loved riding the bay gelding. It was a gaited horse, one gifted at birth with naturally smooth movement and stamina. A fast walk approached the speed of a lope. Atop such a horse, a rider could easily endure the animal trotting for miles in comfort. Yulin had gained possession of the bay during a bounty hunt. The dead man was no longer in need of a horse other than one to sling his body across. Yulin was instantly taken by the beauty of the horse and swapped it for his own. The smooth gait was an unexpected bonus.

Yulin boarded his bay gelding at the livery stable in town. Armando Gomez, the stable owner, took care of feeding and grooming the horse. It was already saddled and tied to the hitching rail next to the corral when Yulin walked over. He checked the tightness of the cinches. Gomez knew how he preferred them but Yulin just liked to make sure.

Gomez was inside the corral with a rake gathering horse manure into piles for composting. "Señor Temple— "

"*Sheriff* Temple," Yulin corrected.

"Sí, *Sheriff* Temple," Gomez corrected himself, "I hear you and the Señorita Delgado are in the same casa now, es verdad?"

Yulin kept his hands on the front cinch and looked through the corral boards. "Yes, it's verdad. You heard mighty quick, Gomez."

"I can't help how fast I hear, Sheriff Temple," smiled Gomez. The short, stocky Mexican could be a pain in the ass sometimes, but no one knew horses or could take better care of them than Armando.

Yulin untied the bay, swung up over the saddle and rode over to his office. Mayor Carson was sitting in a chair outside waiting for him with his customary cigar in his mouth. He removed it but continued to sit. "Good morning, Sheriff," he said.

"Mornin, Mayor," answered Yulin.

"Now, Sheriff, I'm a man who doesn't like to beat around the bush so I'll get right to it. I personally don't care what somebody does in their own private life—but my wife does which means I have to as well. She says it ain't seemly for our county sheriff to be cavorting with an unmarried woman—even if she does own her own business. It don't look proper."

Yulin stood there for a moment using his utmost self-control to stay calm. Had the news already spread all over town? "Ain't *seemly*, Chet? It ain't none of your wife's business or yours what I do in my private life. You can have a say in what I do as sheriff if you don't think I'm doing my job—but that's it. And who came up with *cavorting*—you or your wife?"

Carson stood up from the chair. "Now, Yulin—I mean Sheriff—I didn't mean— "

"Oh yes you did, Chet," snapped Yulin, "every one of those words. And I warned you about letting that dog bark all night. I'll be living with Reva until further notice or until that dog is gone, and most likely *after* that dog is gone. Now this discussion is over."

With that, Sheriff Yulin Temple strode into his office and slammed the door shut, leaving the mayor standing alone on the boardwalk.

Still fuming and muttering to himself some additional comments he should have fired at Carson, Yulin went to the potbelly stove, lit it, and picked up a coffee pot sitting atop it and opened the lid. Seeing the coffee pot was still about half full, he put it back on the stove to reheat. He sat down in the swivel chair behind his desk. Taking the makin's out of his shirt pocket, he rolled a cigarette, lit it and blew a perfect smoke ring.

From inside a desk drawer he took out a small leather case containing his tax ledger and receipt book, also taking out an empty canvas bag for the collected tax payments. First grabbing a Spencer carbine from the rifle rack on the wall, he walked outside. To his relief Carson had departed. He put the leather case and the canvas bag inside one of his saddlebags and thrust the carbine into the scabbard. He untied the bay from the hitching rail and swung into the saddle. Reining the horse over into the street, he touched his bootheels to its sides. He couldn't wait to leave town.

No matter how much Yulin enjoyed riding through the countryside, he always timed his tax collection rounds so that he was back in time to eat a late lunch at Reva's. Later at the café, Reva Delgado was serving Yulin at his reserved table against a wall in a corner of the room. She saw some of the customers casting furtive and not-so-furtive glances in their direction. She ignored them. She said to Yulin, a little too loudly, "I heard about your conversation with Carson. I'm proud of you for standing up to him and that shrew of a wife of his."

"No one runs my life but me, Reva." He cut into his steak, took a bite and smiled. "You cook the best steak this side of Kansas City."

"It's a gift." She paused for a moment. "Yulin, what did you mean by you living with me *until* the mayor's dog is gone? I didn't think we set a time limit on living together."

Yulin paused and set down his knife and fork, took Reva's hand in his and looked up at her. "I also said most likely *after* that dog is gone." He paused. "But, Reva, you know my past. Family and relationships haven't exactly worked out for me. It took me a long time to find a place I wanted to settle down in again. And I had to agree to be sheriff to do it. This is a quiet town with not much for me to do except drink too much. But that could change with the next stranger or gang that rides into town. Nothing in life has a guarantee. All we can do is enjoy what we have now for as long as it lasts."

He stood up and led Reva out of the dining room and into the kitchen, then wrapped her in his arms. "I think I could fall in love with you, Reva. It would only be the second time in my life. But I need to take it slow. I've been on my own a long time. You kinda get used to riding a trail alone. So, don't rush me." He smiled down at her and gently pulled her tighter against him. "Is what we have now so bad?" He lifted up her chin with his hand so that her lips were right beneath his. He lowered his head and kissed her. She pressed her lips back against his with the full force of her love for him. After the kiss ended, he softly said, "This is the best I can give you for now. Is it enough?"

Reva looked up at him and smiled. "It'll do...for now," she said, taking his head in both her hands and pulling his lips down onto hers, kissing him passionately as if it would do forever.

CHAPTER 5

Garrison and Ike Fleck were born on a forty-acre farm in Jackson County, Missouri, Garrison on November 19, 1850, Ike on January 3, 1861. In August of 1862, their father rode off on the family's one saddlehorse to join the 8th Missouri Cavalry and fight in the Civil War, expecting to return victoriously in less than a month. Instead, he was killed at the Battle of Poison Spring on April 18, 1864. Their mother wasn't notified of his death until four months later when she received a letter from the captain who had commanded his unit.

Devastated by the loss of her husband and overwhelmed by unbearable anguish, their mother was emotionally unable to care for her two young sons. On a very cold and snowy Christmas Eve after the boys had been put to bed, she set up something for Garrison to find in the morning. Finishing that, she went outside to the front porch, sat in the swing she used to share with her husband, wrapped around herself a daisy-yellow cotton lace shawl that he had given her one summer, and froze to death during the night.

When Garrison awoke Christmas morning, he saw a small, carved wooden box with a hinged lid on top of the dresser in his room. Sitting atop the box was an envelope addressed to him. Inside the envelope was a note written in his mother's hand. The note said she was sorry to ruin Christmas for them, but she had gone to be with their father. But not wanting to leave her sons destitute, she had sold the farm to a neighbor who had always coveted their land. Inside the box was $800 in cash, the price she had been paid for the land. Also in the note she told Garrison for the first time about her brother Roy Parker. He lived in the Territory of Colorado where he owned a gunsmith business in Boulder. She had already written to advise him of his nephews' impending journey to come live with him.

Alarmed by what he had read, Garrison ran down the hallway calling his mother's name. He looked in her empty bedroom and rushed to the stairway, running, almost falling down the stairs. Frantically looking around the front room, his eyes caught sight of what looked like a yellow shrouded figure through one of the front windows. Settling his eyes on it, he recognized his mother's body affixed to the porch swing.

Church members held funeral and burial services for the boys' mother, but Garrison didn't attend either service nor did he let neighbors take Ike. Garrison also refused all invitations for them to live with nearby families. He talked to the new owner of the farm, getting an agreement to allow them to remain in the house until the spring. By then the weather would have improved enough so they could travel west to find their Uncle Roy. Garrison had just turned fourteen years old; Ike would turn four the following month.

In mid-April, Garrison hitched their plow horse to a buckboard wagon. With Ike sitting in the seat beside him, he pulled up in front of the house. He went inside to grab an old Enfield rifle-musket he had used to go hunting with his father. It was a chore to load but would provide some protection along the way, besides ensuring they would have fresh meat on their westward journey.

He also found a cartridge pouch with extra bullets that his father had left behind. He walked into the bedroom he shared with Ike and grabbed the blankets off their beds. He looked over his collection of books, choosing a few to pack into the wagon. He left the carved wooden box behind.

Taking a final look at the family home, Garrison headed the wagon for Independence, Missouri, the starting point for the Oregon Trail. His plan had been to travel down the Trail in the wagon, but when he went into a general store to buy some provisions he was talked out of it. The store proprietor told him the journey was far too hazardous—what with the threat of Indian attacks and crossing rivers swollen with spring runoff—to risk traveling by themselves. Doubting the buckboard wagon could make it all the way to Colorado, he offered Garrison one hundred dollars in store credit for the horse and wagon.

"I'm paying too much for the wagon but not enough for the horse. I call that a fair deal all around," said the proprietor, whose name was Van Middlesworth. Garrison accepted the offer and the deal was closed with a handshake.

Van Middlesworth added, "I suggest you try catchin' a ride on this wagon train just outside here. They're headin' to the Willamette Valley in Oregon in about an hour or so. It'll reach the Upper California Crossing near Julesburg in a few weeks. You'll be in Colorado then, an' you can get off there."

Garrison gratefully thanked him for the information. He didn't know how to catch a ride with a wagon train, but he had an hour to learn. Taking Ike's hand, he led him about the store while deciding what to buy for their journey.

At the front counter, a man named Hollings was trying to buy some supplies for his family. They were part of that wagon train headed for Oregon. Hollings had given Van Middlesworth a list of supplies he needed. The proprietor had just given him the estimated total bill.

"It'll cost that much? But why are prices so much higher here than they were back home?"

Van Middlesworth answered, "Supply and demand, my friend. I've got the supply you're demandin' and you can't get none of it elsewhere 'round these parts. Besides, it costs more money to have stock shipped to me here than to your shopkeepers back home."

Hollings stared at the written estimation. "Fifteen dollars for a barrel of flour, a dollar a pound for potatoes? I mean, look at this. Forty cents a pound for sugar, sixty cents a pound for coffee and butter. Oh my God, look at the price of bacon. I thought we'd set aside enough money, but I wasn't counting on your prices being this high. What will my wife say? Please, sir, we can't even make it to Fort Kearny without more food and provisions." He began fumbling about his body. He pulled a Bowie knife out of its belt sheath. "How much will you give me for this?"

The proprietor was resolute. "Sorry, friend, but I'm not set up to barter. This is a cash only business."

Garrison overheard all this and walked back to the store counter.

"Mister," he said to Van Middlesworth, "if it's all the same, I'd appreciate it if you'd take my hundred dollars store credit and give it to this gentleman so he can buy his family some food and provisions." Both men looked dumbfounded at him.

"Young feller," said the proprietor, "that's the Christian thing to do but a bit foolhardy. You and your brother are going to need your own supplies for the Trail."

"Don't worry about us. We'll be fine." The money his mother had given him was hidden inside one of his boots.

Hollings kept staring at Garrison. "As this gentleman said, it's Christian of you to make the offer but I can't accept charity. And it would buy more than we need anyway."

Garrison's expression was earnest. "It ain't charity. My brother Ike and I need a way to get down the Oregon Trail to the Colorado Territory. We got family to meet there. The way I figure it, if you let us ride with you, well, that hundred dollars will buy a lot of food and then some. Besides, I got me a rifle that'll come in handy if we run into Indians. I can also provide us with meat along the way." He paused for emphasis. "It ain't charity."

Hollings thought it over for a moment. He then smiled and extended his hand to Garrison. "Sir, you got a deal. Welcome aboard the Hollings Family Wagon." Garrison had never been called "sir" before and tried not to blush. He shook Hollings' hand.

The Hollings Family Wagon was the type called a Prairie Schooner. Even with nine family members, there was still plenty of room for Garrison and Ike and their belongings. Even so, Garrison spent most of the time walking beside the wagon or riding one of the two heavy draft horses pulling the wagon. Ike stayed inside to play with the four youngest children, but also out of his fear that Indians would attack the wagon train. None ever did.

Still, the wagon train made stops at both Fort Kearny and Fort McPherson, allowing the emigrants to rest more easily under the protection of the Army outposts. At the Fort Kearny supply depot, Garrison saw a gray horse for sale. Thinking it was best for he and Ike to have their own means of transportation besides the Hollings wagon, he purchased the gelding. Gifted with a knack for bargaining, he convinced the owner to throw in an old saddle with the deal.

When he rode the horse back to the wagon, Ike meet him with glee. Hollings met him with shock. It wasn't just that someone as young as Garrison had expertly managed a horse purchase. He hadn't known that Garrison was carrying that much money. But as he had witnessed at the general store in Independence, there was a lot more to Garrison than appeared on the surface.

On the wagon trail, Garrison had kept his word to provide meat as often as he was able. But he had otherwise remained aloof from the Hollings, giving no information about himself and Ike. Yet an instinct had prompted him to buy ten pounds of salted pork for the Hollings family as a gesture of something he wasn't quite sure about.

"I reckon eating all that cottontail and squirrel has become a mite tiresome for you all," he said, avoiding Hollings's stare as he handed him the large sack of pork.

"Don't you just surprise a person," Hollings said, a smile slowly crossing his face. "Garrison, if things don't work out at the Crossing, we'd be more than proud to have you and Ike accompany us to the Willamette Valley. You're family, now."

As much as Garrison wanted to be part of a family again, the Hollings were not the family he wanted.

*****

Roy Parker was waiting for the two young pilgrims about three weeks later at the Upper California Crossing. He received his sister's letter in February, informing him his nephews were on their way. She didn't tell him the reason why they had been forced to leave home.

Roy had thought it strange that his nephews would be heading west during the heart of winter. Not with blizzards closing the plains to all travel for weeks to months. Wagon trains, large and small alike, waited for the spring thaw, heralding the arrival of the warmer months. He figured it more likely that his nephews would depart sometime in early April.

He also figured the route they would take to Boulder would lead them to the Crossing. In fact, he had been counting on it. But had the wagon train forded the South Platte at the Lower California Crossing in the Nebraska Territory, he might have missed them for good.

Five months earlier, Cheyenne Dog Soldiers leading warriors from the Arapaho and Oglala Lakota tribes had looted and burned Julesburg to the ground for the second time since the beginning of the year. The attacks were in retaliation for the ambush massacre of a Cheyenne village at Sand Creek by a band of Colorado volunteers commanded by Col. John Chivington the previous November. Wagon trains still flocked to the Crossing, but fear ran endemic among them and the local inhabitants. Mounted cavalry from Camp Rankin regularly patrolled the Crossing and the Overland Trail to prevent further Indian attacks. It was for this added protection the wagon master had chosen to cross the South Platte River here.

Roy had set out from Boulder in a buckboard wagon drawn by a two-horse team about the same time the Fleck brothers left Fort McPherson. While he had to travel a farther distance, he was able to make faster time than the wagon train, arriving at the Crossing a week before the wagon train rolled up to the Crossing.

In addition to his profession as a gunsmith, Roy sold both new and refurbished firearms. He had earned a solid reputation throughout eastern Colorado and western Kansas for his meticulous craftsmanship and fair dealings. He had driven a wagon filled with weapons he knew would sell quickly at the Crossing: ten wooden crates of .44 Henry repeating rifles—one hundred rifles total—and one hundred boxes of cartridges.

The Camp Rankin commander ordered the purchase of almost the entire stock for his men, still carrying the old muzzle-loading Enfield rifle-muskets issued to them at the beginning of the Civil War. Roy sold the remainder of the rifles and ammunition to Julesburg townsmen, living temporarily within the safer confines of the Army camp along with their families.

But all the while he kept his eyes constantly searching the wagons and horses arriving from Nebraska throughout each day, searching for two young boys who might resemble his sister. He had no idea if they would be traveling on horseback or by wagon. He spent hours riding around the Crossing, repeatedly calling out "Garrison and Isaac Fleck" until his voice grew hoarse. After sunset, he would continue riding among the campfires spread throughout the migrant camps, calling out their names.

*****

The Upper California Crossing was situated on the South Platte River about a mile to the east of Camp Rankin. It was here that thousands of wagon travelers crossed the river over to the north side to continue on to Oregon. Or, a great many wagons stayed to the south side, following the Overland trail to Denver, and from there headed westward to California.

Julesburg had also been nearby. Burnt to the ground twice by Indian attack, it was at this time being rebuilt three miles to the east, just outside the eastern boundary of the Army post. The Indian villages along the river, where travelers waiting to cross the river had traded with the friendly tribes, were gone. The following year, after peace had been restored, they would be back.

When they reached the Crossing ten days after leaving Fort McPherson, Garrison was not prepared for the scene that lay before him. The south shore, where the Hollings wagon train had stopped, was a busy place. Long lines of wagons waited hours to ford the river. Here, it was a half mile wide and no more than four feet deep, less than that in the middle. Even with several columns of wagons and horses wading across the river at once across the quicksand-like bed, it could take two hours to cross to the other side.

In June, the white sun had blazed down from clear blue skies, turning the winter snow into vast puddles of mud and water. Now in July, the weather was cooler than normal and there had been a series of heavy rainstorms. The ground near the river was slick and muddy, and the entire area was barren of trees, all of them chopped down for firewood long ago.

Many emigrants chose to wait until evening or the following day to cross the river. On the high, drier ground above the river, groups of covered wagons had formed their own protective circles. Volunteer militias augmented the military in patrolling the camping areas, their eyes looking for any place an Indian warrior could hide.

Inside the wagon, Ike had been lulled to sleep by the rhythmic rumbling of the wooden wheels and the swaying of the wagon bed along the trail. He was awakened by the sudden jerking motion of the wagon as the team of horses was reined to a stop. Whenever he was unexpectedly roused from sleep, he would cry out for his mother. Garrison, who had been riding the gray alongside, quickly dismounted and climbed over the back of the wagon to comfort his brother. After Ike was calmed, Garrison helped him out of the bed and down to the ground. He then gathered the blankets they had brought with them.

The Hollings wagon train had halted behind two long columns of wagons that had not moved forward a foot in hours. Hollings looked back and saw Garrison lowering Ike out of the wagon. He set the brake on the wagon, jumped down from the seat and walked over to Garrison. Extending his hand he said, "Garrison, it has been a pleasure. God be with you both meeting up with your uncle."

Garrison, despite himself, was overcome with emotion at parting with this good man and his family. He and Ike would have never made it to the Crossing without them. He grasped the hand and shook it warmly. "Thank you, Mr. Hollings" was all he could manage.

Hollings placed his other hand over Garrison's, then turned away as he released his grip. Garrison might have detected a tearful eye before the man went to climb back onto the wagon.

The Hollings children gathered around Ike, embracing him all at once. Mrs. Hollings, displaying the same reserve as her husband, gave him a quick hug. Her stiff embrace of Garrison was accompanied by the most emotion she would show anyone. "You're a fine young man, Garrison. You take care of your brother, now. He needs you more than you know."

As she walked away, Garrison looked at Ike. He was standing in place, not knowing for sure what had just happened. Garrison lifted Ike up onto the gray, and then swung into the saddle behind him, stuffing the blankets between them. Then he sat there, not knowing where they should go.

Garrison realized he hadn't planned beyond this point. Ike was complaining that he was hungry. Garrison knew they were out of the food. The Hollings hadn't thought to pack any for them before they left the wagon. Garrison couldn't blame them, not with all those mouths to feed. He certainly would never beg for food anyway, not when he had his Enfield. There had to be deer or rabbits in the area.

But he was almost out of ammunition, having forgotten to buy more black powder and paper cartridges back at the supply depot. He had a few Minié balls left in his cartridge pouch. He had dug them out of the carcass of every animal he had killed, but quite a few had been lost when he missed.

He had been told there was an Army fort nearby. They might have the ammunition he needed, but he couldn't chance leaving the Crossing because he'd have to take Ike with him. What if Uncle Roy were to come looking for them after they left? The same thing might happen if he went off hunting for game. With all these people and wagons all around, Uncle Roy just might turn around and go home.

And what did he really know about Uncle Roy? He didn't even know what his uncle looked like. All he knew was that Uncle Roy lived in a town called Boulder, but he had no idea where that was. Even if he did, with Ike and him riding double on the gray they'd be easy targets for Cheyenne Dog Soldiers. He couldn't place his little brother in such jeopardy, not with Ike's fear of Indians.

Garrison looked again at the hundreds of wagons waiting to cross the river, and the hundreds more camped along the low hills. For the first time since they'd left their home in Missouri, he felt alone. He was only fourteen, yet the responsibility for taking care of Ike was crushing him. In the Greek myths he had read about Atlas carrying the weight of the skies on his shoulders for all eternity. He now knew exactly how Atlas must have felt.

He was so deep in thought he barely heard a voice calling. It was almost drowned out by the sounds battling each other in the air: men and families shouting, horses snorting and whinnying, whips cracking, and wagon wheels creaking over soft, wet earth.

It was a male voice, indistinct at first, then slowly building in clarity as the voice drew nearer to them. And then he began to make out words. No, they were names shouted repeatedly in a deep, somewhat-raspy baritone voice: "Garrison and Isaac Fleck! Garrison and Isaac Fleck!"

Garrison was now able to discern which direction the shouting was coming from, far to their left, slowly getting closer. He looked in that direction but there were too many wagons and riders on horseback to cull from his vision. If he didn't call out soon, the man looking for them might move off in another direction. He shouted, "Here! Garrison and Ike Fleck here!" He kept shouting and waving his hat high above his head, looking in the direction of whoever was calling their names.

Garrison saw a man on a brown horse look over and then spur his horse toward them. The man pulled up hard when he reached them. Leaping to the ground, he grabbed the brothers and pulled them from the gray and down onto the ground.

Ike started to cry, frightened by this strange man who had his arms fastened tightly around him and his brother. Garrison felt the hard-muscled arms grasping him against an equally muscular body smelling of sweat, wood smoke, and gunpowder.

"I was afraid I might never find you two," said Roy, almost in a whisper. "If you'd stayed north into Wyoming, if the Cheyenne…"

By now Garrison was sure this was their Uncle Roy Parker, the man their mother had sent them to live with. Roy held them away from his body and crouched down to look at them. Garrison saw a man with thick brown hair spilling down from his gray, wide-brimmed hat, brown eyes that looked like his mother's, and a strong face that reminded him of his father's. But where his father had worn a thick, drooping mustache, his uncle's face, except for a few days' growth of beard, was clean shaven. He wore a plaid cotton shirt and blue jeans, the pants cuffs stuffed inside mud-splattered, knee-high leather boots.

"At first I didn't know who Isaac Fleck was," said Garrison. "I've only called him Ike his whole life."

"Well," smiled Roy, "at least I got the Garrison part right. Let's head over to my camp."

Roy mounted his horse and waited for his nephews. Garrison lifted Ike back onto the gray and swung into the saddle behind him. The blankets had fallen into the mud. Garrison decided to leave them there.

Roy spurred his horse, wending his way past wagons and horses as the brothers followed behind. At the campsite stood a buckboard, the green paint on it faded from years of traversing prairieland and mountains alike.

Hobbled near the wagon was a second brown horse, eating hay that Roy had forked down from the wagon. A white canvas tarpaulin was pulled back halfway across the wagon bed and tied down with hooks on both sides. Next to the wagon was a canvas wall tent, ten feet long with seven-foot tall walls, the guylines attached to wooden pegs sunk deep into the mud. A second tarpaulin had been laid down as a tent floor. It was a castle compared to many of the makeshift shelters erected by other travelers who hadn't quite thought their journey through. Outside the tent was a fire pit, its embers warm and still faintly glowing.

Roy led the brothers into the tent. "Home away from home," he said. "I've already got bedrolls fixed up for you. May not be as comfortable as you're used to, and I apologize for that."

"Sleeping in a covered wagon with nine other people wasn't all that comfortable," said Garrison. "This'll do us fine by comparison."

Roy smiled. He instantly liked Garrison. Ike, on the other hand, was still clinging to Garrison and not saying a word. He'd come around in time, or at least Roy hoped he would.

As Roy left the tent to relight the fire pit, Garrison grabbed Ike's hand and followed his uncle outside. Roy threw a few wood slats from some busted-up rifle crates onto the coals, gave them a few hearty puffs, and the fire reignited. Straddling the fire pit was a steel tripod. A cast iron Dutch oven hung from a hook attached to a chain hanging from the top of the tripod. Using a bandana to protect his hand, he lifted the lid of the Dutch oven and stirred its steaming contents with a ladle. "Warmed up beef stew out here can taste better than the finest steak served in Denver. Unfortunately, we're having rabbit," he said with a sly wink.

Eating from tin plates, Garrison and Ike didn't mind at all, having eaten their fair share of rabbit along the Oregon Trail. Garrison hadn't had much time yet to observe his uncle, but he could already tell Roy was a man of few words. He would also learn that Uncle Roy had just told one of his rare jokes in an attempt to put them all at ease. He seemed to be doing all the right "uncle" things so far, but Garrison could also feel his uncle's discomfort. The man had been obligated to care for nephews he knew nothing about.

That evening after finishing what remained of the rabbit stew, they sat around the campfire staring intently at the flickering flames. A shower of sparks rose each time a burning log slipped down into the glowing red coals. Ike had fallen asleep leaning against his brother. Garrison gently lowered Ike's head to his lap and, lost in thought, absent-mindedly stroked his little brother's hair. It was then he told Roy about their father's death in the war, and of their mother's suicide.

Roy was silent, not knowing what to say. He gazed at the brown-haired older boy stroking the blond hair of the sleeping younger brother like a loving, protective parent. With a bit of hesitation he said, "Your folks would be proud of what you've done. You should be proud too. Getting you and Ike here all this way on your own. It takes a real man to do that."

"Well, I ain't proud of any of it," Garrison shot back. "I did what had to be done for Ike. It's not like I had any choice."

Roy paused, taken aback by the sharpness, the anger and pain in his nephew's tone. Then he spoke his first words about his sister, carefully choosing those words. "What your mama did…surprises me. But I'm not one to judge her for what she did or for what your daddy did by goin' off to fight. Most folks try to do what they think is right at the time. Some put their families first. Some don't." It was the last time he would mention their parents.

Garrison managed to steal a sideways glance at his uncle. He got the feeling that Uncle Roy *had* made his judgment. And that *he* would always put family first. He would also learn that Uncle Roy had no family of his own, never having married nor fathered any children. As his uncle would tell him later, selling guns was no vocation for a family man.

CHAPTER 6

They left the Crossing the next day, taking the Overland Trail to the stagecoach cut-off past Camp Wardwell, then following the trail which led past the abandoned Fort Lupton towards Boulder. Riding in the buckboard was harder on Ike than riding inside the covered wagon since there was no soft bedding and no Hollings children to play with. Even though it added a few extra days of travel, Roy chose to break up each long day with frequent stops to rest and eat before making camp for the night. They reached Roy's ranch outside of Boulder a week later.

Besides the gun shop, Roy owned forty acres of land in a small canyon outside of town. The ranch house was made of wood and stone, with a large front porch that extended the length of it. The house stood on a rise, below it a line of box elders growing near a creek. The only other structures on the property were a horse barn with a few stalls, a corral attached to the side entrance of the barn, a smokehouse and an outhouse behind the main house.

There were no other animals on the ranch besides the two mares that pulled the wagon. Roy was not a farmer. He did not milk cows nor gather eggs. Farm work was an abhorrence born of his childhood days growing up on a farm. He was a businessman who enjoyed living on a ranch, albeit one with just two horses. He trained and fed them, which kept the mares loyal to him and the land. No need for fences to keep them from wandering off.

He didn't mind performing repairs and doing maintenance on the buildings and on the well he had dug himself. He had even run pipe from the well to the hand pump over the horse trough. Someday he might even run pipe into the house. Someday, when he was through selling guns.

Roy unhitched the mares from the wagon and led them over to the corral. He opened the gate and unbridled the horses who then leisurely sauntered inside. Garrison led the gray into the corral and removed its bridle. The gray wasted no time in joining its new companions at the water trough. Garrison handed the bridle over to Roy and lowered Ike down from the wagon seat. Roy hung the bridles over the corral fence, unloaded the gray's saddle from the buckboard and hung it alongside the bridles and reins.

"We'll leave all this here for now," Roy said, closing the corral gate. "I'll unload my stuff from the wagon later. Just give me a few minutes to fork some hay out of the barn here, and I'll get you and Ike inside the house."

With the horses contentedly watered and fed, Roy walked his new charges into their new home. Ike held tightly onto Garrison's hand. Pointing to an overstuffed sofa, Roy said, "You two can take a load off there." Despite his calm demeanor, Roy was a bit nervous. He rarely had visitors, and now he had committed to sharing his house with two young nephews he knew nothing about.

Roy scratched the back of his neck. "Afraid you boys'll have to share a room. I built this house just for me but when I got your mother's letter, I added on an extra room. Figured you boys wouldn't want to sleep in the same room with a snoring old goat like me."

On the sofa, Ike clung to Garrison, who was a mix of emotions. Now that they were finally in Uncle Roy's house, it was more real that their family home was gone forever.

Roy took another stab at being a good host. "I bet you boys are hungry. That's how I get after a long trip. I'll see what I got in the smokehouse and the icebox to turn into dinner for us. But first things first."

He squatted down in front of a cast iron cook stove and opened the firebox door. "Yeah, these ashes are just where I left 'em. I'll get a fire started and then we will see what we will eat. Sound good, boys?"

Garrison remained silent. He hoped his uncle's cooking was better than his jokes. But he clearly did mean well. Ike, almost burrowed into Garrison's side, did not understand what this Uncle Roy person was saying.

Roy took a couple of sticks of firewood from underneath the stove and fed them into the firebox. As he lit the fire, he had an idea for helping his nephews acclimate to their new home. "Garrison, maybe after dinner you and Ike can help me bring in two to four or five buckets of water? No more 'n' eight or nine at the most."

He closed the firebox door. "We'll heat enough water to fill up the bathtub." He smiled at the brothers. "Nothing like a good hot bath to make us feel like men again."

Never having had a family of his own, Roy at first was not sure he was up to the task. Garrison made it that much harder. Whether holding Ike during a night terror or attending to him after a skinned knee, Garrison was always there before Roy could attempt to comfort the younger boy. Roy was in a quandary, sometimes wondering if it was worth putting his business on hold if he didn't seem to be needed at home. But he was a patient and deliberate man. This was still a new situation for all of them. It would take time to get used to living with each other. He would take that time, because he wanted to do it right.

Garrison was doing his best to extend that time. He had accepted his uncle as family, but not as their guardian. For almost six months, *he* had been the sole family for Ike. It was a duty he had willingly taken on to the point where it was part of his identity. It had also kept his mind from dwelling on the surreal fact that he was an orphan, with no idea what he would do with his life other than provide for and protect Ike.

The older nephew presented another problem for his uncle. Garrison burned with an inner rage over being robbed of his parents. He couldn't blame it on anyone, so he took it out on everyone. In the fall, Roy enrolled Garrison in the Pioneer School. From the first day, he was subjected to the standard verbal hazing of a new student. But Garrison was stronger than the town boys, years of doing chores on the family farm having added layers of hard muscle to his young frame. By midweek, he responded to the taunts with his fists, breaking the jaw of one of the schoolboys. He also took a swing at schoolmaster Brown, who promptly expelled him from school.

That night, after Ike was put to bed, Roy sat in his favorite chair reading *Harper's New Monthly Magazine*, glancing occasionally at Garrison. The glowering boy was slumped on the sofa, his arms crossed in front of his chest. Inwardly, Roy was proud of how his nephew had defended himself against the school bullies. But there was a deeper problem to attend to.

In a conversational tone Roy said, "Those boys were pretty rough on you. I understand that. But my question is, did breaking that boy's jaw and getting expelled from school change the fact your folks are gone?"

Garrison said nothing. He tightened his crossed arms and folded himself further into the sofa.

Roy lowered the magazine. "Garrison, I asked you a question, and I'd appreciate the respect of an answer."

After a few moments to establish that it was his own idea, Garrison answered with a muttered, "No."

"Seems to me, then," Roy said, "you might want to try another tactic. Anger can't change the past. But it can prevent you from having a future. Just something you might want to think on."

Roy lifted the magazine and glanced at an illustration. Almost as an afterthought, he added, "You have family here, Garrison."

For Garrison, that was the night he first felt his anger slipping away. And he became less protective of his younger brother, allowing Roy to develop his own relationship with Ike. Roy would come to have a profound influence on the lives of both brothers in ways none of them could imagine at the time.

The Pioneer School refused to accept Ike on the grounds that the physical belligerence displayed by the older Fleck brother might be genetic. As there were no other schools in town, Roy was forced to educate both boys at home. With his gun business keeping him in town or on the road much of the time, Roy was fortunate that Garrison took responsibility for his own education as well as Ike's. Roy provided the boys with textbooks covering spelling and grammar, arithmetic, and history. Garrison loved schoolwork, immersing himself in his studies and grading his own papers.

Ike, on the other hand, had a limited attention span for learning his letters and numbers. Garrison considered it a good session if Ike lasted ten minutes before running outside to play solitary games of his own invention. Eventually, Ike grasped the basic concept of the three 'R's, but it took several months.

As the months drifted into autumn on their way to winter, Roy noticed that after Garrison finished his studies and his chores, he read the newspapers and magazines Roy brought home. Garrison was always reading something it seemed.

Garrison's love for reading gave Roy an idea. Two months before Garrison's fifteenth birthday, Roy walked into the general store owned by his friend Bill Benbow.

"Tell me, Bill," Roy said, "what are the boys reading these days?"

"Depends," Bill replied, "if they're reading for themselves or for school."

"I need both," said Roy.

"Well then, Edgar Allan Poe's got some great stories filled with blood and horror. They're real popular. And Mrs. Finlayson over to the schoolhouse got her older kids reading Shakespeare. She says if they can read that they can read anything."

Roy gave it a few moments thought. "How about choosing some books you think a boy about to turn fifteen would like and order some for me?"

Bill smiled at Roy. "Pardon me for sayin' this, Roy; you can go back to school but you ain't never goin' to be fifteen years old again."

"They're not for me, you idiot," said Roy, slightly annoyed. "I got someone else in mind who might like 'em."

On the day of his birthday, Garrison walked into the house after finishing his chores and saw two stacks of books on the dinner table. The first stack was a two-volume set of Edgar Allan Poe's *Tales of the Grotesque and Arabesque*. The second stack was *The Complete Works of William Shakespeare*, volumes one and two.

Roy was in the kitchen preparing the night's dinner.

Garrison picked up one of the Poe books. "What're these?"

Roy was preparing venison stew from a deer Garrison had killed. He stifled a grin as he sprinkled salt and pepper on cubed and floured venison meat in a bowl. "Oh, I thought I'd try to get a little culture into my brain, but I can't make hide nor hair of them books."

He spooned a couple of dollops of lard onto a hot cast iron skillet and poured the venison into the pan. "Maybe you can," he said with false indifference. He sneaked a glance at his nephew.

Garrison didn't buy the ruse at all, especially since his uncle never talked that way. But he was overjoyed by Roy's thoughtfulness—although he didn't dare show it. "Well, if I get some time, maybe I'll look at a page or two, see if I can help you out," he said, attempting the same indifference of tone, and failing just as his uncle had.

Roy sneaked another glance at Garrison and smiled. The boy had picked up all four books in one stack, holding them lovingly in his hands as he gazed warmly at the embossed titles. A smile crossed Roy's face as he chopped up carrots and onions on a cutting board.

The joy Garrison felt over his uncle's gift was palpable. Before he and Ike set off from their Missouri farm, he had packed his favorite books into the wagon: the English translation of Charles Perrault's *Tales of Mother Goose*, and Thomas Bullfinch's *The Age of Fable, or Stories of Gods and Heroes* and *The Age of Chivalry, or Legends of King Arthur*. These were the books his mother had read to him, and he had learned to read himself. Because of their bulk and weight, he had been forced to give up those works when he sold the horse and buckboard in Independence.

Reading was one of Garrison's great pleasures. He would finish reading a book and immediately start another one. For Christmas, Roy gave him all four volumes of *The Works of the Late Edgar Allan Poe*. The C. Auguste Dupin short stories greatly appealed to Garrison's natural ability for deductive reasoning. Some years later, Garrison would buy the Bullfinch books himself.

For Garrison, Roy had proven his loyalty after the school expulsion episode and had proven his love with those treasured gifts of books. As his Christmas gift to his uncle, Garrison gave him the remainder of the hidden money.

Roy sat at the table, staring at a pile of greenbacks. Not one to show his emotions, he found himself unable to speak.

"It's the money our mother gave us from selling the farm," said Garrison. "I had to spend some of it to get to Camp Rankin. I also bought that gray horse and some salted pork at Fort Kearny, so this is what's left. There's seven hundred and fifty dollars. I counted it."

"Garrison— "

"I would've given it to you sooner," Garrison broke in, "but I thought Ike and I might be needing it if things didn't work out here."

Roy raised an eyebrow. "If things didn't work out *here*?"

"Well, I didn't know you would be so, so—well, here's the money. Merry Christmas. Take it or leave it."

"Oh, I'm taking it," said Roy. He folded the stack of paper currency and stuffed it in his pants pocket. "Bet the next thing you tell me, you got a goldmine on Pike's Peak your granddaddy left you."

Garrison smiled. "No, sir. I surely wouldn't tell you if I had one of those."

Right after Christmas, Roy opened a joint trust fund for his nephews at a local bank. He just didn't let Garrison know about it.

The bond between Roy and Garrison had been solidified. He never preached or lectured, delivering wisdom and guidance to Garrison in succinct, quiet statements. He lived by example, and by that example Garrison quelled his rage, finding the self-confidence within himself to become a man of honesty and compassion.

Roy was too modest to take credit for any of it. As he said to Garrison once, "I had nothing to do with it. Your moral character was there from birth."

Ike was a different story. He never displayed the anger shown by Garrison. In fact, he never seemed to need disciplining at all, or need anyone else in his life besides Garrison. With the same close observation Roy had applied to Garrison, he watched Ike play games of war at the dining table. The games would last for hours with Ike using silverware and salt and pepper shakers as his opposing armies.

On the Christmas when he gave Garrison the sets of books, Roy gifted Ike with a metal toy soldier set imported from Germany. The figures looked strange to Ike at first, but he fashioned Army uniforms out of strips of cloth and tied them around his soldiers. Union soldiers wore dark uniforms, the Confederate army was adorned in what passed for gray. Overjoyed with his new toy soldier set, Ike waged tabletop battles that lasted for days.

Roy eventually sent away for more toy soldier sets along with toy naval ships and sailors. The collection grew so big that Ike moved his ongoing wars onto the hardwood floor in the main room. For the next year, he spent long hours every day waging his wars, oblivious to everyone and everything around him.

Roy knew he had not yet connected with Ike as he had with Garrison. Considering it a personal failure, he strived to find some way to get through to Ike, something that would excite the boy and bring him outside of his head. That something turned out to be someone on the cover of a magazine.

Ike happened to see the February 1867 edition of *Harper's New Monthly Magazine* on the dining table along with other mail his uncle had brought home from the post office. On the magazine cover was a picture of a tall mustachioed man, long hair flowing from beneath a flat-brimmed hat, his hand on a long-barreled gun tucked under his belt. Roy was still getting out of his coat when Ike picked up the magazine.

"Uncle Roy, who's this man?" he asked, holding the magazine up for his uncle to see.

Roy hung his coat on the dowel of a wall-mounted coat rack and walked over to Ike. "James Butler Hickok. Otherwise known as Wild Bill. Best man with a gun there is. If he ever stopped by the shop to buy a gun or two from me, I'd be set for life. Everyone would want to buy a gun from where Wild Bill bought his."

Something clicked inside Ike. There was something about the confidence this Wild Bill Hickok exuded on the magazine cover. The confidence came from the guns he wore, and how good he was with them. From that point onward, Wild Bill Hickok became Ike's idol. He became less involved with playing war, choosing instead to stage imaginary gunfights. His hands became six shooters and he made gunshot noises with his mouth. He was determined that someday he'd be the equal of Hickok—a fast and deadly shot. Perhaps if they met as equals, he could convince Wild Bill to visit the gun shop and make Uncle Roy famous, if that was what being set for life meant. Ike did indeed love his uncle; he just didn't know how to show it.

For Ike's seventh birthday, Roy gave him a wooden toy gun. Over time, the handle became worn from constant play. When Ike turned eight, Roy gave him an old .31 Colt Pocket Model revolver. The small-caliber cap and ball percussion revolver with the four-inch barrel was a perfect fit for Ike's small hands.

"Ike," said Roy, "I've put a lot of thought into this. A young man needs something in life to grab onto. A gun ain't always the answer but it was for me. At least selling them was. Let's see how you feel about it."

Ike was apprehensive at first. But when he took the gun from Roy and wrapped his fingers around the grip, something clicked inside him again. The way the gun felt in his hand, the balance of the small revolver seemed perfect, like it was meant for only him.

For the first time since Ike had come to live with Roy, he embraced his uncle tightly, burying his face in Roy's abdomen. In a muffled voice he said, "I love you, Uncle Roy." It was also the first time he had ever spoken these words.

With Ike's eyes safely pressed against his chest, Roy allowed his own eyes to well up with tears. He wrapped his arms around Ike and quietly said, "I love you too, son." It had just naturally come out. Roy wasn't sure how Ike would react. His nephew just tightened his embrace around his uncle. Roy held onto Ike as he held onto the moment.

The toy soldier sets were now forgotten. Ike had found his identity, the foundation upon which he would build his own self-confidence and chart the course of his life. Naturally blessed with quick hand-eye coordination and reflexes, he became obsessed with the gun. Wearing it under his belt, he practiced quick draws and target shooting for hours on end each day. Within a few months he could both draw the weapon with speed and shoot with accuracy. He could hit anything he aimed at with all five shots. In his mind, he was Wild Bill Hickok shooting outlaws through the heart from over a hundred feet away.

When Garrison turned nineteen, Roy hired him to work in the gun shop as a clerk. Gifted with a mind for mathematics, he was soon in charge of doing the books. Within months Garrison was running the business under his uncle's guidance. As for Roy, he began to flirt with thoughts of retirement—someday.

Garrison had gathered enough knowledge of guns and rifles to be able to sell them, but he never took to them the way Ike had. His .50-70 Springfield

Model 1866 rifle was his weapon of choice for hunting, which continued to be his passion.

This is where Ike came into the business. Working as Roy's assistant, he absorbed everything about firearms his uncle had to teach at the workbench. As with Garrison, Ike quickly proved he could work independently, handling repairs and maintenance by himself. He was soon loading ammunition on his own, including cartridges for Garrison's rifle. He even learned how to make cap and ball paper cartridges for the Pocket Colt.

This freed Roy to run the other part of his business. He traveled to towns and military installations, selling guns and performing minor repairs. He journeyed alone, staying away from home for weeks at a time as he visited customers in parts of the Colorado Territory, Nebraska, and Kansas. He had no worries about Garrison. The lad had a cool, confident independence about him.

It was Ike who concerned him. While Roy loved both boys like they were his own sons, he had to admit Ike was unique. He would sometimes say things that were inappropriate, thinking he was just being funny or honest. He never developed the awareness of other people finding his words odd or downright offensive. Ike couldn't figure people out, so he stayed to himself, spending hours on his fast draw and target shooting or working on firearms at the shop.

Roy was seldom home these days. Ike seemed so troubled, and Roy felt guilty over this. He needed to find a way to spend more time with the boy. The annual trip to Fort Collins was coming up. The military post had been decommissioned two years ago, but the town was thriving. Sales were always good there.

Since war parties of hostile Indians were no longer a problem, Roy decided to take his nephew along with him. Ike had never been one to talk much, but perhaps during the long drive Roy could find a way to have a meaningful conversation with him. He didn't know what else to do.

As they rode in the green-painted buckboard pulled by the two mares, Ike was lost in thought. It was a sunny day, and they had been on the road for a little over two hours. Ike was looking at the Rocky Mountains to their left, thinking he wouldn't want to be lost inside any mountains because he'd never find his way out.

To the right of the trail was the yellow green vastness of the Great Plains. The endless miles of open grassland reminded Ike of the journey with Garrison from Independence to the Upper California Crossing five years earlier. He really didn't remember much of it. He did recall meeting Uncle Roy and how afraid he had been of the big man. He turned his head to glance at his uncle sitting next to him. How could a man he loved so much have been so scary?

But he also remembered the Hollings family and playing with the children. Children who had parents. He always felt strange when Roy took him into town, seeing the families all about, especially on Sundays after church. He wished his own parents were still alive. It gnawed at him not being able to remember what they had looked like.

The wide-open expanse they drove along had not yet succumbed to the fenced off divisions of sprawling ranches and homesteads, and the growing incursion of towns. The land was all so strange, yet Uncle Roy seemed to know it like his own ranch. He would have the horses trotting straight ahead for miles then turn off onto a road that broke off to one side or the other. This confused Ike.

"Uncle Roy," he asked, "how do you always know how to get where you're goin'? Have you already been everywhere?"

It took Roy a moment to answer. He allowed himself a little grin but the last thing he wanted was for Ike to feel foolish over any question he asked. "Well, son," he said, "I ain't been everywhere by a long shot but I do always know where I'm headin' and how to get there. Know how?"

"No, I don't. That's why I'm askin' you."

Roy, holding the reins, lifted his hand and pointed a finger at the dirt road stretched out ahead of them. "See this trail headin' way out further than we can see? This was made by game animals first, then by Indians hunting them and then by everyone who came after. That's the way trails are made, Ike. Mostly by people who figured out the best way to get from one place to another."

Ike could remember how his fear of Indians had kept him inside the covered wagon on the Oregon Trail. "Are we gonna be attacked by Indians?"

"Nope. Army's pretty much got them moved over onto the reservations. And any of them wants trouble sure don't want to mess with a couple of sharpshooters like us, do they?"

"Nope, I don't think they would, Uncle Roy."

"Well then, all we need to think about is gettin' to Fort Collins. And this trail will take us there. Always keep to the trail, Ike. That way you'll never get lost. It'll always get you to your destination."

Always keep to the trail. Ike decided that was something he needed to remember. And so, he would.

CHAPTER 7

The brothers' lives abruptly changed again in June 1871 when Roy was shot to death inside the gun shop. The killer's intent had been to steal a weapon to use in a bank robbery. He set fire to the shop to cover up the murder and to distract the town as he rode off, only to be killed at the bank an hour later by the armed manager.

The volunteer fire department had to let the shop burn to the ground, not daring to enter the building with all the ammunition and black powder exploding like artillery shells in a battlefield. Sparks were flying everywhere; black smoke was billowing over that entire part of town. The raging fire soon consumed the entire block, taking out all the adjacent businesses.

Roy had stocked a lot of ammunition behind the sales counter and in the back storeroom. It wasn't until early evening the explosions finally stopped. The fire continued unabated the next day, finally settling down into smoke and scattered flames by the afternoon. The fire department brought the firehoses out then to drown the still-burning wreckage in water.

Mercifully, the fire was out. Steam, more than smoke, rose from the ashes and cinders of what had been Roy's gun shop. The business was a total loss. When the firefighters were finally able to make their way through the rubble, they found the charred remains of Roy's body lying behind what had been the sales counter.

Roy left a will stipulating he be laid to rest on his ranchland. Garrison chose a spot among the box elders by the creek. Bill Benbow paid for the custom-made oak casket for his old friend, hand rubbing the oil finish himself.

The funeral was well-attended even though it was held so far out of town. Roy had been a respected businessman, and the town officials and merchants came to pay their respects. Most of the men in town had purchased weapons from him, and they brought their families with them to the burial service.

Once again, the Fleck brothers were alone. Garrison was now twenty; Ike was ten. At least they still had a home. Roy had left them the house and land in his will. But that was followed by a surprise. According to the lawyer reading the will, Roy had bequeathed the joint trust fund to his nephews.

Garrison was speechless. He was angered at first, but he had to admire the logic behind the action. Although Uncle Roy had hidden the existence of this fund from Garrison, he had given his nephews full access to the money just when they needed it most.

But, Ike's dream of having Wild Bill Hickok purchase guns from his uncle's shop was gone. Again, he withdrew into himself. Burying his sorrow, he practiced drawing and firing the Colt with an increased fervor. He didn't speak to anyone, not even Garrison.

All business records had burned up with the gun shop. A week after the funeral, Garrison gathered together what business files and possessions of Roy's he could find in the ranch house. Ike walked in after an afternoon of gun practice and went to his room. On his bed was the magazine with Wild Bill Hickok on the cover. He picked it up and stared at his hero.

Garrison was suddenly at the doorway. Ike saw him, dropped the magazine on the bed, and rushed to him. He hugged his brother tightly, his face pressed against Garrison's chest. And then all the grief, all the tears poured out of him like a deluge of water gushing from a burst dam.

"Why'd he have to die, Garrison? Why'd he have to die?" Ike cried for his uncle, he cried for himself. And he cried for all the things in the world he didn't understand.

Garrison held his brother, just letting the tears spend itself out. "I don't know Ike. Bad things don't always need a reason to happen. If I'd been working in the shop that day, it might have been me who got killed."

Ike looked up at Garrison, his eyes leaping with fright. "No, Garrison," he said, alarmed by the mental vision of his brother being shot. "You don't get to die. Promise me you won't die."

Garrison held his brother closer and began caressing his hair. "I promise you I won't die anytime soon. We'll be together quite a while yet."

That seemed to calm Ike. His tears began to subside.

Garrison stood there, comforting his brother and wondering what he was supposed to do next.

CHAPTER 8

With the death of his uncle, Garrison's rage might have returned, but he couldn't afford to succumb to it now. He needed to figure out how he was going to support Ike and himself now that Uncle Roy's business was gone. There was the trust fund, but that wouldn't last forever. He had to find steady work, but doing what? There were people who would hire him, but he couldn't see himself clerking in a general store or hiring on as a ranch hand.

Truth was, Garrison wasn't sure what he wanted to do with his life. And he was frustrated. If it wasn't for Ike, he could do any manner of things. He could wander freely and endlessly with no one to answer to. But raising Ike was his responsibility, and so his frustration also filled him with guilt.

Within a month an opportunity presented itself. Garrison had just about decided to sell the ranch, take Ike and move to Denver when he saw a help wanted ad in the local paper. The J.K. Binghamton Stage Line, with a stage station in Boulder, was looking for a shotgun messenger. Based on his skills with a rifle, Garrison was hired, and handed a 12-gauge double barreled coach gun. He had never shot one before but he figured it was a lot easier to shoot than his big Springfield rifle. All he had to do was point the barrels in the direction of a hold up gang and squeeze both triggers.

Before he could start his new career, Garrison realized he couldn't leave Ike on his own. His brother didn't like being left alone in the house; he said it scared him. He refused to take a bath if Garrison wasn't home. He wore his shirts inside out, saying they felt better that way. He didn't understand how to start a fire in the cook stove so he couldn't feed himself. Garrison wryly thought that if it wasn't for Ike's shooting ability, he'd be one hundred percent helpless.

Then there were the horses to think of. Thanks to Uncle Roy, Ike could ride, but that was all he could do. He couldn't saddle or put a bridle on a horse himself. While he had an affinity for animals—and they seemed to love him—he wasn't too keen on taking care of them. He knew how to water the horses at the trough and let them out of the corral to feed on grass, but that was about it. No, there was nothing else for it but find someone to look after Ike and the horses.

Once again, Ben Benbow stepped in to help. He just happened to know a stove-up chuck wagon cook by the name of Taggart. The old man was down on his luck, in need of a job and a place to live. But as it fortunately turned out, he was still in good enough shape to cook Ike's meals and to look after the horses. Ike would have to handle his own baths.

Garrison paid him ten dollars a month and, as the house cook and Ike's caretaker, he bunked inside the house. It was easy money for Taggart and cheap peace of mind for Garrison when he was away from home, which was just about all the time.

As it turned out, Taggart and Ike grew very close. The old man had lots of cattle drive stories to tell, and tall tales of gunman he had seen in trail towns. Ike loved every story and had to show off his own gun skills. After witnessing an impromptu exhibition, Taggart exclaimed he had seen no one better with a gun in his entire life.

On his first day as a shotgun messenger, Garrison found himself paired with Duke Ferrell, the best whip, or driver, in the company. Duke handled the on-the-job training, explaining to Garrison exactly what his job entailed, and how to stay alive doing it. Over time, Garrison allowed himself to open up a little, and talked a bit about his past, and the loss of people he loved. He told Duke about Ike, and how much he hated leaving his little brother for days or weeks at a time, although he was being well-cared for.

Over the long hours and months of riding the stage together, Duke became more like a father figure to Garrison, filling the void left by Roy's death. He had the same gentle way of giving sage advice that resonated with his young partner.

Garrison had been on the job for a year when he was paired with another stagecoach whip for a run carrying passengers to Greeley. J.K. Binghamton had just bought out a rival stage company and Duke had been assigned the task of riding the new routes on horseback to map them out for the other drivers. The existing route maps had been part of the acquisition, but Duke insisted on drawing up new maps himself.

The stagecoach on this run was carrying $800 in gold. Up to that point, Garrison had never been the shotgun messenger on a stage with a cargo that valuable. He could tell that the tight-lipped driver was very nervous about it. As it turned out, the driver's nervousness had been warranted. En route to its destination the stage was held up by a masked gang. The driver threw his gun down when given the order, but Garrison refused to let go of his shotgun. The gang opened fire on them both, killing the driver instantly. Garrison was the lucky one; the sound of gunfire spooked the stagecoach's team of horses. When the leaders reared up on their hind legs, the stage moved just enough so that a bullet fired at Garrison hit him in the shoulder. The force of the impact knocked him sideways before he tumbled to the ground below. He lost consciousness from both the shock of the bullet wound and hitting the hard-packed dirt. Miraculously, the bullet had gone clear through the shoulder, missing the vital arteries. Thinking he was dead from the blood spilling out from his body onto the ground, the gang ignored him. After robbing the passengers of their money and valuables, the holdup gang went riding off with the stolen gold.

The local sheriff, advised by the station agent that the stage was over an hour late, rode up with his posse about forty-five minutes later. They found Garrison lying unconscious on the ground. He had lost a lot of blood but was still alive. They lifted him into the stage and laid him across one of the seats. A deputy climbed up to the driver's box and drove the stage to Greeley while the passengers stayed inside the stage with the wounded shotgun messenger.

It took Garrison a month in a hospital to recuperate from his wounds. But instead of going home to Ike, he set out to track down the gang who robbed the stage, killed the driver, and left him for dead.

Naturally gifted with a brilliant, deductive mind and a memory for detail, he gathered clues to the gang's whereabouts and tracked them down. Within a few weeks, Garrison led the local sheriff and his posse to the gang's hideout in Clear Creek Canyon. After a brief shootout where two of the gang members were killed, the sheriff arrested the survivors. Inside the house they found $13,000 in gold and cash stolen in a string of robberies, including the stage Garrison had been guarding.

In return for recovering all the stolen loot, he received cash rewards that had been posted by other stagecoach lines and the banks the gang had robbed. J.K. Binghamton himself handed Garrison a check for a hundred dollars and promoted his young shotgun messenger to stagecoach detective.

This new change in his career excited Garrison, and he found he was reluctant to ride back to the ranch. When he arrived, he found that Ike had no inkling anything had been wrong. He was used to Garrison being gone for weeks at a time.

Taggart, on the other hand, figured something bad had happened. "Garrison, if you don't mind me saying, but I know it don't take no two months to get from Boulder to Greeley by stagecoach. I'm bettin' you found some trouble along the way."

Garrison was forced to admit he'd almost been killed during the stagecoach robbery, and that after his recovery he had tracked the gang back to their hideout. He allowed himself to brag about his new position with the company. "But don't tell Ike any of this. He doesn't need to know I got shot. That's too close to me dying as far as he's concerned."

Handing Taggart extra money as back pay for the time he'd been gone, he then peeled off a ten-dollar bill as a pay raise. No telling how long this new job would keep him on the road, and he wanted to keep the old man happy.

Garrison was now assigned to the company's stage station in Pueblo. He immediately began to formally educate himself about detective work. Building upon what he had learned from the C. Auguste Dupin series by Poe, he studied the investigative techniques of the Pinkerton National Detective Agency, reading up on their case histories as he compiled his own file of notes and ideas. The hard, painstaking work paid off. Garrison was highly effective in tracking down holdup gangs and recovering most of their stolen loot.

But as he had figured, the job continued to keep him on the road for extended periods of time. The J.K. Binghamton Stage Line had purchased other stagecoach companies with routes throughout the Territory. It seemed like a stagecoach was being held up every month. Garrison was tracking a solitary robber when he came to a realization: he enjoyed being away from the ranch. With Taggart taking care of Ike, Garrison was also enjoying his freedom from responsibility. And then it struck him: had Uncle Roy felt the same way about leaving Garrison to watch Ike when he was off selling guns?

CHAPTER 9

It was just shy of seven years since the death of Uncle Roy. Garrison was twenty-seven and Ike had just turned seventeen. Taggart, the old chuck wagon cook, had decided to mosey on down the trail the previous year. He had achieved a personal triumph by managing to teach Ike how to fix steak and beans. In addition, he had gotten Ike to accept taking baths twice a month and had helped him accept putting shirts on with the buttons facing out.

Ike was old enough to take care of himself, but his lack of maturity worried Garrison. He needed to learn responsibility and act like an adult. There was only one fix for it: his brother would have to find a job in town. Ike had to grow up sometime.

The brothers were standing in line inside the Boulder City Bank where Garrison kept their accounts. Garrison stood behind Ike so he could keep an eye on him. He had opened a separate account for depositing his pay from Binghamton and had long ago converted the trust fund into a joint savings account with his brother.

Drawing on his bookkeeping days from the gun shop, he carefully budgeted for expenses and purchases. While the mares still pulled the green buckboard for trips to town from the ranch, the gray had been retired to pasture. Garrison had borrowed from the joint account to buy two new horses and expand the tack room in the barn. The loan was almost paid off, and the deposits would soon all go towards savings.

Still, there were times to ignore the budget. Garrison was making more money now, so he splurged on a Winchester Model 1873, and the new Colt Frontier Six Shooter for himself. His old Springfield was a big, heavy hunting rifle, and the smaller caliber repeating rifle was better suited for his line of work. The Colt was a highly accurate single action revolver and used the same .44-40 bullets as the Winchester. That made good financial sense.

Ike's Pocket Colt was still a treasured gift from Uncle Roy, but for his birthday the previous year Garrison had bought him a pair of .36 Remington New Model Navy percussion revolvers, mainly because the dealer had no Navy Colts on hand. Ike was very disappointed that they weren't Hickok's .36 Colt Model 1851 Navy cap and ball revolvers but agreed they were a very good second choice. Quickly mastering the guns through daily practice, Ike decided most people couldn't tell the difference between the two anyway.

Ike was wearing one of his brother's old shirts, slightly too big for him but he liked the soft, broken-in feel of the fabric against his skin. On his head was an old, wide-brimmed hat that had belonged to Uncle Roy, also slightly too big for him. Tucked under his belt were last year's birthday gifts, worn gun butts forward in the style of Hickok.

He was practicing the Cavalry Draw, drawing the two revolvers from under his belt and twisting them right side up with the barrels facing forward. He practiced it over and over as he stood in line, making gunshot noises with his mouth as he pretended to shoot at random targets. Then he would flip the revolvers back under his belt in their original gun butts forward position.

A woman standing in front of Ike turned towards him twice, looking annoyed and nervous whenever he made those gunshot sounds.

Garrison, watching from behind Ike, whispered, "Leave those guns alone, please."

Ike pretended not to hear and kept practicing the two-handed twist draw.

The woman turned around a third time and said sharply, "Young man, will you please stop playing with those—things—and put them away? If one of them accidentally goes off and kills someone—that someone will be me! "

Ike didn't pay attention to her so Garrison stepped in. "I'm sorry, ma'am, I'll take care of it." Garrison turned Ike around to face him. "Ike, look at me. Look at me," he said calmly but firmly. "Can't you see you're upsetting this nice lady?" He nodded toward the woman Ike had worked into a state of agitation.

Ike slowly brought his eyes up to his brother's face. "No. You got me turned around so I can't see her. Besides, I wasn't playing with my guns. I'm practicing my Cavalry Draw."

Garrison was firm. "Well, you're upsetting her. I'm going to need you to keep those guns under your belt, walk over to that bench and sit down and wait for me. I'm almost done here and when I am, I'll come get you. OK?"

"Can I still practice with my guns?" Ike asked.

"I'm sorry, Ike," Garrison answered. "Let's keep 'em under that belt for now."

"Can I practice just using my fingers?" asked Ike.

"Fingers, yes. Guns, no. Guns kept under the belt," Garrison repeated, looking at the revolvers still in Ike's hands. "Now, put your guns away and go sit on that bench. Quietly."

Guns secured under the belt, Ike walked to the bench and sat down. Garrison turned to look at the line in front of him. The nervous lady was now being helped by one of the tellers. He was next in line. Behind him on the bench, Ike was pretending his fingers were the Remingtons, pointing them at customers while making the same gunshot noises as before.

In a few minutes Garrison had completed his deposit and finished counting the cash he had asked for. He stuffed the bills into his wallet and put the wallet in his inside coat pocket. As he turned away from the teller window, three men wearing bandanas over their lower faces burst into the bank. One of the robbers stationed himself at the door, his feet spread apart in a wide stance. His gun was pointed at the ceiling.

The two other men waved their guns from side to side, pointing them at everyone inside the bank. The one wearing a grey floppy hat shouted out, "OK, ladies and gents. This is a holdup. Raise your hands and line up in front of these teller windows. Do what you're told and nobody gets dead."

His partner, stifling a laugh, quickly walked over to stand in front of the tellers. Gun in one hand, he grasped a leather valise and some large burlap bags in the other.

Floppy Hat looked over at the bank manager, sitting at a desk a few feet behind the teller windows. "You, Mr. Bank Manager over there. Come over to this door next to these teller windows and open it. Stand where I can see you and keep your hands up. Do anything else and you get a third eye hole between the other two."

Floppy Hat's partner snickered again.

Shaking with fright, the bank manager nervously walked to the door, both hands held high in the air. He lowered one hand to open the door then immediately raised it above his head. Behind him was the open bank vault.

Floppy Hat looked at his partner standing a few feet away. "Hand them burlap bags over to this gentleman here," he said, pointing his gun at Garrison, "so he can give them to those bank tellers to fill up from their cash drawers."

His partner held the bags out to Garrison, who started to grab them with his left hand. The robber said, "Uh uh," pointing his gun barrel at Garrison's other hand. Garrison had started to lower it toward the gun he wore on his right hip. He now had no choice but to take the bags and try to stall while he figured out a plan of action.

"What about the money in the vault?" the robber asked over his shoulder.

Floppy Hat exhaled a very peevish breath. As if he were talking to a child, he said, "We just went over it this morning. You never listen, do you? You just gave the bags to Mr. Trickster here. He hands 'em out to the tellers to fill up. Meanwhile you and Mr. Bank Manager over there walk into the vault. You hold the gun on him while he fills the leather case with all the cash he can stuff inside it. I grab them burlap bags from the tellers, they get inside the vault with Mr. Bank Manager and you lock it up tight. Just be sure to grab that leather case first. Now be right quick about it. We got about three minutes to get this done."

Floppy Hat's partner had just started to move when a loud voice sounded. "Drop your guns and hands up!" It was the voice of a young man.

Garrison froze, the burlap bags still in his hand. The robber guarding the front door turned his head toward the voice. Floppy Hat and his partner looked around, searching for the person who dared interrupt their carefully planned bank robbery.

Ike was on his feet, facing both men with his hands poised over his guns. His words were straight out of the Wild Bill Hickok dime novels Garrison had read aloud to him many times. However, there was a coldness in his voice that Garrison had never heard before; one suffused with absolute confidence.

Floppy Hat looked at Ike, wearing his two guns Hickok-style. "Why, it's Wild Bill Hickok come back from the grave. And lookee here at them guns ol' Bill's wearin'. They look older than *him*. Hell, I bet they don't even shoot no more."

His snickering partner turned back to face Garrison. Pointing his gun at the burlap bags he said, "I want them handed out—pronto!" As he turned his head, the bandana slipped down from his face. He looked down at his nose for a moment, looked up at Garrison and then lifted the bandana back into place again.

Ike stood there looking at the two men. The robber to his left guarding the door turned to face him, his gun pointed at Ike's body. Ike wasn't nervous or scared at all. He was locked in a zone where it was just him and the bank robbers. His face was blank, something he had practiced in front of a mirror for years. His hands were held motionless just above his guns.

Ike eyed Floppy Hat coldly. "My name isn't Wild Bill Hickok but thank you for sayin' so. It's Isaac Fleck but I go by Ike. And I said drop your guns and hands up."

Garrison, trying to keep his eyes on all three robbers, glanced over at Ike. The last thing he wanted was for Ike to identify himself to everyone inside the bank. How bad was this going to get?

"You're Hickok, alright," said Floppy Hat. "You're about to be a dead man two times over. C'mon, dead man, get me to drop my gun." He lowered his bandana and pointed his gun directly at Ike. He wanted Ike to see who he was dealing with.

The second robber looked at his partner, the smile vanished from his face. "We don't have time for this now, Avery. I still got to get inside the vault. Just shoot the kid and be done with it."

Avery turned his head slightly toward his partner. "Damn it, Coughlin, I told you not to say our names. I'll deal with you later. Go take care of that bank vault." He turned his attention back to Ike. "OK, Wild Bill, show me what you got."

Ike was confused. "I'm showing you my guns. I don't got anything else."

Avery started to laugh.

Garrison saw Avery's finger loosen on the trigger of his gun. He mentally weighed if he could drop the bags and pull his gun fast enough to shoot Avery before taking a bullet himself. He concluded he could not. He didn't have nearly the gun speed he had seen Ike display during shooting practice.

The laughter gone, Avery raised his gun and pointed it at Ike's head. "Go ahead an' open the ball, Wild Bill. But you'll have to kill all three of us."

Before the last words had left Avery's mouth, Ike drew both guns with blinding speed, firing at the two robbers in front of him. Avery clutched his stomach with one hand. He attempted to raise his gun again, but Ike shot him in the chest, the force of the bullet driving him backward against the line of teller windows. His gun still in his hand, he fell face forward to the floor, and lay still.

Coughlin had dropped the valise as he was bringing his gun around to shoot Ike. Ike's bullet hit him in the throat. Coughlin dropped the gun and clutched his throat with both hands, blood spraying in rhythmic beats between his fingers. He was both gasping and choking as he dropped to his knees. He fell backward, his legs folded underneath his body. The back of his skull cracking against the wooden floor echoed loudly in the room. His choking breaths stopped within a few seconds, his hands falling away from his neck.

The robber guarding the door made the mistake of looking at his two partners who had just been killed. It gave Ike just enough time to draw back the hammers on both guns, make the pivot and fire two rounds into the robber's chest and belly. The double blow from the bullets knocked the man backward and down into a sitting position as his gun dropped out of his hand. He sat there, staring down at the blood spreading across his shirt. He brought his hands down to press against the shirt as if that would stop the bleeding. He raised one hand up to his face, somewhat in disbelief that the blood was his. He then slumped down onto his side, dead.

Ike stood there as if in a trance, his guns pointing at where the third bank robber had stood. There had been no conscious thought. Instinct, utilizing the reflexive and deadly guns skills he had honed over years of practice, had taken over when he had drawn the revolvers. It took him a moment to realize what he had just done.

He looked down at the guns in both hands. Five shots had hit their targets, three bank robbers dead in a matter of seconds. "Thank you, Mr. Remington," he said quietly. He twirled the guns and thrust them back under his belt, butts forward.

Garrison, along with everyone else in the bank, stared in amazement at Ike. Quite a few times, he had watched his brother practice that two-handed twist draw and then fire both guns at the same time. He had just never seen Ike this fast—nor this lethal. He had killed three men in less time than it took most men to draw a gun from its holster and aim. He realized he had to get Ike out of there—fast. Dropping the burlap bags, Garrison quickly walked over to Ike and whispered, "We gotta go—now."

"But I just killed them all. Why do we gotta go?"

Garrison took Ike by the arm and, maneuvering around the body of the third robber, pulled him toward the front door. "Because we have to, that's all. Now, c'mon."

Garrison led Ike to the door and pushed him out. On the street, he dragged Ike to the hitching rail where their horses were tied.

Ike's voice was loud and excited. "He called me Wild Bill Hickok, Garrison! Did you hear him call me that? And did you hear me talk like Wild Bill? Son of a bitch I did!"

Garrison hastily untied the reins of both horses, handing one set to his brother. He quickly stepped into the saddle and backed his horse away from the hitching rail.

Ike was in the saddle and turning his horse toward Garrison. "I don't know what you're fussing about. They were trying to rob the bank."

Garrison didn't answer. He was still processing what had just happened. He had known Ike was fast, but this was beyond belief. Yet he had seen it with his own eyes.

Garrison was afraid of word getting out about a kid who was lethal lightning with a gun. It would probably be tomorrow's headline in all the newspapers. Damn it all—it might even be picked up by the *Police Gazette*. If Ike's fame went national, fast guns would be coming out of the woodwork to seek their own fame by killing him. Did a faster gun exist? He wasn't sure. All he knew was he had to get Ike away from Boulder—immediately. As they galloped off, he had an idea.

CHAPTER 10

The J.K. Binghamton Stage Line was headquartered in Denver because its owner, J.K. Binghamton, was married to a woman from a wealthy Denver family. Preferring to live near her family, she had forced J.K. Binghamton to run his company from an office in Denver while the main hub of his stagecoach business was in Pueblo, one hundred twenty miles away (Binghamton often muttered that he could have paid off the company debt with what he paid in telegram fees). From there, stage routes fanned out over central and southern Colorado.

The stagecoach business had been very good to J.K. Binghamton who had founded the company with his wife's money. Problem was, he had never told her about it, and she was never one to read bank account statements. As long as she could sign for her own purchases and the bills were always paid by her husband, she gave no thought to that account.

But now, his business was facing increasing competition from the burgeoning railroad industry. More people were choosing to ride passenger trains, enjoying how much faster—and more comfortably—they reached their destinations than any stagecoach could. Business firms were now shipping more goods and materials by train because of the faster speed of delivery and their capability to carry a lot more freight than a stagecoach. The railroad lines were moving in everywhere, taking business away from the stagecoach companies.

Business had gotten bad—very bad. Stage lines were going under, with Binghamton picking up the ones with routes he deemed still profitable. But those routes had turned out to be not that profitable. In fact, red ink was gradually replacing black ink on the business ledger pages. A grand plan had to be created, one that would take a failing business and turn it back into a gold mine.

And so, one presented itself to the mind of J.K Binghamton—and gold mine had been the keywords.

There were many pockets of small-scale gold and silver mining operations in the San Luis Valley and in the San Juan Mountains to the west. These claims were owned by lone prospectors or a partnership of two or three miners. Their mines were generating enough metal-laden ore to make a nice living, but it was a challenge to remain alive to be able to make a nice living.

The challenge was not so much earning a cash return on their labor but making it back to their diggings with their lives and the cash returns on that labor intact. The corporate mining operations had small armies of hired guns to deposit payments from smelters into company bank accounts and to guard the transportation of the monthly payroll back to the mines.

The small mining operators had no such protection. They had to travel long distances over mountain trails to a town with a railroad station where they could ship their raw ores off to a smelting company. When the payments for the assayed value of the extracted gold and silver were sent back, these miners had no bank accounts in which to deposit the cash fruit of their labors. It was on the return trip back to the mines when they were subject to attack by outlaws, and often killed for the large amounts of money they carried. With a one-man operation, a miner returning to his diggings could be murdered by a gang who had jumped the claim during his absence. Because of this double jeopardy to their health and livelihood, quite a few of these miners were sitting on tons of rock laced with considerable amounts of rich ores. They were too afraid to leave their claims.

J.K. Binghamton had read newspapers accounts of these killings. And he had wondered how he could capitalize on the misfortunes of those miners in a way that would greatly enrich himself. And this is where "gold mine" came into play, for that is how he envisioned how wealthy his business idea would again make him.

His stagecoaches could travel to places in and around the San Luis Valley the railroads could not yet reach. True, the Denver & Rio Grande Railroad had built track over the Sangre de Cristo Mountains which would ultimately terminate at Alamosa—the new town it was constructing to be the regional railway center—but that was still several months away. If his new plan worked, Binghamton would not have to worry about Alamosa or the D&RG anymore. The plan was not only foolproof—it was railroad proof.

Using the last of his wife's money, Binghamton created a subsidiary of his stage line that he named the J.K. Binghamton Stage Line Special Express Delivery Service. The goal was to become the exclusive gold and silver ore transportation and cash delivery service for all the small mining operators in the San Luis Valley—to start with.

The plan was broken down into two parts. First, ten freight wagons in fairly good shape had been purchased at auction for $1000. A total of two thousand dollars a month would be paid to ten two-man teams hired to drive those wagons. Duke Ferrell had negotiated pay for the men and insisted on nothing less. Loaded with raw gold and silver ores from the sixteen contracted mines, the wagons would travel on a stagecoach road over the Sangre de Cristo Mountains to the railroad station in Walsenburg. From there, the ores would be shipped by freight train to the Boston and Colorado Smelting Company in Black Hawk. Binghamton had calculated some of the mines were closer to

Walsenburg than others, and so several wagons could make at least two round trips to service all clients within the same month.

The initial return on this investment came from fees—lots and lots of fees he would charge the miners. Fees for the pickup service that would transport their raw ore to the railroad, and another fee for having the ore transported by train to the smelting company.

The second part of the plan was where the real profits would flow into the pockets of J.K. Binghamton. While the Boston and Colorado had its own fees and charges for extracting and refining ores, Binghamton had his own list of fees as well. While he passed on the smelting fees to the miners he also charged a fee for having the smelter payments shipped back by train.

But his biggest—and most lucrative fee—was the "administrative" fee he charged in addition to his other fees. It was one percent of the payment each mining operation received from the B&C. If the average payment was $25,000, Binghamton's cut was $250. With sixteen mines signed up, he stood to make $4000 on each delivery. His only real expense was that eight hundred dollars a month he paid the men who drove the freight wagons. The horses pulling the wagons practically ate for free.

Binghamton had his clients sign contracts designating him their legal representative for all delivery service financial transactions. Wielding this authority, he had instructed the smelting company to send the payments—by check—to his bank in Pueblo. There it would be deposited into a special business account opened for this very purpose. Binghamton and his bookkeeper would sort through the paperwork included with the payments, and the cashed checks would be converted into the new U.S. Silver Certificates bundled in the amount due each mining operation.

The bundled silver certificates, packed inside bank deposit bags with the identification of each mine, would be loaded onto a fleet of specially designed stagecoaches manned by heavily armed security guards. The stagecoaches were to set out from the Pueblo stage station and deliver the money to the miners' banking accounts set up in four secret destinations. And this is what made paying all those fees worth it to the miners: they would remain alive to spend their money.

With this new venture, J.K. Binghamton stood to rake in more profits than from his existing stagecoach business. That business had been built on money he "borrowed" from his wife's personal savings account—unbeknownst to her. Now he could begin to pay it all back, with her still being none the wiser. The first delivery to the banks would total $400,000—and that was after Binghamton had taken his $4000 one-percent administrative fee off the top.

And those sixteen mines were just the start. Yes sir, the return on that fee could easily be doubled once the delivery service was in full swing. Binghamton figured once it was proven how easy the delivery service made it to receive cash money *and* remain alive to spend it, independent miners throughout the Valley and the San Juan Mountains would be flocking to sign up on his dotted line.

There was just one catch: while Binghamton had ten wagons with which to haul the raw ore, he had only one stagecoach for the money deliveries to four different and widely scattered towns. It was an old, somewhat tired and creaky Abbot-Downing Concord Coach purchased at another auction for five dollars. After hiring the drivers of the freight wagons, he had no money left to hire all the stagecoach drivers and all the heavily armed security guards promised in his sales pitch.

Binghamton assigned Duke Ferrell and Gully Walton, his most trusted and experienced two-man crew, to the stagecoach delivery run. Duke negotiated another four hundred dollars for himself and Gully to drive the stagecoach. This necessitated the imposition of a stagecoach delivery fee to somewhat offset the payroll expense Binghamton was forced to pay out of pocket.

Still, J.K. Binghamton was full of ideas for how he could bleed every dollar possible from his new venture, especially since he literally couldn't deliver on most of his sales pitch promises.

One of them was a "business enhancement" fee he had convinced merchants in those delivery towns to pay him. After all, wasn't *he* delivering money *his* clients would spend at *their* establishments? There were fortunes to be made, he had told them. His own fortune would be made by positioning himself smack dab in the middle of it all, collecting fees from both sides—the mine owners and the town merchants.

J.K. Binghamton was not about to let all that glorious income slip through his fingers, not with the very existence of his stage line at stake—and his wife finding out he had emptied her bank account. But time was running out. He needed the service up and running before the Alamosa railway center was completed.

Binghamton had bragged about the new business venture to his wife. "My dear, some men work hard all their lives to discover a gold mine. I invented my own." He just didn't tell her whose money he was using to invent his gold mine.

He also waxed enthusiastically to Garrison at the Pueblo stage station about his visions of greater success for the company. Why, he had plans for expanding into new and virgin territories once the delivery service was in place. Then, in a few years he would sell off the entire business and retire to enjoy the good life in Denver. No, that's where his wife lived. He'd travel the world—alone--instead.

While Binghamton was expounding on plans for his own future, Garrison had started thinking that with Ike's deadly skills with a gun, his youthful looks, and his apparent lack of fear in a confrontation with violent men, he would be perfect for guarding the delivery money. Garrison even came up with a job title: secret stagecoach guard.

When Garrison first broached his idea to Binghamton, the stage line owner wasn't so sure Ike was suited for the job. He was just too…young and untested. However, Garrison had the gift of persuasion among his arsenal of talents. He convinced his boss to watch Ike put on a shooting demonstration at a secluded spot outside of Pueblo.

Binghamton watched alright. He watched Ike stand in place while employing the Cavalry Draw to shoot bullseyes at stationary targets. He watched Ike move and tumble, firing both handguns and hitting every can Garrison tossed in the air or near the ground. And then came the pièce de résistance. Garrison threw two silver dollars into the air at roughly the same height but about ten feet apart from each other. Shooting with both revolvers, Ike put a hole through each coin at the same time.

Binghamton hired Ike on the spot—at a modest salary, of course. After all, the boy had no professional experience to speak of.

The J.K. Binghamton Stage Line Special Express Delivery Service now had its first slate of clients and it had its secret security guard. Given the large amount of money the stage would be carrying, the entire project was kept tightly wrapped under full secrecy. Or so it was thought.

CHAPTER 11

Tonight was the maiden run of the J.K. Binghamton Stage Line Special Express Delivery Service. Heading out from Pueblo, the stagecoach would make deliveries to four towns, starting with The First National Bank in Trinidad. From there it would backtrack up the trail to the FNB branch in Walsenburg, then travel through the San Luis Valley to the Means and Ashley Mercantile in Saguache. The final money drop was at the Bank of Leadville. Afterwards, the stage would return to Pueblo and repeat the entire run the following month. This same routine would be followed until Binghamton signed up additional clients for the service.

Binghamton had mandated the entire run—five hundred miles over mountains and through valleys—be completed in under four days. *One hundred forty miles per day.* This tight and highly unrealistic schedule gave no allowances for bad weather or an unfortunate encounter with a marauding band of Indians or a holdup gang. Even the fastest cross-country stagecoaches traveled no further than one hundred twenty-five miles in a single day. This stage run could easily take days longer if roads were washed out or blocked due to rockslides or avalanches. Anything could happen when traveling across valley flatlands and through mountainous country. J.K. Binghamton knew he was taking an immense gamble, but he felt he had chosen a first-rate stagecoach crew. He had absolute confidence the money would be delivered intact and on time.

It was after eight o'clock in the evening, three weeks after the attempted bank robbery. The Fleck brothers were inside the restaurant of the Pueblo hotel where Garrison had booked a room for them.

Garrison had not wanted Ike seen by anyone connected with the stage line, so they had arrived by train about an hour earlier for Ike's first night on his new job. He was also wary of Ike being seen around town, so they had gone straight to their room, and from there down to the restaurant.

The waitress who brought the menus had not been happy about having to serve a table when the place was about to close. But it had been a slow day and a slower night and the restaurant needed the business. Garrison ordered two large dinners. He figured that eating would be the best way to kill time until Ike was to leave on the nine o'clock stage.

Problem was, Ike said he didn't want anything to eat and left his food untouched. He sat across from Garrison, continually lifting his new handguns from their holsters and lowering them back down. The side arms were twin .44-40 Merwin Hulbert 2nd Model Frontier double-action revolvers Garrison had bought him for the new job. Ike was again disappointed that the guns were not Navy Colts. But they were both beautiful and accurate—and used the same rounds as the .44-40 Winchester '73 Garrison occasionally let him shoot.

Ike felt better about his brother's other gift: twin reversed Slim Jim holsters on a cartridge belt that were perfect for working the Cavalry Draw. He had asked Garrison to buy them, having read that Wild Bill Hickok had worn these same holsters when riding the plains.

Garrison took his time eating and drinking, stretching out the clock until it was nearly time for the stage to depart. He cut into a thick slab of beef ribeye steak on his plate that, along with two sunny side up eggs and a serving of biscuits and sausage gravy, was his late dinner. Ike sat opposite his brother with the same meal in front of him on two plates, both untouched. There was also a coffee cup, the coffee inside it growing cold.

Garrison forked a piece of steak into his mouth and started chewing, then sat back in his chair with his eyes closed, hands resting on the table as he held the knife and fork erect, savoring the taste of the pan-seared beef. After a moment he opened his eyes and swallowed the delicious beef. "Sure you're not hungry?" he asked Ike. "You don't know what you're missing."

"I already told ya I'm not hungry, Garrison," Ike said.

"Then at least drink your coffee," said Garrison, "you'll need to stay wide awake for that long stage ride to Walsenburg tonight."

"I told ya before I don't like coffee. It looks all dark and I know it won't taste good."

"And I've told you before," Garrison replied, "that you can add cream and sugar so it's not so dark. It would make it taste sweeter, too."

"But it would still be dark underneath," said Ike. "I'm not going to drink it."

"OK," said Garrison, taking a sip of coffee from his own cup. He knew there was no changing Ike's mind once it was set. Ike had a strange aversion to some food and drink based on the way they looked. He loved biscuits and sausage gravy for breakfast but if the gravy touched the biscuits on the plate, he wouldn't eat any of it. Same thing with steak and sunny side up eggs. Ike loved both, but not if the egg yolks had spread to the steak. Garrison had tried to convince him to eat the eggs scrambled but Ike didn't like the way scrambled eggs looked on the plate. Garrison could never understand why, but the solution had been to have the eggs and steak served on separate plates.

Stabbing another bite of ribeye with his fork, Garrison stirred the meat in the egg yolk and hoisted it into his mouth. Ike looked away, not wanting to see it. "If you're worried about the job, don't be," said Garrison, talking as he chewed. "Duke Ferrell and Gully Walton are the best whip—that's another name for stagecoach driver—and shotgun messenger we've got. No one's been able to rob them even once, no matter how many times it's been tried—and that's a fact."

He looked at Ike, whose attention was on the new guns Garrison would not let him fully draw from the holsters. With Wild Bill Hickok dead, Ike's goal was to be the fastest man with a gun in history. To this end, he had been practicing the Cavalry Draw for hours every day with the Merwin-Hulbert revolvers until the maneuver had become as natural to him as it had been with his old single-action Remingtons.

Garrison went on. "You'll like them. Duke's my best friend; I started out riding in the shotgun seat with him. He was a mapmaker for the Union Army during the Civil War. That's still one of his jobs with the stage line. Now just so you know, Gully's an ex-slave who also fought for the Union Army. A good man and the best shotgun messenger we've got. Not saying they'll be any attempts on your first run. But if there is, you'll be in the best of hands over the next few days. Hey, what's that look on your face? Time'll pass so fast you'll be back here in Pueblo before you know it."

The look on Ike's face wasn't in reaction to anything his brother was saying to him. Although he was listening to everything Garrison said, his visual attention had shifted from his handguns to his clothes. He was wearing a gray-and-black checked suit with a pale-yellow vest, matching tie, and a brown derby. He was supposed to look like a dude visiting the West for the first time. The jacket was cut a little large to minimize the bulges of the holstered revolvers at his waist. At his feet was a duffel bag packed with his own clothes.

Ike hated derbies. He hated his disguise clothes. The boots weren't too bad, but the rest of the outfit wasn't anything like the clothes Hickok wore. Wild Bill had dressed in an expensive three-piece suit, and had worn a round, wide-brimmed hat. Then there were those twin single-action, long-barreled .36 Colt Navy revolvers with the ivory handles. Hickok had been so fast and deadly, thought Ike, there'd been no need for fancy, double-action short barreled guns like the ones Garrison had bought him. The only thing he wore in common with his idol were the reversed Slim Jim holsters. Someday he'd have his own outfit and would look just like Wild Bill Hickok. The moustache might take some work, though.

Suddenly, he heard Garrison saying," So, what do you think?"

"What do I think of what?" responded Ike.

Garrison smiled. "I knew you weren't listening to me," he said as he sliced off a bit more steak, swirled the beef in the egg yolk, and forked it into his mouth. "But let's keep your hands away from your guns, please. It's making that waitress over there nervous."

"I can't watch when you eat that steak with the egg yolk on it. So I gotta do something to take my eyes off it."

"Well anyway," continued Garrison, "I was asking if you think you'll like the job. You've never done anything like this before."

"You told me you thought I could do it, Garrison. So, I can do it, right? You ain't never steered me wrong before. Besides, maybe no robbers will know we're be coming down the trail with lots of money. Not all stagecoaches carry lots of money, right?" Ike asked in a loud voice.

Garrison looked at him and made a shushing sound as he gestured with his free hand. "Ike, pipe down. You want the whole place to hear us? You never know who's around. What if a gang's got someone planted here listening in on our conversation?" Even though they were the only customers in the restaurant, he looked around and then moved his head closer to his brother. "No one outside the company is supposed to know about this, OK?"

Ike didn't like it when his older brother scolded him. "OK," he said, somewhat defiant but chastened. "But, son of a bitch, Garrison, I don't like being around strangers without you. You know I don't."

Garrison picked a biscuit up off his plate, mopped up a bit of the sausage gravy and bit off about half of it. He was now eating more out of nervousness than hunger. "I told you, Ike, you'll be fine." He could see his brother needed a little bit more convincing. "There shouldn't be any trouble, but if it does happen you'll have Gully sitting right above your head with that double barrel shotgun of his. No one messing with Gully has lived to tell the tale. And besides, remember how you took care of those three bank robbers? Not even Wild Bill Hickok himself could've done it as slick as you. Naw, you'll do just fine." He paused and forced a smile. "Wild Ike Fleck. Now, how does that sound?"

Ike, still worried, didn't even crack a smile.

Garrison pointed his fork toward the duffel bag that was on the floor beside Ike's feet. "I still think it's a mistake to take along that bag of yours. You know how you tend to forget things."

"I already told you before we left Boulder my real clothes are in there. I won't forget those 'cos I ain't wearin' these son of a bitch duds any longer than I have to," Ike said. "I'm changin' in Leadville soon as we get done with everything."

Garrison chose another battle to fight. "Now that's been bothering me, Ike. Where did you learn to say 'son of a bitch'? Uncle Roy sure never talked that way. And I don't either."

Ike flashed a goofy smile. "I learned it from Mr. Taggart. He was sayin' it all the time."

"Well I wish *you'd* stop sayin' it. It ain't a polite thing to say in public. Or anywhere else for that matter." Garrison took a spoon and piled more sausage gravy onto the half-eaten biscuit, stabbed it with his fork, and deposited the biscuit into his mouth.

As he was chewing he spread his thumb and index finger across his carefully-trimmed moustache and down the sides where it extended below his mouth. It was a habit he'd developed, not wanting to be caught with bits of food stuck in the hairs of his moustache. He returned to the subject of Ike's new job. "Anyway, it's just once a month to start, but it's very important to Mr. Binghamton. If this thing's successful we can expand out to the Ten Mile district, and even further out to places like Silverton, Ouray, and Columbia. That country's too tough to lay out railroad tracks so we're gonna be sitting in the catbird's seat, and you'll be set for life."

"Catbird's seat?" asked Ike, not looking at his brother while slightly raising the gun butts from their holsters. "I don't know what that means."

"It means we'll be sitting pretty. Uh, have it all sewn up." Garrison could tell that Ike didn't know what any of these phrases meant because he took everything literally. The mental images conjured up by such words confused him. "Ike," he began again, "it means, we'll be going places no one else can go. We'll be the only company doing it and it'll make all of us very rich."

"I wouldn't mind being rich," said Ike. "We could go west and see Deadwood."

"Well, Deadwood's actually north of here, but yeah, you're right. We could go see Deadwood, and you could see the exact chair Wild Bill was sitting in when he was shot in the back of the head by Jack McCall. They got it on display from what I read. Yep, just stick with this new job and it'll help get us there."

Truth was, Garrison didn't feel nearly as confident about what he had gotten Ike into. He himself had almost died from the gunshot wound he suffered in that stagecoach robbery. Still, he had absolute confidence in Duke to keep close watch over Ike's safety.

He and Duke had agreed the new stage run was poorly planned. They weren't convinced the route could be traveled within the three-and-a-half-day timeframe. It had been a compromise. J.K. Binghamton had initially demanded the route be completed in three days. It was miraculous that Duke had been able to get a concession for another twelve hours. It was within the very small realm of a possibility—if the weather held and luck remained with them in avoiding stage robbers or Indians. But with the snowstorms of winter, the entire run could very well take a week—or more.

Duke allowed as seeing how he was on Binghamton's payroll, he had to follow the boss's orders, especially after the deal was sweetened by paying both Gully and him a $15 monthly bonus as hazard pay. Still, he was even less sure Ike was right for the job. He told Garrison it was a bad idea to put a seventeen-year-old kid, with no prior experience—and no matter how fast he might be with a gun—in a job as dangerous as guarding that amount of money on the stagecoach. Garrison had disagreed, but inwardly he put those same doubts in a place where he wouldn't have to think about them until after Ike was safely back in Pueblo.

If any outlaws did stop the stage, Garrison wondered how long Ike would be able to carry off his disguise before they figured out he was a ringer, being the only passenger riding the stage. He hoped Ike would have his guns drawn and shooting by that time. He knew he could easily be sending his younger brother to his death, but he didn't know of any other type of work Ike could do. He again ran his thumb and index finger across and down his moustache as he chewed another bite of yolky egg. He looked across the table at his younger brother.

Garrison was slightly over six feet tall, Ike was more than a few inches under that. A drooping moustache adorned his face, while Ike's upper lip barely supported peach fuzz. And while the blond hair of Garrison's youth had turned dark brown, Ike's had so far remained blond. While Garrison made it a point to get a haircut once a month if he was in town, his brother's hair hung below his ears.

Ike acted younger—and looked younger—than his age, and that helped make him dangerous. No one expected a kid like that to be as fast, accurate, and deadly with a gun as he was. Ike had been naturally gifted with exceptional hand/eye coordination, honed by hours and hours of daily shooting practice. He pursued being the fastest gun alive with a single-mindedness that scared even Garrison.

Garrison looked over at the untouched food on Ike's plate. "You should eat something," he said. "When you're out on the trail and run out of grub, you'll start dreaming of all the food you refused to eat back in town."

"I told you I can't eat. I just want to get this over with." Ike kept fiddling with his guns.

The waitress came back to their table. By now it was almost 8:30 PM and, seeing as how the brothers were her only customers, she clearly wanted to close up for the night. Garrison was sure that the kitchen was already closed. "You boys won't be wanting anything else, will you?" she asked in a tone that clearly said the only acceptable answer was "no".

Garrison, however, wanted to make one last effort to get Ike to eat something before he got on the stage, knowing that the first stage stop would be about an hour after that. "What kind of pie do you have?" he asked.

"We don't," she said. "All been sold today."

Garrison looked over toward the pie case, tins of pies still on display. "What about those over there?"

"You're just determined to make my life a joy, aren't you?" said the waitress. She stood glowering at him.

Garrison broke eye contact first. "On second thought, just bring us the bill."

"With pleasure,' she said, slapping the bill on the table before walking back into the kitchen.

Ike looked at Garrison. "Do you know her, Garrison? Why would you want to make her life a joy?"

"She didn't mean it that way," said Garrison. "She was being ironic. I mean, she said it but she—well, sometimes people say one thing but mean something else."

"I don't understand. How can you tell?" asked Ike.

"You can't always."

This answer confused Ike even more so he refocused on the pie. "Do you still want pie? I see some over there."

Garrison wiped his hands and mouth with the napkin next to his plate, giving a bit extra attention to his moustache. He picked up the bill, looked at it, and got his wallet out from his inside coat pocket. "Forget about the pie, Ike. It's time to go, anyway." He decided to leave a nice tip for the waitress. It wasn't fair to have taken up so much of her time while they were just using up the clock before heading for the stage station. He had also wanted to stretch out the time he had remaining with his younger brother. He laid his money on the table and stood up as he returned the wallet to his coat pocket. As he turned to walk to the front door, Ike stood up and followed his brother. "What time is it, Garrison?"

Garrison glanced at the clock on the wall. "It's eight twenty-eight."

"Don't we have to hurry to make the nine o'clock stagecoach to Trinidad? You said I had to be there by eight forty-five, said Ike, earnestly. "I don't want to be late."

"It's a short walk. We have plenty of time to get there."

"OK. But I don't want to be late for my first day—" Ike looked around and saw the darkness and the town lights outside the restaurant windows— "night on the job."

As they were about to walk out, Garrison noticed that Ike had forgotten his duffel bag. It was still on the floor under the table. He quickly walked back to retrieve it as Ike stood near the front door. After Garrison returned to the door, he said, "Ike, if your head wasn't attached to your neck…"

"I can't help it, Garrison," said Ike, "I'm not used to having this bag so sometimes I forget I have it. It takes me time to remember stuff like that." He then opened the front door, leaving Garrison to hold his bag.

After they closed the door behind them, the waitress rushed to quickly lock and bolt the door shut. She was glad to see the two of them leave so she could finally end her long day. She walked over to their table and saw the large tip Garrison had left. Hmmm, maybe she shouldn't have hurried them out so quickly. A slice of warmed-up apple pie might have been good for an additional two-bit tip.

From Pueblo it was a fourteen-hour journey to Trinidad, including stops at a home station and several swing stations along the route. J.K. Binghamton had decided that a stage pulling up to a bank in mid-morning would attract less attention than one arriving just after dawn, which was why they were departing at 9 P.M.

Garrison knew that the stage office was only a short walk from the restaurant. He wanted to get Ike there early to meet with the stage crew. Ike had already said he was more nervous about riding alone with strangers than he was about the stage being held up. Garrison also wanted to ease his own nervousness about this whole money delivery project of Mr. Binghamton's. But he still chuckled as he watched his brother walk ahead of him down the boardwalk.

"Nice to see you know where we're going, Ike," said Garrison.

Ike looked confused. "But I don't know where we're going. I thought you knew."

"I do. So how about you walking *with* me instead of ahead of me?" Garrison said, swinging the duffel bag against Ike's buttocks.

"Hey! Watch it, Garrison!" cried Ike. He jumped forward and turned slightly to look at his brother. He fell in beside Garrison as they both stepped off the boardwalk and into the street.

The stage station was only about fifty yards ahead of them on the opposite side. As Garrison walked he continued to swing the bag of clothing, occasionally bumping his brother on his side. Ike, fairly oblivious to Garrison's playfulness, was practicing his Cavalry Draw, continuing to work on quickly drawing the twin revolvers out from under his coat. As they neared the station Garrison said, "Ok, Wild Ike, time to holster them six-shooters. Better button up that coat, too, just to keep them hidden for now."

"OK, Garrison," Ike answered, as he practiced the twisting double draw one more time more before following his brother's instructions.

When they reached the stagecoach, Ike stood back and watched the scene unfolding before him. Garrison walked up to Duke and Gully, who themselves had just exited the stage office. He lowered the duffel bag to the boardwalk and reached out his hand to Duke. The stage driver, a tall man in his mid-forties, slapped Garrison's hand aside and moved in to give him an enthusiastic embrace. Years of driving teams of horses had endowed him with steel bands for arm muscles, and a trim body. Garrison could hardly breathe within the vise grip that was a Duke Ferrell bear hug. When the stage driver finally relaxed his grasp, Garrison took a couple of deep breaths and then extended his hand to Gully. About the same height as Garrison, Gully, had a slimmer build but his grip was almost as viselike as Duke's hug. When his ensnared hand was released, Garrison shook the pain out of his fingers, but not all that good-naturedly. These stagecoach guys just had to show off. Had *he* been like that?

But you had to like Gully and forgive him practically everything. Beneath the faded blue kepi he had worn since his Civil War days there was a warm, beaming smile. It was rare that anyone saw the bad side of him. On those occasions, they were usually standing opposite the business end of the double barrel shotgun the shotgun messenger was pointing at them during a holdup attempt.

Clarence Conley, the station agent, also came out to talk a bit. Everyone was chatting with each other except Ike who stood off to the side, looking down at the hidden guns beneath his suit coat. He wished he could pull them from their holsters just one last time. Conley took a long look at Ike. Then glancing at a pocket watch in his hand he said, "Well, boys, it's time to go."

Duke climbed up to the driver's box and sat down. He took something out of his coat pocket and unfolded it. It was a map drawn with great skill on a large rectangular patch of deerskin. "Thought I lost this last week. Clarence over there said he found it on the floor. Don't remember dropping it but no harm done, I reckon." He looked over the map to get the route and stage stations set in his mind. He folded it up and put it back in his shirt pocket. As he took hold of the lines, Gully climbed up and sat to his left. The shotgun messenger checked the loads in both barrels of his twelve-gauge coach gun as well as the bullets in his revolver.

Conley nodded his head toward Ike. "Who's this smartly-dressed young feller?" he asked Garrison.

Garrison quickly saw that Conley didn't know the reason for Ike's presence. "Oh, special assignment Mr. Binghamton gave me. He's Mrs. Binghamton's nephew. Sent out here after a bit of trouble back East.

Conley appeared skeptical. "With the cargo you're carrying, Mr. Binghamton still gave his approval to put this boy in possible harm's way?"

"Oh, he ain't goin' the whole way. Duke'll be dropping him off at Cottonwood to see what Marie can do with him. If she can't straighten him out, nobody can."

"Ok, said Conley, "just so's Mr. Binghamton's approved it." He walked back into the office.

Duke glanced down at Garrison with a questioning look. Garrison looked up at his friend. "Just a gut feeling. If Conley doesn't already know why Ike's onboard there's no reason to let him know about it now."

"Makes me wonder about him finding my map," replied Duke, nodding toward where Conley had gone back inside. "But it's too late to change anything now anyway."

Ike wasn't listening to the conversation. When he first saw the shoddy-looking stagecoach he was to ride in he was disappointed. "Son of a bitch," he said to Garrison. "This isn't how I pictured it. It's smaller and it looks as wore out as Uncle Roy's old buckboard wagon."

Garrison sighed. First, his brother had been afraid to ride alone on the stage. Now he was complaining that it was smaller and shabbier than he imagined it would be. "Well, it has to look like this, Ike," said Garrison, thinking quickly. J.K. Binghamton had spent bottom dollar on an old-but-still-serviceable stagecoach he had bought at auction. "It has to look like it's carrying nothing special so's any stagecoach bandits might take a pass on it. You're carrying $400,000 on this buggy."

"That's a lot of money, isn't it?"

"Yeah, that's a lot of money." Garrison took a moment to look at his younger brother. He saw a young kid dressed in ridiculous clothes…wearing a derby. He wondered again if he'd made a mistake. Then he noticed that Ike had unbuttoned his coat again, the powerful handguns in their holsters visible underneath. The vision of Ike killing those three bank robbers quickly invaded his mind and departed. "And if they choose to hold up the stage they'll never see you coming, little brother." Again, Garrison sounded more confident than he felt.

"They couldn't see me coming. I'll be inside the stagecoach," Ike said.

Duke, pulling his buckskin gloves on, called over to the brothers. "Time to leave, gentlemen."

"Oh—time! Right." Garrison fished through one of his coat pockets and brought out a round gold pocket watch. "When you're working for a man who pays you a wage you gotta make sure you show up to work on time. When you're working for a stage line it's double important to be everywhere on time. So, I got you this, little brother." He gently opened Ike's hand and placed the watch in his palm. "Here, you open it like this." He helped Ike find the crown, and then showed him how to push down on it to open the watch's hinged cover. "See? It shows you it just turned nine o'clock."

Ike looked at the watch face and then up at Garrison. He felt he was about to cry, and that was the last thing he wanted to do in front of his brother and the men on the stagecoach. He didn't say anything because to open his mouth would've started the tears flowing. He had no choice but to keep his eyes fixed on the watch.

Duke called down again, a bit more firmly this time. "Garrison, I got a schedule to meet." He looked at Ike. "Son, you either board this stage now or you stay here. It's your choice."

Ike managed a sigh and quickly looked at Garrison. Grabbing the handrail, he climbed into the stagecoach, and began to sit in the seat below the driver's box.

"You're sitting on that back seat, Ike," said Garrison. "The strong box is right underneath it. Now, Duke really gets his teams flying down the road so I'm afraid it's going to be a rough ride for you. You'd get bounced around less sitting up against the front wall but it can't be helped. Mr. Binghamton wants you sitting on top of the money and facing forward so you can look out the window and see any road agents up ahead."

Ike switched over to the other seat. He looked dolefully out the window at Garrison. The watch was still lying open in his hand "What are road agents, Garrison?"

"Another name for stagecoach bandits. Robbers no different from those jackals you killed at the bank." He climbed inside the coach, placing his hands on Ike's shoulders. "Ike, listen to Duke. He won't steer you wrong. I'll see you back here in less than a week, OK?" He repositioned Ike's coat over the revolvers and re-buttoned it. "You're gonna have to keep these excellent examples of Mr. Murwin and Mr. Hulbert's fine handiwork hidden until you need to use them. Gives you the element of surprise over any road agents."

Garrison stepped back through the open door of the stage and down onto the boardwalk where he felt Ike's duffel bag behind him, almost tripping backwards over it.

"Ike—wait!" He quickly picked up the bag, leaping from the boardwalk and landing next to the still open stagecoach door. "You almost forgot this again! If you head wasn't attached…"

Ike watched as Garrison placed his foot on the step and leaned inside to set the bag on the front seat opposite him. Quickly looking down at the stage floor he said, "I can't help if I forget stuff." Sneaking a glance at his older brother, he added, "Sorry, Garrison."

Garrison patted Ike on the knee. "It's OK, Ike," he said softly. "No harm done." He backed out of the stagecoach and closed the door, his hands resting on top of it. "Duke, you take good care of this brave man, hear?" he called to the driver, his eyes on his little brother.

"Took pretty good care of you when you was sittin' up here, didn't I?" Duke said. "Now, damn it, Garrison, we gotta go."

Ike was looking sadly at his big brother, as if asking Garrison not to make him do this terrible thing. For Garrison, it would have been easier if Ike had been openly crying. This was far worse, and it tore at his heart.

Garrison patted the door twice. "Well, what are you waiting for, Duke? Get this crate moving! Can't have you showing my brother it's OK to run late his first day on the job." He stepped backwards and up onto the boardwalk, keeping his eyes on Ike.

Duke spat a high arc that landed besides Garrison's feet. "When we get back, you're buyin' the first round."

Garrison looked up at his friend who, besides the reins, would have Ike's life in his hands. "When you make it back I'll buy you a bottle."

"Just one?" Duke asked, with a grin. He shook the lines with a "H'yaw!" as the stage pulled away from the stage station, two white mare leaders pulling in front, two larger gray geldings in the swing position and behind them two even larger and heavier gray geldings providing the real muscle as the wheelers.

Garrison stepped forward into the street, a smile pasted on his face as he waved to his brother. "Adiós, Wild Ike!" he called out.

Ike just kept looking out the window at him. Garrison waved again but Ike didn't return it. As the stage began to move down the street, Ike leaned out the window and began to wave his hand in earnest, still holding the watch. He was afraid that his brother wouldn't see him holding it. Garrison waved back, keeping his hand in the air until the stage disappeared down the road beyond the lighted streetlamps.

"Hasta mañana, little brother," Garrison said quietly, lowering his arm.

He walked back to the hotel and climbed the stairs up to their room. Early tomorrow morning he would catch a ride on a freight train that was delivering mining equipment to El Moro. It could cover the eighty-mile distance in a little over two hours. There he would rent a horse and ride over to Trinidad to surprise Ike when the stage pulled in at 11 A.M., knowing that Duke would be right on time.

Inside the room Garrison undressed down to his blue jeans and got into bed. He drew the Colt from its holster and laid it next to him, his finger just off the trigger. His mind was troubled, and when he finally fell asleep, he had a nightmare that he would remember long after he woke up in the morning. But before sleep came, he realized he had forgotten to show Ike how to wind the watch.

CHAPTER 12

"Let's go over the plan again so everybody knows it," said Hank Bellum. He and three other men were inside an abandoned cabin in the Sangre de Cristo Mountains. They were gathered around a wooden table on which a map drawn on the back of a wanted poster was laid flat. It was a crude copy of the map Duke had made for the new stage run, the same stage Ike would be riding later that night. It just showed the route from Pueblo to Trinidad, with the stage stops marked. Walsenburg was circled.

"We ride out to the stage road just outside Walsenburg after we finish up here. We'll pick out a tall, bushy pine to chop into sections and lay them across the road before daylight tomorrow. When that stage comes down that incline it'll be moving faster than a Texas prairie fire. The driver won't see the roadblock till the last minute and have no choice but to pull off the road, just where we want him to. After that stage stops it'll be like shooting ducks in a barrel: driver, shotgun messenger, any passengers inside. There's $400,000 cash money inside a strong box hidden under the back seat. I'll be the one to open it. Afterward, we ride out to La Veta Pass where Dave Mackey's holding fresh horses. We split the loot and all go our separate ways. Piece of cake. Any questions?"

"That's one easy way to make close to half a million bucks if you ask me," said Jesse Bellum, Hank's younger brother. Both Hank and Jesse were big men. Hank topped out at six-foot-seven and two hundred sixty-five pounds, none of it fat. Jesse was just a shade over six-foot-six but about twenty pounds lighter.

Rossi sneered at Jesse. "Nobody asked you, kid. You call this easy? From what Hank said when Skellenger and me joined up, Binghamton's bet his whole company on this run. You think he's goin' to let it go easy? I 'spect he'll have double the guards on it." Rossi looked at Hank. "You never told me how you happen to know how much'll be in that strong box."

"It don't matter how I know. And don't worry about no extra guards," said Hank. "Binghamton can't afford 'em."

Rossi glared back. "It does matter how you got your information if you're cuttin' someone else in for another share—cuz it ain't gonna be taken out of mine!"

Hank glared at him. "How I get the information is my business—and I pay my own debts. You havin' second thoughts?"

"The only thought I've got is who knows about this job besides us." answered Rossi. "Whoever gave you that map, maybe their price to stay quiet goes up after the robbery."

Grinning sardonically, Hank said, "And maybe if they try that I pay 'em a visit and don't owe 'em nothin' afterwards. Christ, Rossi, you worry too much. A worried man makes mistakes."

"I ain't worried about nothin'," said Rossi. "I just like to know who I'm working with is all. But I'm telling you this thing better be on the up and up or you won't want *me* paying you a visit afterwards."

Hank narrowed his eyes at Rossi. Jesse grinned and gave a short laugh.

Rossi quickly glanced at Jesse, then back to Hank. "And how do I know whoever gave you that information won't pull a double cross cuz he don't trust you? Maybe he makes a deal to turn us over to the sheriff and collect a fat reward from Binghamton."

Jesse chuckled contemptuously. "Rossi, if you was any more yellow I'd mistake you for a canary bird."

Rossi's hand dropped down to his gun butt, ready to draw.

"ROSSI!" The shout came from Hank. His gun was already out of its holster, hammer pulled back. Bellum had drawn himself up to his full 6'7" height, the long barrel of the heavy .44 Colt Russian pointed directly at Rossi's chest. The smaller man was petrified, knowing death was just seconds away. No one moved.

Skellenger finally broke the tension. "If you all don't start acting like we're in this together no one's gonna get a share of anything. Hank told us the plan and it seems foolproof to me. So why don't we all just back off a bit from each other? We just might make some money off this deal yet."

Hank kept his gun leveled at Rossi, who slowly moved his hand away from his own gun. Hank then released the hammer on the Russian and slowly returned it to the holster. Jesse was still grinning at Rossi.

Hank Bellum spoke, his voice betraying only a bit of the anger he had just shown. "Just follow the plan and it's $100,000 for each man."

Skellenger spoke up. "You mean $80,000 for each man, don't you, Hank? You're forgettin' Dave Mackey. He's with the horses at La Veta Pass."

"Right, with all this blather from Rossi I forgot about Dave," Hank said with slight irritation.

Rossi wanted to again bring up the additional cut for the mysterious partner but didn't dare. Instead he asked, "You're sure about that stage not having extra guards, Hank?"

He tried to maintain as calm a tone as he could manage, trying to hide his fear of the big man. But the beads of sweat on his forehead and his slightly labored breathing gave it away.

"You doubtin' my word *again*, Rossi?" Hank's voice was pure menace.

Rossi was not about to tempt fate twice. He pulled back. "Just makin' sure is all."

"I've about had it with you and your yellow mouth. You better be in all the way because now it's too late to back out. And no one's backing out," said Hank. He kept his eyes fixed on Rossi.

Rossi glanced at Skellenger and then nervously back at Hank Bellum. If it came down to it, he thought he might be able to beat the big man to the draw. He hadn't been ready this last time, he'd been about to shoot a hole through Jesse instead. He knew for a fact he couldn't beat both Bellums at the same time. He'd need to count on Skellenger to back his play and take out Jesse. But Skellenger wasn't known for his speed with a gun. Rossi decided he'd just have to wait for the right opportunity to take them both out at the same time. His eyes shifted back to the map.

"Oh, Rossi don't get cold feet," said Skellenger, trying to maintain peace within the gang. "When we ambushed that cavalry unit escortin' them horses to Fort Garland, didn't Rossi shoot that Yankee lieutenant clean out of the saddle? And two or three of them other soldier boys? Now, we been partners since back in '75 when we was ridin' with the Kinney Gang. Why, John Kinney hisself told Rossi he had more guts than any man he ever seen. Ain't that right, Rossi?"

"I don't need you defendin' me, Skellenger," Rossi said, scowling at his partner. He turned back to Hank. "Stealin' horses from Yankee soldiers is one thing. The Army figured some Utes on the warpath done it. Robbin' a stage of $400,000 is somethin' else. I don't want no screw ups cuz I don't wanna be lookin' down my back-trail the rest of my life."

It took all of Hank Bellum's self-control to prevent him from delivering a huge fist to Rossi's jaw. "Me and Jesse put a lot of careful plannin' into this. I hear one more word from you..."

Hank turned his glare to the other man. "Any more concerns?" Skellenger wisely chose to remain silent. "OK. Get your gear together so that we're ready to ride out in ten minutes. We got a lot to get done if we're gonna be ready for that stage tomorrow mornin'."

Hank folded up the map and put it in his jacket pocket. He looked at his brother. "Jesse? I think your horse was walkin' funny today. We need to check to make sure he ain't tryin' to throw a shoe."

Jesse looked at his brother and saw a barely perceptible wink. The others wouldn't have seen it since they had moved off to begin packing their few belongings into their open bedrolls. "Yeah. I thought his gait felt a bit off."

The two men went outside to Jesse's horse, walked around its far side, and then knelt down behind the horse's right rear leg. "I swear, Hank. Goddamn those two gutless wonders," said Jesse.

Hank spat. "Don't worry about them. Soon as everyone on that stage is dead we shoot 'em both. That's $400,000 split two ways."

"TWO ways? What about Mackey and Conley?"

"Don't worry about Conley," Hank said. "He'll get his when he rides out to the meetin' spot for his share of the loot. Just won't get what he was expectin'. That's why those two birds in there don't need to know about him. They'll be dead already. As for Mackey, we take care of him when we come for our remounts. We'll just set the other horses loose."

Jesse was silent. Hank hadn't told him this part of the plan. "I never liked Conley anyway. Seems a shame about Dave, though, him bein' a decent guy and all. Bigger shame we can't take them extra horses with us."

"Well, if you want to keep Mackey alive and pay him out of your share that's your business." Jesse remained silent. "Thought so. As for the extra horses, they'll just slow us down. We just need the two horses for the ride back here from the Pass. They'll get plenty of rest while we settle in and count our money."

Jesse nodded his head toward the cabin. "But what if them two in there are figurin' to do to us what we're figurin' to do to them? Then what?"

"Just keep your eyes open and stand behind them when I pull that strong box out from inside the stage. I'll shoot the lock open and while those two yellow bellies are lookin' inside the box you shoot Skellenger in the back. I'll take care of Rossi."

"OK, big brother. You ain't been wrong yet."

Hank looked back towards the cabin. "I'm goin' to make sure Rossi is facin' me when I kill him. I want to see his face when the bullet hits his chest. And then I'll put a bullet through his mouth to shut him up for good." They walked back into the cabin and saw the other two men sitting at the table.

Rossi was defiantly checking the load in his gun. Looking up as the brothers entered the room, he gave the cylinder a spin, flipped it closed, and holstered the revolver.

"How's that horse lookin', Jesse?" he asked.

"Had a small stone caught inside the hoof. Lucky it didn't cut him."

"Yeah," said Rossi. "Real lucky."

Hank ignored him. "Finish packin' what you need cuz we're spendin' the night out there. Jesse, make sure you grab them axes before we head out. "

As Hank and Jesse were across the room gathering up their gear, Rossi and Skellenger were kneeling together tying up their bedrolls. "Make sure you keep 'em both in your sights at all times," Rossi said under his breath. Skellenger nodded as they sneaked a glance at the two brothers.

CHAPTER 13

After seven hours on the road the stage pulled into the Cottonwood home station, which was the halfway point between Pueblo and Trinidad. Two hours earlier they had stopped at a swing station but only long enough to swap for a team of fresh horses. A home station was different from a swing station in that it served meals and drinks to stagecoach passengers, which made the stop longer.

Cottonwood was named for a stand of cottonwood trees growing beside a creek running through the property. Inside a circular corral behind where the stage had stopped, six black geldings were milling and jumping about, filling the night air with snorts and whinnies. These were the fresh team for the stagecoach. Penned in since early evening, they were ready to be harnessed to the stage and be sent galloping down the road.

The station master, Will LeMay, was standing there to greet them. Binghamton had personally sent a telegram advising him of this late-night stage arrival. He was holding a railroad lantern that gave off a dim light. Fully capable of walking the path to the corral blindfolded, he carried the lantern to light the path back to the station house for stagecoach passengers.

Before the stage came to a full stop, Gully grabbed his shotgun and jumped down from the boot. Will walked over and extended his hand. "Hey, Gully, I could barely see you up there in the dark."

Gully smiled as he shook hands. "Yeah and you make a mighty fine target no one could miss in this moonlight, Mistah Will."

Duke remained up on the box. He removed his buckskin gloves and dropped them on the seat. He turned up the light from the running lamp below him and took a logbook and pencil out of his coat pocket. Looking at his watch, he wrote down the time they arrived at the home station.

Will looked up at him. "Heard you were drivin' this route, Duke. Thought you gave up driving stagecoaches for a healthier line of work," said Will.

"Ain't no such thing in this world so ya might as well do what pays the most. For me, this is it." After placing the pencil inside, he closed the logbook and returned it to his coat pocket. He climbed down from the box and lowered the wick on the lamp, then walked over to Will and extended his hand. "Good seeing you again, Will," he said as they warmly shook hands.

When they released their handshake, Will stepped back, eyed the aged stagecoach and slowly shook his head. "'Twas ever thus," he murmured. Binghamton was still trying to get by with broken-down crates. Even in the moonlight he could tell it had seen *much* better days—and he knew Duke was aware of this. "How long you boys fixin' to stay?"

Duke gave an ironic chuckle. "Binghamton's given us thirty minutes to tie on the feedbag. That means we'll probably be here about forty or so, dependin'."

Will asked, "Dependin' on what?"

Duke smiled. "Dependin' on how much grub there is to eat and whether we like it or not."

Will put his hand to the side of his mouth. "Better not let Marie hear you say that," he said in a mock whisper.

"Oh Lord, no!" said Gully, laughing.

Will pointed his thumb at the stage. "No passengers?"

"We got one," said Duke. "A young feller. Otherwise, this is just a freight run."

The curtains were open, so Will looked inside the stage window. "Yeah, I see him now. Couldn't before. Why is he just sittin' there?"

Duke also looked through the window. Ike was on the back seat, his back straight, his hands over his coat where it covered the two revolvers. "Yeah," said Duke, "I'm going to talk to the kid and see what's goin' on."

As Will started to unhitch the horses from the stage, Duke stuck his head in the window. "Ike, why the hell you still in here? There's grub thataway," he said, pointing his thumb toward the long ranch house where the meals were served.

Ike, still holding the watch, quickly slipped it into his pants pocket. "Mr. Binghamton," he replied, "told me it's my job as a secret stagecoach guard to stay inside this coach until it reaches Trinidad."

"He didn't tell you about the stops?" asked Duke.

"No sir," replied Ike, "and neither did Garrison. All Mr. Binghamton told me was it's my job as a secret stagecoach guard to stay inside this coach until it reaches Trinidad."

This conversation interested Will, who left the horses to stand next to Duke. He held the lantern up, raising the wick to, as he often put it, "shed more light on the subject."

"I heard you the first time," said Duke. He tipped his hat back on his head with an index finger and softly whistled. "Well, don't that beat all. Now, listen. You stay with the coach when we're on the road. But when we stop at a home station where they serve food you go inside with Gully and me to eat."

He could see confusion still on Ike's face. "Look, we got contracted home stations where we stop to eat and change horses and such. This here is

Cottonwood and gettin' out to eat is part of your job. It's part of all our jobs, you, me and Gully. If we don't stop to eat and rest, no way can we stay alert on the trail."

"But Mr. Binghamton told me— "

"Son," said Duke, a little sharply, "*Mr.* Binghamton never meant you couldn't get out and eat at a home station. Besides, I'm the boss of this stagecoach run and I'm orderin' you to get out and go inside and get some mighty good grub down inside ya. It'll be another five hours after we leave here till we reach Trinidad and I ain't havin' no secret stagecoach guard of mine die of starvation on the way." He stepped back and opened the door. "Now you git inside an' eat, son. That's a direct order."

"Yes sir," said Ike, meekly. His body was stiff and a little sore from the long ride inside the bouncing stagecoach. He had unbuttoned his coat, enjoying the freedom his body felt without the coat tightly stretched across the handguns. He still wasn't sure about disobeying Mr. Binghamton's direct order, but he *was* hungry. Anyway, Duke had just told him he was the boss on this stagecoach run, probably because Mr. Binghamton had told him he was. He thought it over and decided it was OK to follow Duke's direct order even if it did conflict with what Mr. Binghamton had previously told him. But he decided to leave the derby inside the coach. He wasn't facing any road agents yet.

As Ike stepped down from the stage, Will eyed his two-gun rig, now visible under the open coat. Although he'd never seen Merwin Hulbert handguns before, he could tell they were extremely well-made. He whistled. "Son, that's some mighty serious hardware you're wearing."

Ike stopped and looked at him, confused. Then he looked down. "My guns? Oh. Thank you, sir. My brother Garrison Fleck bought them for me."

"Your brother's got a fine knowledge of weaponry."

Ike didn't know what "weaponry" meant so he just nodded. "These aren't my real clothes. I got those in there," he said, pointing to the stage. Will didn't know what to say to that, so he let the remark go unanswered.

"Don't just stand there. Grub's thataway," said Duke, again pointing his thumb toward the station house. Bright lights flickered from two lanterns mounted near both sides of the front door.

"I heard you the first time," Ike said, walking toward the house.

Duke stood there, staring after Ike. He clicked his tongue against his teeth, and then reaching behind his back he shut the stagecoach door.

Will said, "Marie didn't know which you boys liked best, her biscuits with sausage gravy or steak and eggs so she made both."

"I'll eat it all," said Duke as he followed Ike up the path to the house.

"Not if I get there first," said Gully.

Ike waited at the front door for the men to catch up. Duke arrived first, opening the door for Ike. After Ike nervously walked in, Duke continued to hold the door open for Gully. As the shotgun messenger was about to enter, Duke stepped right in front of him and walked to the dining room.

"Now that ain't fair, Duke!" Gully called after him.

Duke hurried passed Ike. "All I know is grub's in here."

Gully slammed the door shut. Ike was walking behind Duke, but Gully brushed past him. After being overtaken by both men, Ike looked back to make sure there was no one else behind him, and then entered the room.

Once inside, Ike saw a large rectangular dining room. On one side was a long wood plank bar on top of three whiskey barrels. At one end of the bar was an oaken keg with a beer tap on a wood stand. Screwed to the wall behind it were wooden shelves holding bottles of liquor, with beer and shot glasses grouped at both ends of the bottom shelf. In the middle of the room was a long dining table made of polished mahogany. Around it were matching ladder back chairs, enough to seat eight people, three chairs alongside each side and one chair at each end of the table. Gully was already sitting in one of the middle chairs, his shotgun leaning against his chair.

Duke sat down opposite Gully and pointed to the chair next to his for Ike to sit in. Ike was about to sit down when a short, plump woman with salt-and-pepper hair called out, "Duke Ferrell and Gully Walton! Don't you dare set your lazy asses down at my table till you've washed your hands and faces! And that goes for your young friend, too. I know you had to have seen those wash basins outside the door so go out and find 'em again. And put that hand pump to good use. We got plenty of water and lye soap so don't be stingy with either one. I'll be checkin' under your fingernails so wash 'em up good."

This was Marie, Will LeMay's wife, standing with her hands on her hips, her white apron stretched across her ample bosom and stout body. In that position, not even a team of stagecoach horses would dare run past her.

"No use checkin' under my fingernails, Mizzus Marie. Dirt don't show," said Gully, smiling.

Marie pointed a finger at Gully. "Don't you think for one minute I won't be able to see dirt under your fingernails, Mr. Smart Ass! One more word from you and I'll take a wire brush and wash those fingernails down to the nubs myself! Now git!" She pointed to the door. "And don't be stingy with the soap!"

Gully gave Duke a mock serious look. "I thought I didn't have to listen to white folks no more."

"We *all* gotta listen to Marie," said Duke. He grinned over at Ike. "C'mon, son. Makes no sense fightin' a she-cat in her own lair."

He led the way outside to two large porcelain washbasins that were sitting on a tall wooden bench on the covered porch. Two thick bars of tallow soap were lying between the washbasins. A hand pump stood next to the bench; a large clay ewer filled with water sat on the end of the bench in case the basins needed refilling during the wash. After they had finished washing their faces and hands, they dried them on cotton towels hung on long, heavy nails driven halfway into the wood porch post.

Feeling confident of their clean-up job, Duke and Gully returned to the dining room with Ike in tow. The two men held up their hands for Marie's inspection. Ike, looking at them both, awkwardly held up his hands in the same manner. Marie made a great show of examining close-up the three pairs of hands and gruffly pronounced them barely fit to handle food at her table.

On the way back to their chairs, Gully and Duke, with Ike walking behind them, stopped at one end of the table where plates, silverware and napkins were in separate stacks. After Duke and Gully grabbed their plates and silverware, they returned to their chairs where they had been sitting. Ike, having had many a meal with Garrison, picked up a napkin along with his plates and silverware before walking back to his chair. Duke went back to grab three coffee cups and set two of them down in front of Gully and Ike, and then placed one behind his own plate.

Ike noticed there was already a place setting at the far end of the table and wondered who else would be eating with them. He then took his first look at the spread Marie had laid out for them, and his eyes opened wide in amazement. The table was covered with food: a large round china platter piled high with fresh baked biscuits still warm from the oven, a couple of small plates with mounds of freshly-churned butter, a large tureen of sausage gravy with a ladle, two platters heaped with thick, charbroiled Kansas City Strip steaks, and two more platters stacked with eggs cooked sunny side up. On both sides of this mass of food were polished sterling silver coffee pots filled with steaming, freshly brewed coffee.

Gully, wasting no time, was already making headway through food he had piled high on his plate. He paused from eating long enough to gulp coffee from his cup, and quickly resumed chewing an enormous chunk of food that was threatening to burst through one of his cheeks. Duke, who was in the process of dropping eggs on his plate with a spatula, stopped what he was doing to gaze at his partner in disbelief. Gully stopped chewing long enough to grin back.

Ike kept staring at the abundance of different enticements to eat laid out on the table, never having seen anything like it before. He was glad he had listened to Duke and had followed him here. He was also happy because the sausage gravy wasn't on the same plate with the biscuits—it was in its own serving bowl with a ladle sticking out of it—and there was plenty of butter. The steaks and eggs were on separate platters, too.

But then he was struck by an unsettling thought: he hadn't brought any money with him. He didn't know how he was going to pay for his meal.

As Duke was helping himself to more of some of everything he said, "Damn, Marie. Times must be gettin' hard around here. I remember when you used to really lay out a spread."

Marie threw him a phony glare. "If you got any complaints about how much food I set out for ungrateful bastards like you, why don't you just bring your own next time?"

Will came in through the front door. "What's all this about ungrateful bastards?"

"I said Duke was an ungrateful bastard," said Marie.

"We already knew that," said Will. He was about to sit down in his chair at the head of the table when Marie turned on him.

"Willis Eugene LeMay! What do you think you're doing?" she thundered.

"I'm fixin' to eat my supper, Ma."

"You'll be fixin' to wash your filthy horse-stinkin' hands and face before you sit down to eat at MY table!" Marie roared.

Will rose up and gave the others a "what ya gonna do?" look and went outside to the washbasins on the porch. Marie looked over at Gully and Duke and frowned. She picked napkins up from the table and threw one down on the table in front of Gully, then reached over and slammed a napkin down in front of Duke. Noticing that Ike already had a napkin next to his plate, Marie grunted her approval. She then returned to stand by the entrance to the dining room, arms crossed in front of her formidable breasts. Gully and Duke continued to eat, leaving their napkins untouched.

Duke was cutting through a thick slab of steak when he glanced over at Ike, who was still sitting with his empty plate in front of him.

"What are you waitin' for, boy? Dig in!" said Duke.

Ike leaned close to Duke and said in a hushed voice, "Garrison didn't give me any to money to pay for me to eat here."

Duke stared at Ike and then erupted into laughter. "Why, son," he smiled, "you don't have to pay for any of this. None of us do. Binghamton pays *Willis* out there and Marie to provide us with food and drink along with taking care of the horses."

Ike now began to understand. "You mean I can eat for free? Can I eat as much as I want?" he asked.

"Like I been sayin', grab your knife and fork an' dig in, boy!" answered Duke.

Ike didn't have to be told twice. "Son of a bitch!" he said with delight. Picking up his plate as he got out of the chair, he traveled around the table, filling his plate from the various platters and bowls. When he sat back down in his chair, he ate ravenously from the stack of food that dwarfed his plate.

Gully looked over at Ike. "Hey, slow down. kid!" he said, trying to hide a smile. "You'll give yourself a bellyache."

"I tell ya, one thing, said Duke, "the only thing Marie hates worse than unwashed men comin' to her table is throwing out food. Ain't that right, Marie?"

"I can't stand you washed or unwashed, Duke Ferrell!" she said from her guard post near the door.

Will walked back in and stood in front of Marie, his hands held up for inspection. She grunted her approval and he quickly slid into his chair, making a show of picking up his napkin from the place setting, unfolding it with a great flap, and setting it down over his lap.

Giving her husband one of her patented warning glares, Marie said, "I'll be back with *your* dinner, Willis Eugene, so keep your hands off what's on the other end of the table. That's all for the working men." She turned and started back toward the kitchen.

A thought suddenly popped into Ike's head. "Thank you, ma'am," he called out to Marie.

Marie stopped in her tracks and turned to look at Ike. "Young man, did you say *thank you?*" she asked.

"Yes, ma'am. Thank you for the grub and food, ma'am," he said.

"Well, I'll be," Marie said. "This young feller's the first of you wretched scoundrels ever to show manners and proper breedin'. You all could take a lesson from him," she said, shooting a mock scowl around the table that could almost pin a man to his chair. She took all the platters and tureens from the table and placed them directly in front of Ike.

"What the hell?" said Gully.

"None of you ungrateful bastards get a second' helpin' until this fine young man finishes his first one." The men at the table started to voice their displeasure at this pronouncement. "And maybe not even then," she said with a wink at Ike. "What's your name, young man?" she asked sweetly, placing an arm around his shoulders.

Ike answered, "Isaac Fleck, ma'am. But I go by Ike."

Marie gave him a warm smile. "Well, Ike Fleck, you may call me Marie. And you are welcome to eat at my table whenever you come this way, whether you work for J.K. Binghamton or not."

"Yes, ma'am—I mean, thank you, ma'am," said Ike, sheepishly.

Marie gave his shoulder a quick pat and a squeeze and stepped away to stand guard over the plates she had piled in front of him.

As Ike started to help himself to more food, Gully said, mimicking Marie's voice, "Young man, would you mind passin' one of them platters of beef over this way before you eat 'em all yourself?"

Ike continued to eat and then lifted his head to look at Gully. "Were you talking to me?" he asked, innocently.

"No," answered Gully, "I'm talkin' to that durned coffee pot, over there. Hell yeah, I'm talkin' to you, Mr. Has-All-The-Grub-And-Food-In-Front-Of-Him. Now, pass those beeves over here! Wait, I'll do it myself." Ignoring Marie, he reached across the table with his steak knife, speared one of the thick steaks on the platter and flicked it onto his plate. After ladling sausage gravy over the steak, he sat back down to enjoy his culinary creation. "Now I can *really* dig in!"

Ike looked at his empty coffee cup and then at Marie. "Marie," he said, "do you have any milk I could drink? I don't like coffee all that much."

"Well, I suggest you start," said Duke. "We got a long road ahead of us tonight and all of us"— looking directly at Ike— "need to stay wide awake the whole trip."

Marie gave Duke a real glare this time. "I don't know what you need a durn young'un awake for on a freight run." She turned to Ike. "Young man, I got a bottle of milk in the icebox. I'll go get it and be right back." When she returned from the kitchen, she made a big show of placing a drinking glass in front of Ike, prying the cap off the milk bottle, and filling up the glass. She left the bottle in front of him.

"Thank you, again, Marie," said Ike.

"You just let me know if there's anything else you need," Marie said sweetly. Her eyes blazed at the other three men. "And *only* you!" And with that she went back into the kitchen.

During the meal, both Duke and Gully looked over at Ike, who was running his thumb and index finger across the blond peach fuzz adorning his upper lip and down each side of his mouth in the same manner as his brother.

"Uh, whatcha doin' there, Ike?" asked Duke. "With your fingers, I mean."

Ike looked up, a bit surprised. "Trying to make sure no food's caught in my moustache."

The two men again looked at each other and then down at their plates in an attempt to stifle their laughter. "Looks just fine to me," Gully said, emitting a slight giggle in spite of himself.

Ike grinned. "Gee, thanks, Gully. My brother Garrison always says a man with a moustache can't be too careful when it comes to eating food."

Duke smiled. "I reckon so. All us men with moustaches got that same problem."

Will ran his fingers over his own snow-white moustache and gave a soft chuckle.

While Marie was in the kitchen getting a sour cherry pie out of the oven, Will took a pipe and a packet of tobacco out of his shirt pocket. After filling the bowl he lit the pipe, tamped down the tobacco with a small deer antler prong and enjoyed a few puffs. "Had a feller from New Mexico stop here on the stage a few days ago. Said he'd been down in New Mexico Territory and things are looking awfully troublesome in Lincoln County. They got all this shootin' and killin' goin' on between ranchers and what they call Regulators. I'm sure ol' Spotted Wolf's heard about it; those Indians got a way of communicatin' that puts our telegraphs to shame. And I'm sure he likes it just fine with the territorial governor's attention diverted elsewhere cuz he gets left alone. And let me tell you, he and his band of Utes have built themselves quite a village up on Bear Mountain. Utes still leavin' the reservation all the time to join 'em. Army can't do much about it cuz they're busy runnin' around fightin' the Sioux, the Cheyenne and the Arapaho north a here."

"Well, can't say I blame the Utes any," said Duke, sitting back in his chair while sipping some coffee. "Just about all their hunting grounds have been given away or dug up by the miners. And with new towns springing up all around, the Utes got no choice but to live on the reservation. I'm surprised more of them ain't gone to join up with Spotted Wolf on that mountain. Besides, there's some great deer and elk hunting down around there. I wouldn't mind seeing that country again myself someday."

Will took a few more puffs on his pipe. "I hear there's a place down that way called Three Rocks. Trace Pedras the Spanish call it. Supposedly years ago some Frenchmen buried stolen gold around there that's never been found. I like to play around with the idea of headin' down there someday to go find the Frenchmen's gold. Maybe if Ma ever lets me get out of this business." From his facial expression, it was doubtful she ever would.

Ike was fascinated with the idea of a place nearby where Frenchmen's gold was buried. "I never been out of Colorado, least since when we got here from Missouri when I was a kid. Never knew where I wanted to go. Is this Three Rocks Trace Pedras far from here?"

Duke smiled. "Tres Piedras. Yeah, it's a bit of a ride, about a week or so."

Ike wasn't totally listening. In his mind he was already seeing a place called Three Rocks Tres Piedras with the Frenchmen's gold peeking out of the dirt. "Is it a hard place to find?"

"Nope," replied Duke. "If you head out from Stovepipe, there's a trail that takes you down past the border straight to it. Keep Bear Mountain on your right and Ute Mountain on your left. Just keep to the trail and you'll get there. But about that buried gold—"

Just then Marie came out with the pie and placed it on the table. "Now you all just let it set right where I put it. It still needs to cool a bit. I'll be right back with more plates and forks. And *you*, Will LeMay, I'll know if there's even one crumb missing." And with that she went back into the kitchen.

"No she won't," said Will as he reached for the pie.

"WILLIS EUGENE LEMAY!" shouted Marie from the kitchen. "You dare touch my sour cherry pie and I'll be serving you your hand on a plate instead of pie!"

Will quickly drew his hand back from the pie. "I don't know how the hell she does it, but that woman can see through walls."

Marie brought out the plates and forks, walking over to where Ike was sitting to give him his plate and fork first, and then walking over to Duke and Gully. When she had given Will his plate and fork, she gave him a stern look and then glanced over at the pie. Satisfied that it had remain untouched, she cut the pie into large wedges, handing the first and largest wedge to Ike.

"Thank you, ma'am," he said, gaping at the huge slice of warm sour cherry pie on his plate.

"Good manners will get you a long ways in this world," Marie said. Her glare spread around the table. "*Some* men I know would do well to learn that."

As she was serving the pie to the others, Ike was still thinking about what Duke had said. *"Keep to the trail"*. That was what Uncle Roy had once told him. All he had to do was find the trail and follow it to where the gold was buried. There and then he made up his mind that someday he and Garrison would make it to Three Rocks Trace Pedras and dig up the Frenchmen's gold. He couldn't wait to see his brother again to tell him. Feeling jubilant, and with a mouthful of pie he said, "I bet anyone who finds that gold will never have to work another day in his life."

Gully, also with a pie-filled mouth, said, "Well, Ike, if you do decide to head down to find it, let me know. If we find the gold we'll split it fifty-fifty and Duke here can find himself another shotgun messenger."

Ike couldn't tell if Gully was serious or kidding, but he was smiling when he said it so he might have been both serious *and* kidding. Ike thought if Garrison was busy hunting down road agents and couldn't come along, Gully might make good company. Thinking about Gully made him think of the stagecoach and—he had to get back! Garrison had said he had to be everywhere on time. Duke had said that Mr. Binghamton had only given them thirty minutes to eat. He hadn't checked his watch when he left the stagecoach, but it felt like it had been at least thirty minutes. He stood up from the table.

"Thank you very much for all the food, Marie. It was the best meal I ever ate in my whole life. But I got to get back to work. My brother Garrison said I was expected to be everywhere on time so I don't want to be late."

Duke was about to tell him to stay put and eat, but he was already getting the idea that Ike thought differently from most people. He decided to just let Ike do what he felt he needed to do.

Ike was about to leave the table when Marie told him to wait just a bit and she'd be right back, then went into the kitchen. She returned a few moments later carrying a bundle from which emanated a wonderful savory aroma. It was wrapped in a couple of large kitchen towels tied together in a large, handle-like double knot. She motioned for Ike to walk over to her. When he did, Marie gently pulled him closer to her.

"You are the sweetest young feller. Here," she said, handing the bundle to Ike.

It felt steamy and warm. He lifted the bundle up and sniffed it. It smelled like everything he had just eaten for dinner. It smelled...delicious.

"You take these vittles with you but don't let them two have any of it. This is just for you. A gift from Marie."

Ike looked at the bundle and then looked at Marie. Suddenly, he hugged her tightly as if she were his mother. "Thank you, Marie," he said, softly.

Marie felt both slightly surprised and a little uncomfortable with Ike's strong, almost loving embrace. She wasn't one for physical contact or for displays of emotion; it just wasn't part of her upbringing. She thought Ike was a nice young man, one she felt very friendly toward but not affectionate.

Gently disengaging herself from Ike's embrace and just as gently pushing him away, Marie said, "You have a safe ride, Ike Fleck. Come back and visit us soon." She was wholly sincere.

"Yes, ma'am," said Ike, "I will." He turned and practically ran out of the room, swinging his kitchen towel bundle by the handle.

Duke and Gully rose from the table, walked over to Marie, and made a show of thanking her for the meal by bowing low as best they could, each sweeping an arm across his body. "Thank you, Marie," they said in unison.

Marie laughed and gave her head a little shake. Both men mimed giving her a hug and said their goodbyes. They left the room, Will walking right behind to escort them back to the stagecoach.

Marie was thinking about Ike. "Lord," she said softly, "please watch over that young man. Somethin' tells me he's gonna need all the watchin' over You can give him."

Outside, Will put his pipe back in his mouth, and then picked up the lantern he had left on the porch, turning the knob to raise the lighted wick.

Duke stopped and turned to face him. "What I was trying to say in there about Tres Piedras was that there's two of them. The Tres Piedras with the story about the buried treasure is up in Oklahoma, not in New Mexico."

Will took his pipe from his mouth and scratched the top of his head with the stem. "Gee I didn't know that. Got the boy all worked up for nothing."

Duke said, "It's OK. I'll set things straight with him at the next stop. And you ain't the first one to get the two places confused."

When the three men walked up to the stage, Ike was already sitting inside. After Gully and Duke climbed up to their seats, Duke raised the wick on the running lamp, took out his logbook and made his departure time entry. He replaced the logbook in his coat pocket, lowered the wick to give off a dim, soft glow and pulled on his gloves. Will gave the horse harnesses a last check, making sure he had done his usual fine job. Fully satisfied, he walked to stand next to the front boot below Duke.

Ike had set the bundle on the seat opposite him next to the duffel bag. If he wasn't already stuffed up to his chin, the aromas of Marie's cooking rising up from the seat would have made him hungry again. She had said there were vittles in there. He'd never heard that word before. Maybe vittles were also food and grub—which he was pretty sure were the same thing. In any case, he hoped that the two men seated overhead wouldn't smell what was inside the bundle and ask him to share it. Marie had made it clear the vittles were for *him*.

Duke called down to him from the driver's box. "Marie don't normally cotton to most folks much. She can barely tolerate Will. Don't know what you said, Ike, but her allowing you to give her a hug? Never seen the like. That's a lot for Marie, I tell ya."

Will said, "A-men to that."

Ike didn't know what to say. He thought Marie was just fine.

Will glanced through the window at Ike and chuckled a little. Then he took his pipe from his mouth again, looked up at Duke and got serious. "I don't know what you boys are really carrying on this stage and I don't want to know. You just keep a close watch on that trail ahead of you." He gestured towards the running lamps on each side of the stage. Only the one next to Duke was lit. "I'd keep both those lamps dark. They make it real easy for someone to draw a bead on you at night. And you take care of that youngster on board."

"It's kinda supposed to be the other way around," said Duke, as he extinguished the flame on the running lamp next to him. Will looked at him quizzically. "We'll be OK," Duke continued. "See you next trip. Make sure you thank Marie for us again in case she don't remember."

As Will stepped back from the stagecoach, Duke shook the reins, and with a "H'yaw!" the six black horses easily pulled the stagecoach out of the yard as Will waved them off. Duke steered the horses back onto the road leading to Trinidad. Will gave them a last wave goodbye as he walked back to the station house.

It was two-thirty in the morning. Duke would never tell Ike about the two Tres Piedras. There was something else on his mind.

CHAPTER 14

Around that same time the Bellum Gang was working by both moon and lantern light putting Hank's stagecoach robbery plan into action. Among a stand of trees near the edge of a gentle, grassy slope leading down to the stage road, they had chosen a bushy ponderosa pine about one hundred feet tall and three feet in diameter. Two men chopped the tree down; all four chopped the fallen tree into three sections. Ropes were tied around each of the sections with the other ends of the ropes tied to horses pulling the tree logs down the hillside to the road. The sections were dragged onto the road and laid one on top of another to form a barricade almost ten feet high. The logs were set at an angle extending into the clearing and out to the other edge of the road so that a stagecoach would be unable to drive around either side of the barricade.

The spot where Hank Bellum had picked to set his trap was well chosen. It was at the bottom of an incline, a bit past a curve in the dirt road. The driver would not see the wall of logs until he rounded the turn—only sixty feet from the barricade. His only choice would be to steer the team of horses into the clearing on the left where further passage was blocked, right where Hank wanted the stagecoach to be.

Standing at the top of the slope Hank saw Jesse, Rossi and Skellenger working to untie their ropes from the roadblock. "Just cut the ropes at your end and leave the other ends hanging from the logs. Hell, you boys will be rich enough to buy new ropes. Right now we gotta get ourselves hid."

The three men followed his orders and rode their horses up the slope to where Hank was already concealed behind the trees. They swung down and tied the reins to the horses around some slender young pines. From their vantage point, they had a complete view of the stage road from the roadblock on up to the mountain curve. Shooting the driver and the shotgun messenger would be like shooting tin cans off a rail fence.

By now the deep rose of sunrise had begun to glow from beneath the horizon, coloring the few white clouds floating across the dawn sky in shades of red and orange. Hank kept checking his pocket watch every five minutes. The sun would barely show itself until around half past six, less than twenty minutes away. With the sunrise would come the stage heading down the road towards Trinidad with—as Conley had assured him—Duke right on schedule. Hank whistled softly. That was the signal to extinguish the lanterns that could give them away. Besides, there was now enough natural light to see the stage approaching. All four men worked the levers of their rifles to chamber a round and checked their revolvers to make sure they were loaded with six cartridges.

Hank had checked his watch three more times when the growing sound of horses' hoofs was heard from up around the bend. Hank looked again at his watch and smiled. 6:45 AM. The stage was running slightly late. He didn't mind waiting a few extra minutes to collect $400,000. In a matter of seconds, when the stage rounded the curve, he had even more reason to smile. The driver wasn't even trying to check the speed of the horses but driving the stage like it was one of those Roman chariots he had heard about as a kid. Hank wondered if the stage would topple end over end if the driver, trying to brake before hitting the log wall, reined up too hard on the horses. Good. Let 'em all be killed. It would save on bullets.

Inside the coach Ike had somehow dozed off despite being lurched and bounced about in all directions as Duke sped the horses down the road. After leaving Cottonwood Ike had still been nervous but found himself enjoying what he could see of the dark countryside passing outside the stage windows. He enjoyed looking into the star-filled night sky. He'd heard of the Big Dipper but had no idea where to look for it.

Marie's huge feast combined with the rocking and rattling around of the swaying coach had lulled him into a light sleep. His drowsy ears had heard Duke shouting to Gully they were way behind schedule and needed to make up the lost time. Besides staying overlong at Cottonwood, there had been an unscheduled stop along the road between swing stations. Rounding the curve, Duke was pushing the horses hard, barreling down the road at breakneck speed.

Just clear of the bend, Duke saw the roadblock up ahead. "Oh shit!" he cried aloud, followed by Gully's softer "Holy Jesus." Duke only had seconds to assess the danger. If they hit that tree wall, the horses would be crushed against each other by their own weight and momentum, with over a ton of stagecoach slamming into them from behind. The stage's forward momentum upon hitting the solid barrier could send it tumbling over the blockade and crashing down onto the road. If that didn't kill them all, the holdup gang behind this ambush would finish the job.

With all his strength Duke pulled back on the six sets of lines to slow the stage down while at the same time pressing his foot down on the wooden brake lever. He saw the clearing to the left, knowing this was a trap. He had no choice but to steer into it as the stage slid down the road. His commanding but frantic shouts of "Whoa!" to the horses were barely heard above the agonized screeching of the wooden brake grinding against the iron rim of the wheel, the jangling of the heavy trace chains, the pounding hoofs on the hard-packed dirt, and the whinnying cries of protest and fear from the horses. The quick, sharp turn of direction lifted the stage wheels on one side off the ground before they came crashing back down again at the edge of the clearing. Duke redoubled his efforts to keep the stage on all four wheels as he worked to bring it safely to a stop. After that they would all take their chances with whoever lay in wait. Using every bit of his skills honed from his long years as a stagecoach driver, he managed to bring the horses and the stage to a skidding stop inside the clearing—precisely where Hank Bellum had planned.

Ike was jolted awake as the stage veered from the roadblock. In his sleep he had heard the shouting of the two men on the driver's box. With Duke yanking hard on the reins as he turned the horses away from the blockade, Ike was thrown back against his seat, then forced to his right when the wheels lifted off the road. When the wheels slammed back down onto the ground, he was thrown to the floor between the two seats. The food bundle slipped off the seat and fell on top of his head.

Although terrified, he quickly gathered his wits. When the stage came to stop, he climbed back onto his seat. His derby had fallen off when he had been thrown backwards. He quickly placed it back on his head, then buttoned his coat over the revolvers. OK, he was back in his disguise as a city dude, but he was sure breathing hard.

Bellum's gang, hidden behind the trees, had already drawn a bead on the driver's box. As part of the plan, Hank and Rossi targeted the driver. Jesse and Skellenger were to take out the shotgun messenger. At Hank's whistled signal, their rifles unleashed a brutal fusillade on the two exhausted men. Duke's body was pushed back against the driver's box by the sheer force of the bullets hitting him. He died where he sat, his body slumped against the box with his head thrown back. Gully was blown off the seat and fell to the ground. He died sprawled on his back. The leaders on the six-horse team, panicked by the rifle shots and the smell of gunpowder mixed with blood, neighed and jumped around. They made a couple of half-hearted attempts to run away with the stagecoach but there was nowhere for them to run.

Hank whistled again for the men to stop firing and motioned for them to head down the slope. They stepped warily out from the trees, their rifles pointing at the scene of carnage below. As they moved down the hill, they split into two groups to stand on each side of the stage. Once they had it surrounded, the men looked inside. They saw a young boy, dressed in a ridiculous-looking suit and wearing an equally ridiculous-looking derby, taking deep breaths in and out.

Ike had seen and heard the cascading rifle fire issuing from the trees and had seen Gully blown to the ground. He saw four men walking down the hill and flank him on both sides. Still in shock, he knew instinctively that now was not the best time to trust his fast draw. He had to buy some time until he was calmer and more clear-headed.

Hank looked inside the coach and saw Ike sitting on the seat under which the strong box was supposed to be hidden. "Who the hell are you?" He looked disgustedly at Jesse. "Conley didn't tell me nothin' about no passenger on board." He looked Ike up and down. "Boy, you picked the wrong day to ride this stage." He turned his head slightly, keeping his eyes on Ike. "Jesse, Rossi. Get him out of there so I can get to that strong box."

While Rossi hung back a few feet, Jesse walked up to the window as ordered by his brother. He peered inside at Ike. "Ah, Hank, he ain't nothin' but a Fancy Dan. He looks like he don't know nothin' 'bout nothin'. Hey, Fancy Dan, your daddy own a bank? How 'bout a goldmine?" He laughed as he looked at the other men, who remained silent, their eyes and rifles trained on Ike. Jesse stopped laughing and turned back to the window. "C'mon out, Fancy Dan," he said, "I want to take a look at them clothes you're wearin'. Bet you smell just as sweet as you look, too. Open the door slowly and come out this way with your hands up."

By now Ike had gotten his breathing under control. But he was thinking about what the road agent named Hank had said. Ike didn't remember who Conley was but he knew one thing: the silver certificates were no longer inside the strong box.

About an hour after leaving the last swing station before Walsenburg, Duke began to express to Gully his concern that something didn't feel right. He knew he hadn't misplaced that route map. He kept it inside his coat pocket at all times. But there was that saloon girl a few days before who had taken him upstairs and had somehow gotten him to pass out after a couple of drinks from a bottle in her room. He was still woozy the next morning when he woke up alone. As he was getting dressed, he never thought to check his coat pocket for the map. And then later that day Conley handed the map back to him, saying he had found it lying on the station floor. Duke said to Gully that he had had some suspicions about Conley making a copy of the map but couldn't prove anything so he had kept quiet.

Still, Conley already knew that Binghamton had ordered the strong box holding the money to be hidden inside the seat where Ike would be sitting. Binghamton was convinced that robbers would first look for the strong box inside the front boot under the driver's box where it was usually kept. With the strong box moved, Binghamton's thinking was that during the ensuing confusion the kid could get the drop on the bandits until Gully could level his shotgun at them.Conley would have told his partners about the hiding place for the strong box, and by handing them a copy of the map, the gang would also know the stage's location on the road at just about any given time. Duke said to Gully that he couldn't do anything to change the delivery route, but he damn well could do something about those money bags.

Reining the six-hitch team over to the side of the road, Duke had stopped the stagecoach in the early morning darkness. He said that if a holdup gang was planning on robbing their stage he was sure as hell going to make them work for it. He fired up a match and lit the running lamp on his side, raising the wick for maximum light and having Gully do the same with the other lamp. They both climbed down from the driver's box and Duke opened the stage door. After telling Ike to get out of the stage, he and Gully removed the false side of the seat, took out the strong box and laid it on the ground. After Duke took out a key and opened the padlock, he lifted four canvas bags out of the strong box. Grasping them in one hand, he climbed up over the driver's box onto the stage roof where empty wooden crate decoys had been stowed. Using the gun butt of his revolver, he struck upwards against the overhanging lids of four of the empty wooden crates to pry them open. He dropped a canvas bag into each crate, and then used the gun butt to hammer the lids back down. The strong box was again locked and placed back inside the seat.

This was why Duke had been driving the horses down the road so hard, to make up for the time lost in moving the canvas bags up onto the roof of the stagecoach.

Sitting inside the coach surrounded by the holdup gang, Ike was nervous about how angry they would get after they opened the strong box and found the bags gone. But he was suddenly enveloped in a strange calm. He was getting back inside the zone, just as he had been at the bank. He had no doubt that if he could set himself up just right, he could take all four men.

Rossi called out. "Hey, Hank, why don't you and Skellenger walk over to this side and join Jesse and me so we can all look at this dude together? We got him covered so he ain't climbin' outta that stage."

Skellenger looked over at Hank. "After you, Hank." Hank didn't like being ordered around but he saw no other choice. It wouldn't hurt any to pretend to swallow his pride—just this once. Being so close to pulling off his plan, he didn't want to arouse any suspicion. Those two saddle tramps would get theirs soon enough. He kept his rifle pointed in the direction of Skellenger, who did the same to Hank. Both men walked around the front of the stage.

Rossi and Jesse both turned their attention to the two other men walking to stand next to them. Noticing that for the moment no eyes were on him, Ike carefully unbuttoned his coat with one hand, letting the two sides fall away to barely conceal the handguns.

"Jesse, get that kid out of there and finish him off," Hank said impatiently. "We ain't got all day here."

Jesse opened the door. "Come on out, Fancy Dan and join the party. Just keep your hands up where we can see them."

Ike stepped out the door and climbed down the step with his back to the men. He was wearing that derby hat and dressed in a gaudy suit that was slightly too small for him. Jesse started to laugh and turned to Hank. "Well what have we got here, Hank? Hey, Fancy Dan, turn around. I want a good look at them duds of yours."

Ike turned around with his hands up. But as he did, the coat lifted away from the holsters, revealing the twin .44-40 Merwin Hulbert Frontier revolvers.

Jesse, stunned at the incongruous sight of the formidable weapons beneath the suit coat, muttered, "What the hell?"

That was the momentary distraction Ike had been waiting for. In a blur of action, he pulled the handguns from their holsters using the Cavalry Draw. Twin stabs of flame leapt from the barrels of the two revolvers. He shifted his aim slightly and fired again. Four shots—and all four men went down. They never had a chance.

With the sound of the gun blasts still echoing and the smell of gunpowder hanging in the air, Ike stared down at the four dead men lying on the ground. Blood was seeping out of their bodies onto the dirt. It took him a moment to realize what he had done. He stood there with the revolvers held outward, their weight growing heavy in his shaking hands. He was again breathing heavily.

Ike, almost in a state of disbelief, looked at the guns. "Thank you, Mr. Merwin…and Mr. Hulbert," he said softly. Once again, instinct had taken over conscious thought as he had drawn his weapons. He twirled the guns and thrust them back inside the holsters, butts forward.

The stagecoach horses were still unsettled, neighing and blowing while pawing the ground. Ike heard answering neighs from among the trees up on the hill. He turned his head slightly toward the sounds but then walked back and sat in the open doorway of the coach. What was he to do now? He had been hired as a secret stagecoach guard but no one told him he might be the only one left alive. With his breathing once again returned to normal, he thought about the money. Some of it was supposed to be delivered to Trinidad, their first stop. But again, what was he to do now? He didn't know how to drive a horse-drawn wagon, let alone a stagecoach pulled by six horses. And if he couldn't drive a stagecoach how could he get those bags of money to Trinidad, wherever that was?

And then he thought about the attempted holdup. It was his job to prevent a robbery and that's what he had done. But Duke and Gully were dead. Would Mr. Binghamton and Garrison both be mad at him for that? What if Mr. Binghamton thought that he had something to do with the robbery? That maybe it had been *his* idea to kill everyone and steal the money for himself? He could tell everything that happened but what if Mr. Binghamton thought he was lying? Here he was, still on his first day as a secret stagecoach guard, and everyone dies but him? Would Mr. Binghamton have him arrested? Would *everyone* think he'd been part of the robbery and killed the gang members and Duke and Gully to keep all the money for himself? Even if he showed them the money was still all there, what if no one believed he'd had nothing to do with the stagecoach holdup?

He wished Garrison was here to tell him what to do.

Well, son of a bitch, he thought. If people were going to think he was in on the robbery and would throw him in jail anyway, he might as well take the money. He could ride off some place where no one would ever find him except Garrison.

Ike climbed up to the driver's box where Gully had been sitting—turning his head away as he climbed past Duke—and crawled onto the stagecoach roof. He made his way to the four wooden crates containing the hidden silver certificates. Garrison had said there was $400,000 on this buggy. Copying what he had seen Duke do earlier that morning, he took one of his revolvers and pounded upward against the lid of the first crate. Once it was loose, he threw the lid aside. Inside the crate he saw a canvas money bag with a labeled metal tag tied to the drawstrings. On the tag was written the name of the bank where the money was to be delivered. He untied the bag, spread it open, and looked at $100,000 in United States Silver Certificates, ten bundles each of $10,000. "Son of a bitch," he said, softly. It was the most cash he had ever seen in his life. Inside the bag he found deposit slips for the different accounts for which the certificates were to be deposited. He dropped the bag down to the ground and then opened the other three crates to retrieve the remaining three bags. He threw all the bags down and lowered himself onto the driver box. From there he jumped down off the stage and onto the ground.

Ike again heard neighs from the horses hidden among the trees. He trudged up the hill to where the horses were tied. He untied two of the horses led them down to the stage, tying the reins to one of the rear wheels. He retrieved the other two horses and tied them to the other rear wheel. At least this way if anyone came by after he was gone they'd see the horses and make sure they were taken care of. Ike had learned as much as he could understand about horses from Uncle Roy, who had been almost as expertly knowledgeable about horses as he had been about firearms. He looked at the horses and chose a giant palomino Belgian stallion as the best of the four. Not only was it the biggest horse he'd ever seen, it was by far the most beautiful.

With its cream-colored mane and tail, a white blaze down the middle of the face, and four white socks, the animal seemed to glow in the early morning sunlight. *That* was the horse he'd ride away on. It also had the best saddle of all of them, and there were two large saddlebags behind the cantle. Ike looked over at the four dead holdup men. One of them had been called Hank. He was the biggest of the four so he had to have been the leader. This giant horse was most likely his. Ike saw that the rifle scabbard was empty.

He walked over to the rifles lying on the ground near each of the bodies. Three of them were Henry repeaters. But he recognized a Winchester '73 next to Hank's body. It was the same kind Garrison owned! The best rifle ever made was about to become his—and his brother hadn't even bought for him.

As he bent down to pick up the Winchester he heard a slight, almost indiscernible sound. He glanced past Hank and noticed that one of the men was still barely alive. He was the one called Jesse. He looked like a younger and slightly smaller version of Hank. Ike figured they were brothers, just like him and Garrison. Hank, being the older brother, probably did everything for his younger brother, too. A lot of good it had done Jesse.

The younger Bellum was lying on his back, shallow breathing mixed with a gurgling sound rising from his chest. His head was turned slightly towards Hank but his vacant eyes were just gazing outward. Ike took a few steps over to Jesse and looked down.

"I didn't have no choice but to shoot you an' your big brother Hank an' those two other guys. An' I'm not a Fancy Dan. This is just the clothes they made me wear. I'm a secret stagecoach guard."

Jesse just continued to stare, the breaths growing more and more shallow. A few moments later, the breathing stopped.

Ike walked back to the Winchester and picked it up. He worked the lever to eject the spent cartridge and load another bullet into the chamber. He knew that the rifle could hold up to fifteen rounds but he wasn't sure how many were left in the tube magazine. He could find out later. He searched the dead men for bullets that would fit his revolvers and his new rifle. He found some extra bullets on Hank and could tell they were .44-40 cartridges. He slipped those into his jacket pocket. A posse was sure to come after him and at least he now had more spare ammunition.

Then a thought struck him: if he were to get killed by some posse he didn't want to die dressed like a Fancy Dan. That's why he had brought that duffel bag with him, planning on changing back into his own clothes when the stage reached Leadville. His job would be finished and he'd no longer have to dress like a dude until the next delivery run.

He climbed back into the stage and opened the duffel bag, still on the front seat. He got out his own plaid long-sleeved shirt, short brown leather vest, blue denim jeans, and a light-gray wide-brimmed hat with a leather strap. The dude suit was quickly stripped off. After he was back in his own clothes, he stuffed the bullets into a jeans pocket. He jammed the suit back inside the duffel bag, leaving it on the seat. He grabbed the derby hat and flung it out the open door.

What to do about all that money? He had seen two saddlebags on Hank's horse. He decided he would stuff it all into those saddlebags and ride to…where? He needed to think of a direction, let alone a destination.

Ike climbed back up onto the box but this time he forced himself to gaze at Duke's blood-soaked body. He thought back to when the canvas bags had been moved. After Duke was back in the driver's box, Gully muttered he'd drank too much coffee that night and couldn't hold it till they reached the next swing station. While Gully was off taking care of personal business, Duke had lit the running lamp next to him and called Ike up to sit in the driver's box. Ike wasn't sure why Duke had wanted him up there but he did what he was told. After taking Gully's seat, Ike saw the stage driver holding what he was sure was

the route map. Duke said that since Ike was part of the team he should know
where they were going.

Duke handed the map to Ike to look over. Even by lamp light he could
see it clearly enough. The map showed the entire route for the bank deliveries.
Duke remained silent, looking into the distance. Gully's head suddenly popped
up next to Ike, and with mock anger he demanded to know what Ike was doing
in his seat, and to kindly step down before Gully picked him up and tossed him
twenty-five feet through the air to the ground. That had seemed to brighten
Duke's mood a little. Ike handed the map back to him before jumping down to
the ground, maybe jumping a bit too close past Gully.

Now, holding his breath and steeling himself to the task, he reached inside
the Duke's coat pocket and felt for the map he knew would be there. He
grabbed it and quickly jumped down from the boot, exhaling a great burst of
air and gulping more back into his lungs. He climbed back inside the coach and
sat down.

He unfolded the deerskin map and held it near his face. Wet blood
covered almost half the map, but he could still read it. With Duke's detailed
craftsmanship the map showed the stage route from Pueblo to Trinidad, and
from Trinidad back up to Walsenburg, over the Sangre de Cristo Mountains,
into the San Luis Valley and back through the mountains for the last two stops.
It also showed the distances between all the towns. He set the map down on
the seat opposite him and after a bit of study found his current position on it.

He knew he couldn't ride too far in the direction of Trinidad. What if
someone from the stagecoach company was riding toward him to find out why
the stage was late? What if there was a sheriff with him? He couldn't take that
chance. He sure couldn't ride back to Pueblo because he'd have to answer
questions there as well, besides having to give back the money. On the map he
saw the Walsenburg turnoff a few miles down the road from where the
stagecoach stood. They were supposed to make a delivery to a bank there but
not till after Trinidad. No one in town would be expecting the stage this early
so it seemed safest to head that way. He saw that by heading west—or to his
right—from Walsenburg and on past Fort Garland the trail would lead to a
town called Stovepipe, which lay just across the Rio Grande. That was the
town Duke had mentioned at the home station. It wasn't on their delivery
route. Maybe it was one of the places the regular stagecoaches went to.

A town named Stovepipe—how big could it be? It looked remote out
there all alone with no other towns nearby. Ike thought news of the robbery
probably wouldn't reach there for maybe a week. From looking at the map, he
figured it wouldn't take longer than a few hours ride to reach the town. But he
had no experience reading maps. He didn't know anything about the scale of a
map, or even about miles, so he didn't realize that distances were much farther
than they looked.

Although Ike only had basic reading skills, he could sound out words in
both English and Spanish thanks to Taggart. The map showed he could take

La Veta Pass through the Sangre de Cristo Mountains and then down into the San Luis Valley. But, he'd be riding past a place called Fort Garland. What if the soldiers saw him ride past their fort and arrested him? Ike decided it'd be safer if he rode past the fort at night.

He took his finger and moved it downward. From Stovepipe, Duke had drawn a trail that ran down to a perpendicular line. Above the line were the letters "CO", below the line were the initials "NMT". At first he didn't know what those letters meant but then he remembered what Will had said: New Mexico Territory. And what was that place that Will had mentioned—with the Frenchmen's gold? Three Rocks Trace Pedras! He couldn't see it on the map. But Duke had said it wasn't hard to find. All he had to do was follow the trail from Stovepipe and keep two mountains on either side of him. Ike guessed there was a posted sign or something letting you know when you got there, like the town sign that told you that you were entering Boulder.

Gully had said they would ride out there together. He looked over at Gully's body. He had just begun to figure out when the shotgun messenger was kidding him. He thought Gully had sounded serious about riding with him to find the gold. Well, that wasn't going to happen now. He would miss Gully. He had felt safe with Duke and now he was gone, too. At least he had Duke's map. He had to follow it because otherwise he had no idea where he should go.

But then another thought came to mind. What if even Garrison was convinced he was guilty of murder and stagecoach robbery? He wouldn't be safe anywhere because Garrison would find him. But he *needed* Garrison to find him. He couldn't do this alone. Once he was with his brother, Ike would convince him that he hadn't planned any of this and the only people he had killed were Hank and Jesse and their gang. Garrison would believe him. He'd *have* to believe him.

Ike got an idea. He'd leave a written note for Garrison explaining how it all really happened. That would do it. It'd *have* to. He didn't want his brother to think he was a road agent and a cold-blooded murderer. He tried to think where he'd find paper and a pencil. Then he remembered Duke's logbook—but it was still in Duke's pocket. Son of a bitch. Why hadn't he thought to grab it when he'd gotten the map? Well, there was nothing else for it but to climb back up to the box and get it.

After folding the map and stuffing it into his back pocket, Ike drew a huge breath and climbed back up to the driver's box to retrieve the logbook from Duke's body. As he climbed back down, he gripped it by a corner where it hadn't been splattered with blood. When he was back inside the coach he tore out a blank page, thought a bit, and wrote out the note using the pencil that had been inside the book. He cried as he wrote out the words. When he finished he dried his eyes with his shirtsleeve. He left the logbook and pencil

on the seat next to the duffel bag and climbed out of the stage. He stuck the
note in the doorway and closed the door, giving the note a tug to confirm it
was tightly affixed in place. Ike took out the pocket watch Garrison had given
him and pushed on the crown to open the cover. It was almost 8:00 A.M. He'd
been there for over an hour. He had to get moving before someone came
down the road and saw him. Ike figured that if he rode into Walsenburg and
stayed to the back streets he might get through unseen. He closed the cover
and put the watch back in his pants pocket.

He picked up the four canvas bags and carried them over to where
Bellum's horse was tied. To him, the big, muscled palomino looked like it
could run fast and far. He didn't notice, nor would he ever, the US brand on
the stallion's left shoulder. If he had, he wouldn't have known what it meant
anyway.

He set the canvas bags on the ground beside the horse. The saddlebag
was slightly above his head, so he had to reach up to untie the flap. One by one
he took the bundles out of two of the canvas bags and stuffed $200,000 into
the saddlebag. He repeated the process with the saddlebag on the other side.
When he was done and the flaps were tied down, four empty canvas bags lay
on the ground.

With that task done, Ike began his attempt to climb up into the saddle.
Suddenly, he felt like he was going to be sick. Pressing his head against the
saddle fender he managed to keep it all down. Then he started to cry, letting
out all the built-up emotions of the morning. The deaths of Duke and Gully.
The outlaws he had killed. The money he was stealing. He was all alone for the
first time in his life. It was a few minutes before he was able bring himself
under control and regain his composure.

Ike remembered the Belgian was still tied to the stagecoach wheel.
Untying the reins, he led the horse away from the stage. He still found it hard
to comprehend the immense size of this golden beast. The stirrups hung down
low enough for him to reach them, but the saddle horn was so high up he
couldn't easily reach it with his hands. The road agent called Hank had been a
big man, bigger than Garrison, so it must have been no problem for him to get
into the saddle. Still, this horse looked to be the best of the bunch. And from
now on he was going to enjoy the best that life had to offer. $400,000 could
buy all the best things in life he had ever wanted. Add the Frenchmen's gold to
the $400,000, and he could buy things he didn't even know about yet.

But first he had to reach that saddle. Ike gave it some thought and came
up with a solution. He grabbed the reins and threw them up over the Belgian's
head. Grabbing them in one hand, he lifted his foot and slid it into the stirrup.
Then reaching up, he grabbed the nearest edge of the saddle fork with both
hands. Lifting his body up from the stirrup and switching his hands to the
saddle horn, he swung his leg over the saddle. He was sitting on the horse!
Perched at that height, Ike felt like he was looking down at the ground from

the top of a giant mountain. The stirrups were too long for his feet to reach. He'd just have to tightly grip both sides of the horse with his legs as he rode.

He lightly shook the reins and tapped the horse's sides with his bootheels. He had a moment of panic when the horse began moving forward, but it really wasn't that hard to stay in the saddle, at least when the horse was walking. At the edge of the roadblock, he saw a gap between it and the hillside, just wide enough for the Belgian to pass through. He took a last look around. He figured the other horses would be OK. He also looked over at the four dead gang members. Garrison would show up later and take care of everything. He always did. He didn't look back at Gully and Duke.

He kicked the palomino forward and slowly walked it through the gap. Reining up at the edge of the road, he looked both ways. No one was coming from either direction. It was now or never. With the best kick of his heels he could manage, Ike shook the reins and with a "H'yaw!" set the horse in a gallop towards Walsenburg. This wasn't like walking a horse at all. Fearing he'd be thrown from the saddle he leaned forward and drew his legs up firmly against the Belgian, holding onto the reins for dear life.

After several miles of worrying if he would be bounced from the horse or not, he saw the sign for the Walsenburg turnoff. He figured no one would think to follow him that way. Chancing a quick look ahead and back down the road he saw no sign that riders were approaching. With another "H'yaw!" he had the Belgian galloping towards Walsenburg and the trail to Stovepipe. It wasn't until then he realized he had left Marie's package of vittles inside the stagecoach. He didn't dare go back for it.

PART II

AFTER

CHAPTER 15

It was noon. Garrison Fleck had been in Trinidad for two hours, having ridden in on a brown mare rented from an El Moro livery stable earlier that morning. He paid for the rental out of his own pocket since the J.K. Binghamton Stage Line had no contracted stables in town.

His plan had been to surprise Ike when the stage rolled into town to make the first money delivery. It had been scheduled to arrive at the bank at eleven o'clock but hadn't shown up. When the clock in the bank tower struck twelve and the stage still hadn't arrived, the Binghamton station agent named Mankiewicz and the bank president were both worried, as was Garrison.

The two townsmen walked down to the sheriff's office while Garrison rode the mare down the street to meet up with them. The three men entered the office and convinced Haines, the county sheriff, to ride out along the stage route to find out if the driver had gotten into some trouble, like perhaps a broken stagecoach wheel or axle. No one yet suspected a robbery might have occurred since the new route was supposed to have been a tightly kept secret. But at the same time, they acknowledged that nothing could be ruled out. Garrison introduced himself to the sheriff, volunteering to ride with him. The sheriff welcomed him along. Haines was an older man, and his widening girth amply displayed he hadn't done much vigorous law enforcement in years. His gray hair, spilling out from under the curled brim of his tan Stetson, was way past due for a trim.

They walked outside to where Haines's chestnut gelding was tied to the hitching rail. "Lotsa reasons why a stage can be late comin' into town," said Haines, untying the reins with his gloved hands. "We'll probably find it with a busted wheel somewhere along the road like you boys figured."

"Maybe," said Garrison, As he untied the reins to the mare he thought, but my little brother's on that stage so I hope you're right.

The two men swung into their saddles and set their horses into a lope out of town. They decided to keep riding until they either reached the stage or until it got too dark to go on. They could always turn back and spend the night in Walsenburg and head back up the trail the following morning, but they hoped to find the stage tonight. There was still the chance it had broken down before or after the turnoff to Walsenburg. But then why hadn't Duke or Gully ridden one of the stagecoach horses into that town and sent a telegram from the Western Union office?

There was a little over four hours of daylight left to ride the forty miles to the Walsenburg turnoff. The men hoped it would be enough time to find the stage before the sun went down. It took extreme self-control to keep from spurring the horses into a full gallop down the road. The mare and the gelding both seemed to sense the urgency of their mission, several times pushing a lope into a gallop only to be reined back. The riders did their best to hold the horses to an ambled gait. With sunset coming on they did not want to be forced to ride into Walsenburg for fresh mounts, only to resume their search in darkness.

As Garrison and Sheriff Haines rode on they tried to think things out. "I can't believe the stage didn't make it down this far, said Garrison. "We should've seen it by now."

"Maybe, maybe not. We don't know yet what happened, if anything," said Haines. "But I'm beginnin' not to like this."

They rode another fifteen miles and they chanced fifteen miles more, making it to the Walsenburg turnoff by late afternoon. Both horses and riders were about done in. The men reined up to consider their options.

"We go much further and we're taking a chance with these horses. I don't want to be walking back to town," said Haines.

"Me neither, but I just want to push on a bit, no more than a couple of miles," said Garrison. "If we haven't found them by then we'll head back to Walsenburg for the night."

"OK," responded Haines, "but if I have to walk back I'll be a might peeved at you."

Garrison gave a heavy sigh. "I might as well tell you my little brother Ike is on that stage. I was in Trinidad expecting to surprise him there."

Haines looked up the road. "Well, I guess we better try to find your brother then."

They continued on past the turnoff. A few more miles turned into ten, and daylight began to inexorably turn toward sunset. With the stagecoach on their minds, neither man noticed the hours-old tracks of a very large horse ridden down the road in their direction.

They had gone three more miles when Garrison said, "I see something." With Garrison's heels digging into its sides, the tired brown mare bounded ahead in a labored gallop, Haines's horse struggling to keep up.

As he rode closer Garrison was able to see the log blockade in the middle of the road. From the saddle he could just see over the top of it. To his right he thought he could make out the stagecoach. His heart started to race, and he began to grow anxious. He saw the gap behind the trees and the hillside and quickly walked his horse through it, Sheriff Haines following behind. In the clearing they saw the stagecoach. The six black horses were still hitched in front, three other horses were tied to the rear wheels.

Reining up, the two men looked the scene over. The bodies of the Bellum Gang lay side by side on the ground near the stagecoach. They saw Duke's body slumped in the driver's box. A few feet away Gully's twisted body lay in the dirt as if he'd been carelessly tossed there by a giant hand. Blood was everywhere. Garrison loped his horse over to the stage, pulling up sharply on the reins and leaping from the horse before it fully slid to a stop. He ran to the stage.

"Oh my dear God," said Haines, still astride the chestnut. He had seen stagecoach robberies before but none with carnage like this. It took him a moment to choke down both emotion and a feeling of sickness. He gently nudged the horse with his spurs and walked it further into the clearing. It was still light enough for him to notice footprints and horse tracks leading from the stage up the hill. The tracks led into the trees. He dismounted to take a closer look on the ground. The tracks led both ways. But within the main grouping of large footprints he found a strange set of smaller footprints. These prints showed that someone had twice walked to and from the trees. Four sets of horse tracks followed the footprints leading down from the woods.

At the stagecoach, Garrison saw the note Ike had left sticking out of the door and quickly took it down. He glanced at it long enough to recognize Ike's scrawled printing. After checking to make sure Sheriff Haines was occupied elsewhere, he folded the note and stuffed it inside his shirt pocket without reading it.

Haines followed the footprints up to where the Bellum Gang had hidden behind the trees. There he saw the axes and lanterns on the ground where the gang had left them while waiting for the stage. He also saw where horses had relieved themselves among the trees. That meant they had been up there for a long time, perhaps for hours. He gathered up the axes and lanterns and walked back down, following that one set of smaller footprints where they led back to the stage. He set his load down on the ground. "Evidence," he called over to Garrison.

Garrison, his mind only on Ike, climbed into the stage. On one of the seats was the duffel bag. Lying on the seat next to the bag were Duke's logbook and pencil. On the floor he saw the toweled bundle of food that Ike had forgotten. He picked it up, untied the knotted cloth handle, and saw two small tin containers with lids. Next to the containers was a small glass soda bottle with a cork stopper. Inside the bottle was milk. He opened one of the containers and saw the serving of biscuits and sausage gravy Marie had given Ike. In the next container were slices of steak. Everything had begun to turn, the result of being left inside the coach on a very and unseasonably warm day. The first day, it turned out, of an even more unseasonable heat wave.

During this time Haines had squatted down to take a closer look at the dead outlaws. He rose up and walked back over to the open door of the stagecoach. "Out of the four I think I can identify the two Bellum boys. Hank was about as big as they come and Jesse not much smaller. Got wanted posters back in the office for the both of them. Don't know those other two lying with 'em." He nodded his head up and to the side. "It's a shame about the driver and the shotgun messenger." His eyes quickly scanned the inside of the stagecoach. "You said your brother was ridin' on this stage? I just looked around and there ain't another body anywhere. Any idea what happened to him?"

"I don't know," said Garrison. "He left that bag of clothes there. He was going to change into them after he finished this job."

"What job?" asked Haines.

Garrison realized his slip of the tongue. He wasn't ready to let the sheriff in on the entire money delivery plan just yet. "Oh, I helped get him this bank teller job in Leadville. He didn't like the suit I bought him very much. He was going to change into his own clothes after he got back to his room."

"Kids today," replied Haines.

"There's also this." Garrison showed him the abandoned food.

"That's peculiar. That must have been pretty tasty some hours ago," said Haines. "You sure your brother didn't just up and quit and is waitin' for you at a swing station up the road aways?"

Garrison looked Haines in the eye. "Ike's no quitter," he said. As he set the food bundle down he glanced over at the duffel bag. Something was protruding from the open bag and he pulled it out. It was that ridiculous striped suit coat. Had Ike taken the time to change back into his own clothes? Why here? Still, this could mean he was alive. But where was he?

Garrison remembered the hidden strong box. "Sheriff, there's $400,000 in United States Silver Certificates inside a strong box hidden under this seat. Help me get it out." He was sure the money was still there. So again, where was Ike?

With the strong box on the ground, Garrison shot the lock off. After opening the lid he sat back on his bootheels, stunned. "What the hell is this?"

Standing behind him, Sheriff Haines looked over Garrison's shoulder and inside the strong box. He pushed his hat back on his head. "Sure looks empty to me."

Garrison fell forward onto his knees, trying to make sense of it all. He then got an idea. Standing up, he stepped onto the leather thoroughbraces beneath the coach and opened up the side flap on the front boot. It was empty. He walked around to the rear boot and looked inside. Also empty. There was only one more place to check. Keeping his eyes averted from Duke's body, he climbed up past the driver's box and gazed at the stage roof. There were the four opened wooden crates. He crawled over to them. As he looked inside the first empty crate, Sheriff Haines called up to him. "Find anything?"

"None of it's here. I don't understand."

Haines was still looking over the robbery scene when he spotted something on the ground. He walked over and bent down to pick it up. It was a derby hat.

"More of your brother's bank teller clothes?" he called out.

Garrison looked over at Haines and recognized the hat Ike had been wearing when he had left on the stagecoach. He crawled back down to the driver's box, again avoiding looking at Duke, and jumped down from the boot. He walked over to where Haines was standing and took the derby. Holding it in front of his face, he was dumbstruck. "What the hell? I don't understand."

"Well, I'm beginning to," said Haines.

The sheriff had also spotted the four canvas bags Ike had left on the ground. Garrison's mind was reeling, careening through and around thoughts. There were just no logical reasons for what he was seeing and why Ike wasn't around. He didn't know what Haines had in mind, but whatever had happened, one thing was certain: Ike had nothing to do with it. There was just no way he could have.

"If you walk around a mite you'll see some interestin' footprints," Haines continued.

Garrison looked down and saw the smaller set of footprints among the larger ones. Those could only be Ike's. A few inches shorter than his big brother, Ike had average sized feet. The dead outlaws were all big men; he could see that from where they lay.

"Fleck, I think we just found out what happened to the money and your brother," said Haines.

Garrison remained silent. He had a hunch about what the sheriff was thinking, because he was now thinking it himself. Adding all the visual clues together, the only logical conclusion was that, somehow, his brother *was* involved in all of this. He didn't believe Ike had killed Duke and Gully, but no one else could have killed Hank Bellum and his gang. Then for some reason, he had stolen the entire cash delivery and ridden away on one of the horses. Garrison just couldn't understand why.

Haines picked up the empty canvas bags, walked over to his horse and stuffed them into one of the saddlebags. "Evidence," he said as he finished tying down the leather straps. He walked back to Garrison. "You gonna want to be keepin' that derby hat? That's evidence, too."

Garrison absent-mindedly handed it to him. His focus was on a set of Ike's footprints leading away from the stage. He walked over to the spot where Ike had struggled to climb onto the tall Belgian stallion. Following the horse tracks, he walked past the gap between the hillside and the end of the logs to the edge of the road.

"Sheriff," said Garrison, "I know where Ike took off to."

Haines, after putting the derby hat back in the duffel bag, walked over to stand beside Garrison. He also had missed seeing the tracks when they first rode into the clearing because, like Garrison, his attention had been on the abandoned stage. The large hoofprints of the Belgian were easy to discern from other imprints on the road. Even in the gathering dusk, Haines could also see the direction in which they led, which was south.

Haines said. "I believe you're right. Seein' as how he rode out on this side of this roadblock, and we never ran into him coming up from Trinidad, the only way he could've gone was into Walsenburg." He looked at Garrison. "You might not want to admit it, but everything points to your brother stealing the whole kit and kaboodle and then takin' off on one of these ponies to make his getaway."

Garrison, who had been gazing at the tracks, quickly looked up at the sheriff. "I already came to that conclusion myself," he said coldly. From the evidence gathered so far, everything pointed to Ike as the prime suspect. He, the money, and one of the horses were gone. Ike had taken a horse that, judging from its hoofprints, had to be huge. Try as he might, he couldn't picture his little brother on top of a horse that must have been the size of the stagecoach or thereabouts. Despite the magnitude of what his brother had apparently gotten himself into, that one vision was still a bit humorous.

Haines seemed to echo his thoughts about Ike atop the Belgian. "Mighty big horse left those tracks. No idea how your brother's goin' to stay on top of a horse that size unless he's as big as Hank Bellum was," said Haines, with a slight grin. "But I think we just found some of the horses stolen from a string headed to Fort Garland about a month back. A cavalry detail leadin' them to the fort were all killed. Everyone thought a band of renegade Utes done it but now it looks like it was this Bellum Gang."

Haines looked up at the darkening sky. "We'll never make it back to Trinidad tonight. Let's unhitch that team from the stage and gather them together with these three. I drove a few Mexican remudas 'cross the Rio Grande into Texas in my day," he said with a slight wink. "We can run 'em over to Walsenburg and board 'em at a livery stable till they can be dealt with. Then you and me can spend the night at the hotel. County's payin'. Meanwhile, I'll let Sheriff Tolliver know to send some boys out here to cart these bodies to the undertaker's. At first light tomorrow mornin' we'll ride back to my office. I got an Army bulletin back there on those stolen horses. Shouldn't be no trouble to figger out if these are the same ones. It'll also give us a description of the horse your brother's ridin'."

After they had unhitched the stage team, they gathered the nine horses together. Both men remounted, Haines taking up the reins of one of the Bellum Gang horses and leading it behind him. Garrison could easily picture the sheriff decades ago as a young man running caballos stolen from Mexican ranchers across the Rio Grande into Texas. He brought the mare around behind the others to ride drag behind the assembled string.

Haines looked over at the trees still blocking the road and stopped, dropping the reins of the horse behind him. Remaining mounted in the saddle, he walked his horse over to the roadblock. "We can't leave an obstruction standin' like this. This road needs to remain open all the way to Trinidad. Between the two of us it shouldn't take too long to move these logs off to the side there."

Garrison was frustrated. "We ain't got time for this. And besides you said earlier our mounts were about to keel over dead."

"We got it to do and we're gonna get it done. And if our horses do keel over we got plenty more to choose from right here. I know Huerfano County ain't my jurisdiction, but Sheriff Tolliver would do the same for me."

Haines swung down, took a coiled rope from his saddle and mounted the Bellum Gang horse. At the roadblock, he uncoiled the rope and tied one end around the saddle horn. He tied the other end of his rope around a thick limb protruding from the top log. Garrison reluctantly followed suit on another horse, tying his rope around the log just beneath the first one. They soon cleared the road of all three logs. They decided to remain on the fresher horses for the ride into town.

By this time, the sun had dipped behind the peaks of the Sangre de Cristo Mountains, but the moon had already risen. Garrison motioned his head toward the stage and the bodies on the ground. "What about them?"

"They ain't goin' nowhere. They'll keep till we can send a wagon for them tomorrow."

Garrison thought for a moment. "Just a sec," he said, swinging down from the saddle. He untied the bedroll from his horse, and then took the bedroll off one of the other horses. Holding them under each arm, he walked over to where Gully's body lay. Dropping the bedrolls to the ground, he unrolled one of them and took out the blanket. He draped it over Gully, tucking the ends of the blanket underneath the broken body. He did the same thing with the tarpaulin, making sure it would not blow away during the night. Picking up the other bedroll, Garrison walked over to the stage and climbed up to the driver's box. Spreading it out as he had done with Gully, he gently laid the blanket over Duke's body, securing the sides underneath the body of his old friend and mentor. Giving the blanket a gentle pat, he held his hand there for a moment. It seemed like the death toll of people he loved kept piling up. He draped the tarpaulin over the blanket and secured it around Duke's body. He climbed down from the boot, walked to his horse and swung back into the saddle.

"OK," he said, "let's go."

CHAPTER 16

Early the next morning the two men were back at the stagecoach to have a last look around before riding back to Trinidad. Haines had decided not to tell Sheriff Tolliver about the robbery. He was facing a tough election in the fall. Cracking the bloodiest and largest stagecoach robbery case in Colorado history would enable him to coast to an easy victory. It could even make him a statewide name.

The night before, Garrison had sent a telegram to Mankiewicz, the Trinidad stage station agent, about the robbery. It had taken him a few moments to decide if he should mention Ike's disappearance or not, but it was his job to report exactly what happened. He just didn't volunteer any conjectures connecting Ike to the stolen money. Both were missing, and he left it at that.

When Garrison and Haines again arrived at the bloodied scene of the holdup, a few buzzards rose from where the outlaws' bodies lay. They flew up to circle overhead, remaining there until the intruders left and they could return to their grizzly feast. Garrison kept his eyes off the four bodies, looking instead at Gully on the ground, and Duke in the driver's box. A light wind had blown during the night but, thanks to Garrison's efforts of the previous day, their bodies remained unmolested under the bedrolls.

Sheriff Haines swung down from the chestnut and walked over to the stage. His intent had been to gather up the food and the duffel bag but then decided against it.

"Best to leave all this evidence stay put for now," he said. "I'll send my deputy and some boys out here later to bring it back to town." Haines then climbed back into the saddle.

Garrison, having remained on the brown mare, looked over at Haines. "I'm not going back with you. I've gotta go find Ike. I found his tracks this morning. He rode through town alright, but he kept to the back streets 'til he joined the stagecoach trail heading west. Those tracks will lead me to him."

Haines leaned in the saddle toward Garrison, his gloved hands folded over the saddle horn. "Ordinarily I'd say do what you think is best. But, son, that might not look so good to your boss. Now, having talked to you I don't think your brother was part of the deal to rob the stage. But there are others who *ain't* talked to you." The sheriff narrowed his eyes. "Your brother and the money are both gone and that's a fact. You go ridin' off and it could look like you were in on it with him."

Garrison was dumbfounded. "Are you saying folks would think this whole thing was planned by Ike and me? That we hired the Bellum Gang? Then why would Ike kill them?"

"Maybe he decided not to share the money after all. Or maybe they was fixin' to double cross him and he got them first. Now, I ain't sayin' that's what happened. I'm just sayin' that's what folks might say happened before they send Sheriff Tolliver and a posse out to arrest your brother. That's right after Tolliver arrests you," the sheriff said.

"He has no reason to arrest me—and the telegram I sent to Mankiewicz last night should exonerate me. Why would I have reported the robbery and Ike missing if I was in on the whole thing?" Inwardly, Garrison regretted sending the telegram to the Trinidad station agent but it had seemed like the right thing to do at the time. He should've left out any mention of Ike. He just wasn't thinking clearly. The truth was, Garrison was in a state of shock. He had been thrown into a nightmare he couldn't wake out of. But the bottom line was he had no time to waste on this. He had to start down the trail to track down his brother.

"That telegram might work," said Haines. "But if it was me who was the stage detective with a brother and $400,000 gone missing, I'd ride back to Trinidad and file an official report. Let your boss know exactly what happened and that you'll be goin' to find your brother. I'll back up everything you say, to your boss and to Tolliver if it comes down to it."

Garrison was silent for a moment, wrestling with the decision of what to do. Haines had asked him to hold off saying anything to Tolliver just yet about Ike and the robbery, which was fine with him. He had other concerns. What if it snowed or rained and Ike's tracks were lost? How would he be able to follow Ike then? Right now the sky was clear and it was getting hot, but weather in this country could shift on a dime.

But Garrison had to admit that Haines was making sense, even though an entire day would be lost riding back to Trinidad. It was best to go back and file that report. He could also better provision himself for the search since he had no idea how long it would take. He knew he'd need a fresh horse, one that would not tire easily and would be able to withstand the long hours and miles of the journey ahead. Besides, he'd tracked men through rain and snow before—and found them. He felt that Ike wouldn't veer off an established trail in country he'd never been in. He should be easy to track in any kind of weather. "OK," was all Garrison finally said.

They arrived back in Trinidad by midday. Haines's deputy came out of the office to greet him. The sheriff swung down and tied the chestnut to the hitching rail. He placed his hands on his waist as he arched his aching back and emitted a pained groan. Garrison remained astride the mare.

"Pete," said the sheriff to his deputy, "We got a stagecoach robbery up the road close to fifteen miles past Walsenburg. Six men dead. Why don't you scare up a wagon and a couple of men and go bring those bodies back here to the undertaker's? I've started the investigation."

The tall, lanky deputy reached up to scratch his shock of wheat straw-colored hair. "Up where, sheriff?"

Haines was trying to sound casual. "Up a ways past where the road branches off towards Walsenburg. Easy to spot."

Pete kept scratching his head. "Walsenburg? That's Sheriff Tolliver's jurisdiction, ain't it?"

Haines began to fidget slightly. "Well, ah, um, technically it is but since Mr. Fleck and I come acrost it first I'm taking control of the case. In special cases like these the law allows for me to expand my jurisdiction."

"Whatever you say, sheriff," said Pete. "When you going to tell Sheriff Tolliver?"

"*When I tell him*," responded Haines, with some annoyance.

"Okee doke, Sheriff," said Pete. He walked into the office to grab his hat.

Garrison stared at Haines. "Thought you said last night Huerfano County ain't' your jurisdiction?"

"I changed my mind," said Haines, a bit sharply. Then his tone softened. "We got our own county election comin' up in November. I ain't as young as I used to be. I gotta show folks I can still do the job."

Haines turned to walk away but then turned back to Garrison. "I'm gonna scare up an early dinner," he said, pointing over his shoulder towards a nearby saloon. "The sign outside a Charley's said they got elk steak with mashed potatoes an' gravy on special. That's some good eatin' right there, I tell you. County's payin' if you're hungry."

"Thanks, but I'm not hungry," said Garrison. "I'm gonna check in at the stage office and file that report. And then I gotta get this worn out mare over to the stable and pick out another horse to ride out on today."

Haines looked at Garrison as if he were crazy. "Well," he said, patting his generous belly, "suit yourself." He started to turn away again, then turned back as he remembered something. "Before you leave town, stop by my office. I'll show you that report on the stolen horses. At least, I should be done with dinner by then. Charley sure knows how to fry up elk." His gaze drifted off to a mental vision of pan-fried game meat. "That man works magic with a skillet."

The sheriff began to walk off a third time and then remembered something else. He turned to Pete, who had just walked out of the office. "Oh, scare up a second wagon. Back to where that stage is at you'll see axes and lanterns sittin' on the ground and some ropes tied to logs. There's a bag of clothes and some leftover chow inside the coach, too. All evidence I don't want blood from those dead bodies contaminatin'."

He gestured backward toward the chestnut with his thumb. "Meanwhile, I got some empty canvas bags in my saddlebags that need attendin' to. They's also evidence for the robbery investigation. Well, I think that's about it. Take 'em into my office and drop 'em on my desk. I'll deal with 'em later."

"Okee doke, Sheriff" said Pete, stepping off the boardwalk and walking over to the sheriff's horse.

Haines began to walk away a fourth time but hesitated, appearing to resolve some internal struggle, and turned back to his deputy. "Eh, Pete, on second thought, no use stirrin' up bad blood between me and Tolliver. You go ahead and check in with him after you collect up those dead bodies. See what he wants to do with him. But tell him that I'm happy to take the stagecoach robbery investigation off his hands—if he wants, that is. Yeah, tell him that."

"Okee doke, sheriff."

With that, Sheriff Haines turned to face Garrison again, touched the brim of his hat in parting, and finally walked off toward the saloon, envisioning the pan-fried elk steak with mashed potatoes and gravy dinner he was about to enjoy. Garrison swung the tired mare back into the street as Pete was opening the first saddlebag.

Trinidad was a J.K. Binghamton Stage Line stop. At the contracted livery stable, Garrison was able to pick out a sturdy, well-muscled buckskin gelding and leave the brown mare in its place. For now, he wasn't going to worry about returning the horse to El Moro. He rode the buckskin halfway down the street to the stage station. In front of the office, a black mare stood harnessed to an elegant black brougham carriage. Garrison instantly knew it belonged to J.K. Binghamton, who had arrived in town during Garrison's absence. When he walked through the door, he saw his boss pacing back and forth, stopping occasionally to shout and grumble at Mankiewicz, who was sitting behind a paper-laden desk.

"I had them load my horse and carriage onto the train because Lord *knows* what I'd find for transportation down here." In his late-forties, J.K. Binghamton was a large man, both in height and girth. He had removed the silk top hat he usually wore, and the few gray hairs remaining on the top of his head were plastered to his scalp by sweat. His moustache, filled with gray, grew into mutton chops. He was dressed in a black suit and waistcoat, with an open, tan woolen greatcoat worn over the suit. The coat, along with Binghamton's scalp, was spotted with white coal ash. He was chewing on a large, unlit cigar poking out of a corner of his mouth. He removed it when he saw Garrison. The cigar would go in and out of his mouth throughout the conversation.

"Garrison! Thank *God* you're here. Where the hell have you been?" Binghamton stopped his pacing and stood in front of Garrison. "That brother of yours—which I hired per *your* personal endorsement—has sent this company into certain bankruptcy! And it's *your* fault, Garrison. It's *all* your fault! Telling me how good he is with a gun. You forgot to tell me he was just another common crook, like the ones he killed."

Garrison, frozen by this onslaught of venom and verbiage, remained silent. He had never seen Binghamton this angry. He had also never seen him this afraid.

Binghamton again started to pace the floor. "$400,000 in cash that *I* personally vouched for! I don't *have* that much money. Everything I have—including my wife's money—is invested in this delivery business. What else could I do? No insurance company would sell me a surety bond! They said carrying that amount of money on a stagecoach was too much risk. Then what the hell are they in business for if not to insure too much risk? Isn't that the *point* of insurance? But I had to tell the mine owners I was bonded or none of them would sign with me. What if they find out about the robbery? What if my *wife* finds out? What happens to me then?"

He stopped pacing and started jabbing his finger in Garrison's face. "Your brother was hired to prevent this very thing from happening—and now he's ruined me! For all I know he was working with that gang and killed them so he wouldn't have to share the money. For all I know you're tied up in this with him." Breathing heavily with white spittle on his lips, he stared at Garrison, who hadn't moved from inside the doorway.

Garrison was stunned. Sheriff Haines's words had come true all too quickly. But for those words to first come issuing from Binghamton was unsettling. Stepping into the office, Garrison reached behind his back and closed the door. He knew that Binghamton had not yet worked himself up to his maximum volume.

"Well?" asked Binghamton. "What do you have to say for yourself?"

"Mr. Binghamton," he said with controlled rage, "You're damn lucky I don't punch you in the mouth for what you just said." He took a few moments to calm his temper, taking cruel delight in watching the stunned look on the stage line owner's face. "Now, let's back off and try to have a reasonable conversation about this. First, you shouldn't be here. Wait—why *are* you here?"

"Lucky for me *someone* keeps me in the loop so that I know what's going on within my own company." said Binghamton. "Thank *God* for Mankiewicz here. He seems to be the only employee who actually does what I pay him to do! After he received your telegram last night, he had the good judgment to wire me. Now, seeing as how this is *my* company it seems only right that I should be told immediately about one of my stagecoaches being robbed *of $400,000!* Especially this one! Why the hell didn't you take the time to send me a telegram before you went riding off with Haines?"

Garrison was still trying to recover from Binghamton's verbal onslaught. "I was going to wait until after I filed my report, Mr. Bing— "

"You were going to *wait*? $400,000 in United States Silver Certificates on the loose and you were going to WAIT? Thank *God* Mankiewicz sent me that wire last night. I took the Denver and Rio Grande this morning from Denver to El Moro. It got me there in five hours. *Five* hours! If I'd taken one of my own stages I'd still be on my way here. God damn it but I'm in the wrong business!" Binghamton was looking somewhere into the future. "Railroads will be everywhere someday and right soon," he said solemnly.

"I've just opened my investigation, Mr. Binghamton," said Garrison, trying to get his boss re-focused on the issue presently at hand. "As I said I was just coming in to file my report. And I was hoping to keep a lid on this for a few days."

"A few DAYS?" thundered Binghamton, now reaching his maximum volume. "I had to cancel all stagecoach runs because I can't make payroll! The J.K. Binghamton Stage Line will no longer exist if I don't get all that money back—in full—by tomorrow!"

Garrison couldn't believe what he was hearing. He pointed in the direction of Walsenburg. "*Two* good men were killed yesterday, Mr. Binghamton. And I don't know for sure yet *what* Ike did—if anything. But it's my job to find out."

Binghamton stood looking at Garrison for a moment, then looked away and sat down on the corner of the station agent's desk. "It doesn't matter. I'm ruined, anyway," he said quietly. "Even if I can recover the money there's no way anyone will trust me again." He got up from the desk and shook his finger at Garrison. "But I still want all of it back!" He collapsed back down again on the corner of the desk. "I'll never hear the end of this from my wife. She warned me against this venture. 'You're going to bankrupt us both' she said. All she needs to hear is that she was right and there will be no living with her, if you can call the past nine and a half years of married life living. Living hell is more like it. If my first wife hadn't passed away…"

"I'll say it again," said Garrison, interrupting him, "you shouldn't be here. It's a mistake. Besides, I just may be able to bring back your money and my brother yet."

Binghamton's face brightened with hope. "You know where my money, and uh, Ike, is?"

Garrison thought about what he had read in Ike's note. "Well, I might have a lead."

Binghamton stood there, his face reddening to the point where it appeared his head would explode. "*Might* have a lead?" he thundered, reaching a higher maximum volume. "God damn it to hell! 'Might' isn't a comforting word at a time like this, Garrison. But after tomorrow, what Mankiewicz *will* do is the spread news about my stolen money throughout the West. I want every lawman and bounty hunter between here and the Pacific Ocean out hunting for your brother. After I get through with him, he'll wish he were dead—unless someone takes care of that before I get my hands on him."

Garrison glared at Binghamton. It took great control to keep himself from drawing his gun and shooting Binghamton right between his two piggish eyes. But since he couldn't afford to be thrown into Sheriff Haines's jail, he had to keep his anger under control. "Don't send those telegrams just yet," he implored. "Give me a week to find Ike and return with the money." Despite Garrison's anger, his eyes were pleading with the company owner to give his approval. "All I ask is that you give me a chance to handle this myself. If you don't hear from me by next week you can do what you like."

"How the hell do I know you *will* find him?" asked Binghamton.

"Because he's riding a horse the size of a damn elephant," Garrison snapped. "I *think* I can track him. Sheriff Haines and I found a set of large hoofprints leading away from the stagecoach. Haines has every reason to believe Ike's riding one of the horses that the Bellum Gang stole from the Army. He'll give me a full description of it before I leave town. Only one of those horses could've left tracks that big. That's the horse that's missing so that's the horse Ike's riding."

"Who's to say your brother won't abandon that horse and steal another and then another one after that? He'll no longer have to cover his tracks because you won't know what horse you're supposed to be following," fumed Binghamton.

Garrison leveled his eyes at Binghamton. "I've solved every stage robbery I set out to investigate. You always got your money back—and that's a fact. And besides, I told you; I got a lead." He paused before making the next statement he knew he had to make. "I swear to you right now, Mr. Binghamton, I'll return with the money, with or without my brother. If Ike doesn't come back with me, it's because he's dead."

Binghamton lowered his head and thought, pacing back and forth. He finally stopped. "OK, tell me what you need."

"Just give me that one week."

"One week?" asked Binghamton. He shook his head as he resumed pacing the floor. "Seven days. I—I don't know. Your brother could be down in Mexico by then and we'd never find him."

"Five days, then," replied Garrison. "Just give me that much time to find Ike."

"I just don't know," said Binghamton.

"Then you need to know this," Garrison said, shadowing Binghamton as he continued his pacing. "You let it be known Ike's out there with $400,000 in silver certificates and I *guarantee* you he'll be ambushed. You'll never see your money again."

Binghamton stopped pacing, standing in one spot as if unsure in which direction he should move next.

"My way is the best chance you have of getting it all back." Garrison grabbed Binghamton by the shoulders and turned him so that they were looking eye-to-eye. "I'll return all of your money to you. You have my word on that. Do I have yours?"

Binghamton heaved a sigh and looked down. He mulled over his detective's argument. "OK, Garrison," he said, moving out of the detective's grasp. "We do it your way. You have five days to find him. You have my word on that. But God help you and your brother if you fail to honor yours."

Garrison said, "I have never once failed to honor my word, Mr. Binghamton. You just keep this off the wires till you hear from me. I handle this my way, on my own. We got a deal?" He held out his hand to Binghamton.

J.K. Binghamton looked beaten. He took Garrison's hand and gave it a perfunctory shake. "Yes, we have a deal."

"Good," said Garrison, "I'll leave in ten minutes. Just gotta stop by the sheriff's office on the way out of town and tie up a loose end."

CHAPTER 17

Ike was riding up the moderately steep grade of La Veta Pass on his way to the San Luis Valley. Despite all the mixed emotions he was feeling, he was smiling. Here he was riding through mountains, and he wasn't afraid of getting lost. Uncle Roy had said to always keep to the trail, it will always get you to your destination. He was carrying Duke's map, and it showed the trail he was following would lead to Stovepipe. From there the trail would take him to Three Rocks Trace Pedras and the Frenchmen's gold.

Actually, Ike wasn't so much riding a horse as managing to stay in the saddle. With the Belgian trotting along the trail, it had been a very hard twenty miles. Every few minutes, Ike reined the stallion to a halt to give his body a respite from pounding against the saddle. After four hours they hadn't yet made it to the Pass summit. An experienced rider would have been through the Pass by now, but it was all Ike could do to keep from falling onto the road. He kept turning around in the saddle to check his backtrail. No sign of a posse on his trail—yet.

His feet couldn't even reach the stirrups. Hank Bellum had been well over six feet tall and the stirrups were adjusted to fit his long legs. Ike didn't want to waste valuable time stopping to readjust the stirrups length to fit his much shorter limbs. He tried to compensate by bending forward in the saddle and hugging the sides of the palomino with his knees in the manner of horse race jockey. Gripping the reins as tightly as he could along the back of the horse's neck, he still was afraid of being bounced out of the saddle.

His entire body was in pain from the beating it had taken as the horse galloped through Walsenburg. The stallion had slowed as the grade up the Pass grew steeper, but the trot was even worse. His buttocks felt raw and sore. His inner thighs were chafed from rubbing against the horse. His hands were cramped and tired from gripping the reins. Still, Ike kept looking behind him to see if a sheriff's posse was catching up.

The Belgian, up to the past half hour, had more or less taken the uphill grade in stride. The trail wasn't overly steep, but it kept rising as it stretched before them to the summit. Ike didn't know horses, but he now felt the big stallion was laboring a bit. The horse hadn't eaten or drank anything since the day before at the hideout cabin. Tied to the pine tree above the clearing, it could barely reach anything edible. The horse's thirst and growing hunger were sapping its strength and endurance. Sweat was beginning to form along its sides. But it stayed true to its military training and kept pushing forward up the mountain trail. Ike had grown just as thirsty and hungry and was nearing exhaustion. But he knew he had no choice but to keep pressing onward.

Ike rode past a trail branching off from the stage road that led to the planned rendezvous site for the Bellum Gang and Dave Mackey. After the gang had failed to arrive at the agreed-upon time, Mackey, unaware of how fate had issued him a reprieve from his death sentence, had set the horses free. After that he had headed north to Rosita, the most recent silver boomtown to spring up in the region.

The old trade route the J. K. Binghamton Stage Line was using for a stagecoach road was leveling off a bit as it neared the top of the Pass. Following the map, Ike had been afraid to veer off onto another trail because he knew he would be lost. He felt safer following the upward and winding road to the summit. Below him now, he could see the train tracks for the new Denver & Rio Grande Railway. He was also able to see a small settlement below as well. It was Muleshoe, a water stop for the railroad steam engines. He reined up the stallion, and it seemed like the horse was grateful for a rest stop. Ike pulled out the stage route map, found his location, and saw there was a winding trail off to his left that led to a horseshoe curve around Muleshoe. The trail led to down to a much larger horseshoe curve before it resumed its meandering path to Uptop at the crest of La Veta Pass. From there, the trail rejoined the stage road.

Uptop was the tiny station for the Denver & Rio Grande Railroad. The new, narrow gauge rail line that began in Walsenburg had made its way over the Sangre de Cristo Mountains, ultimately to reach Alamosa, the town the D&RG was building to serve as its regional rail center. From there travelers would eventually ride the rails to places like Santa Fe and Salt Lake City, driving more nails into the coffin of the J.K. Binghamton Stage Line. Who would choose to undergo the rigors of stagecoach travel when instead they could sit back in a comfortable railroad passenger car seat, arriving at their destination in half the time?

Ike folded the map, stuffed it into his back pocket and kicked the stallion into a lope. He rode alongside the railroad tracks as he wended his way up the circuitous path to Uptop. To call it a town was being charitable. It was a few scattered buildings built near the train station. It was past noon but there was almost no one in sight. The next train wasn't due for some hours yet.

Near the train station, Ike reined up as he decided which was the safest route through the hamlet. He chose a path that led past a two-story log building, hoping he wouldn't be seen. But as he drew even with the building, something caught his eye. He turned the Belgian and walked it up to within forty feet of the structure. There, cooling on the windowsill was a freshly baked pie. Sliding down the very long side of the horse, he took the reins in one hand and led the horse right up to the window. He didn't dare let go of the reins for fear the horse would run off. But hunger overruled his common sense. Ike grabbed the pie from the sill and jammed it down inside his jeans. He then climbed up the side of the horse as he had back at the clearing. With one foot in the stirrup, he grabbed the saddle horn with both hands to boost himself back into the saddle.

As he took the reins in both hands, a woman stuck her head out the window. Seeing Ike and the now-empty windowsill, she yelled, "How dare you steal my rhubarb pie! Help! Stop, thief!"

Ike was fully aware of his crime but there was no way he was going to obey her command. He dug his bootheels into the stallion, setting it in a gallop down the road away from Uptop. The Belgian seemed to love the downhill run. Ike, however, was lying flat against the back of the giant horse. In that position, he wasn't able to pull back on the reins with enough strength to slow it down. As the trail descended onto ground that was more level, the stallion drifted off the trail. Ike could see railroad tracks directly ahead. The Belgian easily crossed over them as it galloped toward a stand of trees.

Ike, his body pushed backward on the saddle, pressed his calves and heels against the palomino's sides while clinging to the reins with all his strength. How he wished his feet could reach the stirrups! The pie tin was held taut against his belly. He hoped there would be something left of the pie to eat when he finally had a chance to get down off the horse.

The Belgian was now running through a stand of cottonwoods. Ike could now see where the stallion was heading. Just beyond the trees was a great winding creek curling its way through vast wetlands. Cottonwoods and willows growing along the banks shielded the area from the railroad track and the stagecoach road.

The Belgian mercifully stopped at the edge of the creek. As it lowered its head down to drink, Ike swung an aching leg over the saddle and dropped to the ground. His thirst being greater than his fatigue, he hobbled over to the creek bank. There he flopped onto his stomach on the downstream side of the horse, gulping mouthfuls of water. When he had finally quenched his thirst he sat up, trying to recover his breath and his strength. He had never before felt this physically exhausted. He sat there for a few minutes until his heart stopped racing and his breathing returned to normal. Beside him, the horse continued slaking its thirst. Years ago, Uncle Roy had warned against a thirsty man or horse gulping water. He said they could get gut sick, which was a very painful stomachache. Right now, Ike didn't care. Let the horse drink; he was too tired to do anything about it anyway.

The palomino started to move away from the creek's edge. Ike, alarmed at first that the stallion was walking away with the money and his Winchester, leapt to his feet and ran behind, waving his hands. "Hey, you stupid horse!" he cried, "Stop! Stop!" The horse seemed to pay him no mind but stopped to nibble at some wild grass growing next to the creek.

With the horse appearing to have chosen to stand in one place for a while, Ike looked at the stirrup facing him. He recalled how Uncle Roy had adjusted them to fit his legs after he had climbed into the saddle. He lifted the stirrup up, moved the fender out of the way, and found the buckles and holes. Remembering how Uncle Roy had made the adjustment, he slipped the buckle through those same holes, shortening the length of the stirrup. Climbing back up into the saddle, he found he had done a pretty good job. After sliding down from the saddle, he repeated this procedure with the other stirrup. Now both stirrups looked similar in length to what Ike was used to. Maybe it would be easier to stay in the saddle from now on.

There was a fallen log nearby and Ike sat on it. He felt the squishiness of the smashed pie against his body. He unbuckled his belt and unbuttoned his jeans, then lifted out the pie tin. Somehow, the rhubarb pie—although compressed—had remained largely intact. He scooped out some pie with his hand and stuffed it into his mouth. It was still edible—and delicious. After he had eaten it all, he smiled as he flung the pie tin into the water. Road agents didn't wash their dirty dishes! He watched as the pie tin floated downstream and then wedged itself between two jagged rocks in the middle of the creek. To get at it he would have to walk down the bank and wade across the water over to the rocks. He decided not to even try. No one will ever see it, he thought.

He looked down at the sticky remnants of the rhubarb filling and pie crust on his belly and inside his jeans. He decided he needed to wash himself off. He unbuckled his gun belt and laid it across the log. After removing one of the revolvers from its holster, he took off his boots and socks. He also remembered to take out the pocket watch, laying it on top of the gun belt.

Spring runoff had swollen the creek. Holding the revolver above his head, Ike waded waist deep into the water. Having started its journey from a source high up in the mountains, the water was ice cold. It burned the deep red rashes on his inner thighs as it also numbed them. As much as he wanted out of the gelid water, he forced himself to stand there for as long as he could. He used one hand to push his jeans down below his waist. Dipping his body a bit lower in the water, he used the same hand to wash off the sticky smear of pie remnants from his body.

A soft breeze was blowing as he emerged from the creek. He stood on the bank, letting the sun warm his body as the breeze helped to dry him. He buttoned his jeans, walked back to the log and plopped down onto the sand, using the log as a back rest. The fatigue of the past two days descended upon him like the curtain falling at the end of a stage performance. He felt as if he could fall asleep sitting where he was. But he knew that he couldn't stay there safely for long. Although he didn't think anyone from that little town would hunt him down for a stolen rhubarb pie, they might have heard about the stagecoach robbery. What if they figured he was the one who done it? There might even be a price on his head.

He had to get back on the trail. According to the map, Fort Garland lay just down the road. But he was so tired. He really hadn't slept since—how long ago had he been in Pueblo with Garrison? They had arrived by train yesterday, spending almost the whole night inside that restaurant until it was time to walk to the stagecoach. That was last night. That meant the shootout with the holdup gang had been this morning.

He picked up the pocket watch and opened the cover. It was 2:37. He knew he had to get back on the horse, but he could barely move. The Belgian was still chewing on the wild grass. Ike thought that it should be okay to sit up against the log and close his eyes for a little bit. The rippling of the creek rushing by and the chirping of the birds among the trees combined to relax him. Under the willows, he was hidden from the stage road and the railroad track. He heard an engine whistle in the distance but couldn't tell from which direction it came from. Then suddenly he was on the train. It seemed strange that he should be riding it with the sound of the train whistle so far away. He looked around. He was alone inside a passenger car. Out the window he could see Garrison riding a horse alongside the train. He was waving his hat and shouting but Ike couldn't hear what he was saying.

CHAPTER 18

Ike awoke with a start. He opened his eyes to discover it was night. Still, the light from a gibbous moon high above lit the area bright enough for him to see the area around him. The air was filled with the echoing choruses of chirping crickets and croaking frogs. He could hear the stallion breathing softly as it stood next to the creek a few feet away, remaining in place as if standing guard duty.

The pocket watch was still in his hand, the cover still open. He closed it and put the watch back in his jeans pocket. After pulling his boots on, he stood up and grabbed his gun belt. After he buckled it around his waist, he felt more secure wearing the revolvers again. He put on his hat and walked quickly over to the horse to check the saddlebags. He opened each one and placed a hand inside. The silver certificates were still there. He felt relieved, yet silly. Why shouldn't they be there?

Ike had no idea what time it was. In fact, he had been asleep for ten hours. The moonlight was bright enough for Ike to find the trail back to the stage road. He led the Belgian by the reins until they were clear of the trees. He put his foot in the stirrup, grabbed the saddle fork and, lifted himself up, grasping the saddle horn as he swung into the saddle. The palomino seemed eager to hit the trail again. It was well rested and had drunk its fill at the creek. On its own the horse started to trot along the flat ground then fell into an easy lope up the hill to the railroad track. Sitting high up in the saddle, Ike felt as if he were flying through the night air as they crossed the track. He reined the Belgian over to the stage road. They were back on the trail leading to Stovepipe and the Territory of New Mexico.

Ike was feeling much better. He had needed the sleep. The rhubarb pie had eased his hunger, and the creek had quenched his thirst. He figured no posse would be chasing him at night because their horses could trip over rocks and maybe not even see the edge of a cliff.

And speaking of night, what time was it? The moon was bright, but not enough to see a watch face. He only knew it was dark, and it had gotten very cold. His clothes were dry, but the night air made them feel cold and brittle against his skin.

As he rode out of the Pass and onto flatter terrain the moon bathed everything in its cold, silver light. Desert land stretched away in all directions from him. In the distance, he could make out the dark shapes of mountains sleeping under the stars. The night sky was so full of glittering stars that when he looked up, he imagined himself rising up off the horse and dragged off into the furthest reaches of space by the gravitational pull of the universe. He enjoyed the momentary fantasy until a thought struck him: if he went millions of miles out into the universe, how would he find his way back to earth and Garrison? The thought of being lost for eternity scared him so much he decided to concentrate on the trail ahead of him. Since that didn't fully do the job, he decided to picture how he would spend $400,000.

Down the trail he could see flickering lights sandwiched in between the low dark hills. These were the lights of Fort Garland, still ten miles away. Despite the hours of rest by the creek, Ike's body was still sore and tired. Trotting was painful to endure so he kept the stallion to a walk. Besides, he wanted to conserve the horse's strength as much as possible. He didn't know how far past the fort he still had to go until he reached Stovepipe.

As he rode, Ike pictured himself and Garrison finding that Frenchmen's gold at Three Rocks Trace Pedras. Maybe with all that gold they wouldn't need the $400,000 after all. Maybe they could bury the money there and tell Mr. Binghamton where to find it. Then he and Garrison could ride off with the gold and nobody would be hunting them ever again. They could even go to Deadwood. See the very chair Wild Bill had been sitting in when he was shot in the back of the head by that no-good skunk Jack McCall. They'd finally hung him last year. "Wish I'd had the chance to shoot him myself," Ike said aloud. Yes, they would make that long trip, just him and Garrison traveling alone together like when he was little.

But then Ike's thoughts darkened. He wondered again if Garrison and Mr. Binghamton now considered him an outlaw. He didn't feel like one. When he had killed those Bellum brothers and the other two, he'd just done what he'd been hired for. Sure, he knew it had been wrong to take the money and now he wasn't quite sure why he had. But it was too late to go back. Besides, he'd left that note for Garrison that explained it all.

Yeah, finding that gold and giving the money back would fix everything. And if Garrison never showed up, he'd ride out to Deadwood himself. Maybe become the law, just like Wild Bill. He could see himself as town marshal: long hair down to his shoulders, and a long droopy moustache. And he'd finally own a pair of those .36 Navy Colts. Or maybe he'd just be a gunfighter and keep on killing bad men. He was good at it.

A quarter mile out of Fort Garland, Ike could see the trail would lead him too closely past the Army post. The torches and campfire lights grew brighter as he approached. He pulled up on the reins to halt the stallion. He needed to figure a way out of this unexpected trap. He wished it were daylight so he could look for another trail. Off to his side, the ground appeared to be flat. All he had to do was ride out a short distance from the stage road and travel parallel to it. He reined the horse over to his right and walked it about a hundred yards beyond the road. The ground here was sandy and fairly soft. He just needed to get past that fort. If he just kept the horse to a walk, chances were the soldiers wouldn't hear him pass by.

Ike took off his hat and held it up between his head and the lights from the fort. It made it easier to see his moonlit surroundings as he tried to keep the horse moving forward in a straight line. As he passed by the sentries standing at the entry gate, he held his breath. Please don't make any noise, he thought to the horse. But what if the guards could still hear those giant hoofs clopping on the ground? Ike pictured a company of cavalry riding out of the fort with bugles blaring and pennants waving as they encircled him.

He was almost past the still-silent fort, and the sentries remained where they were. No bugles blaring, no pennants waving. He waited until he was well beyond the fort before reining the stallion back over to the stage road. He kicked the Belgian into a full gallop. With the stirrups adjusted for his legs, he was no longer bouncing around in the saddle nearly as much. He also felt like he was getting the hang of riding a horse.

Back again on the trail to Stovepipe, Ike allowed himself to relax a little—which was a mistake. Those hours of sleep hadn't given him enough rest after all. He still felt literally bone tired. And, he hadn't packed a coat, not thinking he'd need one on the stagecoach. But as hot as the days had grown, the desert nights were unbearably cold. Now he wished he had kept that dude coat instead of the short vest he was wearing.

Ike reined the horse back into a lope, a gait that appeared to be its favorite. He just didn't know how or where he was going to feed it when the horse got hungry again. He wished it wasn't so dark so he could check the map. He felt he had gotten better at reading it. Even though he couldn't correctly judge distances, he could still pick out where he was. Fort Garland was behind him, but he didn't know how far he still had to go to make Stovepipe.

He wondered how many miles he and the horse had traveled together. He thought it seemed like way over a hundred when in reality it was about fifty miles. Still, there was one positive aspect to his situation. Having spent so many hours in the saddle, Ike was feeling more attuned to the Belgian, as well as proud: he and the big palomino had crossed a mountain range today.

He allowed the horse to remain in a lope for a few miles. When he felt it starting to tire, he reined it back into a walk until he again felt nervous about a posse overtaking him. He alternated the two gaits over the next five hours, stopping occasionally to dismount and stretch the tightness and fatigue out of his body. As the morning sun was rising, he was barely keeping his eyes open. He was also very thirsty and hungry. He figured the horse, plodding wearily with its head lowered, was in the same shape, too.

Ike had been leaning against the pommel dozing. He was startled awake
by the stallion, who had given a couple of snorts while tossing its head up and
down. Newly energized, it surged forward, first in a trot and then breaking into
a lope. Ike tried to look ahead as he struggled to rein in the horse. About a half
mile away, he managed to see a thicket off to the side of the road. As he got
closer, he could see that the trees were the entrance to a larger forest. No
armed guards here; arboreal sentinels stood in silent watch as he reined the
stallion to a halt at the edge of the woods.

Ike slid down the side of the Belgian to the ground. Grabbing the reins,
he led the horse into the woods past growths of willows, cottonwoods,
dogwood and chokecherry. Shafts of amber light shot through breaks in the
canopy of leaves to dispel areas of dark shade gathered among the evergreens.
A woodpecker somewhere above loudly tapped away at a blue spruce, trying to
reach its breakfast within. The songs from what seemed like hundreds of birds
chirped and trilled from tree branch to tree branch. Just beyond where he was
walking, Ike could now hear the sound of a rushing stream as the water
tumbled over and between the rocks impeding its way. The Belgian must have
heard and smelled the water from that half-mile distance. That explained the
snorts and the head tossing.

Ike led the horse over to where a single cottonwood stood by the bank of
a wide, clamorous tributary stream of the Rio Grande. Almost forty feet across,
it was only several feet deep but with deeper pockets where groups of brook
trout gathered. The morning sun was brighter here. Broken sunlight danced
and played upon the white, churning of the rushing water; continuous rows of
tiny ripples lapped against the rocky banks.

He let his body collapse to the ground against the cottonwood. He had to
slightly raise himself up again off a thick root, but a small shift in his sitting
position fixed that. He was now on soft, dry earth. Long blades of elk sedge
growing near the base of the tree tickled his elbows. He closed his eyes. All the
horrors of the previous day, the aches and pains suffusing his body, the
crushing stress of running from arrest weighed down upon him. Yet, the sound
of the burbling stream caressed his spirit like a soothing hand.

He could still feel the rolling motion of riding in the saddle. Keeping his
eyes closed, he could imagine the feel of the tree against his back was like an
arm holding him. It took him back to the times of sitting on the porch swing
next to his mother at the old family home. He could feel it all; the gentle
swinging motion, his mother's arm across his shoulders and her hand caressing
his hair. He could hear her sigh, but her face would not come into focus. Try as
he might, he couldn't see her face.

Ike opened his eyes at the sound of a horse whinny, taking a few seconds
to remember where he was. He realized he had fallen asleep, but he had no
idea for how long. All he knew was the sun was higher up in the sky than it had
been when he had first sat down against the tree. It was now late morning, and
the air had grown considerably warmer. It was going to be a very hot day.

He looked around for the horse. The Belgian had made its way down to
the stream bank and was drinking the fresh, cold water. First shaking its head
side to side to fling bits of cooling water over its face, the horse snorted and
nickered contentedly, exulting in the relief from the thirst and sweat of the past
night's journey.

Ike was still thirsty and hungry but first things first. He stood up and
walked over to where the Belgian was drinking. As he had done at the creek
the day before, he checked both saddlebags. The silver certificates were still
there. But after looking at both sides of the saddle, it struck him that there was
no water canteen. Despite Hank Bellum's careful planning of the stagecoach
robbery, he had forgotten to bring one to the holdup site.

Well, there was the stream right in front of him. Ike walked over to the
slanted bank where the horse was drinking and laid on his belly so that his
mouth could touch the cold, rippling water. It was delicious, and despite what
Uncle Roy had warned about gulping water, he kept drinking and drinking. If
he was to get a stomachache later on, at least he was quenching his hours-long
thirst now. When he raised his head to take a breath, he saw young brook trout
swimming and leaping out of the water near the bank. That reminded him that
he hadn't eaten since early morning yesterday at Will and Marie's home station.
That made him think about the food he'd left inside the stagecoach. That was
the problem. If he wasn't using to having something, he forgot all about it.

He thought about shooting a few of the fish with one of his revolvers but
the bullets would probably just blast them to tiny, bloody pieces. He didn't
know how to cook fish anyway. With his stomach growling noisily, he stood
and looked around for something to do to take his mind off his gnawing
hunger. Finding nothing, he looked again at the brook trout. Maybe he could
just aim for the heads...

Meanwhile the Belgian having quenched its own thirst had walked over to
the cottonwood tree where Ike had been sleeping. Pulling some leaves off a
low-hanging branch with its teeth, the stallion began eating its morning repast.
Ike, still standing by the water, looked on in frustration at the horse. OK,
somebody had found something to eat. What was there for *me* to eat around this
place? What he wouldn't give for some steak and eggs—even with the egg yolk
touching the steak.

He looked up in frustration. He saw high up among the green foliage of
the cottonwood where he had been sitting—a bird's nest! Were there bird eggs
inside there? He hoped that if there were, there were no baby birds inside those
eggs. He thought about the best way to get up to the nest. The thick tree trunk
of the cottonwood branched out into a second, smaller trunk, forming a vee a
little over six feet up from the ground. The nest, snuggled within a cluster of
spidery branches and broad, green leaves, was high up on a stout limb growing
upward from the second trunk. He could try to shoot off the branches holding

the nest, but what if the eggs spilled out of the falling nest and broke? Ike thought that there had to be some way to climb up and safely retrieve the nest and all the eggs—if there were any—at the same time.

Wait—the horse! He was easily as tall as the old six-foot stepladder in Uncle Roy's barn. Ike walked over to the big stallion and led it by the reins to stand underneath the cottonwood where the two trunks branched off from each other. The saddle was at the same height as the vee. Ike climbed up into the saddle and reached his leg out to slide it across the juncture between the tree trunks. Wrapping an arm around the second tree trunk, he slid his body off the saddle and onto the tree. He cautiously stood up and leaned his body against the tree trunk. Gazing upward, he tried to determine his best climbing route to the bird's nest.

A few feet above him was that stout limb, curving upward and large enough to support the weight of his body. As his eyes scanned the network of limbs and branches overhead, Ike felt slightly discouraged. The nest didn't look much closer up here than it had on the ground, situated about nine feet above his head. He mulled over different methods of climbing up to the limb, deciding he would shimmy his way up. Wrapping his arms and legs around the trunk, he slowly reached his arms out, grabbing the trunk further up, then scooted his knees up from behind to propel himself forward. The rough bark cut into his arms and the side of his face as he slowly moved up the tree, but he made it up to where he was able to reach out his leg and curl it around the limb. He carefully moved his body over until he sat straddling the limb with his legs.

Well, so far so good. He sat there for a few moments to catch his breath and then inched his way up the limb, pulling himself along with his hands, his thighs scooting up from behind. Fortunately, the growths of broad leaves here weren't as dense as they were in the upper reaches of the tree. He slowly but steadily shimmied up the curved limb until he reached the bird's nest. Ike gingerly lifted himself above the nest to look down inside. There huddled at the bottom of the skillfully woven nursery built of twigs, leaves, and mud were five eggs! He thought he could hear the mother bird squawking at him from some place, but he didn't pay her any attention. His hunger had him focused on those eggs.

Now to get this nest out of the tree. Ike cautiously reached his hands through the tangle of spidery branches to grab the nest from where it was embedded among the leaves. Extending his arms, he grasped the sides of the nest with both hands and slowly worked it free of the branches. Breathing a sigh of victory, he slowly scooted back down the limb to where it grew out from the trunk, keeping a firm hold on the nest. When he looked down from his sitting perch, it seemed like it was a lot higher up than it had looked from the ground.

The problem was that with him holding the nest, he couldn't use his hands to make it back down to the vee. He was also on the side of the tree opposite the horse. What to do? He looked down and figured he was no more than ten feet off the ground. Telling himself that it was just slightly higher up than sitting on the big horse, he gathered his courage, wrapped his free arm around the limb and slid one leg off the limb. He was now hanging by one arm with the nest pressed up against his chest with his other hand. He held his breath, closed his eyes, and let go. Landing on his feet, the jolt from hitting the ground dropped him back down onto his butt. He sat there for a moment, catching his breath and waiting for the world to stop spinning. After everything was more or less resolved, he lowered the nest away from his chest and glanced down. The eggs had survived intact! Breakfast was about to be served.

Ike went back around to where he had been sitting against the cottonwood. The Belgian was standing in his spot, so he grabbed the reins and led the horse a few feet away from the tree. With his spot once again vacant, Ike slid his back down the tree to the ground, the bird's nest in his lap. Now, he had to figure out how to crack the eggs open. The Merwin-Hulbert 2nd Model Frontier revolvers! He withdrew one of the guns from its holster and examined it. He bet that if he tapped the eggshell gently enough with the front sight on the gun barrel, he could crack a small hole in the eggshell. Then all he had to do was suck out the yolk and white stuff. But what if a baby bird flew out of the hole? Just picturing it made him squirm. He made up his mind: there would just have to be no baby birds inside those eggs.

Screwing up his courage, he held one of the eggs upright in his hand and tapped the gun sight against the larger end. It left a small dent. He tapped the egg again and this time the shell cracked open enough for Ike to see inside the egg. There was only egg yolk!

He laid the gun across the bird's nest and held the cracked egg up to his lips. He sucked its raw contents into his mouth and gave it a few chews. Swallowing the yolk and albumen in a couple of gulps, he began to hiccup but that soon subsided. The raw egg didn't really taste that bad--but not that good, either. It was something he would prefer not to repeat after today.

As he ate, he absent-mindedly ran his finger and thumb across and down the blonde peach fuzz he called his moustache. When he had eaten all the eggs, he took the nest in both hands and ceremoniously dropped it on the ground next to him. With the gun in his hand, he stood up and walked over to the stream. He carefully rinsed off the gun sight, wiped it on his shirt, and then holstered the revolver. He plunged his hands into the stream. The water was ice cold, making his hands numb. He furiously rubbed them against his jeans, the friction helping to bring some warmth back to his fingers. It was also a further help that the day was steadily growing warmer as the sun rose higher in the sky.

As he stood in the wet sand, Ike wondered what time it was. Wait! He had the pocket watch that Garrison had given him. He dug it out of his jeans pocket and pushed down on the crown to flip open the cover. The time was still 2:37. That couldn't be right. That's the same time the watch had shown yesterday. It couldn't be the exact same time again. He looked up; the sun was lower in the sky than it was at 2:37 yesterday. Then he remembered the other times he had looked at the watch. The second hand had been moving every time, making a noticeable ticking sound. The second hand was not moving now, and the watch was silent. Somehow, he had broken the new watch.

Ike didn't know what else to do so he closed the watch and threw it into the middle of the stream. He stood there feeling worthless. How could he have been so careless with such an expensive gift? Garrison was going to be really upset when he found out.

In his peripheral vision Ike saw something red and black flit across the stream less than twenty feet away. In an eye blink he drew both handguns and fired. The body of a red-winged blackbird, minus its head and tail, dropped to the water. The gunshots roused flocks of birds to escape from the trees. Two quick shots and two more birds fell dead into the rushing current. He watched as their tiny bodies were carried downstream by the swift current, then he holstered his guns. He ignored the squadrons of squawking, would-be assailants flying in frantic agitation overhead.

He took the reins and led the stallion to the edge of the woods. Peering out at the road, he saw no riders approaching from either direction. He lifted himself up into the saddle. There was no need to check the map anymore. Ike set the Belgian in a gallop toward Stovepipe.

CHAPTER 19

Inside the Silver Strike Saloon that afternoon the town businessmen were gathered together for the weekly town council meeting. Burt Owens, the saloon owner, had set them up with free beer from the tap. The tap was connected to a barrel containing draught beer that had been diluted with about five percent well water. The water made the difference in minimizing his losses from providing free beer to the town council and maximizing his profits when serving it to his paying customers.

The town council members were seated around several tables near the bar. All were drinking beer from glass mugs in various states of fullness. Some of the members were on their second round of beer, a few on their third, and all were talking loudly. The only person without any drinking vessel in front of him was Ernest T. Bowersox, the feed store owner and a confirmed teetotaler.

Yulin Temple was leaning forward against the corner of the L-shaped bar, one foot on the rail. Positioned where he was, he could see the entire saloon, the gun on his right hip facing the batwing doors. He was drinking from a shot glass filled with bourbon, the bottle on the bar in front of him. He set the glass down, took the makin's out of his shirt pocket and rolled a cigarette. Lighting it, he took a drag and blew a perfect smoke ring. He decided he didn't want the cigarette after all, dropping it on the floor and grinding it out with his boot. He grabbed the bourbon bottle, poured a healthy shot into his glass and downed it in one gulp.

Mayor Chet Carson stood up at the front table and rapped his knuckles loudly on the tabletop. With no one paying attention to him, Carson picked up his prepared notes which were lying in front of him next to a half-filled beer mug. Reading from those notes, he opened the meeting.

"Gentlemen, gentlemen... it's time for the weekly Stovepipe Town Council meeting to come to order." Everyone heard him but still took their time quieting down. Carson may have been elected mayor, but they refused to grant him much authority. Carson looked at the assembled men, wishing he had the power of an absolute dictator so he could have them all shot.

Dwight Phipps, owner of the mercantile store, said "Come to order? Sure, I come to order." He yelled to Owens who was standing behind the bar. "Hey Burt, put another beer on my tab and bring it over here, willya?" He dissolved into laughter as did the men surrounding him. All the men, that is, except

Mayor Chet Carson. Phipps looked at Owens. "Hey Burt, I was serious. Bring that beer over here pronto."

Owens was writing down on a sheet of paper every drink poured for each man. He said, "Phipps, nothin' more comes your way until you pay off that tab you already owe me from the last meeting. "

"Tell you what," answered Phipps, "you come by the store tomorrow and I'll make it right."

Owens said, "You put that in writing right now so that the sober you knows what the drunk you promised me. Here, I'll even supply the paper and pencil."

As Owens walked over to Phipps, Carson drank some of his beer, composed himself, and continued. "I now call the town council to ord— ". He looked at Phipps. "I now convene this meeting of the Stovepipe Town Council. Our first order— "

Phipps snickered just loud enough to be heard as he signed Owens's promissory note.

"—of business is my proposal to form a chamber of commerce for our town."

Blake Dooley, the town banker, said "A what?"

Carson replied, "A chamber of commerce. All great cities have them. They're made up of the most prominent men in the business community."

"Oh hell, Chet— "said Dooley.

Carson interrupted him. "Blake, when I'm presiding in my official capacity as this town's chief executive, please grant me the respect for my office by addressing me as 'mayor'."

Dooley continued, "Oh hell, Chet—*Mayor*. Every one of us on the town council already functions like a chamber of commerce, you know that."

"That's not the point, Blake."

"That's *exactly* the point!" We're a small town, population five hundred and thirty-two.

"Don't forget Sally Levine's new baby girl, said Phipps."

"OK. Five hundred and thirty-*three*," said Dooley. He turned towards the other men. "Stovepipe's a real boomtown now, boys!" he said sardonically.

Upon the ensuing laughter, Carson started to fidget a little. "Uh, funny you should mention that, Blake, because you just touched upon the next item on our agenda for this afternoon. We'll just table the chamber of commerce proposal for now."

He cleared his throat, drank more of his beer and placed the mug back down on the table. He continued to read from his prepared notes. And he was beginning to sweat.

"Yes, we're a small town now but Stovepipe is primed to grow. And when we do, the *sky's* the limit." At the word "sky's" Carson raised his index finger above his head. He quickly looked around to see the reaction of the council. There was none. He awkwardly lowered his hand back down to his notes.

"When I first arrived here back in 1861, this town was nothing more than a byway for gold and silver prospectors passing through here to seek their fortunes up in the mountains. Well, we all found our own fortunes here— "

"I'm the managing partner of the bank," said Dooley, "and I can tell you there ain't no fortunes in there, *Mayor.* 'Ceptin' maybe if you're talking about yours."

That drew a round of snickering from the men.

"—growing this town up around Stovepipe Monaghan's old trading post." Carson then paused to let the snickering subside. "When the gold played out in '65, did I leave? No, my friends, I stayed put because my roots here were dug in deep."

"That's because you bought up most of the roots in town here, Chet," said Phipps.

Carson shot him a glance and kept reading. "I was one of the visionaries who stayed to rebuild this town and to maintain the legacy left by Stovepipe after his death in '67."

Dooley looked at Phipps. "Didn't we just have an election? Sounds like Carson's already running for the next one."

"I'm waiting for the other shoe to drop," said Phipps.

Carson stood there, picked up his beer mug and downed the remaining beer in one huge gulp. He slammed the mug down on the table, right on top of his stack of papers. Taking a moment to recompose himself, he continued. "Now silver mines are booming again, thanks to the federal government's new issuance of silver certificates to prop up the silver market. But it's not just silver that will put us back on the map. Oh no, my friends. There's talk of the railroad coming our way, possibly building a major railway facility right here in Stovepipe—just like the one they have on the other side of the mountains in El Moro. I see us doubling, no *tripling* our population in the next few years and after that—the *sky's* the limit!" He raised the same index finger as he had the first time he had spoken that line, and he got the same non-reaction. He quickly lowered his hand, but paused the speech to let his last words sink in. Judging by the faces of the men sitting around him, they weren't sinking in very deep.

"Seein' as how the sky's pretty low 'round these parts," said Dooley, "exactly *who's* talkin' about a railroad comin' to town, *Mayor?*"

"I am, Blake," said Carson, glaring at the banker. He doubted there was another man he hated more. Then he glanced over at Phipps and decided he hated him just as much. He returned to his prepared remarks. "I've been in contact with the board of directors at the Denver and Rio Grande Railroad. Every day they're expanding into new routes, laying down tracks to new destinations. I told them 'Bring it on this way, boys; bring your railroad tracks to Stovepipe. And, after they do, well, the sky's the limit," he said, rushing through that last phrase. This time he kept his index finger firmly on the table.

"You already said that twice before," Phipps said. He leaned his head closer to Dooley sitting next to him. "And I bet this limitless sky will only rise above the properties Chet owns in town."

"No, Dwight. This is all about *us*," said Carson, stretching his arms out to encompass the gathered assemblage of businessmen. "Therefore, I next propose that you, the town council, vote to unanimously authorize me, your mayor, to negotiate with the Railroad the terms for bringing both its tracks and unimaginable wealth to our growing town and business community."

"Not a chance," answered Phipps and Dooley in unison.

"Alright," responded Carson, "we'll also table that proposal for now." Undaunted, he continued his sales pitch from his sheets of written text. "But after they finish building that railroad to our town, my friends, we'll be on our way to becoming the biggest rail center this side of Denver. Once that happens, you will witness our presently small town grow into a major metropolis. And with that metropolis will come art, culture, theater and fine dining. Gentlemen, we'll be known as the San Francisco of the High Plains!"

Despite all indications to the contrary, Carson felt he had hit his stride. As long as he kept pushing, he thought, he just might close this deal yet. "Think about it, gentlemen. Right below us is the Territory of New Mexico. I guarantee you it will be a state someday. And when it does, trains leaving our massive rail center will carry passengers and freight there and throughout the entire southwest and beyond—all the way out to the Pacific Coast!" That last paragraph must have impressed them, he thought. He had worked so hard on perfecting it.

"Well, that's all well and good for someday, Chet," said Dooley. "But for the here and now, we'd be doin' good just to be known as the Stovepipe of the San Luis Valley."

The men laughed at Dooley's quip. Then he turned more serious. "Nobody knows who we are *now*. OK, being a major metro-whozits someday may be fine and all. But right now I ain't seein' a lot of new accounts being opened in my bank and I sure ain't writing a lot of new business or home loans. Being a partner in the bank, you should know that, Chet. Sure, we've grown bigger than the old trading post but we're still not big enough to even be called a small town." He stood up and looked at the men seated around him. "Big cities have big names and we sure ain't got one of *those*. And anyway, besides El Moro there are already rail centers in Salida, Cañon City and Leadville. The talk *I* hear is that the new rail center is gonna be in Alamosa once the rail line reaches it in a couple of months. What they gonna build another one all the way out here for? Sure, we got mines scattered around here and there, but not like in Leadville and those other towns." He sat back down again.

Carson scowled at him. Instead of closing the deal he was starting to see the door of opportunity closing on him. He verbally stuck his foot in the doorway. "Blake, you're missing the point. That rail center in Alamosa hasn't been built yet. I still have time to convince them—if I start right now—to build it in Stovepipe." He returned to his prepared arguments. "We've got a fully mature town here with commerce and banking and industry and..."

The mayor came to the end of the page and looked down to see the empty beer mug sitting on top of the other sheets. He lifted it up, only to find several papers sticking to its wet bottom. He angrily ripped the papers away, only to have them stick to his fingers. Slamming the mug down on the table, he pulled a couple of the papers away with his other hand, only to have them adhere to those fingers. Not knowing what else to do with the pages sticking to both hands, Carson grabbed one set of papers with his mouth and blew them back onto the table. He was about to rub his brow in frustration when he saw the page he wanted stuck to his fingers. He grabbed it with his free hand and resumed reading his presentation aloud. "...a growing and ready clientele. Alamosa has none of that—yet. Time is indeed ticking away so we have to act now. Gentlemen, just think of all the people who will flock here if they can ride a fast, shiny new *train* pulled by the latest in powerful steam engines over the mountains, instead of a slow as molasses, old, broken-down stagecoach pulled by...a team of *horses*."

Carson was really feeling that beer. He looked longingly at the empty beer mug on the table in front of him. God, how he needed a refill! But that could wait. He was going to finish his presentation come hell or high water. Searching among the pages on the table, he found the statement he was confident would drive his point home. The final point that would close the deal with what he considered these morons of the business community.

"By becoming a rail center, our fine town will be known as the Gateway to the Southwest," Carson said proudly.

Dooley again stood up and said, "First you said we'll be known as the 'San Francisco of the High Plains'. Now you're sayin' we'll be the 'Gateway to the Southwest.'" He looked around. "I don't know about you boys, but I've lost track of what and where the hell we are now!" The town council members erupted into laughter as he sat back down.

Carson cleared his throat as he pretended to shuffle through the sheets of papers, trying to re-recompose himself. Succeeding somewhat, he trudged onward. "Now, back to the subject at hand, which is guaranteeing the growth of Stovepipe into a major metropolis and railroad center. As Blake surprisingly but factually pointed out earlier, 'big cities have big names'. When you say, 'New York City', everyone instantly knows what city you're talking about." He returned to his prepared remarks. "In order to continue this growth, I propose changing the name of this town to one a big city can grow into, one which will enable us to reach our manifest destiny. And as members of the town council—" (adding 'and chamber of commerce' in sotto voce) "—your Yea votes will put you in on the ground floor of the rising of this future great metropolis!"

"There's that other shoe I was waiting for," smirked Phipps to Dooley.

"No, let him speak," said Mac Sampson, the town barber.

"Thank you, Mac," said Carson. "And I've come up with such a name."

"Oh…my…god," said Phipps to Dooley. "We're about to hear a third shoe hit the floor."

Mayor Chet Carson was now in the home stretch. "I propose a name change that will immediately put this town—no, this *city*, on the map. "

He reached down and picked up a long roll of heavyweight blue paper lying on the table in front of him. As he unfurled it, he said, "Gentlemen of the town council, my friends, I give you…" he paused as he displayed the opened paper. It showed a map of the town with a name emblazoned in large, ornate, capitalized gold lettering at the top. "…Carson City."

Every member of the Stovepipe Town Council sat there, speechless. It was Ernest T. Bowersox who managed to speak first. "Chet, this is a joke. Right?"

"It's no joke, Ernie, I'm serious. Carson City. I'm both the mayor and the legal counsel for the town. I also own a big chunk of the properties, including a partnership in the bank, as Blake said earlier. I masterminded our incorporation into Rio Grande County and made Stovepipe the county seat. I'll be doing all the paperwork and the proper filing with the state to make the name change legal. Surely I should be rewarded for my labors."

"*Carson* City, Chet?" asked Dooley. "Not only do I think that's a mighty big display of balls but ain't you forgettin' there's already a Carson City out Nevada way? Ain't folks goin' to laugh at us for stealin' that name?"

Carson quickly tried to come with a reason for supporting his proposal. It never occurred to him that anyone would object to it. Fortunately, that reason came to him—or so he thought. "Of course not. Why should they? There's lots of towns with the same names throughout our great nation. Take Bloomington, for example. There's Bloomingtons everywhere. Bloomington, Illinois; Bloomington, Indiana. Bloomington…well I'm sure there's more. And speaking of Illinois what about Cairo? There's already a damned Cairo in Egypt but that didn't stop Illinois—sians—from giving their town the same name. And, besides, who remembers Kit Carson anymore?"

"I do," answered Dooley. "and so does everybody else in the entire country. They teach little schoolkids about him. And I'm tellin' you we'll be known as the Laughin' Stock of the High Plains with a name like that."

Stan Waxworth, British owner and editor of the daily newspaper said, "When I studied English literature at Oxford there was a word, Greek in derivation, I came across called hubris. It means arrogance or conceit." He paused and lifted his glass mug towards the mayor. "Hubris, thy visage is Carson."

The mayor was sweating even more now and looking slightly frantic. He took a handkerchief from his coat pocket and mopped his forehead. Somehow, it only served to turn beads of sweat into rivulets of sweat. He started to argue with the town council members, and they with him. The resulting cacophony grew and grew in volume until there was heard a loud, sharp report of glass shattering on the bar. Everyone immediately fell to silence and looked toward the source of the sound.

Carson, jolted by the unexpected suddenness of the breaking glass, gave an involuntary gasp. Just at that precise moment, his long-suffering watch chain, stretched across the torturous rack of Carson's expanding abdomen, chose to succumb to its years of extraordinary maltreatment and snapped in two. No one, not even Carson, noticed. All eyes were on one man.

Sheriff Yulin Temple held a wadded-up bar towel above the broken shards of what had been a shot glass. He threw the towel on the floor, then took his foot off the bar rail. Straightening himself up to his full six-foot-three height, he turned and stepped forward to face the men.

"Gentlemen, you hired me to be the sheriff of Stovepipe. Now, I'll be the sheriff of just about any name you choose for this town."

Yulin walked past the tables to the batwing doors. He stopped to turn and face the men. "But no way in hell will I ever be the sheriff of Carson City, Colorado." With that, he walked out.

The men all sat in silence. It was Phipps who broke it. "Well," he said, "I guess that proposal is tabled, too."

CHAPTER 20

Later that night Yulin Temple was still angry over the idiocy of Chet Carson. He had returned to the Silver Strike sometime after the town council meeting had broken up and spent the entire night at the bar. At 12:30 A.M., Burt Owens advised Yulin he should take himself home in case he was needed as sheriff later in the day. Yulin couldn't dispute that logic so, grabbing the bottle of bourbon he had been working on, started walking back to Reva's Café.

When he had moved in a couple of days ago, she had told him to come home to her after he finished his rounds instead of going to the saloon. Then she had kissed him as only she can, so what could he do? He hadn't had a drink in those two days.

That had ended tonight. Now, drinking as he walked, he kept thinking about Carson. It was Chet Carson's type that drove him from town to town when he'd been a deputy marshal. At least with the drunks, bank robbers, and killers he'd dealt with, Yulin had been very clear as to who and what they were. An outlaw like Clay Allison might represent himself as a rancher and businessman, but Yulin could still see the cold-blooded killer who hid behind the civilized façade. With men like Carson, the façade was pretty thick, but it was a façade all the same.

As mayor, Carson's salary was paid from business and property taxes. He also collected a monthly salary—and any profits—from his co-ownership of the bank. Unbeknownst to Blake Dooley, Carson had developed a covert, virtually untraceable system for redirecting a percentage of mortgage payments made to the bank into his own pockets. He had also taken possession of every business property that had been foreclosed on by the bank or had shut its door after the owners decided to move to another town.

Yulin knew that Carson's ultimate goal for growing the town was more a scheme to grow his own wealth than to increase commerce. Still, the man had shown admirable patience waiting for his opportunity. But after what the mayor had pulled at the town council meeting, it was clear that Chet Carson's patience had worn thin. He was anxious to start seeing huge returns on his dormant real estate investments right now.

Yulin, didn't want Stovepipe to get any bigger than it was now. Small towns were easier to control. A rowdy, drunken cowboy thrown into jail at night was usually a very sober, contrite cowboy in the morning. A tinhorn gambler using marked cards and an ace up his sleeve was easily discouraged by strongly advising him to choose another town for his next game. Yulin delivered this advice with quiet menace and his hand resting on the .44 Scofield.

But big towns attracted big money—which attracted big violence. It seemed like guns were everywhere. Shootings at the gaming tables, and shootings in the streets as rival factions fought for control of all the gambling in town. In some towns, a gambling boss would put local law enforcement on his payroll. When other ambitious gamblers moved into town, either a bidding war ensued or an all-out shooting war broke out between the opposing factions.

Yulin had worked as a deputy marshal in one of those towns. When he refused to join his colleagues in going on the take, he became the target of back shooters on both sides of the law. He may have had a death wish, but that was not the way he wanted to die. A half dozen would-be assassins met their deaths before he was persuaded to leave town immediately and never return.

Here in Stovepipe, Yulin had hoped it would be different, that this small town would remain small. When he was first appointed sheriff, he had sworn to maintain law and order. He had most certainly accomplished that; most criminals and tinhorns gave Stovepipe a wide berth. But now after hearing Carson prattle on with his goddamn dreams of becoming a national legend from growing the town into a major rail center, it brought back memories of those cow towns where you couldn't tell the badmen from the town marshals and politicians. He'd be damned if he was going to allow it to happen here. At his age, he had no place else to go.

He raised the bottle to his mouth, only to discover it was empty. Another thing Carson was to blame for. Yulin threw it high into the air. Just as it reached the peak of its upward flight, he drew his Schofield and fired, shattering the bottle into multiple pieces. He followed up with shot after shot, sending the diminishing glass shell of the bottle skipping and dancing through the air as it plummeted to the street. After he holstered his gun, he staggered over a carpet of glass that seconds before had been a whiskey bottle.

Reva heard the gunshots. She was lying awake in bed when Yulin shuffled into the room. He was breathing loudly and heavily. She could smell the bourbon emanating from his body as he walked from the bedroom door over to the bed. She wryly thought to herself that if he had made his rounds tonight it had been from inside the Silver Strike.

There was an oil lamp on a small table next to the bed. Reva always lowered the lighted wick, leaving a soft glow just bright enough for Yulin to avoid bumping into furniture after he entered the bedroom at night. She remained lying on her side facing away from him, pretending she was asleep. She heard his hat fall to the floor as he threw at and missed the ear of a chair across the room. She then heard the creaking of his leather gun belt as he unbuckled it, followed by the sound of the Schofield as he slid it out of its holster before dropping the gun belt onto the chair. From his long years among the violent men of the Northern Plains and the Southwest, he always slept with his gun in his hand lying across his chest.

Reva always left the bedcovers drawn back on Yulin's side so he could just slip into bed no matter the time or his condition. Yulin slid his feet under the covers as he got into bed. He lay on his back, noisily mouth breathing. He hadn't even taken off his pants or boots. Damn that man if his boots ripped her new silk bedsheets!

But at least her man was in bed with her. She began to slide her feet over toward him; it was her way of feeling close to him. She needed and loved the reassurance of physical contact with him, even if it was just her feet touching the calves of his legs.

Just then she thought she heard something downstairs, but with Yulin's loud breathing—almost to the point of snoring—she couldn't be sure. She listened again but all she heard was Yulin.

Reva moved her feet over to rest against his legs. As soon as she made contact he moved his legs away. She edged slightly closer to him and pressed her feet against his boots. He jerked his feet away as he brought his knees up.

"Don't," said Yulin in a gruff, breathy voice.

"Don't what? I'm not doing anything…yet," said Reva, trying to sound coquettish.

"Not in the mood."

Reva tried to put a smile in her voice. "This is how I get you in the mood." But she could tell something was wrong. This was the first time since he had moved in with her that he'd gotten drunk. And it was not like him to turn down the opportunity to make love. She wanted to help him overcome whatever was bothering him. She turned over and placed her hand on his chest.

"I SAID DON'T!" bellowed Yulin. He threw off her hand and swung his legs onto the floor, sitting on the edge of the bed with his back to her. "God damn it," he said in a slurred voice. "First Carson and now you. Why can't everyone leave me the hell alone?" He was silent for a moment. "Lillian knew when to leave me alone."

Reva wasn't frightened of Yulin in the least. She had long ago learned how to handle angry, drunken men. But she froze at the mention of Lillian's name. She knew the ghost of Lillian was always there, ready to rise up between them. So far, there was not one thing she had been able to do about it.

"Lillian knew when to leave me the hell alone," he repeated, softly this time.

She lay there, almost unable to breath, watching him. Yulin picked up his gun belt and shoved the Schofield back into the holster. After having some difficulty in buckling the gun belt around his waist, he bent down unsteadily to pick up his hat. Straightening himself, he swayed as he placed it on his head.

"Where are you going?" she asked.

"Home. I'll pick up my stuff tomorrow."

"Yulin, come back to bed. You don't need to do this."

Yulin, against his will, was sobering up. "It's not going to work. Maybe I'm not ready. Maybe I'll never be ready."

Reva half rose out of bed. "Yulin, Lillian's dead. I'm here. I'm alive, and I love you." Her eyes began to well up with tears.

"I know she's dead, Reva. And that's the problem. I don't know if I can love another woman. I thought I could but I'm not sure anymore." He walked over to the bedroom door and stood there, head down with his back to her. "I'll be by later to get my things. It'll make it easier if you're downstairs in the kitchen."

She was crying now. "Yulin, you don't have to do this. Please stay with me, we can talk this out." She looked at him. "I love you," she said again, softly.

Yulin stood in the doorway for a moment, as if wrestling with a decision. He then walked out, closing the bedroom door behind him, and trod down the stairs. Reva heard the front door open and slam shut. Throwing herself back down on the bed, she cried into her arms.

She was caught between anger and sorrow. She lay in bed, fighting a battle to see which emotion would emerge victorious, finally calling a truce when she felt herself drifting off to sleep. She lifted herself up enough from the bed to blow out the flame inside the oil lamp.

In the darkness before she fell asleep, she again thought she heard faint sounds coming from outside the window. But she wasn't sure and right now, she didn't care.

CHAPTER 21

Garrison Fleck left Trinidad that same afternoon after talking to Sheriff Haines. He had written the description of the Belgian stallion on a sheet of paper, stuffing it in the same shirt pocket where he kept Ike's note. He rented a buckskin mare from the company-contracted stable and purchased supplies from the general store. He filled his new canteen with hot coffee. It would serve the dual purpose of quenching his thirst and keeping him awake on the trail. At least he didn't have Binghamton to deal with. His boss had already left for El Moro to take the train back to Denver.

On the road back to Walsenburg, Garrison saw a rider heading the opposite way toward Trinidad.

 Filled with anger towards Binghamton and worry over Ike, he paid the rider little mind. He took Ike's note out of his pocket. He hadn't had time to read it, what with having to bunk with Haines last night in the hotel room and the ride back to town this morning. Haines had seemed to be everywhere. But now he was rid of the sheriff and could read Ike's words openly and undisturbed. He slowed the mare to a walk and took out the note. It was written in Ike's scrawl but was legible enough.

The note began: "I kilt those robbers who kilt Duke and Gulle. Don't be mad I tuk the money."

Garrison read those two sentences several times. So, Ike admitted killing the Bellum Gang and stealing the $400,000. He read the rest of the note. At least he now knew what Ike's plans were. Whether or not Ike could see them through was another question. But he was grateful he had been the one who found the note and not Haines.

How could he have not seen this coming? That whole business with Duke losing the map and Conley finding it should have tipped him off that something wasn't right. He should have acted that night to cancel the stage run, shut down the entire operation. It had already been compromised. Even if Binghamton had reversed that action, it might have bought a few hours to figure out a plan. At the very least, *he* could have ridden the stage instead of Ike.

But he hadn't done any of that that, and now Gully and Duke were dead. Ike was somewhere miles and days ahead of him by now. Once word got out that Ike was carrying a fortune in negotiable silver certificates, he would be an easy target for any tracker with a rifle. What have I done? Garrison thought. My God, what have I done?

His eyes welled up with tears. Even if Ike were somehow captured alive, he'd undoubtedly serve the next twenty years at the territorial prison in Yuma. Binghamton would see to that. Ike would never survive prison. His chances were better out here, but for how long?

He was jarred out of his thoughts by the buckskin, who had wandered over to the side of the road looking for some long tufts of grass to eat. Garrison folded up the note and put it back in his pocket. He then gathered up the reins and spurred the horse into a fast lope. Right now he couldn't dwell on the stage robbery or on what might happen to Ike. He had to track down and intercept his brother before anyone else did. Ike's tracks led through Walsenburg and the note had told him Ike was headed for the New Mexico Territory. Garrison was aware of the stage road that ran over the mountains and through the San Luis Valley since it was one of the company's stage routes. Although he and Duke had never driven it, he knew the trail led past Fort Garland to a small town called Stovepipe. All he knew of the town was that a sheriff had been killed there some years back.

He made it back to Walsenburg after nightfall, stopping at a company livery stable to swap his worn-out horse for a fresh one. It was where Haines and Garrison had taken the horses from the ill-fated stagecoach. He chose a sturdy black gelding that he could tell had a lot of bottom. The horse would need every bit of it for the journey he was about to undertake.

He rode over to Sheriff Tolliver's office. The sheriff was still at his desk and surprised to see any visitors to his office at that late hour. "Office is closed, mister."

Garrison introduced himself, advising that he was investigating the stagecoach robbery. He planned to make this a quick visit. The sooner he was back on the trail after Ike the better.

Tolliver took a moment to put his mind back on duty. "Oh yeah. Sheriff Haines's deputy was in here yesterday askin' where to drop off the bodies. He didn't tell me much about the robbery. But since Haines's already got ahold of it, he can keep it. I ain't even made it out to the stagecoach yet. Guess it'll keep till your people come to retrieve it."

"Well, I was just checking to see if you found out anything new on your end," Garrison said, flopping down into a chair in front of the desk. He tried to sound nonchalant. There was no reason to let this sheriff in on the whole story.

"Nothin' much on my end. But, as it happens, I did find something that might interest you." Tolliver leaned back in an oak swivel chair. "Undertaker found a map on Hank Bellum's body this morning." He smiled and paused.

Garrison sat up, stunned. "What map?"

Tolliver seemed to be enjoying milking the drama from this moment, knowing something that Garrison didn't know. He waited a few beats and then said, "Well, not a real map. More like a drawing of a stagecoach route between Pueblo and Trinidad. That's where your stage had come from and was headed to, wasn't it?"

Garrison just nodded.

"Map had a big circle drawn around a spot not that far from here. Looks like the same spot your stage is located at."

Garrison was on his feet. It had to be a copy. Conley had given the real map back to Duke. "Can I see that map?"

"Nope," answered Tolliver.

Garrison stared disbelievingly at Tolliver. What possible grounds could this fool of a sheriff have for refusing to show him the map?

Once again, Tolliver waited until the right moment to respond. "Can't. Don't have it anymore. After the undertaker give it to me, I wired Haines to see if he wanted it, seein' as how he's taken over the investigation. Anyway, Haines wires me back sayin' he wants it as evidence. So, I sent my deputy down to Trinidad to hand deliver it to him. Shoulda gotten it by now."

Garrison felt his insides collapse. That was the rider he had seen ride past him.

Tolliver went on. "I was happy to give it to him, too. Got enough to deal with already gettin' all them bodies identified and buried. I got no time to investigate no robbery. Haines took that on. I guess you have, too."

Garrison realized there was no use wasting more time here. He quickly thanked Tolliver—for nothing, he thought—and went out to his horse to mount up for the night ride over La Veta Pass.

Even though it was dark, Garrison wasn't worried about losing Ike's trail as long as the weather held. He had tracked men before by moonlight. As long as there was a bright moon out in a clear sky, he could pick his way safely along a trail. Besides, the tracks of that behemoth of a horse Ike was riding would be impossible to lose unless you were blind.

It was about ten-thirty that night when Garrison had to stop a few miles short of Uptop. The trail had been all uphill and now, at over 9,000 feet, the black was clearly tired. He had to admit he was done in as well. It had been a very long and very bad day. No matter how driven he was to push himself onward through the night, sleep was what he needed.

In the bright moonlight he could see a thicket of trees nearby. He walked the horse over to it and dismounted. Finding a small glade among the trees, Garrison took a short length of rope out of a saddlebag and hobbled the black. The horse paid him no mind, already nibbling on the leaves of a staghorn sumac.

Garrison untied the bedroll from behind his saddle and tossed it to the ground. After laying out the tarpaulin on soft ground, he unsaddled the horse and took off its bridle, dropping the saddle and bridle on the tarpaulin. After spreading out the blanket he crawled inside, laying his head against the saddle. High up in the mountains as he was, the night wind was literally ice cold. He reluctantly got out of the covers again, picked up the damp horse blanket, and threw it on top of his bedding. As wet and smelly as it was, the blanket would still give him an extra layer of warmth and protection against the night's below freezing temperatures.

Because of the wind, he didn't try to build a fire in the dark. Wearing the heavy coat he'd bought along with his other supplies, he was sufficiently warm enough tucked under his double layer of blankets. Lying on his back, he reassuringly patted the Bowie knife in its sheath on his belt. He drew his gun from its holster and laid it beside him, finger near the trigger. After positioning his hat over his eyes, he quickly dropped off to sleep. That dream about Ike kept waking him throughout the night.

Garrison finally gave up trying to get back to sleep just as the sky was turning gray with the early morning. The sun had not yet risen when he was eating a cold breakfast of venison jerky and hardtack. He tried to wash it down with the coffee in his canteen, only to find it had frozen during the night.

The sun was still creeping up the other side of the mountains, its reddish-orange glow beginning to light up the eastern sky. There was enough light to saddle up and start on the ride to Fort Garland. Garrison quickly packed up his gear, saddled the black and headed back out onto the trail. The coffee would thaw along the way.

With the morning growing brighter, he easily picked up the Belgian's tracks embedded in the stage road dirt. He remembered the mental image Haines had painted of Ike atop the monstrous horse and chuckled in spite of himself. He saw where the tracks left the trail at Muleshoe and headed toward Uptop. He followed them past the two-story log building where Ike had stolen the rhubarb pie. The window was closed.

A few miles down the road, Garrison spied where the Belgian had veered off to cross the railroad track down to the creek. The horse tracks led him to the exact spot where Ike had spent those hours by the rushing water. As he stood in Ike's bootprints at the creek's edge, the sun glinted off something a few yards downstream. It was a pie tin wedged between two rocks. He now wished he had asked in Uptop if anyone had seen a kid on horseback riding through town.

After ten minutes, he had seen all he needed. He swung into the saddle and followed the tracks back up to the stage road. Ike was truly something, he thought. When did he learn how to leave and return to a trail, especially out here in unfamiliar country? He continued to follow the horse tracks, but when they swerved off the road and away from Fort Garland, he decided it was still best to ride over to the fort to check in with the commanding officer. Maybe at least one of the guards had seen a rider on a giant horse pass by.

It was mid-morning when Garrison reached the fort. After identifying himself to the guards at the entry gate, he asked to see the commandant but was instead shown to the officer of the day, a Captain Richland. Again identifying himself as a detective with the J.K. Binghamton Stage Line, he briefly told the captain about the stagecoach robbery, omitting the identity of the person who had robbed it. Richland told him that none of the guards had reported seeing a rider over the past two days. Garrison inquired how far it was to Stovepipe if he kept to the stage road. Richland told him it was unlikely he would reach the town that day. Watch me, thought Garrison.

Richland also volunteered information about the Rio Grande County sheriff, some old gunhand named Yulin Temple. Garrison filed it away and departed shortly thereafter. And he knew the captain was right; he would never make Stovepipe—some fifty miles away—by tonight. But he was pinning his hopes on Ike, with no experience traveling on his own, making worse time. Besides, his brother had that gargantuan horse to deal with.

When he was back on the trail, Garrison worried over not seeing any trace of the Belgian's tracks. He didn't want to backtrack past the fort. At last he was relieved to see the stallion's hoofprints return to the road almost a half mile past the fort. He set the black into a lope, one the horse could sustain over the very long ride ahead of him. Although he had rested and watered the horse back at the fort, Garrison knew that after a couple of more hours on the trail they would both need to stop again to drink water and to eat. He still had some venison jerky and hardtack left, but the horse would need grass or some brush to nibble on.

Almost three hours later, he found himself outside the same woods where Ike had stopped the previous morning. He dismounted and led the black along the narrow path Ike had followed to the tree near the stream. Yes, the Belgian's sign was all around. He found Ike's bootprints under the cottonwood. But there was something there that didn't belong—a bird's nest on the ground next to where Ike had sat. Garrison crouched down in front of it. Inside there were five empty eggshells. Garrison stood up, walked around and saw where the Belgian had stood while Ike climbed the tree. He walked around again, now noticing where Ike had landed after letting go of the tree limb. Where had Ike learned to do all of this? This little brother for whom Garrison had provided everything and had done all the thinking. He smiled at the thought of Ike apparently learning to take care of himself. But why now? Why had Ike chosen now to become independent and self-sufficient? Why couldn't it have happened back in Boulder where Garrison could have nurtured Ike's new-found independence?

But he already knew the truth. Garrison now understood why Ike had stolen the money: it was finally something he could do on his own. Ike was never going to find that independence in Boulder. And in that town they would still have had to contend with the aftermath of Ike shooting those three bank robbers.

Ike had taken the money so he could stand on his own, yet he still wanted to share it with Garrison. Ike was still Ike, would always *be* Ike. With his back against that same cottonwood tree, Garrison slid down the trunk to the ground. "What have I done?" he said, choking down tears. This whole thing had blown up in his face. In an effort to save his brother, he might have lost him for good.

After a few minutes, he realized he had to gather himself together. Wiping his eyes with his shirtsleeve, he staggered to his feet. Leading the black down to the stream, he carefully let the horse slake its thirst. After dropping the reins to the ground, he took a few steps upstream and knelt to fill his empty canteen. As he dipped it below the surface of the cold, fresh water, he looked around at the beauty of the area, now reawakening in springtime after its long winter slumber under blankets of snow.

A breeze whooshed through the willows and alders along the stream bank. Mountain bluebirds and horned larks chirped and sang among the trees. A woodpecker tapped away at the bark of a tree. The sun's reflection was dancing upon the rippling surface of the stream, broken up into thousands or perhaps millions of shimmering dotted lights.

Garrison thought he would like to have shared this spot with Ike. He happened to look down to see Ike's bootprints in the wet sandy ground. He reached out and gently, lovingly caressed them with his fingertips.

With the canteen full, he pounded the cork back in with his hand and hung it back around the saddle horn. Taking the reins of the black, he led it out to the stage road. Swinging into the saddle, he spurred the horse to a gallop and headed for Stovepipe.

Back at the stream, a pocket watch was lying six feet below the surface of the water and twenty feet away from where Garrison had filled his canteen.

Chapter 22

Almost forty-eight hours after the stage robbery, Ike Fleck crossed the wooden bridge that spanned the Rio Grande outside of Stovepipe. The first thing he heard on entering town from the north end was a dog barking. He quickly brought the Belgian to a halt. He sat there listening, waiting for someone to come out, gun in hand, to check on what or who the dog was barking at. He waited a few minutes more but heard nothing besides the barking. Taking a chance the loud dog was the type people ignored, he nudged the horse with his bootheels to start again down the street.

It had taken fourteen hours for Ike to reach Stovepipe from the woods. The daytime temperatures were the hottest he'd ever felt. Not having a canteen made it feel even hotter. Sweat had clung to his body like a wraparound steam bath, making him feel warm and clammy. The cold night air had relieved much of that, but he still felt sticky inside his clothes. The sides of the Belgian were also drenched in sweat. On the trail, Ike had stopped at every spot where there was even a slight trickle of water with a patch of shade to rest himself and the stallion. After the sun had set and the air had cooled, they had made better time.

So far, he had been lucky in avoiding people on horseback or in horse-drawn wagons along the trail. There were a few close calls where he barely made it to cover in time, but if anyone had seen him there had been no confrontations.

Now, the great Belgian stallion was used up, literally on its last legs. The palomino's walking gait was unsteady, at times stumbling as it willed itself to keep moving forward. In the night stillness the uneven clip clop of the big, heavy hoofs sounded like a loud, staccato drumbeat. Ike pictured men streaming out of darkened buildings, all with guns pointed directly at him, ready to shoot him to pieces.

Ike had to find another horse to make a swap. He also desperately needed to find something to eat. His last meal had been those five eggs back in the woods. During dinner with Garrison back in Pueblo he'd been too nervous to eat anything but had more than made up for it at the Cottonwood home station. He thought again about the food he had left inside the stage; food Marie had personally given him. It seemed like weeks ago but had been just two days. He was literally starving and close to physical collapse. Fear and determination were the only things driving him on.

On his right, Ike saw a two-story building with fancy lettering in a window. With great but very tired concentration, he was able to recognize the word "café". He had seen that word on a sign in Boulder. Garrison had told him it was another name for a restaurant. If it was a place to eat, he might be able to find some food in the kitchen and maybe something to drink. The building, situated on the corner, stood apart from the few other false-fronted buildings on the short block. Behind the buildings was a narrow dirt road, more like an alley for deliveries. He hoped there was an unlocked back door to the café.

Ike reined the Belgian around the corner. He saw a door that he hoped was the back entrance to the kitchen he was looking for. He halted the horse and saw it was standing in ground muddied from dishwater thrown from the back door. As Ike slid down the side of the horse, he pushed his body away so that he landed on dry, dusty ground.

There was no hitching rail so he looped the reins around a wooden bannister that ran along two wooden steps leading up to a small loading platform. With no water nearby to beckon it away, the Belgian would have remained standing in place anyway. Behind the platform was the door. Ike closed his eyes for a moment, picturing himself opening that door. All the inside lights were out except for a dim light flickering from an upstairs window. He stood on the lower step, wiping his boots just to make sure there was no mud clinging to the soles. Under the bright moonlight, he saw well enough to walk quietly up the steps to the door. Holding his breath, he turned the knob, and pushed on the door. It swung inward and hit something against the wall. He remained still, holding his breath and listening. Everything remained silent, but he still gave it a few more seconds.

Satisfied that no one had heard the noise, Ike exhaled and entered the kitchen. Moonlight streaming through the windows made it bright enough for him to look around. He discovered that the door had hit an icebox. This was confirmed when he opened one of the compartment doors and reached inside. He instantly knew by the extreme cold that it was the freezer. It was too dark inside to see anything other than shapes of frozen foods, all wrapped in paper. Forced to guess which would be the best food to take, he chose two packages, hoping the food inside them was already cooked. Although they were frigid, he stuffed them inside his shirt, not knowing where else to put them. He closed that door and opened the one next to it. Not as icy cold as the other compartment, he knew it had to be the refrigerator. Reaching inside, he felt two glass containers that seemed like bottles. Grabbing one, he was sliding it inside his shirt when he heard loud, arguing voices of a man and woman directly above the kitchen.

He held still, waiting to hear if someone would indeed come down to the kitchen. Heavy footsteps stomped down what might have been a flight of stairs. Then a door slammed, and all was quiet. He waited a little longer in case more footsteps came down the stairs. When all remained quiet, he quickly closed the icebox door and hurriedly tiptoed outside, softly closing the back door behind him. Placing one hand over the stolen food under his shirt, he jumped over the two wooden steps, landing with an audible thud next to the stallion. As he was pulling the reins from the bannister, he looked up and saw the upstairs window was now dark. No one was at the window, and he breathed a little easier.

Ike was too tired to struggle with climbing back onto the big horse, and besides, he had that food inside his shirt. He took the reins and led the Belgian back into the street. On one side he saw lights and heard sounds from what looked like a saloon. As he walked the stallion toward there, something crunched under his boots as he took each step. He looked down and saw a blanket of shattered glass glittering on the ground. He had no choice but to lead the horse over the glass as he made his way to the saloon.

In front of the Silver Strike the cacophony of sounds emanating from inside was much louder. Ike could hear the tinny sounds of tacked piano hammers playing an out-of-tune melody, drunken men laughing and arguing, coins and poker chips tossed onto gambling tables, and the clinking of empty beer mugs gathered onto trays. All served to cover up whatever noises Ike and the Belgian made outside. He found it hard to breathe as his nostrils were assaulted by odors of alcohol and stale tobacco wafting from the batwing doors.

Still, Ike's luck was holding. Just shy of two o-clock in the morning there were almost a dozen horses tied to the two hitching rails out front. Ike knew that the stallion was done in. He remembered that years ago Uncle Roy had said an old horse on the ranch was "living on borrowed time", meaning it would be dead soon. Ike didn't know how long borrowed time was, but he knew he had to get rid of this horse fast before it died on him right there in the street.

Ike looked at the horses tied to the rails and decided to make a swap for a blue dun mare, the major selling point being it was the one closest to him. Hidden from the saloon windows by several horses tied next to it was an added bonus. The mare looked OK, but while Ike knew all about guns, he didn't know a thing about horses. He didn't even know that this horse was a mare. Garrison was the one who knew all that. All Ike knew was this horse was the easiest to steal, and it was *a lot* smaller than the horse he had been riding.

There was an empty space between the mare and the horse tied closest to it. Ike walked the played-out Belgian into the space and loosely looped the reins around the rail. At that point, he didn't really care if the reins would slip off or not. Because of the stallion's size there was no way anyone looking through those windows could see him now. He checked the saddle on the mare. Yes! There was a canteen slung from the saddle horn. The saddle was much older than the one he had been sitting on and there were no saddlebags. He would have to move his saddlebags from the other horse.

However, something else caught his eye. From the stock and the hammer sticking out from the rifle scabbard he recognized a .50-90 Sharps. Uncle Roy had taught him it was one of the high-powered rifles used by hunters to kill off the giant buffalo herds. Roy had carried several of these shoulder cannons in his gun shop because they were hot sellers. Though never approving of the wholesale slaughter of the plains bison, money was money.

Ike knew the Sharps was far more powerful than his Winchester, but it was only a single shot and it didn't use the same cartridges. He decided he was better off with the repeating rifle he had taken from the brother named Hank. Slowly sliding the Sharps out of the scabbard on the mare, Ike ducked down as he walked back around the Belgian. He slid the Winchester out of the scabbard and replaced it with the Sharps. He quickly reached up and removed his saddlebags from behind the cantle as fast as he could.

As he did all this, he wished again he'd thought to pack a coat. Now he was shivering in the frigid night air, shivering made worse by that icy food beneath his shirt.

Ike hurried back to the blue dun, sliding the Winchester into the scabbard and throwing the saddlebags behind the cantle. He untied the reins and slowly led the horse away from the hitching rail. He would have to walk the horse past the saloon. This time he pictured no one rushing out with guns a-blazing to stop him. Everyone inside would be staying where they were. Amazingly, they did.

After he was clear of the saloon, he quickly mounted the horse. He was happy to see the stirrups fit his legs. He kicked the mare into a trot. As soon as he got beyond the edge of town he shook the reins, digging his bootheels into the mare harder this time. With a sharp "H'yaw!" he set the dun into a full gallop. This horse felt strong and seemed like it liked to run. He felt lucky that he had chosen a good horse.

CHAPTER 23

Ike swung down from the blue dun and checked its right foreleg. The horse had been favoring that leg for the past few miles and was costing him precious time. After he had stolen the mare from in front of the Silver Strike, he had ridden the horse hard, riding at a gallop. He didn't know how long or how far he'd traveled because he wasn't good with those things. Garrison was the one who knew how many miles or hours or days it took to get to different places. Ike never understood how his brother or Uncle Roy were able to do that. But then Garrison had been to lots of places while *he'd* never been anywhere. Well, there were those gun-selling trips with Uncle Roy, but they were just to towns and forts where they sometimes spent the night before going back home. He'd never been anywhere by himself until now. And he barely knew where he was.

The blue dun at first seemed like it did like to run, galloping at top speed as if it could keep up that pace for as long as it liked. But apparently the mare preferred to run at that pace for only a couple of miles. At that point, the mare slowed down and began to limp at a fast walk. The horse kept it up for another few minutes until Ike, worried that it was pulling up lame, reined it to a halt.

Ike didn't know much about horses, but he had seen his uncle run a hand up and down a horse's leg to feel for any sore or tender spots. He just didn't know how he was supposed to tell if a horse had a sore leg or not. What he didn't realize was that the blue dun was missing a horseshoe and didn't like running on that leg for too long. He didn't know about horses needing horseshoes, so he never thought to look for it. The mare was no help, remaining impassive during Ike's examination of the leg and giving no reaction to any place he touched.

He decided to let the mare rest for a bit while he took the opportunity to look at the map. He thought that by now he should know it by heart, but he kept forgetting what was drawn on it. Unfortunately, the moon had already set and he couldn't see the markings on the deerskin. However, he was sure he was still on the right trail to New Mexico Territory. He folded the map and stuffed it into the back pocket of his jeans.

After a nervous ten minutes, Ike swung back into the saddle and put the mare into a walk. He knew that riding a lame horse could cripple it, leaving him helpless in front of the posse that had to be on its way. But he had no choice; he had to keep nursing the horse along in the hope it was tired, not injured.

The horse seemed to walk just fine without a trace of a limp. After letting it walk for about a half mile, he tapped his bootheels against the dun's sides to settle it into a trot. The mare accepted this pace, so Ike retained it for about the same distance. Then with his heels, he nudged the mare into a lope, which it appeared to enjoy. After twenty-five minutes, the mare still seemed strong so Ike kicked it into a full gallop. Again, after about two more miles the horse slowed to a limping walk, favoring that right foreleg. Ike tried to coax it back into a trot, but it quickly become obvious that the mare wasn't going to stop limping any time soon.

By this time Ike had managed to put almost twelve miles between himself and Stovepipe. With only the stars to guide him, he couldn't see the trail ahead of him very well. He wished he'd thought to take one of the coach lanterns. Then up ahead he saw the dark shapes of a dense thicket. That would make a safe place to rest the horse until after sunrise. He could sure use a rest himself. At the edge of the thicket, Ike dismounted and led the mare into the trees. Using an outstretched hand to guide himself past pines and brush, he managed to find a clearing just large enough for the horse to stand unseen from the trail.

To Ike, the horse must have already been injured, limping the way it was. He wondered how the owner could be so cruel as to ride an animal that was obviously hurt. That was just inhuman. Uncle Roy never treated horses that way. He decided the first chance he'd get to steal another horse he'd shoot this one dead. It was the only kind thing to do, putting it out of its misery. But in the meantime, he'd have to nurse this horse along, hoping it wouldn't delay him too much. According to what he remembered of the map, there were no more towns between here and the Colorado state border. He figured it had to be the same from the border to Three Rocks Trace Pedras. Without any towns from here on out, the chances of finding another horse to steal were slim to none. So, he was back to nursing the horse along.

Ike hid himself and the blue dun among a stand of ponderosa pine, wrapping the reins as best he could around the branches of a large juniper bush. He didn't trust this horse to stay in place as the big horse had. There were some lupines next to the bush and the mare began nibbling on the tall spikes of the flowers. Ike lifted the canteen from the saddle horn and sat down on the cold, damp earth behind the juniper bush. He felt hungrier than he'd ever been. He set the canteen down on the ground and took the cold, wrapped food and the bottle out from underneath his shirt.

The front of his body felt cold and numb from where the food and the glass bottle had pressed against it. He had never felt this cold before. During the hard winters at Uncle Roy's house, he'd lie near the fireplace hearth while playing with his toy soldiers. He sure missed that fireplace now.

He stood up and checked the horse for anything that could provide him with warmth. He saw a thin rolled blanket behind the cantle. He untied it and wrapped the threadbare blanket around him. It smelled like sweaty horses and old tobacco, but at least it made the chilly night more bearable.

And now for the food. Ike decided that no matter what was inside the paper bundles, he would eat it, even if it were raw. The bale and wire stopper on the glass bottle had cut into his chest as he had ridden the trail. With the cold glass no longer pressed against his skin, the irritation began to sting a little.

Too thirsty to care what was inside, he lifted the stopper from the bottle top and swung it out of his way. Bringing the bottle up to his mouth, he took a long drink without stopping to breathe. Only after he finished swallowing did he lower the bottle. Allowing himself to take a breath, he recognized the taste of the liquid. It was milk! He loved milk. He took several large gulps. It had been hours since he had drunk anything and he couldn't stop. But, as Uncle Roy had warned, the flood of cold liquid suddenly making its way down into his stomach began to give him intense cramps. He doubled over, dropping the bottle onto the soft dirt. The scratches on his chest were throbbing. He lay down on the ground, holding his stomach and writhing in pain.

He started to cry. Son of a bitch, he thought, what was he doing out here all alone? Would Garrison track him down or would a posse find and kill him first? He thought about going back to that last town and turning himself in. Yes, that's what he would do.

After a few minutes, the stomach cramps subsided. The scratches seemed to throb a little less, too. Ike sat up and wiped the tears from his eyes, heaving a heavy sigh. He was still a little thirsty but wanted no more of that cold milk.

Then he remembered the canteen. He picked it up, pulled the cork out and took a drink. Instead of water, cheap whiskey burned inside his mouth. He spat it out. But the alcoholic taste brought back a dim memory of that wagon train that had taken them to meet Uncle Roy. There had been a night when he had been so very cold under the blankets inside the wagon. He remembered how—what was his name again? —Mister...Hollings. Mr. Hollings had given him a thimbleful of whiskey to warm him up. It was a nightly family ritual on those cold, prairie nights. He remembered that although he had hated the taste, the hard liquor did warm his body as it moved downward from his throat. He grew to look forward to that little thimble at bedtime.

Ike took another swig, but this time he swallowed it. It still burned and hurt his throat when he swallowed. He coughed a little, but the whiskey did its body-warming trick. He took another drink. He pictured the bundles of money inside the saddlebags. With that kind of wealth he could buy anything he wanted, go anywhere he wanted. Live his life anyway he chose. With Garrison there with him, of course. But he remembered that he was going to give back that money. That's why he was on his way to Three Rocks Trace Pedras: to leave the money behind after he and Garrison had dug up the Frenchmen's gold. The posse chasing him would get all of the bank delivery money back, and he and Garrison would be free to keep the gold.

Soon the intoxicating warmth of the liquor, combined with his physical exhaustion, made him drowsy. He took another drink. Yes, just him and Garrison. That was his last thought before he fell asleep.

CHAPTER 24

That goddamn dog was barking again. Yulin Temple had just returned to his house after the fight with Reva. The argument, along with walking in the cold night air, had sobered him up. That was something he planned to fix—and soon. He remembered he had left a mostly full bottle of bourbon in his bedroom before moving in with Reva. His feelings were a jumble of confusion, but the bourbon would help him block everything out for one blessed night. The expensive bottle of bourbon had come directly from Mayor Chet Carson's private stock at the Silver Strike, courtesy of Burt Owens.

The bottle was conveniently sitting on the small table beside his bed, as was a shot glass with moist remnants of several days old bourbon nestled at the bottom. Sitting on his bed, he uncorked the bottle and poured a healthy shot into the glass. Downing it in one gulp, he felt the sweet, smooth amber liquid slide down his throat. *That* was just what he needed, he thought. He quickly poured another healthy shot and dispatched it just as quickly.

Conflicting thoughts rose and fell, rotating round and round inside Yulin's brain like they were cars on some internal Ferris wheel. If he was totally honest with himself, he knew at his core he was in love with Reva. But he had been in love before and look how well that had worked out? He couldn't go through the pain of such loss again. And besides, as long as he remained alone he could keep his love for Lillian alive in his heart and mind. He just couldn't stand to replace his love for her with a love for someone else. He needed Lillian to remain alive inside him, because if she wasn't, well…he wasn't ready to face that yet. He poured and drank another shot.

So, whether he loved Reva or not was irrelevant. He would go on as he had for years; closed up emotionally, deadening those emotions with as much whiskey as he could swallow every night. All he had was today. If a bullet found him tomorrow, that was fine. Maybe he'd be reunited with Lillian and Weed, if that's how things worked.

Finally, after two more healthy shots, he decided he'd had enough of the thoughts going round and round inside his mind. He would think on it later and set all thoughts of Reva aside for now. Reva…

He yelled at Carson's dog to shut up, which did no damn good. He didn't know how much time had passed, but when he picked up the bottle he saw one lonely swig left. He drank it slowly this time. If that goddamn dog's still barking when I finish off this bottle, he thought, that'll be one dead goddamn dog. The dog's life was again spared when Yulin fell back asleep against his pillow.

Much later that morning, Yulin woke up to one of the worst hangovers in a lifelong series of bad hangovers. His head seemed to pound in time with the pulsations of blood pumping through his heart. Served him right for trying to get through life sober. He'd been a fool to try. What had he been thinking? The answer, he well knew, was Reva. For a short time, she had been worth the attempt at sobriety. Now he felt doomed to see the remainder of his life through bloodshot eyes. He sat up in bed and watched the empty bourbon bottle roll off his chest and onto the floor. The bottle kept rolling until it bumped up against the far wall with a clink.

Through his window, Yulin saw Carson's dog asleep on the front porch of the mayor's house. Well, that won't do, he thought. He got up out of bed, walked over to the empty bottle and picked it up off the floor. Returning to the window, he heaved the bottle at the sleeping canine, scoring a direct hit as the bottle bounced off the dog's back. The dog jumped up awake, yelping more with alarm than pain. "Bow goddamn wow, you shithead mutt," Yulin grumbled.

When he arrived at his office, Yulin saw Sam Gilroy asleep on a chair outside the door. Oh, Christ, Yulin thought, you're the last man I need to see today. Please don't make me shoot you just to shut you up.

An old gold panner, Sam Gilroy lived in a shack a few miles outside of town. He'd staked a placer claim in a stream bed and built the ramshackle abode next to it. Any gold flakes or nuggets he found were soon converted into their relatively commensurate value in beers at the Silver Strike. A few flakes were set aside now and then for food and other items of luxury.

Yulin leaned over and roughly shook Sam by the shoulder. "Sam, go home. You can't sleep it off in front of my office."

Sam's arms lashed out as his body jumped in the chair, his mouth emitting a noise that sounded like "hungagh". It took a few seconds to adjust his eyes and recognize Yulin standing over him. "Gall durn it, give a man some warnin' afore you shake him to pieces."

"Well, you should've chosen to sleep in your regular chair outside the Silver Strike. You can't sleep in front of my office."

"I weren't sleepin'—I was waitin'," grumbled Sam. "I got official business with you, Sheriff."

Yulin dreaded hearing what that official business might be. But he was sheriff and this was part of the job. "Then step into my office and we'll talk about it." As they walked through the door Yulin added, "But not too loud. I didn't get much sleep last night myself."

As Sam sat down in a chair in front of the desk, Yulin lit a fire inside a potbelly stove. He poured water from a pitcher into a coffee pot, spooned in some ground coffee, looked at Sam, spooned in a bit more, and set the coffee pot on the stove. "So, why are you here, Sam?"

"Well, sir, I want to report a stolen horse but then I'm not sure if I should."

Yulin knew the coffee wasn't nearly ready yet but he needed the caffeine jolt now. He preferred to drink it black, anyway. He picked up the pot and began pouring the still-brewing coffee into a porcelain mug. "What do you mean you're not sure if you should? Did you have a horse stolen or not?"

"Well, sir, I did indeed but they left another one in its place. So if I report a stolen horse I also got to report the one they left me, right?"

Yulin stopped pouring and stared at Sam. If he pulled his gun fast enough, he thought, he could shoot Sam and holster it without spilling any coffee. He then resumed filling the mug. "I don't know if it's because I didn't get much sleep or not but I'm having a hard time understanding what you're talking about. Are you saying you had a horse stolen but the thief left you a replacement horse?"

"That's exactly what I'm saying, Sheriff. Well, sir, when I went inside the Strike last night I had Lucy—you know my blue dun mare, don't you? —tied up out front. I stayed 'til closing time at 3 A.M—you'd left way before then— and went out to ol' Lucy to ride her home. An' durn if I didn't see a big palomina stallion standin' where she'd been. Biggest I ever seen. Anyone with eyes could plainly see he ain't no female!"

Yulin, walked over to his desk. "Burt Owens closes down at 2 A.M."

"Well sir, not on the nights I'm there," replied Sam, "I like to help him clean up. Not all the glasses layin' around are empty, if you know what I mean. Hee hee!"

Yulin sat down in the chair behind his desk, mulling over what Sam had said about a palomino stallion of great size. He was also trying to think of a question to which Sam couldn't reply "Well, sir". He took a sip of coffee, set the mug down on his desk, and took the makin's out his shirt pocket. He needed a cigarette. Quickly rolling and lighting it, he inhaled and blew a perfect smoke ring.

"And another thing," Sam began.

"What's that?" asked Yulin, quickly, taking another drag on the cigarette.

Sam continued. "Well, sir"—Yulin winced, his second smoke ring ruined— "you know that .50-90 Sharps buffalo gun o' mine? Won it off a feller in a poker game. He said it was the exact same one Billy Dixon borrowed off 'im at the Second Battle of Adobe Walls. Used it to shoot that Comanch' off his horse at seven- eighths of a mile."

Yulin, knowing Sam, greatly doubted it was the same rifle that killed one of Quanah Parker's warriors.

"Wish he'd put up his claim instead. I'd be a rich man today," continued Sam, 'but I keep 'er well-oiled and the stock polished. Well, sir"—Yulin had now given up and resigned himself to just playing this out to the end— "wouldn't you know that while he stole Lucy *an'* my saddle the varmint left me my Sharps? Now why on earth would he do that?"

Why indeed. "Where's this horse now?" Yulin asked.

"Well sir, I figured I best leave 'im tied up where he is in front of the Silver Strike so you could have a look at 'im, you bein' the sheriff and all."

"Good call, Sam. Let's take a walk."

Outside, he flicked the cigarette away, and followed Sam across the street and down to the Silver Strike Saloon. Sam stopped at the hitching rail where the palomino Belgian stallion was tied. Yulin instantly saw it was a magnificent animal but ridden hard over a very long stretch. White streaks of dried sweat caked along its neck and shoulders and there was white spittle around its mouth.

Christ, thought Yulin, Sam left him out here like this since three in the morning? He felt down the length of each of the legs. No bowed tendons. The muscles felt tight but otherwise the horse appeared to be sound. Gomez would be able to tell for sure. Under his excellent care, the horse would soon be better than new.

Yulin also saw the US brand on the Belgian's left shoulder. From a bulletin that had gone out over the wires the previous month, he was aware of the theft of a string of horses being delivered to Fort Garland. The cavalry unit serving as a military escort had been wiped out. A freak snowstorm occurred after the theft, blanketing all tracks. The case was still unsolved, and now one of the horses had apparently re-surfaced.

"Mighty nice piece of horseflesh," said Sam. "And big, too. Twenty hands high if he's a finger." He laughed at his own joke. "Judgin' by that brand he was prolly gonna be wasted on some Army general. But you know what that horse thief also took that burns my bacon?"

Yulin had walked around to the other side of the horse. Yes, the Sharps was in the scabbard. "No, Sam, what did he take that burns your bacon?"

"Well sir," said Sam, "I wouldn'ta minded if he'd took my Sharps since I don't use it for buffalo huntin' much no more. But at least he shoulda left me my canteen. I had pert near a half-quart a whiskey in there I stole from ol' Burt when he went to see a man about a horse. Snuck the bottle outside and poured it into my canteen clean as a whistle—only to have it stole from me. Dagnabit, I hate dishonest people."

Yulin suddenly heard a series of loud, thumps drawing closer. Mayor Chet Carson was quickly striding down the boardwalk, headed toward them and obviously in a hurry. "Mornin', Sam. What happened to Lucky?"

"Well, sir..." started Sam.

"Nice talkin' to you, Sam." Carson tugged downward slightly on the brim of his hat at Yulin. "Haircut, Sheriff. And I'll talk to you about my dog later," he said, hurrying through the batwing doors of the saloon.

"Who's Lucky?" Sam called after him.

Sam gave a wide grin, took off his hat, and started scratching the back of his head. "Mrs. Carson went off to see her Aunt Sally in Colorado Springs last week. Guess Carson figures she's fur enough away to go see Luann every mornin'. Good thing he ain't really gettin' no haircuts. He'd be bald by the time Mrs. Carson gets back. Hee Hee." He placed his hat on his head and dug into his shirt pocket for a pack of chewing tobacco. He bit off a chaw and pushed it inside his cheek with a finger. About to put the tobacco back inside his pocket, he offered it to Yulin.

Yulin glanced at the proffered pack wet from Sam's bite, his still-moist, tobacco-stained fingers wrapped around it. "Thanks, but no."

"Suit yerself," said Sam, returning the chewing tobacco to his pocket.

Yulin shook his head but smiled in spite of himself. Gilroy had quite a set of manners in his own special, peculiar way. He was done examining the Belgian, anyway. "Sam, do me a favor. Walk this horse over to Gomez's livery stable and ask him to board it for me."

"An' just how am I supposed to git back to my place?"

"Tell Gomez I said to let you pick out any horse you like—not already owned by someone else. He always keeps a few for renting out. Mayor Carson will take care of the bill after I forward it to him."

"Well, sir," said Sam, "that'll do for now, but I sure like that big yeller horse. He's twice the animal Lucy was."

"Maybe the Army has a reward out for his return," said Yulin. "You can claim that instead. Just give me a couple of days to send a telegram to Fort Garland. But first, I need to find out what's going on." Sam began to open his mouth. "Yes, Sam. I'll let them know you're the one who found their horse."

"An' I'll tell you right now about that renter horse from Gomez," said Sam. "It better be a fair swap considerin' the pain and sufferin' it's caused me to lose my Lucy. You know, she was like a daughter to me."

Yulin tried his best to stifle a laugh fighting for release. He barely succeeded, making it sound more like clearing his throat. "Ok, Sam. We can see about Gomez getting you a permanent replacement, one equal to the pain and suffering that having your daughter Lucy stolen has caused you."

As Sam walked the Belgian over to Gomez's livery stable, Yulin headed back to his office. At least Gilroy had helped him clear his head, just from the shear mental task of dealing with the man. Inside the office, he refilled his coffee mug and sat down in his chair. On the desk was a handful of wanted posters. With nothing else to do, he started rifling through them. Maybe some desperado had been reported in the area who could've been involved in both horse thefts.

Among the dodgers there were the usual suspects. William Brazelton was operating out of the territories of Arizona and New Mexico but staying clear of Colorado. They were still looking for Sam Bass, fresh off the biggest train robbery in history. But Bass was rumored to be in Texas. Yulin wished for the first time in four years he was the bounty hunter he used to be. In those days he answered to no one but himself. Now he couldn't even shoot a goddamn dog.

He got up and walked over to the coffee pot. There wasn't much left so he poured in more ground coffee and water and set the pot back on the stove. He thought about rolling a cigarette, but it wasn't what he needed right now. He also thought he didn't really need to drink another pot of coffee.

Even before the fight with Reva, Yulin was finding it hard to sleep through the night again. If it hadn't been for that bottle of bourbon last night he wouldn't have slept at all. He was again dreaming about Lillian and Weed. Years ago, he'd trained himself to put them out of his mind—with the help of two bottles of bourbon—before falling asleep. But now those dreams were back. What did it mean that they had returned? He didn't have a clue. What were his feelings for Reva? He hadn't a clue about that either.

At first it had felt right being with her, making love to her, just being with her. But now it felt like he was cheating on Lillian's memory. It didn't make sense, but he couldn't help how he felt. He could tell that Reva was aware of his confusion as well, choosing not to talk about it unless he brought it up—which he never did. Or at least he didn't think he did.

But right now, he didn't have time to think on any of that. He had to find out who stole Sam's horse last night—and why.

CHAPTER 25

In mid-morning Ike woke up with a start. He was really getting tired of waking up like this. Not deeply asleep anyway, he had heard a rustling sound nearby. It was Lucy foraging for something to nibble on. Ike suddenly felt wet. He sat up and looked down at his body. Some whiskey had spilled onto his shirt during the night. Well, he was going to pour it out anyway, the next time he came across a creek or something. Or maybe he'd just keep the rest for tonight when it got cold again. He pushed the cork back in and slung the canteen around his neck.

The smell from the blanket suddenly filled his nose. It didn't smell any better in the daytime than it had last night. He threw it off him and slowly got to his knees. As his body began to wake up, he realized he no longer felt the scratches on his chest. Peering out from the side of the juniper bush, he found he couldn't see the trail. That meant he couldn't be seen, either.

He slowly stood up and made his way over to crouch behind a tree at the edge of the thicket. Now he could see both directions on the trail. There was no dust, no sign or sound of movement. Maybe the posse had ridden past him in the night while he was sleeping? No, he had learned from Garrison that a posse, like Indians, didn't like to ride at night if they could help it.

Ike was sure he could still make it down to the border without getting caught. He walked back behind the bush and sat down. The wrapped food from last night lay untouched on the ground. He had forgotten all about it, what with the stomach cramps and falling asleep before he could eat anything. The stomachache was gone, replaced by a gnawing hunger. He tore at the paper wrapping, finding a small, fully cooked meatloaf in one package and a few baked sourdough rolls in the other. Better still, the food was mostly thawed. Well now, he and the horse were both going to have breakfast this morning. Ike hungrily shoveled one of the cold dinner rolls into his mouth and chewed eagerly. He had never tasted sourdough before; this was delicious! He polished it off, and then ate another.

Ike had never seen meatloaf before. At first, he wasn't sure about it. The dried marinara sauce on the outside looked like ketchup, and he knew what *that* tasted like. When he took his first tentative bite, he found the meat cold, but very interesting. It turned out that the red stuff didn't taste like ketchup at all— it tasted better. With his second bite, he hit the core of solid mozzarella cheese inside the meatloaf. Here were flavors he had never tasted before, and he loved them. He shoved the rest into his mouth. Finding it hard to swallow so much meat and cheese, he picked up the milk bottle. Some milk had spilled out onto the ground and there was some dirt on the bottleneck. He didn't care. Taking a healthy drink, he swallowed both milk and meatloaf in a couple of gulps. His mouth erupted with a loud, satisfied belch. Maybe someday he and Garrison would ride back to that town and eat at that café. It had the best food he'd ever eaten in his life.

With breakfast finished, he lay back on his elbows. He looked up into the glittering sunlight filtering through the fir trees around him. Thick clusters of pine needles and cones were swaying in the soft morning breeze. In the gaps between some tree branches, he imagined he saw a face. Indistinct at first, it gradually began to resolve itself into something recognizable. It was a woman's face, somehow familiar to him. Was that long hair surrounding the face? So familiar…just on the edge of his memory.

Then he recognized it. It was his mother's face. He *did* remember what she had looked like after all. He must have been two or three, sitting next to her on the porch swing. She had held him close as they glided back and forth for what had seemed like hours. He would look up at her face as she sang to him in her soft, gentle voice. His mother had smiled down at him, the way the face among the trees appeared to be smiling down at him now.

Overcome with emotion, he shifted his eyes away. Was his mother actually here with him? He looked back up at the spot among the pine needles, feeling a momentary panic when he couldn't locate her. No—there she was. He relaxed, keeping his eyes fixed on his mother's face. He recalled that on the wagon train, he'd heard talk about angels up in heaven watching down on the loved ones they had left behind. People in Boulder had talked about this, too. Ike wondered if it were true, that his mother could be an angel up in heaven watching down on him. He remembered a woman in town telling Uncle Roy that he needed to teach "those boys to believe in *something*". His uncle had answered *his* boys would decide for themselves what they would believe in when the time came. Ike wondered if the time had come for him.

Ike wanted to believe he was seeing his mother's face, but was it really hers? Was he seeing proof she was an angel up in heaven? He decided he liked the idea of her watching over him. Besides, after he was dead, he'd know the truth anyway.

The sound of rustling among the bushes brought him back to the situation at hand. He now wondered what he should do with the empty milk bottle and the paper wrappers. Should he leave them here? Yes, that's what he would do. No one would have any reason to think he'd even been here. Just to be safe, he hid them under the bush. Walking over to the mare, he lifted the canteen from around his neck and slung it across the saddle horn. He was about to lead the mare out of the woods when he remembered the blanket still lying on the ground. He quickly rolled it up and tied it behind the saddle.

Outside the woods, Ike swung into the saddle, turning the mare back onto the trail. He put the horse into a trot to test the right foreleg. It seemed strong enough, so he set the mare into an easy lope. Again, the gait seemed fine. He knew the horse needed water. He hoped they would come to a creek somewhere down the trail.

He turned half around in the saddle, looking for any signs of dust besides his own. Still nothing. Last night the horse had galloped for two miles before it had started to limp. He had let it rest, varied the gaits and had coaxed it along for about a dozen miles. The night's rest appeared to have done some good. The blue dun was eagerly taking to the trail. Taking no chances, Ike kept the horse in an easy lope for a few miles at a time before slowing down to a walk. He repeated this pattern as he began to get the feel of the horse.

Hours later, it was Ike who was in discomfort, but from the heat. Sweat ran down his forehead from underneath his hat, stinging his eyes. He didn't have a scarf, so he did his best to wipe away the sweat with his shirtsleeve. He was frustrated. Son of a bitch! It had never been this hot back in Boulder. Not in April, anyway.

Always keep to the trail. How could he keep to the trail if he couldn't *see* the trail? To add to his frustration, the mare seemed to be favoring that same leg again. "Stupid son of a bitch horse," he shouted.

Just then the blue dun picked up speed, forgetting its limp, and led Ike away from the road, down past a great scrub oak to a small, sandy beach next to a shallow creek. Ike grabbed the canteen before he dismounted and carried it down to the water. As the mare settled in to drink its fill, Ike knelt beside the creek. Remembering what happened to him after drinking that ice-cold milk, he watched the horse closely. He couldn't afford to ride a horse that was both lame *and* gut sick.

When he opened the canteen, there was still whiskey left inside. He had forgotten that he was saving it for the next cold night, but it was daytime now. He needed to have drinking water for the ride still ahead of him. After taking a quick swallow, he poured the rest of the whiskey into the creek. "Wait till you see me drink whiskey," he said in an imaginary conversation with his brother. "I'm not a kid anymore, Garrison. I'm a man now, just like you." After the canteen was full, he took off his hat and poured water over his head, then wiped it all over his face. The cold water felt good on such a hot day. After refilling the canteen, he slapped the cork into place, and rehung it from the saddle.

Ike pulled the mare back from the creek and re-checked that right foreleg. He didn't know what to think. The horse had stopped limping when it ran to the water, but what did that mean? If only Garrison were here. He knew horses. Ike decided he'd just have keep switching the horse between a lope and a walk, letting it rest when it started to limp. With every mile he was getting closer to Three Rocks Trace Pedras.

Ike checked his weapons again. Both revolvers and the Winchester were loaded enough with bullets. Besides, he also had the spare bullets he'd picked up from Hank Bellum. That should be enough to hold off a posse for a while if they caught up to him.

Suddenly, he had to see all that money again. He untied and lifted the flaps on both saddlebags. The silver certificates, of course, were still there. He realized that he had never really looked closely at them before. He picked up one of the $10,000 bundles. The bills were held together by an elastic band. He slowly fanned through them with his thumb. He counted ten. Holding the bundle at eye level, he saw that the top bill had a picture of a man on the right side and "1000" printed in a couple of places. He remembered his arithmetic. This meant that there were ten $1000 bills in each bundle. Ten thousand dollars? He counted the number of bundles in the bag. That was as far as he knew how to count. But now he had an idea of how much money was in $400,000.

Ike thought of the watch he had thrown into the stream back at the woods. Perhaps he should keep one of the $1000 bills and buy a new watch just like the one Garrison had given him. That way Garrison would never know he broke the first one. Yes, Garrison could ask what time it was and he would pull out the exact same-looking watch. His brother would never know it was a different one. Ike didn't know how much pocket watches cost, but he was sure $1000 would be enough.

No, Mr. Binghamton would want all his money back. It was safer to keep it all together and find the Frenchmen's gold. Then he'd tell Garrison about the watch and buy them both new ones. He replaced the bundle and tied the flaps down on the saddlebags.

Ike grabbed the reins and stepped into the saddle. He took the map out of his back pocket and unfolded it. It had become easier to read. He found his relative position and ran his finger down the drawn stage trail to the letters NMT. That's where the map stopped. But Duke had said keep to the trail, just like Uncle Roy had also told him. He'd head for Three Rocks Tres Pedras, find a hiding spot and wait for Garrison to show up. He knew Garrison could track a man better than anyone, or at least that's what people said about him.

What had Will called the Indians down there? Band of Utes. He didn't know how many Utes were in a band but they seemed like nothing to worry about. He had killed seven men all by himself. With his two .44-40 Merwin Hulbert Frontier 2nd Model revolvers and the Winchester '73 and the extra bullets, he could handle at least twice that number of Indians. He was the fastest draw anyone had ever seen.

If only it wasn't for this stupid son of a bitch lame horse, he'd have been in New Mexico Territory by now. He didn't know where he could find another one. Maybe there'd be some Indian ponies running loose and he could try to rope one. There was a hair rope on the saddle he could use. He'd start practicing once he found his hiding spot.

CHAPTER 26

It was late afternoon of that same day and Yulin Temple realized he was hungry. His stomach had felt jumbled all morning, the very thought of food making him feel nauseous. But now the hangover was finally gone, mostly due to the morning's encounter with Sam Gilroy, and the dual mystery of the disappearance of Sam's horse and the appearance of the giant palomino Belgian stallion. And, partly due to the pot and a half of coffee he had drunk.

With his appetite returned, Yulin would normally walk over to Reva's for dinner, but today that wasn't an option. The hotel in town had a dining room and kitchen but the cook had just quit to hunt his fortune in Columbia, yet another new silver boomtown. The temporary cook, who was also the bellhop, was making it quite apparent through his lack of culinary skills that he was better at carrying luggage than at cooking meals. Yulin also thought of the food at the Silver Strike Saloon and re-considered the food at the hotel. Then he thought of Reva and the glorious food she cooked. Why'd she have to act like such a damn woman?

As Yulin stepped out of his office onto the boardwalk, he saw a rider on a very tired-looking black gelding approaching. He took out the makin's and rolled a cigarette. He took a drag, blew a perfect smoke ring, and watched as rider and horse slowly made their way toward his office.

Yulin's eyes took in the stranger at a glance. The rider appeared tall, strongly built with broad shoulders. His dark brown hair was visible under a flat-crown, narrow-brimmed hat. He wore a well-trimmed drooping moustache, but there was a couple of days beard growth on his face. Yulin figured him to be a youngish man who looked older than his years.

It was clear that the rider was just as tired as his horse, obviously from riding a very long way. He also wore his gun tied down on his right hip. Yulin decided he already didn't like this guy. Whoever this stranger was, Yulin had a strong feeling that more trouble had just ridden into town.

The rider reined up at the hitching rail in front of where Yulin was standing. With a small bit of effort, he stiffly dismounted from his horse, tying it to the rail. "You Sheriff Temple?" he asked, fatigue hanging from his words.

"I have been for some time, yes," answered Yulin.

The rider, not acknowledging Yulin's response, pulled a Winchester out of the scabbard and stepped up onto the boardwalk. "My name's Garrison Fleck.

I'm a detective with the J.K. Binghamton Stage Line." He extended a weary hand toward Yulin, who grasped and slowly shook it.

Yulin was still sizing up exactly who and what just rode into town. "Detective with Binghamton, huh? Somebody rob a stagecoach?" He released Garrison's hand.

Garrison gave Yulin a quick glance over. For a drunk this sheriff was fairly perceptive. He then looked up and down the street. "Can we go into your office and talk?"

"Sure thing." Actually, Yulin didn't want this saddle tramp—detective or otherwise—within the confines of his office. The smell of man sweat, horse sweat, and woodsmoke emanated from him like an animal in heat seeking its mate. Yulin knew he had smelled exactly like this when he had returned to Lillian during his Ranger days. She hadn't appeared to have minded. But this guy wasn't him and Yulin certainly wasn't Lillian. Still, he couldn't think of any legitimate reason to deny this stranger entry. He turned to enter the office, flicking the cigarette away before walking through the door.

"Got any hot coffee?" asked Garrison, following behind Yulin. "I've been on the trail since yesterday afternoon."

"Your lucky day. Pot's only about an hour old. You been on the trail from where?"

"Trinidad."

Yulin stopped and turned to face him. "Trinidad? That's a hundred and thirty miles from here—straight over the Sangre de Cristo Mountains. You rode it in twenty-four hours?"

"Got a few hours' sleep last night in the mountains. I don't need much rest."

"Did you ask your horse if he feels the same way? It's a wonder he's still standing upright." Yulin gestured toward a chair in front of his desk. "I'll get you that cup of coffee and a bucket of it for your horse." He was *really* not liking this guy.

Garrison sat down in the chair, setting the Winchester on the floor and leaning the barrel against the desk. His facial expression showed him lost in thought as well as exhausted. Yulin studied the stagecoach detective. Yes, he did indeed look older than he was. It was a strong face, but like all men in this line of work, it was hardened. And it looked like this stagecoach detective hadn't had a decent night's sleep in a long while. Yulin knew all about that, yes he did. Still, there was a hint of something in his eyes. Sadness? Over what? He took a coffee mug from a wall shelf near the stove, poured some coffee and handed the mug to Garrison.

Garrison took a sip and his face showed gratitude for its hot, bracing strength. At least this sheriff knew how to make coffee, he thought. He took another sip and set his coffee mug down on the desk. "Sheriff, what I'm about to tell you needs to remain confidential. Just between us, understand?"

"No, I don't. But I'm sure you're about to help me understand." Yulin had to add, "And I do know what confidential means." That'll show that young punk.

He watched Garrison take a shallow breath. More of the sadness appeared in the eyes.

"As I told you, I'm a detective with the J.K. Binghamton Stage Line. We just started a new service delivering mined ore to the railroads on behalf of the miners." Garrison outlined how the pickup and delivery service was to operate. "We had sixteen mines and four banks lined up, all in areas rife with bandits."

The use of the word "rife" did not go unnoticed by Yulin.

Garrison took a sip of coffee and continued. "This was our first run. The stage was carrying $400,000 in new U.S. Silver Certificates."

Yulin was in the middle of pouring himself some coffee when he looked up at Garrison. Coffee ran over the top of the mug and onto the floor. He quickly lifted the pot away, holding it upright. "$400,000—in legal tender that anyone can cash in any bank west of the Mississippi? Serial numbers don't mean a thing out here. And you were carrying it on a stagecoach? Son, if your boss Binghamton never realized how stupid and dangerous his plan was, I'm sure he's gotten the idea by now. Because I'm sure you're about to tell me that stagecoach was indeed robbed." He looked down at the coffee puddle on the floor and stepped over it to put the coffee pot back on the stove. He stepped over it again to walk back to his desk chair and sat down.

Garrison was taken aback. This sheriff might be sharper than that Army captain had given him credit for. "Yes, there was a robbery. Everyone was sworn to secrecy prior to that first delivery run, but apparently there was a breach in security."

"*Apparently?*" Yulin took an angry sip of coffee. If he couldn't unleash his anger at Reva, this—detective—would bear the brunt of it. "There was no way you could keep a stage carrying that much money a secret. What the hell was Binghamton thinking?"

"He was thinking of a way to save his company," Garrison snapped. He didn't have to sit here and be lectured by some drunken old fart of a sheriff. He was already overwhelmed with feelings of guilt over the deaths of Duke and Gully, over what he had pushed Ike into. He was still Atlas, with the weight of the heavens bearing down upon his shoulders. It seemed like he had borne that crushing weight his whole life.

Now, adding further to that weight, he had no idea where Ike was. Horses, wagons, and pedestrians had obliterated any hoofprints the Belgian might have left in the dirt road that was Main Street. Still, he had to keep faith in Ike doing what he figured Ike would do; keep following the trail. It gave Garrison the momentum to drive himself onward, hopefully to intercept Ike before...

He gathered his fears and emotions together and tried to put them some place where he wouldn't think about or feel them. Right now, he needed whatever information this fool of a sheriff might have.

"Mr. Binghamton figured to expand into areas where trains can't go, at least not yet. Everyone involved was sworn to secrecy," Garrison repeated. "This included myself and the stage crew, the mine owners and the bank presidents. The first delivery was supposed to be two days ago. The stage left Pueblo for Trinidad but never arrived. Sheriff Haines and I found it by the side of the road not far from Walsenburg. A roadblock had forced it off the road." Garrison told Yulin about finding the stagecoach with Duke and Gully, and the Bellum Gang all dead. When he told of the missing silver certificates, he left out any mention of Ike.

"Sworn to secrecy," Yulin said, disdainfully. "Too many people already knew about it to keep it a secret. And from what you told me it had to have been an inside job." Yulin took a sip of coffee. "Any suspicions yet?" It was obvious the detective was fighting to keep emotion from seeping into his voice but Yulin didn't yet know why.

"I haven't proven it for sure but the facts lean toward Conley, the Pueblo station agent," said Garrison. He told how Duke's map had mysteriously disappeared, only to be "found" by Conley on the station floor. "I don't know how he became involved, but Conley appears to have been the inside man for the Bellums."

"I know about the Bellums," Yulin said. "Hard customers. Hank was the brains. Jesse did what Hank told him. But what about that station agent? Did he suddenly vanish?"

"No, Garrison replied. "I wired the Pueblo town marshal to keep Conley under surveillance with orders to arrest him if he tries to leave town. I'm going to question him when I get back."

Yulin was trying to take this all in. Why had this Fleck character ridden into town if the robbery had happened on the other side of the mountains? He was sure there was something, some detail, this detective was keeping from him. He decided to probe a little further. "So, let's see if I've got this straight. The Bellums had an inside man feeding them confidential information. They rob the stage but wind up dead—"

"I never said they robbed the stage," snapped Garrison, his exhaustion giving him little patience with this slow-witted sheriff. He paused before continuing, emotion further welling up inside him. He hadn't wanted to bring Ike's name into this, but he had no choice. "At the crime scene, Haines and I found evidence to suggest the actual robbery had been carried out by somebody else."

Yulin let the abruptness of Garrison's initial response slide. He was about to get that missing detail. Again, he observed the detective trying to keep his emotions in check. "OK, your investigation suggests someone other than the

Bellum Gang made off with the money. Were you able to figure out who it might be?"

Garrison sat for a moment, cleared his throat, tried to talk, then cleared his throat again. "We had a secret guard dressed up to look like a city dude riding the stage. The idea was that bandits attempting to rob the stage would think he was the son of a bank president or something. The guard, using the element of surprise, would get the drop on them first. We had full confidence in the m-man we chose. He's so fast with a gun…" Garrison's voice trailed off. Yulin had noticed the slight stammer, and a tear sliding down the detective's face.

Garrison casually brushed the tear away. "We were prepared for a holdup, but no one figured on an ambush. But at least part of the plan worked. After the driver and shotgun messenger were shot dead by the Bellum Gang, the guard killed all four men."

Yulin gave a soft whistle. "That must've been some shooting."

"Yes," said Garrison, "my brother is very good."

This unexpected detail stunned Yulin. "Your brother?"

"Yeah. My little brother, Ike. He was the guard. Just turned seventeen last January, but he's hell on wheels with a gun. Fastest I've ever seen." Garrison reached in his coat pocket and pulled out a folded photograph and opened it. "Had this taken at a photographer's studio last week. Wanted to have a picture of him alone but Ike wanted me in it with him."

He handed the photograph over to Yulin. In the picture, Garrison was sitting on a divan next to a young teenage boy. Both were looking stern-faced at the camera. The boy called Ike had long hair in the style of Wild Bill Hickok, but his hair was not yet as long as the gunfighter's had been. Maybe a slight hint of a moustache above the upper lip. Yet, there was something in the boy's face that struck Yulin emotionally. "How old did you say your brother is?" asked Yulin.

"Seventeen."

Yulin's eyes narrowed and his face reddened with sudden fury. Barely containing his anger he said, "You mean you had a seventeen-year-old boy riding that stagecoach with that amount of money onboard—because he's fast with a gun? What the hell were *you* thinking? Plenty of fast guns are buried in graveyards throughout the West. You should know that."

Duke had practically said as much. If only he'd listened then, thought Garrison. But when he spoke, his voice remained flat.

"I was thinking Ike could handle himself. He had the element of surprise with those guns hidden under his coat. I was positive he and Gully would prevent a holdup. Just didn't work out that way." Garrison leaned forward in his chair. "But I told you Ike was fast. He didn't need any help. He killed those gang members himself." He leaned back, picturing in his mind what it must have been like for his brother.

Yulin looked again at the photo of Ike. He was just a kid. And seventeen? Weed would've been seventeen this year, he thought. His hair had also been blond, just like his mother's. Although Lillian had suggested it from time to time, Yulin had never gotten around to having a family photograph taken. As a consequence, he struggled to hold onto the clear memory of their faces so they would never fade from his mind. He looked again at the photograph. No way Lillian would've allowed their son's hair to grow that long. He suddenly imagined Weed's face on the other boy's body in the picture. Yulin shook the image out of his mind. His eyes fell on the sidearms the kid was wearing in the photograph, two handguns in reversed open top holsters, gun butts facing forward. "Wears his guns like Hickok did," he said.

"He's easily as fast as Hickok was, maybe faster," Garrison said, "and shoots just as straight. That's why I bought him the best guns I could afford. That guard job was going to be dangerous and I wanted Ike to have as much of an advantage as possible."

A sudden realization dawned on Yulin. "If your brother killed the entire gang after they killed the driver and the shotgun messenger, then you mean your brother…?"

Garrison gave a deep sigh, steeling himself for the response that was painful for him to utter. "Sheriff, I don't know for sure what transpired out there, but yes, everything points to my brother Ike taking the money. I just don't understand why he did it. I just know I have to find him before anyone else does. I'm sure I can talk him into coming back with me and return every dollar he stole. We'll see what happens after that." He picked up his coffee mug, took a sip, and frowned. It had turned lukewarm. He placed the mug back on Yulin's desk.

Yulin noted the use of the word "transpired".

This time it was Garrison's turn to examine the sheriff. He could smell last night's whiskey still radiating from the man's body, along with the smell of tobacco mixed in with all the coffee he had been drinking. Tiny red tendrils spread out from the deep blue eyes, set in a face with a bit of extra flesh that came with age. The nose had grown a bit more bulbous, with the same red spider web-like veins as in the eyes.

From what Garrison had learned from the captain at Fort Garland, the word was that while Sheriff Yulin Temple might still be fast with a gun, it was his hard drinking that was driving his reputation now. Yet, the face still showed the strength of the deadly gunfighter the man had once undoubtedly been.

Yulin gave Ike's face a long, final look and handed the photograph back to the detective. Garrison gazed at it before tenderly folding and placing it back in his coat pocket.

"That brother of yours ever been in a gunfight or faced a man shooting at him?" Yulin asked.

Garrison looked away, and then spoke. "About three weeks ago we were inside a bank in Boulder. I'd just made a deposit." He told Yulin how Ike had handled the three bank robbers on his own. He turned back to the sheriff. "That was the first time Ike ever faced anyone holding a gun on him. And he killed all three men, just like"—he snapped his fingers— "that."

Yulin leaned back in his chair, took a sip of coffee and found it also had grown lukewarm. He set it down on his desk. He was dumbfounded. Beneath all that Fleck had just told him, the answer was, no, the kid had never faced a gunman shooting at him. All the morons who had pointed guns at him had lacked enough sense to pull the trigger.

This lame-brained scheme had been doomed from the start. Undoubtedly, details of that "secret" delivery run had been leaked beforehand. But to pit some green kid with a gun against hardened killers—even if he was the fastest gun on the planet—was just insanity. Maybe even criminal. It could easily have gone the other way with the kid shot to pieces. "Any idea what happened to your brother?"

"Possibly. Got something else to show you." Garrison took Ike's note out of his shirt pocket. He unfolded it and handed it to Yulin. Holding it away from himself at eye level, Yulin squinted, trying to read Ike's handwriting as best he could.

The note read: "I kilt the ones who kilt Duk and Gulle. Dont be mad I tuk the money. Followin map to NMT then 3 rocks and the gold. Stay away or Ill kill you. Love Ike. p.s. I got my own Winchestir now."

"Do you believe all this?" asked Yulin.

""You don't know my brother," said Garrison, "He's entirely capable of this."

Yulin was still trying to decipher the note. "What's NMT.? Oh, New Mexico Territory. And three rocks...he means Tres Piedras. It's that buried gold legend. He's got those two places confused, doesn't he? New Mexico and Oklahoma. Your brother steals $400,000 and then goes gold hunting in the wrong spot? And why hunt for gold at all? He already has all that money."

Garrison sighed. "I admit that's yet another thing that baffles me. And I have no idea how Ike ever heard of Tres Piedras. But nothing he's doing makes sense." He stood up, walked over to a window, and stared out. "Sometimes I get an idea of how Ike thinks. Maybe if he finds the gold, he can give back the money, and no hard feelings. I figure that's pretty close. Still doesn't make any sense."

Yulin took a visual assessment of the detective. Fleck was telling the truth about the robbery. And he wasn't surprised the kid brother had run off the money. "$400,000 changes a man's character awful quick. And what was that about a Winchester?"

"Judging from the crime scene Hank Bellum was the only one with a Winchester. Ike took it, and then rode off on what was probably Bellum's horse."

This Ike kid, I swear, thought Yulin. "In the note he says he'll kill you if you follow him."

Garrison turned to face the sheriff. "I don't believe for one second he'd actually do it. I think he threw that in for the benefit of anyone else reading the note is all I can figure."

This sounded plausible to Yulin. Something else in the note caught his attention. "Your brother said he had a map. What map?"

Garrison walked over to the desk. "A map of the new route. Duke had the sole map since he was the only one driving it. He was carrying it on him when the stage left Pueblo. Ike had to have taken it off Duke...after the ambush." His eyes focused on a vision of Duke's body slumped against the box.

"That couldn't have been pleasant," said Yulin.

"Yeah, I saw Duke—Duke's body—still sitting up there." Garrison stayed silent for a moment, working to clear that vision from his mind. "My brother rode out through Walsenburg and over La Veta Pass. I've tracked him here." He sat back down in the chair and paused. He didn't want the sheriff to know that he had lost Ike's tracks. "The horse Ike's riding is so big it was easy to follow his sign. I was gonna ride straight through town till I saw you. Thought I'd better check in to find out if you'd seen him."

Yulin didn't buy that for a minute, having seen the clearly exhausted detective on a worn-out horse. No way was he going any further. Yulin let it drop and moved on. "Your brother expected you to follow him—alone?" He handed Ike's note back to Garrison, who folded and stuffed it back in his shirt pocket.

"Yeah. That's why he wrote where he was headed. He knew I'd track him." That was if Ike had kept to the trail, thought Garrison. What if he had lost the map after riding into Stovepipe?

"Has he been down there before?"

Garrison looked at Yulin. "He's never been anywhere by himself before. I even hired people to take care of him when I'd be gone on a job. You need to understand something about Ike. He may come across as slow but some things come easy to him. Guns are one of them. Reading maps appears to be another one. I'm guessing Ike figured out how to use the map to get himself here. Now he's got the confidence to go the rest of the way on his own."

"You sure your brother will even be able to make it down to the state border?"

"Sheriff, he made it at least this far, didn't he? Ike's displaying guts and skills I never knew he had. Believe me, he'll keep going till he reaches Tres Piedras. And right now I don't know of anyone who can stop him other than me."

Yulin sat back in his chair. He admitted his initial opinion of this Garrison Fleck was wrong. The trouble he had brought into town was tormenting only himself. Yet the torment the man was carrying around felt all too familiar to Yulin, which started to worry him. He didn't want to get involved in any of this. But there was a seventeen-year-old kid out there riding alone into Indian country. And down there the $400,000 he was carrying wouldn't make a bit of difference.

"Sounds like a miracle he made it this far," Yulin said. "But if he's made it through town, the stage road south of here turns into an old gunrunners' trail. They'd ride through town on their way down to the Territory and sell guns to the Jicarilla Apache and the Utes. It'll lead him to Tres Piedras alright if he keeps to the trail. But you've got something else to worry about. A Ute chief named Spotted Wolf has a village on Bear Mountain. And he takes a dim view of white men trespassing on what he considers his land, which happens to be all the land surrounding the mountain. It's a quick way to wind up dead, even if your brother can shoot like you say he does."

Garrison turned back to face Yulin. "Ike may not know what he's riding into, but if he did it wouldn't stop him. I figure he's still on the trail, maybe a day's ride ahead of me. I was hoping he'd still be in town here, but I'm positive if I head out now I can overtake him. That giant horse must be near done in by now."

Yulin now realized what Fleck was saying to him. He held his breath, and then asked the question. "Was this horse an extremely large palomino—with a US brand?"

Garrison eyes narrowed. "Yeah. How did you know that?"

"I think you should be looking for another horse now," said Yulin. He told Garrison about the horse swap in front of the Silver Strike Saloon. "That was a new one on me. I've never seen that before."

Garrison was already halfway out the door. He stopped and turned toward Yulin. "I need your help. I want to talk to the man who found that horse," he said.

CHAPTER 27

"What do you mean you didn't see or hear anything?" asked Garrison Fleck. He was holding the paper where he had written down the missing horse's description.

Sam Gilroy, sitting in a wooden chair in front of the Silver Strike, was in a bad mood because it was late afternoon and he was still sober. Unable to ride back to his cabin, he was waiting for someone he might know to walk up and offer to buy him a drink. Until now, no such person had appeared.

"Well sir," said Sam, with some irritation in his voice, "how am I supposed to see anythin' when I got one eye on my poker hand and t'other on the gents sittin' at the table? Besides, I got the piany playin' in one ear and the calls of those same gents in t'other. A whole durn freight train coulda come rollin' past outside and I wouldn'tna seen nor heared it. Did you expect me to use my durn nose to smell it, too?"

Garrison sighed. He had years of experience in interviewing men like this one but they were never easy. Their information remained locked inside their minds unless the right key could be found. He looked at Yulin, standing next to him.

Yulin, smoking a freshly rolled cigarette, looked at Garrison, shrugged his shoulders and blew a perfect smoke ring. He turned to the old placer miner. "Sam, just remember as best you can."

"I don't remember so good with a dry throat," Sam said, curtly.

Garrison sighed again. The right key had been found. "OK, let's go in and I'll buy you a drink. But just one."

The three men entered through the batwing doors. Sam led the way to the bar and sat down on a stool. Garrison sat down beside him, and Yulin stood behind Sam. Garrison looked at Burt Owens, standing behind the bar, a terry cloth towel over his shoulder. "A whiskey for my...friend here. But not from the top shelf." The detective looked at Sam who stared back at him. "OK," said Garrison, "from the top shelf."

Sam smiled as Owens glared back. He took down a bottle, poured a couple of fingers into a shot glass and set it on the bar in front of Sam, who downed it in one swallow.

"That'll be two bits," said Owens.

Garrison watched Sam, who was wiping his mouth in satisfaction with his shirtsleeve. Sam lifted the empty glass to Owens. "A-heh-hem," he said.

"Maybe you should start a running tab," said Garrison to Owens. "I'll settle my account before I leave."

Owens glared again at Sam. "An account for a no-account if you ask me." He poured another drink. Sam downed it in one swallow, wiping his mouth again with a greater show of satisfaction than before. He lifted the empty glass again. "A-heh-hem." From behind, Yulin blew a perfect smoke ring that broke against the back of Sam's head.

Garrison, resigned to his present fate, nodded at Owens, who poured another shot. Sam again downed it in a single gulp. He belched loudly with great pleasure.

"OK," Garrison asked him, "what did your horse look like?"

"Well sir, she's a fair-looking animal, blue dun mare about fifteen hands high, give or take a finger." Sam gave out a wheezing laugh that ended in a loud snort. "But the funny thing is that horse thief left me a lot better horseflesh than what he took. That palominer's a fine animal—Sheriff here saw 'im. A yeller sonobitch that's gotta be twenty hands high if he's a— "

"Finger," said Yulin and Garrison together.

Sam stared at the two men, nonplussed for the moment, then continued. "Helluva nice saddle, too. Looks right new. Critter was gonna be wasted on some Yankee general, judgin' by the US brand there."

Garrison looked at the paper again. The one Army horse unaccounted for was the palomino Belgian stallion. Along with the horses, the Bellum Gang had stolen an expensive new saddle. Both saddle and horse had been earmarked for the commanding officer of Fort Garland. "Did you say a palomino? With a new saddle? Where's this horse now?"

"Took him over to Gomez's stable, like the sheriff told me to."

Garrison rose to his feet. "Will you show him to me?" he asked.

Sam nodded and rose unsteadily from the barstool and fell back on it again. "Jes give me a moment. But Sheriff's already seen 'im. I showed 'im the horse this morning."

"I would've taken you straight to him, had you'd asked me," said Yulin.

Garrison, at a loss for words, stared at Yulin. "I didn't know to ask. But that horse fits the description of—"

"A horse that was part of a string of Army horses stolen on their way to Fort Garland," finished Yulin. "We have a telegraph in town."

"Sheriff also knows what Lucy looks like. I ride 'er to town ev'ry day," said Sam, followed by a loud belch.

"Then why did I buy him all those— "

"I was wonderin' the same thing," said Yulin. "Sam already told me all he knows."

"That'll be seventy-five cents," said Owens to Garrison.

Garrison looked at Owens, looked at Yulin, looked at Sam, dug three twenty-five cent pieces out of his pocket and placed them on the bar.

"And a dollar for that bottle of whiskey *he* stole last night," said Owens, tilting his head towards Sam. "That's a buck seventy-five total."

Sam turned around on the barstool, his upper body swaying while making the maneuver, and addressed Owens. "Now lookee here, Burt. How do you know t'weren't Luann or Pearl that took it?"

"Because before I went to take a piss it was on the bar in front of you, and when I got back both you and the bottle were gone. Now pay up."

Garrison stepped in. "You said a dollar-seventy-five?"

Owens looked at him. "I did indeed. "

Sam snorted and laughed. "'Tweren't no more than a coupla ta three swallers left in it! And you may've got that bottle off the top shelf, Burt, but the whiskey inside it came from that barrel underneath the bar."

Owens glared at Sam and then looked back at Garrison. "OK, make it a buck and a half."

Garrison reached into his pants pocket, pulled out a silver dollar, and handed it to Sam. Sam looked at the silver dollar, picked up one of the quarters on the bar, and looked expectedly at Garrison.

"That's OK, sighed Garrison, "keep the change."

Sam, grinning a mostly toothless grin, pocketed the quarter, and slammed the silver dollar down on the bar. "One silver dollar and fifty cents! Never let it be said that ol' Sam Gilroy don't pay his debts!"

Yulin blew another smoke ring at the back of Sam's head. Owens, still glaring at Sam, picked the coins up off the bar, rang up the sale on the cash register, threw the coins in the cash drawer and slammed the drawer shut.

Sam slid off the barstool and navigated himself toward the saloon doors. Yulin made a sweeping gesture with his hand toward Sam's retreating figure. "After you," he said to Garrison.

As Sam walked out of the bar he was giggling. "Hee hee! There were *four* swallers easy left in that bottle. I sure snuck one over on 'ol Burt!"

"OK. Where's this livery stable?" Garrison asked, walking behind Sam.

"I'll lead ya there. You paid for it."

Sam stumbled as he stepped off the boardwalk. Somehow retaining his balance, he staggered across the street as Garrison followed at his heels. Yulin, having flicked his cigarette into the street, followed right behind Garrison.

Sam led the two men over to Gomez's livery stable. Gomez had seen them coming and was waiting outside. He led them inside to the stall where the Belgian was standing, the top of its head rising above the stall partitions. Gomez had cleaned and brushed down the palomino; it almost looked like a different horse. Even by the stable's lamplights, the Belgian's golden coat was gleaming.

"Well sir," said Sam, "here he be. I wouldn't mind havin' my Lucy— "

"The stolen horse," Yulin interjected.

"—stole more often if I could get a deal like this," finished Sam.

"Sam," said Yulin, "I told you this horse is going back to the Army."

"A magnífico animal, Sheriff Temple," said Gomez. "Any other horse rode as hard and far as this one drops dead right under the rider. I think this horse is too strong to die. That is what save him."

Yulin glared irksomely at Garrison. "What is it you and your brother have against horses?"

"Also, Sheriff Temple," continued Gomez, "whoever ride him never took the bridle and saddle off the whole time. Who would treat any horse this way?"

My brother, thought Garrison. He looked the horse over. Yes, Gomez was right. This horse was magnificent. He could see why that Fort Garland general had spent so much of the taxpayers' money to get it. He had Gomez open the stall door. He entered and gently let his hand slide along the horse's neck, seeing the US brand on the left shoulder. That confirmed it was one of the horses stolen from the string headed to Fort Garland. He was amazed that Ike had figured out how to ride a horse this size over the mountains from Walsenburg to Stovepipe. Uncle Roy had never taught Ike to ride like this. It was as if his brother had become a person he no longer knew. A feeling of sorrow began to descend upon him, which he managed to push aside.

"But here's what I find interestin', young man," said Sam, walking over to stand in front of the stall. The saddle hung on the door railing, and he pulled a rifle out of the scabbard. "That horse thief run off with Lucy and my saddle— but he didn't take my Sharps, Model 1874. Won it off a feller in a poker game. He said it was the exact same one Billy Dixon borrowed off 'im at the Second Battle of Adobe Walls. Used it to shoot that Comanch' off his horse at seven-eighths of a mile."

Garrison glanced at Yulin who shook his head, meaning no, it wasn't the exact same rifle. He looked again at the Sharps. Why would Ike leave a powerful weapon like this? Then he remembered…Ike had written he had a Winchester—the rifle that was missing back at that robbery site. That's why he hadn't taken Gilroy's buffalo gun. A Winchester was not only a repeating rifle but used the same bullets as Ike's handguns. If cornered, the Winchester would provide him with continuous firepower. The Sharps had to be reloaded after each shot. Ike *was* a smart boy. If only I'd been around more, thought Garrison, I would've known that.

"And he took my canteen, too," Sam continued. "That was a durn nasty thing to do. Keep it full of whiskey for emmerginces, ya understand. But Lucy will give him his comeuppance. That mare might present a problem for that feller."

"How so?" asked Garrison.

"Well sir, she's got lots of bottom but she's lazy. Get her runnin' for about two miles and she'll make like she turned up lame, favorin' her right foreleg. Ya know, I won her in poker game. That was the same day I come outta the Silver Strike and found my mule dead, tied right there to the hitchin' post. Went right back inside and won me that danged mare."

Garrison looked at Yulin. "Don't ask," said Yulin.

"Anyway," continued Sam, "Lucy threw a shoe on 'er right foreleg a while back and I ain't got 'round ta gettin' a new one nailed on. An' Lucy don't like it none. She pulls that limpin' around act outta pure spite. First time she pulled it, I almost shot her dead. I was pannin' for gold in that stream that runs past my cabin and struck some color. So, I'm high tailin' it on Lucy back to town to turn them gold flakes into cash. And whadaya know? Lucy starts limpin' like her leg's broke. Thought for sure she'd gone lame. So I get out my Sharps to put her outta her mizry, and it fires by itself. Missed Lucy's head by a foot or two. And whadaya know? She takes off runnin' like her tail's on fire for about a mile or so. Took me like to an hour to catch her. That was the last time she fooled me, cuz I figured out how to handle her." He looked at the three men with a sly smile. "When she pulls that limpin' stunt, scare the shit out of her. Hee hee! That's what you do. Fire a gun near her head. Or anythin' to spook her'll do. She'll set to runnin' and won't stop till next Tuesday."

"That is no way to treat a horse," said Gomez.

"It's the only way to treat her till I get that shoe put back on. Still get twenty miles outta her at a stretch, though. I'm just glad whoever stole her left me my Sharps. I value it a lot higher than I do the animal." Then Sam remembered what he had told Yulin earlier. "Even though I love Lucy like my own daughter," he added.

Confident that Ike knew nothing about horses, Garrison found himself hoping his brother *had* shot Lucy in the head. It would make it a lot easier and faster to overtake him, with Ike on foot carrying all that money and the rifle.

"OK, I'm through here," Garrison said to Yulin. He turned to Sam. "Thanks for the help."

They left Sam to negotiate with Gomez which horse he'd take to ride home. As the two men walked back to the sheriff's office, Yulin asked, "Do you need me to raise a posse to go after your brother?"

Garrison's answer was a little brusque. "That won't be necessary, Sheriff," he said, "I'm handling this myself."

"Pardon me saying this, Mr. Fleck, but you said when you first came into my office that your brother was headed down into New Mexico. Have you ever been there?"

"Can't say that I have," said Garrison.

As they were about to enter the sheriff's office, Phipps, who was also the town postmaster, walked up to them. He was holding a sheet of paper. "Ah, here you are, Sheriff. A rider just dropped off this wanted poster. Took off right after he handed it to me. Thought you'd want to see this pronto. Says there was a stagecoach robbery over by Walsenburg. Did you know about it?"

"Let me see that!" said Garrison, grabbing the dodger from Phipp's hand. Holding the poster in both hands, he stared at it in angry disbelief.

On the poster was a hand drawn picture of Ike, his name in large print. The J.K. Binghamton Stage Line was offering a reward of $1000 for Ike's capture, dead or alive. There was not a single word about the missing silver certificates. Garrison was outraged. "Damn that Binghamton! He told me he'd give me time to find Ike before he made it public."

"Let's go back inside my office," said Yulin.

"This is insane," said Garrison. "Once they discover Ike's carrying $400,000 that $1000 reward won't mean a thing."

"Yeah, and now you're tellin' everyone in town about it." He held the door open. *"Inside."*

Yulin grabbed his coffee mug and poured the remainder from the coffee pot. Garrison flopped down in the chair in front of the desk, still looking at the wanted poster and muttering to himself.

Yulin sat down behind his desk and tipped the coffee mug to his mouth. The coffee, having sat on the stove for hours, had reduced itself down to pure concentrated molten caffeine. He gloried in its brute strength. Setting the coffee mug down he reached his hand out toward Garrison. "Let me see that dodger again."

Garrison, cold anger toward the betrayal building inside him, reluctantly handed it to Yulin.

"Sounds like Binghamton didn't trust you to get his money back," Yulin said reading the poster. He took another sip of the potent, scorching brew. "It says at the bottom to contact Tate Mallory at the J.K. Binghamton Stage Line. Who's he?"

Garrison got out of the chair and stood next to Yulin. "I didn't see that. Tate Mallory? This isn't good. Binghamton uses him for special jobs. I work with a sheriff's posse to bring stage robbers back alive. Mallory works alone and only brings back the stolen money. He gets a percentage of what he returns."

"Funny I never heard of him," said Yulin.

"He worked for the Pinks," said Garrison. "He might be the only detective Allan Pinkerton ever personally fired. He's a killer and— "

Garrison froze, a realization hitting him dead center in the brain. "Mallory plans to ride with anyone who says they can lead him to Ike. If he finds out they lied, he'll kill them. If they lead him to Ike, he'll try to kill them both. With Ike dead, he takes the $400,000 back to Binghamton and gets paid his cut. Or, maybe he keeps it all for himself."

Garrison walked around the desk to pick up his rifle. "I've got to get to Ike before Mallory finds him." He was doing some calculations in his head. "Ike has to find a place to sleep and that'll cut his lead down to maybe six hours. If I leave now I could gain ground and overtake him before he reaches the border."

"Now just hold up!" Yulin said, loudly. Garrison stopped moving, glaring at Yulin. "First off, you got a used-up horse that ain't going anywhere tonight. Second, you don't even know where your brother is. Third, *if* he makes it that far, that trail he's riding leads past Bear Mountain, Spotted Wolf's headquarters. I told you he doesn't take kindly to white men trespassing on his land unless they're trading for guns. And fourth, your brother— "

"His *name* is Ike," interjected Garrison.

"–*Ike* could start another Indian war once he starts shootin' down Utes. All because he's so fool-headed goin' after gold that doesn't exist. I can't allow that to happen. So, like it as not, I'm riding with you. Maybe I can help keep the peace."

Garrison was stunned, then angered. "No, you ain't goin' with me. This is none of your business. And I travel faster alone."

"He stole a horse in my town. That makes it my business. Now, we do it my way or I don't let you ride out of here."

"How would you stop me?" challenged Garrison.

"I'll put a bullet in your leg for resisting arrest for something I'll think up later," said Yulin.

Garrison looked at him, measuring the man. Yes, this idiot sheriff might just do that. Staying angry would literally not get him anywhere. When Garrison next spoke, it was in a calmer voice. "Aren't you concerned about leaving this town without a sheriff? You're not worried you'll be out of a job before you get back?"

"Despite what you might have heard elsewhere, I've built a reputation around here that keeps this is a quiet town." Yulin took a sip of coffee and frowned. Lukewarm again. "Now, it's about sixty miles from here to the border. It's near sundown, and I don't ride at night. Besides, I never start a journey on an empty stomach."

He watched the detective's body deflating as the anger left it. Friends again. "I'm going to grab a bite to eat, and you're welcome to join me. Afterwards, we'll get our gear together and set out tomorrow at first light."

Now that the sheriff had mentioned dinner, Garrison realized he was famished. He hadn't eaten anything since his meager breakfast that morning. He had pushed on without eating until reaching Stovepipe. "Well, I am starved. Where do we eat?"

Yulin answered, "Well, there's stew over at the Silver Strike. It's decent enough."

"I've had saloon stew. Any better place to eat in town?"

Yulin thought of Reva. He hadn't talked to her since walking out during the night. "Well, there's a café in town— "

"Sounds great. That's where we'll eat," said Garrison.

Yulin shifted uncomfortably in his chair. "Well, I don't know— "

"Something wrong with the food?" asked Garrison. "It'd have to be better than saloon food."

"It is but I'm not sure I'm welcome there."

Garrison smiled. "I'm sure your money's as welcome there as mine is, Sheriff. If we're going to eat we might as well eat now." He stood up while Yulin remained in his chair. Garrison made a sweeping gesture with his hand. "After you", he smiled.

Yulin had calmly faced badmen in gunfights, some men who had been quicker on the draw than him. He'd never been afraid. But, the thought of facing Reva after last night filled his hungry stomach with butterflies something fierce. He hoped he would be able to eat. He gulped down the rest of the coffee before walking out of the office.

CHAPTER 28

Garrison decided that he needed a bath and a shave. Yulin pointed him to Mac Sampson's barbershop where he got both. He bought a new shirt, blue jeans, and socks at Phipps Mercantile. Feeling human again, he met Yulin at the sheriff's office.

The two men entered Reva's Café, Yulin allowing Garrison to walk in first. He felt like he was in enemy territory, even though some of his belongings were still upstairs in her room.

The café was empty. Although it somehow had been quickly known that Reva and Yulin were no longer shacking up together, the married ladies of the town were still bound and determined to punish Reva for her sinful transgressions. They were boycotting the café, forbidding their men to eat there as well. Instead of Reva's food filling empty bellies, silence filled the empty dining room.

Yulin picked a table close to the door in case he needed to make a hasty exit. He was careful not to make a sound while pulling his chair out from the table. Garrison wasn't so careful.

From the kitchen, Reva heard the sound of a chair scraping across the wooden floor as Garrison took his seat. She came out from the kitchen through the swinging door and saw Yulin and Garrison at a table. Picking up two menus, she pasted a smile on her face and walked over to them. A lock of honey-blonde hair had escaped its hair pin and hung loosely at her temple. Her smile dissolved slightly when Yulin stole a quick, apprehensive glance at her. She tried to move the wayward lock of hair back into place but it resisted every attempt. She resurrected the smile when Garrison grinned shyly up at her as he took his menu. He had never seen a woman so beautiful before.

Reva dropped Yulin's menu on the table. "You *gentlemen,*" she said in a sweet tone while coldly glaring at Yulin, "are welcome to take as much time as you need to look at the menu. I'll check back in a few minutes to see if you're ready to order."

"If you serve ribeye steak and eggs—sunny side up—with biscuits and sausage gravy, I already know what I want," said Garrison, still beaming his shy smile at Reva. "And coffee, please."

Yulin opened his menu and stared at it. He already knew what he wanted, but it was a way to postpone the inevitable moment when he'd have to deal with Reva again.

Reva said, "Well, to be honest, my biscuits and gravy have never been as good as my mother's but I make a mean batch of sourdough rolls."

Garrison put on a mock frown. "Well, biscuits and gravy are my favorites, but I've never had sourdough rolls." He flashed a warm, bracing smile at Reva. "But there's a first time for everything. And it will be especially nice when served by such a beautiful woman as yourself. Sourdough rolls it is."

Yulin's mouth noticeably dropped while Reva's face turned pink with an uncharacteristic blush.

"I'll be happy to bring them right out to you, Mr.— "

"Fleck. But please, call me Garrison."

"Alright...Garrison. I'll be back in a few minutes with your order," said Reva, feeling almost girlish in front of this charming, attractive stranger. Why couldn't some *other* men be like him? she thought, giving Yulin a quick glare.

"I'm looking forward to it," smiled Garrison.

Yulin, tired of being ignored, laid his menu down on the table. "I'd like to eat too, Reva. I'll have the same as *Garrison* here, if you don't mind."

Ignoring Yulin, she took the menu from Garrison. When she grabbed Yulin's menu, she knocked his hat askew with her elbow. Smiling sweetly at Garrison, she said, "I'll be right back with your order." Looking coldly at Yulin, she said, "I just sold the last ribeye. I'll see what I've got left." With that, she walked back into the kitchen.

Garrison, unwrapping his silverware from the rolled linen napkin, looked questioningly at Yulin, who was straightening his hat. Yulin responded, "Don't worry about it."

When Reva emerged from the kitchen with the food on a large silver serving platter, she first set a plate down in front of Garrison. The slab of ribeye steak was magnificently pan-seared, fried to a perfect medium rare. The sunny side up eggs were cooked perfectly, a slight graze with fork tines sending rich, golden yolk oozing onto the plate. She poured coffee out of a china coffee pot into a matching coffee cup on the table in front of him. On Yulin's plate, which she dropped on the table in front of him, was a thin chuck steak burnt to the amazing resemblance of a slab of coal. The eggs were flat and blackened on both sides. From the tray, Reva lightly dropped a chipped, ceramic coffee cup on the table in front of Yulin. After she finished pouring coffee into it, Yulin looked down. There was a dead fly floating in the coffee. "Enjoy your meal," she said sweetly to Garrison. Setting the coffee pot on the table, she walked back to the kitchen, the empty platter tucked under her arm.

"She mad at you or something?" asked Garrison.

Yulin stared down at his plate. "Yeah, it's something alright."

"Well, anyway, you were right. These are some great-looking steak and eggs." Garrison cut the steak and forked a piece into his mouth. He sat back, closed his eyes, and put his hands, holding the knife and fork upright, on the table.

Reva walked through the swinging door, carrying a small serving platter of sourdough rolls. Next to the rolls was a quarter pound of butter molded into the shape of a rose. "As advertised, my homemade sourdough rolls. I started out making sourdough French bread, but this is more of a biscuits town. So, I compromised—sourdough rolls! My customers just love them." She placed the serving platter on the table next to Garrison. She looked with concern at him. "Is there something wrong, Mr. Fle--Garrison?"

A slow smile crossed Garrison's lips. "This steak is...excellent." He opened his eyes and grinned at Yulin. "You should taste it, Sheriff. This woman can really cook." He beamed a smile at Reva.

Yulin looked down at his plate and then looked back at Garrison.

"Ma'am," said Garrison, the smile still playing upon on his face, "I want to say you fry up the best steak this side of Kansas City."

Yulin gave Garrison a stunned look, looked up at Reva, then back at Garrison. Was this smalltime Pinkerton trying to jump his claim on his gal? he thought. Only, it now seemed like there was no claim to jump. Apparently, Reva no longer considered herself his gal.

"I mean everything's just excellent," continued Garrison. He went back to cutting his steak. "The way you cook, ma'am, you'd make some man a fine wife."

"Not every man thinks so," said Reva, shooting daggers at Yulin from behind her brick wall of anger. She turned back to Garrison and smiled sweetly. "And please, call me Reva. But...wait till you try my sourdough rolls. Don't ask me how but the same starter the Boudin French Bakery uses in San Francisco fell into my hands. I've maintained it for the past two years," she grinned proudly. Holding a napkin, she took a couple of warm dinner rolls and placed them on Garrison's plate. She then took a knife and buttered the rolls from a petal on the rose-shaped butter. Turning to Yulin, she took a blackened roll in her bare hand from the platter and dropped it onto his plate with a loud plop.

She looked on expectantly as Garrison picked up one of the rolls, gazed at it for a moment, and then bit into its soft, warm sourdough goodness, melted butter lazily dripping down the sides. He started chewing, sat back in his chair, eyes closed as before...and smiled.

"You're not going to do that all through dinner, are you?" asked Yulin, indignantly.

"With a meal this good, I just might," Garrison opened his eyes and smiled at Yulin. He gave the roll in his mouth a few last chews and swallowed.

Reva was ecstatic. She clapped her hands together. "I just *knew* you'd like them!" Heaving a satisfied sigh, she walked back through the swinging door.

The men turned their heads toward the sound of glass breaking in the kitchen. "Luke!" yelled Reva, "you break one more glass and I will personally throw you outside without opening the door first!"

The men heard a young boy's voice saying, "It was an accident, Miss Reva. I swear."

Garrison laid down his steak knife and combed his fingers through his moustache. He turned to Yulin. "Maybe you should say something to her. About your meal, I mean."

Yulin just stared at his plate. "Not when she's like this. Much easier to just catch something to eat at the Silver Strike later on." He took a spoon and lifted the fly out of his coffee, shaking the deceased insect onto the floor. "There'll be plenty of time for talking after our business with your brother is done."

He looked at the Binghamton detective sitting there, eating his perfectly cooked ribeye. He noticed how the man would run his fingers over and down his well-groomed moustache as he was chewing his food. Jesus, he was *too* good-looking, him with those sad brown eyes. No wonder Reva was treating him like a king. He could hate the guy for that alone. But it would only give Reva another reason to be angry at him. Christ, would this meal never end?

Reva walked back to the table. Raising the coffee pot off the table, she smiled sweetly at Garrison. "Would you care for a refill, Mr. Fleck?"

"Yes, I would, Reva. And as I said, I'd appreciate it if you'd call me Garrison. You're too beautiful to be so formal with me."

Reva blushed again as she refilled his coffee cup. "So, Garrison, you really like my sourdough rolls?"

"They were…exquisite. They may be the closest to 'Frisco I ever get."

"Really? Why, I thank you sir," said Reva with a small curtsey, holding the coffee pot in one hand, slightly lifting her apron with the other hand. "You must be quite the connoisseur."

"No ma'am. I just know fine cooking when it hits my plate."

"I'd like to hit something about now," Yulin muttered, glancing at Garrison.

Reva ignored him. "Is there anything else I can bring you?"

Garrison sat back and flashed his warmest, brightest smile at Yulin and then back at Reva. "You could get a decent meal and a cup of coffee for my friend, the sheriff here. We're hitting the trail tomorrow morning and it might be a while before we make it back."

Yulin's face dropped, a slight panic overtaking him. Reva's face darkened as she looked at Yulin. "What does he mean about you two hitting the trail?"

Yulin began to fidget, trying to find words of explanation. He hadn't wanted to tell Reva about tomorrow's journey, but now he knew there was no way out. Damn that Fleck! "We're setting out to find this man's brother, Reva. He came through here sometime last night. Stole Sam Gilroy's horse from out

in front of the Silver Strike. We'll be heading down to New Mexico Territory"
—narrowing his eyes at Garrison— "early."

Reva was stunned. "Oh my god, Yulin, why didn't you tell me?" Then she
was struck by a thought. Turning to Garrison she said, "Last night? Your
brother stole a horse here in town last night?"

"Yes," said Garrison eyeing her closely. "Why do you ask?"

"Oh my god, what a fool I've been. I thought it was you who broke into
my kitchen," she said, turning toward Yulin. Her wall of anger had started to
crumble.

"What are you talking about?" Yulin asked.

Reva took a moment to gather in her reeling thoughts. "Last night after
you left, I thought I heard someone downstairs in the kitchen. When I came
down to the kitchen this morning to prepare today's menu, I found a meatloaf,
some of my rolls and a bottle of milk missing from the icebox. I thought it was
you, that you had taken food from my icebox."

"You really think I would steal milk? And why the hell would you think
I'd steal *any* food from you?" asked Yulin.

"Because I was mad at you!" said Reva. Yulin stared at Reva then turned
his head away, attempting to make sense of what she had just said.

Reva turned back to Garrison. "My point is, Mr. Fleck—Garrison, it had
to have been your brother who I heard last night."

She turned back to the sheriff. "As for *you,* Yulin Temple," she said, a few
angry bricks still in her crumbling wall, "you should've told me about all this
when you came in here. *Of course* I'll fix you a decent meal. And I'll pack some
food for you both to take on the trail." She hurried off to the kitchen.

"Now you don't have to go and do that, Reva," Yulin called after her. He
turned to Garrison, who had already risen from the table and was following
Reva into the kitchen.

Yulin quickly followed behind Garrison "This is exactly why I didn't want
her to know any of this. Now she'll be fussing all over me and crying when she
says goodbye—and it's all your doing!"

Garrison, not really listening to Yulin, was already through the kitchen
and opening the back door. He stepped outside onto the small loading
platform and leapt over the two wooden steps. He crouched down next to a set
of large hoofprints. By this time, Yulin was standing on the bottom step.

Garrison's finger was pointing at the deep-set impressions in the mud.
"See there? Look at the size of them. *There's* your Belgian. And look at these
bootprints. They're Ike's, alright. He must've walked up the steps into the
kitchen. He took the food, and then went to the saloon where he switched
horses."

Yulin stepped around Garrison to crouch down for a better look at the
sizeable tracks left by the stallion. Fleck was right. The Belgian was the only
horse in town with hoofs that size. The bootprints were of an average-sized
man. He turned to Reva. "Wait—you thought those were *my* footprints?"

She looked back at him and shrugged. "I never looked at them. You slammed the *front* door when you left last night."

"Damn, Ike," Garrison said quietly, "you keep surprising me."

Back at their table, both men were beset by their own concerns. Garrison was now even more anxious to ride off, but he was still very hungry and exhausted. He admitted to himself that even if Ike was still on this side of the border, he was in no shape to ride after him without more rest—and a fresh horse.

Yulin, noticing that Garrison was deep in thought, wondered if Reva would keep her word about serving him something edible. It became a moot point after Reva came back into the dining room with Yulin's new plate of food, laid down a china coffee cup in front of him and filled it with freshly brewed coffee.

"Before you leave here I'll pack you some bacon, my sourdough rolls, and some ground coffee to take with you. That should tide you over for a few days. I wish I could do more but business has been slow"—she glared at Yulin— "lately." She rushed back into the kitchen.

Yulin ate his food and drank some coffee. Finally, a decent meal. He set his coffee cup down on the table. "Before we go riding off, I just want to make sure about what your brother wrote in the note, about him heading down to New Mexico. Do you think he meant it, or was it a ploy to throw everybody off while he heads somewhere else? He's got enough money to go anywhere he damn pleases. Hell, he can hop on a train to New York City and sail off to Europe."

"Ike doesn't think that way. I know him better than anyone else," Garrison said, in between chewing his steak and checking his moustache. "He thinks linear. Once he has his mind set on a thing he never deviates from it. It's what's made him so quick with a gun."

Yulin noted the use of the word "linear". Was this Fleck guy going to keep using all these flashy words down into New Mexico and back? If only a bottle of whiskey could make a man deaf without making him drunk...

Now that Reva had served him some decent food, Yulin no longer felt hungry. He'd been right the first time: more trouble *had* ridden into town. Now he'd have to ride out of town to deal with it. "You said he knew you'd track him. Think maybe he figures you'll try to talk him into coming back with the money? Is that what he wants?"

Garrison fell silent for a moment. "I don't know what to think anymore. I thought I knew Ike, but now...all I know is he's scared. And I think he knows it was wrong to take the money but has figured out a way to give it back. You gotta think like Ike, and my gut tells me his plan is to find the gold so he can return what he stole from Binghamton. In his mind all will be forgiven, and that I'll meet him down there and we'll ride off with the gold together into some rosy future. Nothing else makes sense, as if that does." Garrison paused, looking down at his plate, thinking of Ike. He cut another bite of steak. "Damn fool."

Yulin was convinced the detective was telling the truth. He had to be. If he had been in on the robbery, Fleck could've just ridden through town the way his brother had. But he also thought, *this is why you don't hire a seventeen-year-old kid as a stagecoach guard.*

Reva had been listening at the door before bringing out two overstuffed canvas sacks. "This isn't much but it'll keep your bellies full for a few days. There's two pounds of bacon, two dozen sourdough rolls"—she smiled at Garrison— "and two pounds of coffee. I split them equally between two sacks and wrapped everything tight to make sure nothing spills out." She handed the bags to Garrison, afraid that if she spoke to Yulin she'd start to cry.

Yulin eyed Reva. Was he forgiven or not? "Jesus Christ, Reva," he said, "we're just going down to New Mexico, not out to California."

That did it. She looked teary-eyed at Yulin. "Oh, I just know you're going to get killed."

Yulin said, "I'm not going to get killed."

Reva looked at Garrison. "He's going to get killed, isn't he?"

"I'm not going to get killed!" said Yulin, slightly exasperated. He looked at Garrison. "Right? Tell her I'm not going to get killed."

Garrison looked back at Yulin, then at Reva. "He says he's not going to get killed."

Yulin stood up, and with both hands on Reva's shoulders gently pulled her to him. "Now, Reva, I don't want to go like this." She lowered her head. He reached a curved finger under her chin and gently raised her head to look at his face. "I don't know how long we'll be gone but I promise you that if—when—I do come back we're going to sit down and have a talk to set things right. I just need you to wait for me. Will you do that?"

Reva nodded her head, sobbing quietly. She softly pounded her clenched fists on Yulin's chest. "You better come back, you bastard."

Yulin looked at her tenderly. He bent his head down and kissed her parted lips. She softened only slightly, standing rigidly against his chest. But it was in that slight softening that Yulin could tell how she felt about him. She still loved him. And in that moment, he was convinced that he was in love with her. He found himself saying, "Reva, I'm sorry for how I acted last night. A man would be a damn fool not to come back to you."

And he knew he meant every word. So, did she. He forced himself to let her go and walked out the front door.

Garrison wiped his hands and mouth with his napkin. Saying a quick goodbye to Reva, Garrison followed Yulin out of the café, closing the door behind him. Reva walked over to the door, laid her head against it and started to sob. "I love you, Yulin," she said, softly.

The two men walked side by side down the boardwalk. Yulin stopped Garrison and took from him both sacks of food. "Exquisite?" he asked, glaring at Garrison.

It took Garrison a moment to remember the context of his earlier remark. "Yes. In fact, the entire meal was exquisite."

"There are places where you would be shot dead for flinging around big words like that."

"That's why I usually dumb it down for most people," said Garrison, and resumed walking.

Yulin started to walk but stopped, realizing what Garrison had just said. "Dumb it down for *who?*"

After they returned to the sheriff's office, Garrison flopped down into the chair. Yulin set the canvas sacks on his desk and took his Spencer down from the rifle rack. He glanced over at his prospective traveling companion, already fast asleep in the chair with his head thrown back, snoring loudly. Shaking his head, Yulin laid the carbine on the desk and lifted Garrison up and over his shoulder. He carried him into one of the jail cells and deposited him on the cot. Yulin looked down at the supine form of his guest. "Exquisite," he said, derisively. He plucked Garrison's hat from his head and dropped it on the sleeping detective's face in mid-snore.

Leaving the cell door open, Yulin grabbed the carbine and walked out the office to begin his nightly rounds. He saw Garrison's horse still tied up outside. "Damn," he said. As he walked the black to Gomez's livery stable, Yulin's thoughts returned to Reva. Although he felt they had reconciled, he still couldn't tell her that he loved her. Despite what he had felt back at the café, was he in love with her? Yes, he wanted her in his life, but was that the same thing as love? He couldn't think about that now, not with the task before him yet to be completed. After he returned from New Mexico he'd try to figure it out.

Gomez sleepily answered the knock at his door. After delivering the horse into the Mexican's capable hands, Yulin walked back out into the twilight. As was his custom, he walked down the middle of Main Street, visually looking into windows on both sides. Still having other streets and alleys to check, he had already decided there would be no visiting the Silver Strike tonight, not with the early departure of tomorrow morning.

Meanwhile, Yulin had to figure out where he was going to bunk for the night. Spending the night with Reva was completely out of the question as far as he was concerned. And with that goddamn detective inside the jail, sleeping at the house wasn't an option, either. Not that he didn't trust the guy…OK, he *didn't* fully trust him alone inside the jail, asleep or not. No, he'd have to bunk in one of the other empty cells—*if* he could get any sleep. Christ, that guy was a damn roof rattler.

Having made sure that everything in town was calm—well, as calm as things ever got inside the saloon—Yulin returned to his office. Closing the door, he left it unlocked. After placing his carbine back in the wall rack, he entered the empty cell next to the one where Garrison was sleeping, leaving the door open. Unlocked doors didn't worry him. Years of sleeping out on the range at night gave a man a sixth sense, one that was always awake while he slept. The slightest sound of something nearby that didn't belong jolted him from the soundest sleep, finger already on the trigger of his revolver. No one would ever catch Yulin Temple asleep—literally.

As he sat on the cot inside the cell, he rolled a cigarette. He lit it, laid back on the cot, and blew a perfect smoke ring. As he smoked, he tried not to think of Reva or anything else that would keep him awake. Reva…

Garrison slept fitfully through the night. His dream had changed. He was following Ike's trail but never catching up to him.

Yulin did fall asleep that night. For the first time in years, he found himself dreaming of Lillian, but the face he saw was Reva's. He also dreamed about Weed. He was somehow older and wearing a two-gun rig.

CHAPTER 29

Reva Delgado couldn't sleep. And when she couldn't sleep she baked, a habit she had picked up back in the cattle towns. It was after midnight and she was in her café kitchen baking three dozen sourdough rolls. She would wind up freezing them, serving them at a later time when business picked up.

It didn't bother her that her kitchen had been broken into the night before. Well, it wasn't exactly breaking in since she always left her doors unlocked, keeping a loaded .32 revolver tucked under her pillow at night. The intruder wouldn't have been a threat to her. Besides, he had obviously been a frightened young boy. Cold, almost starving to death, one who she might have fed for free. As long as she kept the gun on him.

She thought with pride how she had taken care of her man, and that sweet Garrison Fleck, too. No, they wouldn't starve on their journey, not if her name was Reva…but that wasn't her real name, was it? She'd come a long way from being Eula Mae Sundstrom, the preacher's daughter. She couldn't and didn't want to go back to that way of life. But what was her life now? A moderately successful businesswoman in a small western town.

And *was* Yulin Temple her man? She had fallen in love with him the first time he walked into the café—but she didn't dare tell him that. Was he in love with *her*? Would he ever be in love with her—or was she just fooling herself? She knew she could compete against any other woman alive and win. But how could she win against a ghost? She knew it wasn't a case of Lillian refusing to let Yulin go, it was just the opposite. He was the one clinging to Lillian's memory. Reva kept telling herself to give him time, that he would come around and realize that he was in love with her. But yesterday, despite all his fancy talk about a man being a fool not to come back to her, Yulin had never said he loved her. But then, she hadn't said it to him either, had she? She had waited until after he'd gone, saying it behind the closed door.

She didn't know how much more time she would give Yulin. What she did know was that Reva Delgado and her current life were both coming to an end. Who and what she would be next were yet to be decided. But she would make no decisions until after Yulin came back. No matter how long it took, she would allow herself to wait that long.

CHAPTER 30

It was still over an hour to sunup when Yulin Temple walked into the jail cell to rouse Garrison Fleck from his sleep. Yulin, dressed in a plaid, long-sleeved shirt, fleece-lined cowhide coat and blue jeans had already been to the livery stable arranging with Gomez to rent the detective a sturdy, sorrel mare. Whether the bill would be paid by Fleck or Binghamton didn't matter to him. Let Gomez and Fleck work that out between them.

Yulin had expected there to be a problem waking Garrison from his deep slumber. But to his surprise, Garrison was already awake and sitting on the edge of the cot, yawning and stretching.

"How'd you sleep?" asked Yulin, more out of cordiality than concern.

Garrison smiled sheepishly. "OK, I guess. Somehow I wound up in one of your jail cells. For a moment I thought you'd carried out your threat to keep me in town. Then I saw you'd left the door open."

"It wasn't *somehow*. I carried you in after you fell asleep in the chair." He looked at the disheveled younger man. "You ready to go?"

Garrison took a last yawn and stretch. "Thought you said you didn't like to start out on an empty stomach." He rearranged his clothes slightly to make himself look more presentable. He smoothed his hair back and put on his hat.

Yulin wished Reva could've seen what this guy Fleck looked like right now after waking up. "I don't, and I'm not. With you pulling your Rip Van Winkle act I didn't know whether you'd wake up today or not. I cooked up a can of beans about an hour ago. Still some left on the stove out there if you're hungry." He walked out of the cell and over to his desk.

"No, thanks" Garrison called after him, "I can get my own breakfast." He stood up, gave his arms a last stretch and went over to the desk to retrieve his rifle. He glanced up to see Yulin's bedroll on top of the desk next to the two canvas sacks.

Yulin noticed Garrison eyeing the bedroll as he took his carbine down from the gun rack. "I like to travel with all the comforts of home," he said, "What I've got in there is worth carrying the extra weight." He opened a desk drawer, took out a couple of boxes of bullets and dropped them into his coat pockets. "How are you fixed for bullets?" he asked.

"I still got plenty," answered Garrison. "Stocked up in Trinidad. Didn't take the time to use any on my ride out here."

"I know," said Yulin, "you were too busy trying to kill your horse."

Garrison ignored the remark and nodded over to the food sacks. "We'll have to ration what Reva gave us. When we find Ike, he's liable to be pretty hungry. We might run out of food pretty quick."

Yulin pointed to the rifle in Garrison's hand. "You got that Winchester. You can prove that you don't carry it just to look stylish."

At the livery stable, two horses were tied to the hitching rail. Gomez had already saddled Yulin's bay, as well as the sorrel Garrison would be riding. He had wanted them ready for when the two men rode out at daybreak. The stable owner, wrapped in a heavy woolen blanket, had fallen asleep in a wooden chair near the horses. He had meant to stand guard but had been unable to stay awake.

Yulin, giving the chair a light kick, loudly said, "Buenos días, amigo!"

Gomez jerked awake but upon seeing Yulin, stretched and yawned widely. "The horses are all saddled and ready, Sheriff Temple. And now if you don't mind, I go back to my own nice warm bed." He stood up. "Adiós. Vayan con dios, mis amigos," he said, and shuffled back to his living quarters attached to the livery stable.

Yulin handed one of the canvas sacks to Garrison and walked over to the bay. He tied his food sack to the bedroll behind the saddle. A coiled rope was tied with a leather strap to the right side of the pommel. Yulin shoved the Spencer into the rifle scabbard hung on the left side of the saddle and took the boxes of bullets out of his coat pockets, stuffing them inside one of the saddlebags. Checking his horse, he noticed the front and back cinches already adjusted the way he preferred them. Gomez was worth the premium rate he charged, thought Yulin. He decided that when he got back to town, the county taxpayers would reward the Mexican with a handsome bonus.

Garrison's saddlebags and bedroll were already on the sorrel, having been transferred from the black. He pulled a heavy, fleece-lined coat off the top of the bedroll roll where Gomez had courteously draped it. Following Yulin's lead, he untied the bedroll and laid the food sack across it before tying them together behind the cantle. After donning the coat, he checked both cinches on the sorrel, finding that Gomez had adjusted them perfectly. That was indeed impressive. He thought that if someday he decided to become a freelance Don Quixote, he'd want this man to be his Sancho Panza.

Garrison untied the horse from the hitching rail, gathered up the reins and climbed into the saddle, sliding the Winchester into the scabbard. Out of a coat pocket, he lifted the venison jerky to his mouth and bit off a piece. Grinning at Yulin he said, "Breakfast. "

Just before he untied the gelding, Yulin muttered, "Be right back. Forgot something." He walked back to his office, returning a few minutes later to hang something from the saddle horn. He untied the gelding from the hitching rail and swung up into the saddle. He backed the horse away from the rail and lightly tapped its sides with his bootheels to start it walking forward. Garrison followed behind on the sorrel.

The first tenuous rays of sunrise were creeping up over the mountain peaks. As they walked their horses down the quiet, early morning street, Garrison rode next to Yulin. He noticed a sawed off twelve-gauge Remington shotgun hanging from the saddle horn by a leather thong.

"Scattergun," commented Garrison, nodding his head toward the Remington.

"Comes in mighty handy if a bunch of Indians charge at you," said Yulin. "Takes the fight out of 'em real quick."

"Yeah. Gully Walton used to carry one just like it. He'd still be alive had he gotten the chance to use it."

The vision of Gully's body lying in the dirt flashed into Garrison's mind. It was the last thing he should be dwelling on now. He quickly replaced it with something else. "Ain't you worried about leaving this town without a sheriff?" he asked, more as a distraction from his thoughts than for conversation.

"Already asked me that yesterday. Answer's still the same. But if you're so worried about it I'll make you deputy and you can stay here while I go fetch your brother."

Garrison stifled a grin. "Didn't say I was worried about it. Just askin' if *you* were worried about it." He waited a few beats. "But what happens when they find out they can do just fine without you?"

Yulin glanced at Garrison. "I never should've woken you up."

This time Garrison allowed himself the grin and added a chuckle. But dark visions were still imposing themselves on his mind. Once again he sought distraction. "Stovepipe's a strange name for a town."

"Town's named after Patrick 'Stovepipe' Monaghan. He loved ol' Honest Abe. Wore the exact same stovepipe hat. Every day, rain or shine he'd be wearing that hat. Quite the entrepreneur, too. Found a small gold deposit somewhere west of here by accident, about a few hundred dollars' worth of nuggets. Took 'em up to Piñon City some thirty-forty miles away and bought some beads and trinkets—and some say rifles—to trade with a tribe of Utes for beaver pelts and tanned deer skins—whatever he could get. No one tanned hides like the Utes. The women sewed those beads into the clothing they made. This was when the Southern Utes were still able to hunt in the San Luis Valley. Stovepipe'd ride back up to Piñon City, trade the skins and furs for cash at a trading post, buy more trinkets and beads—and maybe those rifles—and head back to trade with another tribe of Utes."

Yulin holding the reins in both hands near his chest, took out the makin's and with practiced hands started rolling a cigarette. "One time back in 1860, he was headed up to Piñon with a wagonload of fur skins and tanned deer hides when the wagon broke down, out there by the river crossing where the bridge is now. They found gold in the San Juans the year before, and there were lines of wagons and prospectors on horseback traveling to and from the gold strikes. Well, Stovepipe told anyone passing by that since he needed money to get his wagon wheel fixed he'd sell what he had at bargain prices, take a loss on everything. Tanned deer hides from the Utes were real popular back then and so was beaver fur, so he had people lined up waiting for their chance to buy. He actually got an offer from a gent to fix the broken wagon wheel in exchange for one of the hides but ol' Stovepipe refused. He was doing just fine where he was. Sold every one of those hides and fur skins—and all at his regular price. After he got the wagon fixed, Stovepipe went back to the Utes and got himself more of the same and staged a phony breakdown at that same spot, selling out just like the first time. What he didn't figure on was miners who'd gone bust wanting to sell off whatever they could for whatever they could get for it, just to be able to afford to get the hell out of there. He bought it all dirt cheap and resold it at triple the price to people coming in to try their luck or who had run out of what they needed. It was then he figured out he could make more money staying put than he could riding around among the Utes. He had that bridge built, set up his trading post on this side of the river, and the town grew up around it. I'm told he used to hold court at the Silver Strike telling that story night after night. When he died back in '71 they buried him in that hat."

Cigarette finished, he put the makins' back in his pocket. Placing the cigarette in his mouth, he lit it and blew a perfect smoke ring. He remembered Chet Carson's ridiculous idea for the town's name change. Some men were too stupid to live.

"Ain't that how it always goes," said Garrison. "It ain't the men looking for gold who get rich. It's the men making money off the men looking for gold who get rich."

After they were clear of the town, Yulin noticed that Garrison kept kicking his horse into a fast lope, moving it ahead of Yulin's horse. Sitting ramrod straight in the saddle and keeping his eyes on the trail ahead of them, Yulin kept the bay alternating gaits every couple of miles. When the bay appeared to tire, he'd slow the horse to a walk for another couple of miles and then repeat the sequence. Garrison, usually a few hundred yards up the trail, would look back and rein up the sorrel, waiting for the sheriff to draw up alongside.

After several times of this, Garrison said, impatiently, "Sheriff— "

"I'd appreciate it if you'd start addressing me as Yulin and not "sheriff" 'til we get back to town, Mr. Fleck. The title goes with the badge."

"But you're still wearing the badge on your shirt," said Garrison.

"We're still in my jurisdiction. Once we reach the Rio Grande County border I'll take the badge off. Then you and me'll just be two compadres enjoying a ride through the desert. But before that I want you to get used to calling me Yulin for the duration."

"Well, Yulin," said Garrison, "I work for Binghamton and he calls me Garrison. You might as well call me Garrison, too." He smiled. "Reva does."

"Thank God we got that settled," said Yulin.

They rode on a few more miles in silence.

Garrison was getting a bit fidgety with Yulin's pace. He finally said, "Ain't we going a bit slow? I can *walk* faster than this," he asked with an edge to his voice.

"Slow and steady saves the horse. It's something you and your brother would do well to keep in mind. You won't get anywhere on a dead horse."

They rode in silence for a couple of more miles. "You sure Ike went this way?" asked Garrison.

"If he's the one who stole Sam's horse then yes, he went this way."

"How do you know?"

"Because," said Yulin looking down the trail, "if he's headed where he said he's headed, he has to keep riding south from Stovepipe. There's no more towns this way so we're in no chance of losing him." He pointed his hand at the trail. "Besides, I'm following his tracks. See 'em in the dirt ahead of us there? Hoofprints. Three shod, one without."

Garrison saw them and felt stupid. Here he was supposedly an expert tracker and he'd missed the blue dun's sign. He hated to admit it, but he was grateful that the sheriff was riding along with him. With his mind so distracted by thoughts of all that had happened surrounding Ike and the stagecoach, he most likely would've missed seeing the hoofprints.

They followed the tracks to the thicket where Ike had spent the night after riding out of Stovepipe. They swung down and tied the horses to some low-hanging tree branches, then followed the tracks into the brush. After poking around a bit, they found the empty milk bottle and paper wrappings under the bush where Ike had hidden them. Garrison gathered up the discarded trash and stuffed it inside one of his saddlebags. "Ike steals $400,000 and ain't got the sense to clean up his back-trail," he muttered.

"If he'd had any sense he wouldn't have stolen the money in the first place," Yulin said.

When they had started out in the early morning, they had worn their heavy coats. Four hours later they continued to ride without a break as the day started to heat up. By late morning, the sun was beating down upon them from a blue sky dotted with wisps of white drifting clouds. They were sweating along with the horses, both of which they now held to a walk. Garrison was itching to kick the sorrel into a gallop, but he knew Yulin was right to save the horses for the long journey ahead and back. He could only hope that Ike also had the common sense to pace his horse the same way. But then, Ike and common sense seemed to be strangers these days.

He lifted his canteen from the saddle horn and pulled the cork out with his teeth. He was about to take a sip when he looked over at Yulin. The sheriff was riding stoically, sitting erect, eyes on the trail. "Screw it," he said under his breath, took a swallow, pounded the cork back in and rehung the canteen.

He was about to take off his coat when he noticed Yulin, sitting tall in the saddle, still wearing his. Garrison decided, grudgingly, to leave his on as well. Yulin had seen this out of the corner of his eye. A slight smile formed in the corner of his mouth and he kept on riding.

About an hour later he looked over at Garrison, who was making snickering sounds. "What the hell is that issuing from your yap?"

Garrison was wearing a smirk on his face. "I was just picturing Ike on Sam Gilroy's horse when she decides to pull up lame. He'll be so mad he won't know what to do. Ike doesn't know horses anyway. At least it should slow him down some so we can catch up."

"*If* we catch up," said Yulin.

I'll catch up to him alright, old man, thought Garrison, even if it means leaving you behind. But when he spoke out loud, it was to prod more information from Yulin. Hearing that grouchy voice was better than riding in this intolerable silence assaulted by his own thoughts. "Who's this Spotted Wolf that Ike has to watch out for?"

Yulin had been enjoying that brief moment of silence. He should have shot this Fleck in the leg back in town and made this journey alone. But getting this guy to listen was one way of keeping his mouth shut. He took the makin's out of his pocket and started to roll a cigarette. "He's chief of a band of Utes that live on Bear Mountain. Some years ago he was with the Caputa Ute tribe when they lived in the San Luis Valley. He wasn't a chief then, but he was a great leader among the warriors. I'd never want to go into battle against him. I met him a few months after I became sheriff. Some miner was caught trespassing on their hunting grounds trying to poach whatever he could shoot. Spotted Wolf caught him, brought him back to the village and tied him up till the elders decided what to do with him. The guy's foreman rode into town and told me either I spring him from those savages or the whole mining crew would. After I threw his ass in jail, I rode out to the Ute village. They must've known I was coming because when I rode in, there he was still all tied up and sitting in front of Spotted Wolf's teepee."

Yulin put the rolled cigarette in his mouth, then struck a match against his saddle. After lighting the cigarette, he blew a perfect smoke ring. "So, there's Spotted Wolf sitting on the ground next to his prisoner, probably more to intimidate him than anything else. Funny, but I remember a little kid peeking his head out from the behind the door flap. They pulled him back in real quick. Anyway, the Utes were all set to hand that idiot over to me. Seems like the Utes chiefs were in Washington working out some treaty and Spotted Wolf was under orders not to jeopardize it. He was a proud man and made it plain that giving that miner back was not his idea." He rode silently on, reliving that whole scene in his mind.

Garrison found himself exasperated. "Well? What happened? To the miner, I mean."

Yulin gave a wry smile. "One of the braves helped me sit him on his horse. I left him tied up and led his horse back to town. Also threw his ass in jail next to his foreman. I needed new boots so I charged 'em both a $25 fine, just in case I decided to buy a second pair. After their company paid me the fifty bucks, I turned 'em loose. Never did get around to buying those boots." He tossed the cigarette away.

As cold as the early morning had been, it was baking hot by the afternoon. After six hours on the trail they'd traveled about thirty-five miles. Against Garrison's protestations, Yulin had them rein up at a brushy spot by a shallow creek not far from the trail, knowing that both men and horses needed water and rest. Rising up from the brush was a large scrub oak which is where Yulin dismounted from his horse. He decided not to tell Garrison about the hoofprints that led from the trail down to this spot. The blue dun's tracks continued down a low hill to a small, sandy beach next to the creek. The beach was hidden from the trail behind large growths of cattails and wild grass.

Yulin led the gelding down to the water near the cattails. Glancing down, he saw the tracks of both Ike and the blue dun in the sand. That confirmed that Ike had stopped there some hours ago, perhaps even the day before. Bringing Fleck's attention to these tracks would just get him all riled up again and do something stupid, like ride out of here to chase after his brother. Yulin was already expecting to bury the kid's body. Having to bury both brothers and return with their horses was more work than he had bargained for when he signed up for this wild goose chase.

With food and water at hand, there was no need to tie the bay's reins to anything. He slid the carbine from the scabbard, lifted the food sack from the saddle and untied the bedroll from behind the cantle. He walked a little way up the beach and dropped everything onto the sand. After laying out his tarpaulin, he unrolled the woolen blanket and spread it out, revealing a cast iron skillet and a tin coffee pot. Laying the food sack and the carbine on the blanket, he walked back up the hill to gather sagebrush and fallen tree branches for a fire. Ten minutes later, a crackling campfire provided additional heat to an already scorching day. Yulin unsaddled the bay, leaving the bridle on. The horse paid him no attention, enjoying its lunch break. Yulin carried the saddle and horse blanket over to his chosen spot, dropping it onto the blanket.

Garrison swung down from the mare, taking off his coat and hanging it over the saddle. He was angry. This was no time to stop; Tate Mallory could already be in New Mexico and Ike might never know. Mallory had a reputation as a backshooter. Ike's speed and accuracy with a gun would do him no good with a coward like that.

Yulin ignored him completely. Looking inside the sack, he found that Reva had outdone herself. There was bacon, sourdough rolls, and coffee, along with a tin plate, cup, and eating utensils. He smiled. What was he going to do with a woman like that? But then that was the real decision facing him, wasn't it?

After filling the coffee pot with water from the creek, he got bacon frying in the skillet and the coffee brewing, He surveyed his handiwork as he took a bite of a sourdough roll. "All the comforts of home," he said.

His traveling companion was pacing back and forth in front of the scrub oak. After every couple of turns of direction Garrison would stop to look down the trail.

Yulin, having finished his meal and coffee, was lying on the ground with his head against his saddle, facing Garrison and the hill. He was smoking a cigarette and blowing perfect smoke rings.

Garrison stopped pacing long enough to glare at him. "How can you just lay around at a time like this? Every minute we sit, Ike's getting further ahead of us."

"We'll never catch Ike riding worn out horses," said Yulin. "Besides, we need rest as much as those horses do."

Garrison resumed pacing back and forth. "Well, I can't just stay here. Mallory could already be on Ike's trail. I'm going on without you."

Yulin remained calm. "You, know, there are many kinds of stupid and you're all of them. Take that mare, for instance. She's a damn sight smarter than you. She knows what she needs to do to survive in this heat and she's doing it by standing in place over there. If you were as smart as her, you'd sit down and stop wastin' sweat. You're going to need a lot of it later on to survive in this heat."

"You don't understand," said Garrison.

"I understand more than you think I do." He blew another smoke ring. "Now take a moment and think about it. Who else besides you and me knows Ike rode through Stovepipe? All Sam Gilroy knows is someone stole his horse. I didn't telegraph Fort Garland yet so they don't know where the palomino is. Only three people know your brother rode through town that night. Two of them are us, and Reva won't say a thing to anyone. So, how the hell would Mallory know where Ike is now? Even you don't know where Ike is now."

Garrison stopped his pacing and scowled at Yulin. He didn't yet want to admit to himself that the sheriff was talking sense.

"I already told you I won't let you ride alone. Now, if you feel like challenging my authority, you're welcome to try. Last night I told you I'd shoot you in the leg to stop you. Now, after riding in all this heat, I'm a bit tired. I might aim for your leg but hit you a mite higher up. So unless you want to start singing soprano for the rest of your life, you'll stay here til I say it's time to leave. *Comprende?"*

Garrison knew his non-existent speed with a gun was no match for the sheriff's. Drunk or sober the man was a natural born killer. But he also knew Yulin was right. There was no way Mallory would be on Ike's trail this soon. Furthermore, to keep the horses moving without water and rest in this heat could be foolhardy, even lethal. He followed Yulin's advice and led the sorrel down the creek but kept the bridle and saddle on.

The horses, refreshing themselves, stood next to each other while twitching their various muscles. Garrison quietly said, "Shit," walked over and unsaddled the mare. He carried the saddle and blanket over to the scrub oak, dropped it, and then sat down heavily in front of the saddle, arms crossed and still scowling at Yulin.

"We've got about five-six hours to reach the border, said Yulin. "It'll be sundown by then. I know a place along the Rio de los Pinos where we can camp for the night. The trail we're on will take us within a mile of it. There's a line of trees along the river that'll screen us from the trail so we shouldn't expect any visitors. Early tomorrow morning we'll cross from there over into New Mexico. With any luck we'll meet up with Ike in a couple of hours. That's the plan I've worked out so far."

"That's quite a plan," said Garrison. "But what if Ike ain't stopping for the night? He hasn't shown much sense yet. And what if he gets lost off the trail someplace? How do we find him then? What if he runs out of water? And while you're at it, got a plan worked out for if the Indians grab Ike and we gotta go get him?"

"I've got time to do all that. Or I'll make it up as I go along."

Garrison looked annoyed. "I could do that on my own."

This was the spark that lit Yulin's ire. Raising himself on an elbow, he glared angrily at Garrison. "You don't know shit about this country. Tracking holdup men around those towns up north is schoolkid stuff compared to tracking a man down here. And you can't even follow the tracks of a three-shoed horse when they're right under your nose."

Garrison was lost for a moment, then looked down. It was then he saw the tracks of Ike and the blue dun mare. His eyes followed them down to the creek. His initial reaction was to saddle the mare and challenge the sheriff to stop him from riding off. But common sense dictated he had to agree with the sheriff; he was every kind of stupid. He would be no good to Ike if he died trying to reach him.

"Now, I'm going to shut my eyes for the next"—Yulin pulled out his pocket watch— "hour. Then I'll put out the fire, and we'll saddle up. We'll continue to follow Ike's tracks and hope that we find him before the Utes do." Yulin lowered his head back down onto the saddle, flicked the cigarette away and lowered his hat over his eyes.

The pocket watch reminded Garrison of the one he had given Ike. He had forgotten to show him how to wind the watch. Yet another way he had failed his little brother. He had never felt so helpless in his life, not even after the deaths of his mother, and Uncle Roy. No matter what, he had always come up with a plan for him and Ike. He had no such confidence now. For the first time in his life, he felt wholly dependent on someone else. Yet with Ike's life hanging in the balance, the sheriff was taking a nap.

All kinds of threats filled Garrison's mind. If *this* happened to Ike, Garrison would do *that* to the sheriff. Every threat remained unspoken, tossed away with no real consideration. And then clarity came to the mind of Garrison Fleck. Whatever happened to Ike would not be this sheriff's fault. Ike was in control of his own destiny. "Oh Ike," he said quietly.

The smell of cooked food and coffee had finally gotten to Garrison. He was starting to resent Yulin being right all the time. But he decided that feeding his stomach was more important than feeding his pride. He slowly walked down to the sorrel and took his food sack from the saddle. Over at the fire, he sat down with the sack and opened it up. Both sacks were packed the same way. Reva had thought of everything, even down to the eating utensils. He smiled and looked over at Yulin. That man did not deserve a woman like her. While the bacon was frying in the skillet, he poured what remained of the hot coffee into his tin cup and took a sip. It was damn good. He then grabbed a sourdough roll and dropped it into the skillet to warm in the bacon grease. While Garrison was cooking, Yulin managed a sideways glance from under his hat brim. He grinned and closed his eyes.

A bit later while chewing on a slice of bacon, Garrison decided to speak his mind. "You know, I ain't seen you take a drink today. From what I'd heard, you pick up a bottle first thing when you wake up and don't set it down till you pass out early the next morning. I was worried about it."

Yulin's hat was still over his eyes. Damn, why did that guy choose to talk now? "Well, I'm sorry I troubled your mind. There's no accounting for what people say about me. If I only hear the truth once in a while I figure I'm ahead of the game."

"It's just that I need you sharp—and sober."

Yulin pushed the hat back on his head, lifted himself onto his elbow and stared coldly at Garrison. "That's right, you young buck. You need me. And what I need is for you to do every single thing I tell you *when* I tell you to do it. Ike is going where he is definitely not wanted, and they'll feel the same way about us. I didn't want to make this ride but I am one hundred percent committed to it. And get this straight: I don't drink when I'm on a job—and nobody riding with me does either. Now if you'll excuse me, I'm taking that nap." With that, he laid his head back down on the saddle, again placing his hat over his eyes. He took his gun out of its holster and laid it across his chest.

While Yulin dozed, Garrison lost himself in thought. His confidence in his own judgment had been shattered. Everything was out of his hands. Yes, he needed the sheriff. But there was something about this Yulin Temple that was inspiring trust. He felt it to his core. It was now clear that Richland had never met the man. Yulin might be a heavy drinker, but the man was no drunk.

When it seemed to Garrison that an hour had passed, he walked over to the fire and threw dirt on it. He went over to the creek and filled his hat with water. He doused the fire as smoke joined with steam rising in the air. Grabbing the reins to his horse, he led the mare back under the oak, throwing on the blanket and saddle as noisily as he could to roust Yulin from his nap.

When Yulin remained motionless, he moved to within a few feet of the recumbent form. "Ain't it time we got movin'?"

Yulin was already awake. He slowly pushed his hat back from his eyes and checked his pocket watch. "Yeah, you're right." He rose up from the ground and holstered his gun. "It's time we head out if we're going to make it to the river before dark."

Garrison was already in the saddle as Yulin was saddling the bay. Yulin removed the badge from his shirt and stuck it in his shirt pocket.

"We at the county border?" asked Garrison.

"Nope. Passed it, some fifteen miles back. We're in Conejos County now."

Garrison was exasperated. "You coulda told me."

"No reason to. You ain't been calling me sheriff." Yulin stepped into the saddle and trotted the bay back onto the trail. Garrison stared after him, then kicked the sorrel into a lope to retake the lead.

Chapter 31

After leaving the creek, the two men rode in silence for a long while. Garrison was on edge, wishing he could gallop down to the border. He was afraid that Ike had already been captured by a band of Utes and was being held prisoner in their village. Or he was dead.

Yulin was thinking about Reva. Despite what he had said at the café, was he in love with her? Could he love any other woman after Lillian? He had fleeting images of Weed but forced himself not to dwell on them. He was sure he would never have a son again. Even if things did work out with Reva, he was just too old to start raising a new family. He wasn't sure he even wanted to make the effort. Finally shutting down all those thoughts, he just kept his eyes on Ike's trail. Besides, there was no sense in making any plans if he didn't come out of this alive.

Just before sundown, Yulin led them away from the trail to a spot on the Rio de los Pinos just above where it joined with the Rio San Antonio. Here they would camp for the night, just a few miles from the border. As Yulin had said, their campsite was shielded from the trail by a long stand of cottonwoods. The trees, in turn, were hidden behind a line of low, grassy hills. Anyone riding the trail at night would never see the glimmering light from the campfire down near the river.

This time the horses were hobbled so they wouldn't stray from camp while the men slept. As Garrison was laying out his bedroll in the soft dirt, he kept seeing a vision of Ike wrangling with that blue dun mare. He and the sheriff had ridden a little over fifty miles today on two good horses surrounded by the oppressive desert heat. He couldn't imagine how Ike, riding Sam Gilroy's recalcitrant horse, could be that much farther ahead. He told himself tomorrow would be the day they caught up. It had to be. He had a gut feeling that time was running out.

Yulin again gathered up some dried brush and fallen branches and lit a fire. Both men laid out their bedrolls just near enough to the fire to be warmed throughout the night. The two canvas food sacks lay open on the ground near the fire. After making coffee, Yulin forked bacon slices around inside the cast iron skillet. Garrison had fashioned a skewer from a thin tree branch and was warming the sourdough rolls a few inches from the fire. Yulin's coffee pot sat on the rock fire ring, the freshly brewed coffee inside kept hot by the heat of the crackling flames.

When the rolls were done to Garrison's liking, he pushed two off the skewer onto his plate, and two onto Yulin's plate. Then bundling up a handkerchief in his hand, he grabbed the coffee pot, filling both coffee cups. After he took his first sip, Garrison nodded his approval. The sheriff had just grown in his estimation. This coffee was even better than before. A man who made good coffee was a man you could just about trust.

While they were eating, Garrison started the conversation, again to take his mind off Ike. "You sure know how to make coffee. I thought that back at your office."

"It's a gift," said Yulin, quoting Reva's words from the café. He chuckled softly.

"What?" asked Garrison.

"Something came to mind. Forget it."

Garrison tore a roll in two, stuffed some bacon in the middle, and made a sandwich. As he was chewing, he ran his fingers across and down his moustache. "So, what's the story between you and Reva?"

The timing of the question startled Yulin. Recovering quickly, he answered, "The story between me and Reva is none of your damn business." He ripped at a sourdough roll with his teeth, barely missing his fingers.

Garrison started laughing. "But it was pretty funny how she served you that burnt food. And that dead fly in your coffee was an awful nice touch. She's probably about as in love with you as she was mad at you."

"I said it ain't none of your damn business." Having gulped down the first roll, Yulin now took his annoyance out on the second one, attacking it more than just biting into it.

"OK, then," said Garrison. "I'm curious to know the real reason why you rode with me to fetch Ike. This whole thing is none of *your* damn business— and I ain't buying that peacekeeping with the Utes business."

"OK," said Yulin, "I've grown used to your company." He flashed a sardonic smile, raising his coffee cup.

"That's a bullshit answer if I ever heard one," said Garrison, dryly.

Yulin stared back at him. "You think I'm in this for the bounty money? You can go to hell." He flung his plate and cup to the ground as he stood up and walked away.

Garrison hadn't thought that at all, but he still wanted an answer. "That still doesn't tell me why you rode along with me."

"Because enough men have died over Binghamton's horseshit scheme." Yulin angrily pointed at Garrison. "And your damn scheme, too! You had no right to involve Weed and put his life at risk. I won't let him die!"

For a moment, Garrison was dumbstruck. "Wait a minute here. Who's Weed?"

"I didn't say Weed. I said Ike. Your brother."

"You said Weed. What's this all about, Yulin?" Garrison was now wondering if he had saddled himself with a crazy man.

Yulin just stood there, trying to make sense out of his own thoughts. Had he said Weed? He realized he had. His hands relaxed as he lowered his head. He sat down, staring at the blazing campfire as if he could see memories from his past playing across it. "Weed was my boy. He died along with his ma—my wife Lillian—of yellow fever a long time ago. Long time ago." He kept staring into his past for another few seconds. "Weed would've been Ike's age by now. I don't know, there was something about the way Ike looked in that picture. Got me thinkin'. Weed might've looked like that had he gotten the chance to…to grow up."

Yulin paused, using his shirtsleeve to wipe a rolling tear from his cheek. It had been years since he had allowed himself to dwell, at least consciously, on the memories of his lost family, on what saving that one hundred dollars had cost him. Turning away from Garrison, he said, "I'm sorry." He picked up the cup and plate and sat down near the fire. His appetite gone, he just looked into the flames, seeing the ashes of his life.

"I had a ranch once outside of La Grange, down in Texas. Still there for all I know. Started it from nothing. Came time to drive my first herd up to Abilene, Kansas, and I chose to head the drive myself. Left my foreman in charge of the ranch while I was gone for three months. When I got home, Emmett—the foreman—met me at the front porch and told me about a yellow fever epidemic, and that Lillian and Weed were gone." Yulin looked down, coughed and wiped his nose. "Spent a couple of days at their graves. Know what I did next? Deeded the ranch over to Emmett, right then and there, an' rode off. Never been back." He paused. "It was a nice ranch."

Garrison didn't know what to say, so he said nothing. It was all clear to him now. He wasn't yet sure how he felt about the sheriff, even with this new revelation. Ike wasn't some dead kid named Weed, he was *his brother*, damn it. And Ike was alive. But whatever the reasons for riding with him, Garrison was glad to have Yulin's company—and his gun. He knew he could count on the sheriff if things got rough.

But a sudden awareness dawned on Garrison; he realized he was actually growing to *like* this man that he had just gotten to know. There was a connection that they shared; one of regrets, and of the pain that comes from loss. Unexpectedly, Yulin had opened up about the emotional burdens he bore. Garrison would return the favor, but for him it would be a confession of his sins. Not expecting absolution, he still felt compelled to make that confession to somebody. Why not Yulin?

"I never should've gotten Ike that job," he said. "I thought I was giving him what he needed."

"Just like you've always done," said Yulin. "You told me about it back in town."

Now it was Garrison's turn to gaze into the past. "I've had to be both father and older brother to him since we were kids. Maybe I held him on too tight a rein or maybe I just tried to provide too much for him. I don't know. Ike was always different from other kids. He always needed taking care of, even after he got older. I thought by getting him that job with Binghamton I'd be giving him a chance to grow into a man. Maybe it worked. Look how far he's gotten, how he's learned to survive on his own."

Garrison had his knees folded up; arms wrapped around his legs. "I know Ike wants me to follow him. But I don't know what he expects once I find him. Does he want me to convince him to ride back and return the money? Or does he expect me to ride off with him and his gold? And what happens when I tell him there ain't no gold to be found? You know, I gave Binghamton my word I'd bring back his money, and he gave me his word he wouldn't send anybody after Ike. Here, I'm undecided about what I'll do once I reach Ike, and Binghamton's brought in Tate Mallory. Seems like nobody's word is worth shit anymore."

Yulin wasn't sure how to respond. "When the time comes I'm sure you'll do the right thing," he said. It was the best he could think of.

"Well, thanks for the vote of confidence," Garrison said, dryly. "We'll just have to see how this thing plays out, I guess." He decided he'd had enough to eat. He stood up and threw the rest of his food into the fire. He walked back to his blanket and sat down.

Yulin decided to let that remark pass. He stood up. "Just remember to keep that Winchester inside the scabbard tomorrow till I say different." He walked over to the river and started washing his plate and cup.

Garrison called out, "You'll put me at a disadvantage."

"It's better than you puttin' us both in the ground," answered Yulin. Shaking the water out of the cup, he walked back to his blanket and sat down, dropping the tinware. "I make it a point to not look like I'm looking for trouble, but I keep my guard up just the same. I keep the peace in town the same way. Haven't had to draw my gun on anyone since I killed Brink Jeffords. Anyway, gettin' late. We better get some sleep. I figure thanks to Sam's horse we should be gaining on Ike. We should overtake him about midday tomorrow. Hopefully."

A thought occurred to Garrison. "You told me that Spotted Wolf doesn't like trespassers. Then how do we explain what we're doing there?" asked Garrison.

Yulin replied, "I'm kinda hoping we don't have to. But if we do, leave it to me." He took the makin's out of his shirt pocket and started rolling a cigarette. "I get to sleep better when I smoke. Think better, too," he said.

He offered the cigarette to Garrison, who rarely smoked but accepted it. Garrison ignited the end of a long stick with the fire and held the flame to the cigarette. Inhaling deeply, he let the smoke out in a slow, satisfying stream.

Yulin rolled another one for himself, using the end of the flaming stick to light it. They both sat back taking drags on their cigarettes. Yulin blew perfect smoke rings one after another as Garrison looked on in admiration.

"Never could do one of those," Garrison said.

"Trackin' a man down for the bounty on his head can take weeks and I did it a long while. Leaves a lot of time to be filled," said Yulin.

"You don't think I haven't put in the same amount of time tracking down stage robbers? I filled the time by reading Poe." Garrison looked at Yulin. "Edgar Allan Poe. Ever heard of him?"

"Not if I never saw him on a wanted dodger." Yulin leaned his head back and blew another series of smoke rings.

"He wrote some great detective stories. *Murders In The Rue Morgue, The Mystery of Marie Rogêt, The Purloined Letter.* They're like textbooks for teaching you how to investigate and solve crimes. It's helped me in my work." Garrison paused, a distant look filling his eyes. "My uncle gave them to me a long time ago. I usually carry them everywhere. Kind of forgot to pack them in my rush to trail Ike."

"I caught my share of wanted men without reading books. You, however, still can't blow a smoke ring for shit," said Yulin, blowing another one towards Garrison.

"Well then, we're even cuz I bet you can't read for shit." Garrison was silent for a moment. His mood had changed. "I should've been there for Ike. I should've found another line of work that kept me home where I could have watched over him. I shouldn't have left him for weeks at a time."

Yulin looked at Garrison. "It had to be done. When a man finds out what he's good at, that's what he does to support his family. You'd be no better clerking in some general store than I'd be. You can't control everything that happens to your family. You just do the best you can and hope it all works out, that they've had a good life, and maybe in the end they're standing over your grave saying nice bullshit about you."

Garrison thought about this. "Well, maybe you're right. Just like driving that herd from Texas up to Abilene. It was your cattle, your ranch on the line. You had to be the one to do it. You did what had to be done for your family. No way you could've known about the yellow fever. No one can fault you for that."

Both men were silent. For Yulin, a gray, obscuring fog was starting to dissipate. It was like a dim light, or the promise of something he wasn't sure about yet, trying to break through that fog. But Fleck—*Garrison*—was right. Sometimes you can do everything right only to have it turn out bad, but it's nobody's fault. He had said as much to Garrison himself, so he had to have known this all along. Giving voice to these thoughts had helped him realize it.

He just had to decide how Reva fit into all this.

Garrison wished he could fully believe the words he had spoken to Yulin. The truth was that he didn't. Well, that was only partially true. He had so much to figure out. Meanwhile Ike was out there in Ute territory, all alone. Suddenly, he felt the need to share something else with Yulin.

"Remember back in Stovepipe when I told you that Ike knew I would track him?"

"Yeah," answered Yulin. "What about it?"

Garrison hesitated a moment. "Truth is, I didn't know where the hell Ike was. I lost his tracks coming into town. I was beat, no sleep for days. I heard you were a drunk but I was desperate for help."

Yulin spat a bit of loose tobacco from his mouth. "Hell, I knew you'd lost his trail when we first set out from town. But I sure hope you're coming to some kind of point here."

"Yes, the point is I was wrong about you. I hate to admit it, but I don't know what I would've done had you not taken the lead to find Ike,"

"You would've made it fine on your own," said Yulin, blowing another smoke ring.

"I hope you shoot better than you tell lies," said Garrison. "Maybe I might've. I don't rightly know anymore."

The daytime heat had now been replaced by the cold desert night air. After the food and coffee had been packed away inside the sacks, both men lay on their bedrolls, their heads on their saddles, blankets drawn over them. The fire continued to crackle and hiss as it began to burn itself out. They would let it smolder all night. Yulin was smoking a cigarette, but no longer blowing smoke rings.

Garrison looked up at the stars, wondering if Ike was looking up at the same sky. He hoped so. It might be the last connection they'd ever share. He tried not to think how scared his little brother must be right now.

He felt the need to share yet something else with Yulin. "The night I saw Ike off on that stage, I had a dream later on. Still have it most every night. Ike and me are standing in the desert next to a stagecoach. He's holding a bag of money and I'm pointing my gun at him. I tell him to drop it or I'll have to shoot him. He just stands there. I warn him again. 'Drop the bag, Ike, or I'll shoot you.' He goes for his gun and I fire. But he just smiles at me and when I look again, his holster is empty, he doesn't have a gun. Instead he's holding the bag of money out to me. It drops from his hand…and then he vanishes. That's when I wake up." He looked over at Yulin. "What do you think it means?"

Yulin was silent. He wasn't good at these things. Then he said, "I think it's your dream and only you can know what it means."

Garrison realized Yulin was right. Only he could know what the dream meant. And then he looked at Yulin. He had always thought you could learn who a man was by following his trail. He now realized that the only way to truly know a man was by riding the trail with him. "At any rate," said Garrison, "you're OK, Yulin."

"Glad I meet with your approval." Yulin took a final drag on his cigarette and flicked it into the dying campfire. "You're OK, too, Garrison. Just a bit talkative is all."

Both men held a gun in their hand as they lay under their blankets. Yulin's was on his chest, Garrison's at his side. Yulin fell asleep within minutes. Garrison would stay awake most of the night.

CHAPTER 32

Territory of New Mexico

Under the starlit sky, Ike Fleck was fighting to stay awake in the saddle until he ultimately lost the fight. The horse, as exhausted as its rider after a long, hot day on the dusty trail, was managing to just keep walking forward. It was also very hot and thirsty. Ike hadn't come across another source of water since they left the creek hours earlier.

During the night after Ike had fallen asleep in the saddle, the blue dun crossed the border into New Mexico. As the horse kept plodding along in its tired gait, it finally smelled the waters of the Rio San Antonio. Following its nose, the mare had wandered off the trail to the river where it could quench its thirst.

Ike was awakened by the light from the rising sun pressing against his eyelids. He found himself atop the horse—also asleep—standing beside the rushing waters of the river. As luck would have it, he was less than fifteen miles from where Garrison and Yulin had spent the night upriver.

It had taken Ike two days to get to the river from Stovepipe. The horse continued to cost him valuable time. He avoided riding the mare at a gallop for more than a couple of miles, but it seemed to express the same displeasure at staying in a lope for about that same distance. His only choices had been to keep the horse in a walk or in a body-jarring trot. This past week Ike had ridden horseback more than he ever had in his entire life. But all the extra effort taken to avoid being thrown from the saddle by the Belgian had paid off. He no longer bounced up and down when the mare was trotting, but it continued to be hard on his body.

At least the horse had gotten him this far, and he hoped this would be the day he made it to Three Rocks Trace Pedras and the Frenchmen's gold. A realization then hit him: he had nothing to dig holes with! Son of a bitch. He should've looked around that kitchen for a shovel or something.

That realization led to another: it could be very difficult to find the exact spot where the gold was buried. Why hadn't he thought of this before? Ike had pictured in his mind a place with three large rocks, and right in front of them a dark patch of freshly turned earth. But men hiding gold would make sure it wasn't easily found. Still, hadn't Duke said the trail would lead him straight to it? So maybe it wouldn't be so hard to find after all. But he still didn't have a shovel.

All he could do was follow the trail down to where he would see the three rocks, find a hiding spot—one where he could still see the trail in both directions—and then wait for Garrison to arrive. Garrison most likely knew all about the Frenchmen's gold so, planning ahead as he always did, he would already be carrying two shovels.

Nearby, patches of snow lay on the ground, while dollops of it clung to the branches of trees and shrubs. The snow was progressively thawing under the onslaught of the unseasonably hot weather of mid-April. Amid all this beauty, Ike panicked. *Always keep to the trail, Ike. That way you'll never get lost. It'll always get you to your destination.* "Son of a bitch, Uncle Roy," said Ike, "how am I going to find my way back to the trail?" He jumped down from the mare, which startled it awake, and began walking around, trying to think things through. As Ike paced nervously over the snow and mud, he looked down and saw the mare's hoofprints extending back in the direction from which it had wandered off the trail.

Ike let out a loud "Whoop!" and slapped his hat against his leg in joy. Ike swung back into the saddle and kicked the mare into a trot as he followed the tracks. He reined up at the point where the snow and mud gave way to dry soil and brush, bending over the horse's side nearer to the ground in an effort to find the hoofprints. He was able to see them in the dirt. All he had to do was keep following them and he'd reach the trail. He smiled and kicked the horse into a full gallop. Wouldn't Garrison be surprised when he found out his little brother knew how to follow horseprints!

Ike was lucky. The blue dun had only strayed a little over a mile from the trail. It took just minutes to return to the exact spot where the horse had wandered off with its sleeping rider. Ike had hoped that Garrison would have picked up his trail and be waiting for him, but his brother was nowhere in sight. He began to worry, not about the posse following him but that perhaps Garrison just wasn't coming, that Mr. Binghamton had talked him into letting that posse capture him instead. Well, if they did, he was ready for them. But *where* was Garrison?

To make matters worse, the hunger pangs had returned. The food he stole from the café was gone. But he couldn't worry about his hunger now. He was almost to his destination, the end of the trail. He would worry about finding something to eat later. He lifted the canteen and shook it. There was still water inside so he was OK there. He drank some of it, figuring it might help him to feel less hungry.

Riding out from the Rio San Antonio he had come from behind a large mountain, actually a dormant volcano still commonly referred to by its old Tewa name, Bear Mountain. Now back on the trail, Ike oriented himself. Bear

Mountain was on his right. He looked off into the distance straight ahead. There was a tall mountain across the desert that didn't seem that far away. That had to be the other mountain Duke had told him about, Ute Mountain. He pictured the mountain full of Utes crowded all over it. He sure was glad he didn't have to ride past there.

But this meant he was still headed in the right direction towards Three Rocks Trace Pedras. He wanted to reach his destination today—and that unexpected side trip to the river had cost him time. He turned the mare onto the trail and kicked it into a gallop. He had to make up for all that lost time. The son of a bitch horse would just have to limp the rest of the way.

*****

It was mid-morning near Tres Piedras. The burnt orange that had suffused the early morning light had progressively become paler and brighter as the sun climbed higher in the sky. The long shadows cast by the rock formations, and those of the pinion, juniper trees and sagebrush, were growing shorter. The warming air had displaced the cool night air still loitering after dawn. The blast furnace heat from the sun would not come until later.

Even though the days had grown hot, snow still encircled the top of Bear Mountain, the highest point on the Taos Plateau volcanic field. The winters were especially hard on the mountain. Heavy rains blown by strong winds would drench everything in their path. Great blizzards would blanket the entire mountain in snow. But while the forests of pines and aspen slept under their white blanket, the mountain served as the winter home to several thousand elk, the largest gathering in the entire territory. There was plenty of other large game as well. Pronghorns, mule deer, bears and mountain lions wintered on Bear Mountain. Hawks and golden eagles glided along the air currents, searching for food among the white-tailed jackrabbits and other small creatures below.

This abundance of wildlife, trees and grassy meadows teeming with wildflowers nurtured and sustained the small refugee band of Ute Indians led by Chief Spotted Wolf. With natural sources of water scarce, in the winter the women would gather snow into clay jugs and basketry water jars sealed with pitch. During the summer months, the men would ride out across the desert plains to the river and fill the containers with water.

But the primary reason for choosing the mountain as the site for the new village was its unique geological formation. It rose twenty-three hundred feet above the desert floor and its wide, rounded peak afforded a panoramic view of the entire Taos Plateau. Advancing war parties or columns of white soldiers could be seen from miles away in all directions, giving the warriors adequate time to make preparations for an attack.

Spotted Wolf's brothers had urged him to approach their old allies, the Jicarilla Apache, to propose a new mutual protection alliance. But he knew they would reject his proposal. The Jicarilla had long lived in peace with the white settlers and soldiers. In 1873, a delegation was sent to President Grover Cleveland requesting that a portion of their own land be set aside as a permanent reservation. The Jicarilla remained waiting patiently—and peacefully—for that request to be granted.

Spotted Wolf counseled his brothers to adopt the same nonviolent ways of the Jicarilla so that the white soldiers might leave them in peace as well. But they only promised to avoid any contact with white men, other than the ones they traded with for guns and whiskey, and to only attack those who threatened them or the tribe.

And so, it was into this uneasy truce a hunting party rode that morning out onto the sagebrush-dotted grasslands of the desert plains.

Left Arrow was excited this day. It was his first opportunity to go hunting with the men. He had ridden out from their village with his father Chief Spotted Wolf, his older brother, two uncles, and two older cousins. It would be something to tell the other children at the upcoming Bear Dance. Theirs was much smaller than the Bear Dance celebrated on the Reservation, but the men refused to travel there, fearing that once they were on reservation land, the Indian Agent and the white soldiers would not allow them to leave. However, their own Bear Dance in the mountain village would still be festive

Spotted Wolf was a renowned warrior who had opposed the signing of all treaties with white men. His family was a part of a small band of Caputa Utes who had refused to take part in the 1873 Brunot Agreement negotiations. The Southern Ute tribes had agreed to sell their lands in the San Juan Mountains, rich with gold and silver, to the federal government, which essentially deeded the lands over to the resident mining companies. Through a surveying oversight Ute farmland in the San Luis Valley, which was excluded from the treaty, had been combined with the ceded territory. After Congress approved the Agreement in April 1874, towns and settlements sprang up quickly in the abundant, fertile farmland which had been stripped of its federal protection. Within a few years the tribes, forced from their remaining homeland in violation of the treaty, relocated to the Southern Ute Reservation to the west.

Spotted Wolf, however, had led his family away from their village after tribal leaders signed the Agreement in September 1873. The small band, including his brothers and their families, traveled down to their ancient ancestral lands in the northern part of the Territory of New Mexico, settling on Bear Mountain. Over the years, other bands of Utes had followed. Now, all members of this small community had acknowledged Spotted Wolf as their tribal chief.

Left Arrow had been born four years before his family had fled the San Luis Valley. He could barely remember his old home. The mountain was all he knew, and he loved it. During the winter, he was able to watch the men hunt the great elk herds. By mid-spring, the elk along with the mule deer and antelope, migrated to the desert plains below. This is where the hunting party was heading, and he was its newest member.

Left Arrow wasn't yet allowed to carry a rifle. Those weapons were only for the men. But he had his bow and arrows and could hit any target he aimed at—as long as it wasn't too far away. He had already killed his first jackrabbit up on the mountain. Today, Left Arrow hoped to kill his first antelope. Naturally more curious than deer, an antelope would stand and look at a hunter slowly creeping toward it. Once the hunter crossed some invisible line, the antelope would quickly bolt out of range. Left Arrow was not adept at creeping slowly. In fact, he usually scared off any animal he was stalking. It frustrated him, despite his father's assurance that he would become better at it with time and practice.

Chief Spotted Wolf was troubled this day. He and his warriors were running out of bullets for their rifles, and the gun sellers still had not come. Thankfully, his band was not at war with other tribes and the white soldiers were leaving them alone. But war, as it inevitably does, would come, and his tribe was not ready for the fight. Wars could no longer be won with just bows and arrows and tomahawks. They would need those bullets for the rifles.

It was a federal crime to sell or trade guns and ammunition with Indian tribes, whether living on a reservation or not. Intermittent cavalry patrols along the Colorado border had made gunrunners more cautious about crossing into the Territory of New Mexico, their visits to Spotted Wolf's tribe becoming more infrequent. The wagons filled with rifles and whiskey had always arrived with the spring. So far, they had not come this year. The tribe hoarded the ammunition that was left, worried that the traders would not show up at all. Although they carried Henry rifles, the men hunted only with bows and arrows. Rifles were solely for protection against an attack by animal or man.

The tribal chief led the hunting party out to an area of granite rock formations to the east of Tres Piedras. One of the formations stood apart from the others. Shaped like a long, shallow band shell, the Utes called it The Meeting Rock. The gunrunners would set up shop in front of it, trading rifles and bullets for animal pelts and tanned hides. A wide fissure split the rock in two, creating a broad passageway leading between both halves of the band shell. A natural granite wall stood at the head of the passageway; on each side of the wall were gaps that led out to where the trade negotiations took place. During the first meeting, a group of warriors hid behind the wall, ready to launch a counterattack should the gun traders start shooting. Since such an incident would be bad for business, no violence ever occurred. Eventually, mutual trust developed between both parties and no one stayed hidden.

Spotted Wolf had chosen to hunt near The Meeting Rock. In this way, if the gun sellers did arrive he would be nearby. But at the same time, he had looked forward to hunting today. His leadership had been needed for the past months. There were dissidents in the tribe longing to return to the reservation and rejoin families they had left behind. It had taken every bit of his commanding influence, charisma and negotiating abilities to keep them from leaving the village.

Today, he was finally off the mountain and would be riding and hunting in flat, open country. He loved to chase after a small herd of deer, scattering them so he could then pick off which one he would hunt down and kill. In these moments he was no longer the chief of a tribe, weighed down by the responsibilities of keeping the tribe together, fed and safe. He was now only a hunter, riding freely on the desert plain.

But he was not totally free, was he? thought Spotted Wolf. Although his older son could take care of himself, and his daughter remained under her mother's care, there was his youngest child, Left Arrow. After much badgering by the boy, he had agreed to allow Left Arrow to accompany the men on the hunt, more to silence him than anything else.

He loved his son but had to admit the boy was clumsy and loud. If they were to bring fresh meat back to the tribe today, Left Arrow could be nowhere near the hunters. What to do about him? An idea came to Spotted Wolf, a way in which his son might prove himself useful.

Left Arrow was riding his pinto pony close behind the hunting party, not yet fully part of it. When the men stopped to gather in a circle, he moved his pony in to stand beside his father's horse. No one was going to deny him his rightful place next to the chief of the tribe. He had begged his father over and over, asking to join the men on the next hunting trip. His father had finally said yes.

"Perhaps the gun sellers might appear today," said Spotted Wolf. "We shall hunt nearby if they do." He turned toward Left Arrow. "My son, I give you an important task. You shall remain near this rock to hear if the white men are coming. They make so much noise you will be able to hear them when they are still far away. If they approach, you will call out to us with the warning cry. We will be here to meet them."

It was agreed that while Left Arrow would remain near The Meeting Rock, the six men would pair off into three teams to hunt for black-tailed deer and antelope. Spotted Wolf spoke a prayer to the Great Spirit that six horses would carry fresh meat back to the village today. The youngest of his two sons was determined to make it seven.

"Father," said Left Arrow, "may I still hunt on my own? How will I learn to kill an antelope if I have to stay here? My pony is fast, and so if I move too far from the rock and hear the white men, I can gallop back right away. I know I can do both. Please let me do both. Please, Father."

Chief Spotted Wolf looked at his son with a stern face, but inwardly he was smiling. His son might make a great hunter someday. Perhaps this should be the start of his training. He looked into his son's pleading eyes and pondered his decision. After what seemed like an eternity to Left Arrow he spoke. "My son, you know how to kill a jackrabbit that crosses your path, which is good. But hunting on the open desert is different from hunting on the mountain. To be a great hunter you must seek out your kill. And you are right; you cannot learn to do that from behind this rock. You may ride alone but keep within close distance of The Meeting Rock." The internal smile vanished before Spotted Wolf spoke again. "For today, learn only to follow the antelope's tracks. If you come upon one, do not kill it. We will handle the antelope."

"But Father— "

"Left Arrow," said Spotted Wolf, "I have told you how it is." He was not in the mood for listening to any more of his youngest son's endless pestering. He then remained quiet, pondering over an even greater decision. A Henry rifle hung from a leather thong behind his back. He lifted it over his head. "I have decided to give you my rifle—just this one time. But you are not to hunt with it. If you are in danger, you will fire this rifle twice as a signal for us to come help you. Do you understand this?"

Left Arrow did not betray a smile as he nodded his head, but inside he was beaming with pride. "Yes, Father," he said, solemnly. "If the white men come, I will call out to you. If I am in danger, I will fire the rifle twice." He was proud to show his father how well he remembered what he had been told. And he thought, it would not be his fault if he was practicing shooting arrows and one accidentally found its way into an antelope.

Spotted Wolf leaned forward and extended the rifle to his son, who took it with his left hand. Spotted Wolf then sat erect in the saddle, pointing his finger overhead. "Keep watch on the sun. When it is straight above you, return to The Meeting Rock." But, knowing his son, he added, "If you have become lost, stay where you are. We shall find you by following your tracks. This is why it is an important skill to learn."

Although Spotted Wolf knew that white men had not been seen for months, he also knew the tribe could not relax its guard. Only the white men who brought guns and bullets to trade were allowed onto their lands. All others were unwelcomed and would be chased away or killed. The hunting party would not stray too far from Left Arrow. He would make sure of that.

Left Arrow hung the rifle behind his back as his father had done, but on the opposite shoulder. He had to reposition it so the motion of the pony wouldn't move the rifle butt around as he rode. When he had first been taught to hold a bow and arrow, he had naturally held the bow with his right hand and pulled back the bowstring with his left. His father and brother tried to teach him to reverse his hands, but that ended the first time the boy drew back his arrow left-handed and cleanly hit a running jackrabbit from thirty yards away. That had been last fall. Now he was allowed to join the men as they hunted for bigger game. Not bad for having lived only eight winters.

Now, where to start his own hunt? As he looked around, he thought about his new name, Left Arrow. His father had given it to him after killing the jackrabbit. He was still getting used to it. For the longest time, his name had been Walks-Too-Loud. His older sister had bestowed that upon him the first time he had gone trapping with her and their mother. As the women set about laying snares to catch small animals, the noise the boy made trampling through the brush scared away all animals in the vicinity. Twice they returned to the village with empty traps. Before they set out a third time, his mother gave him a woven basket and the task of collecting piñon nuts that had fallen to the ground. It kept him out of the way, and little Walks-Too-Loud had fun pretending to be a mountain lion hunting deer among the trees. He returned to the village, only to be sent back into the forest to retrieve his forgotten basket.

Left Arrow enjoyed riding in the cooler air of the spring morning. The heat was gradually building; he hoped they would not be hunting this afternoon when the Great Spirit brought on the burning heat. His older brother had told of a trick played by the desert spirits, making heat shimmers look like bodies of water in the desert. These illusive small lakes seemed to be within riding distance yet they always moved beyond reach no matter how far you rode toward them. Left Arrow decided the desert spirits would not fool him if they tried to play that trick on him today. Besides, he was hunting for antelope, not water.

Searching along the ground, he noticed fresh animal tracks leading to The Meeting Rock not too far from where he was sitting his pinto pony. A wide natural passageway split the rock in two halves and stopped at a granite wall with gaps on either side. He moved his pony closer to the passageway, dismounted, and bent down to more closely examine the animal tracks. What luck! They went through the passageway. He hoped they were from an antelope.

As he moved closer, Left Arrow suddenly heard a gunshot from the other side of the wall, followed by what sounded like a man shouting in a language he had never heard before. His moccasins made no sound as he crept along the dirt passageway. Reaching the wall, he stopped to listen. The loud man did not sound very old, maybe as old as his brother or his cousins.

Left Arrow lifted the Henry from behind his back and slowly worked the lever to load a bullet into the chamber. He placed his finger on the trigger so he would be ready to shoot at whoever was on the other side. He was just a little too short to be able to look over the wall, so he slowly inched his way over to one of the gaps. Sneaking his head partly out from behind the wall's edge, he saw a young white man kick an obviously dead horse lying on the ground. The young man shouted again as he hopped on one foot. Left Arrow wished he could understand the words so he would know what about the dead horse had gotten the young man so angry.

Still not being able to see all that he wanted Left Arrow stuck his head out a bit more. The young man was on his knees, pulling something out of a large leather pouch attached to the dead horse. Trying to get a better look at this strange scene, Left Arrow extended his front leg as he stepped further away from the wall. Suddenly, he lost his balance as some loose pebbles skidded under his foot. As he fell, he let out a grunt. His finger pulled the trigger on the rifle, causing it to fire once.

The hunters, spying a dozen elk walking in a single line toward an arroyo, had ranged five hundred yards from the Meeting Rock. From this distance, Chief Spotted Wolf and the men heard three gunshots. The first shot was from a handgun, but it was unclear from which direction it had been fired. A little over a minute passed before they heard a second gunshot, followed a split second later by a third one. Spotted Wolf recognized the second gunshot as coming from his Henry rifle. The third gunshot had been from the same handgun as the first. Now sure of the direction from which the gunfire had sounded, they set off galloping toward The Meeting Rock. Spotted Wolf cursed himself for not keeping his promise to himself. He had allowed his group to drift too far away from his son.

Coming up to the rear of the long rock, they saw Left Arrow's pony standing outside the passageway. Spotted Wolf raised his hand and signaled the men to split into two groups and circle around both sides of the rock. With bows in hand and drawing arrows from their quivers as they rode, they quickly rounded the formation. Now in front of the great rock, they saw Left Arrow lying on the ground, and a white man holding a handgun bent over him.

*****

In the middle of a sagebrush plain, Ike Fleck was cursing himself for his rotten luck in choosing horses to steal. The mare had pulled up lame again. "You had all night to sleep, you dumb horse!" he yelled. He had hoped the animal could gallop all the way to Three Rocks Trace Pedras to make up for all the lost time. But as mad as he was, Ike couldn't bring himself to further injure the horse. He pulled back on the reins to bring the mare to a halt. "Don't nobody know how to take care of their horses around here? There wasn't this many lame animals in the whole Civil War, I bet!" He dismounted and checked the blue dun for an injury. But as every time before, there was none to be seen. He swung back into the saddle and allowed the horse to walk as best it could. He kept turning in the saddle to check his back-trail. Still no sign of dust, but he felt as if he was on borrowed time. No telling how many men would be coming after him.

He was still bothered about robbing the stagecoach. Even when he was stealing the money, in his gut he had known it was wrong. But he couldn't have his older brother always giving him everything—like the .44-40 Merwin Hulbert 2nd Model Frontier double-action revolvers—and the secret stagecoach guard job. He was old enough to stand on his own. That's why he had written that part in the note about killing Garrison if he followed him. It was so Mr. Binghamton would know that stealing the money had been all his idea, and Garrison had nothing to do with it.

Ike wished he knew where Garrison was. But Ike wasn't exactly sure where he was, either. Duke hadn't marked where Three Rocks Trace Pedras was on the map. This was a long trail, and he was already past the two mountains.

In fact, he was only a mile to the east of the area of rock outcroppings known as Tres Piedras.

Ike wondered if he should stop here and wait for Garrison to show up? No, there wasn't any place to hide if that posse or some Indians saw him first. He would keep riding just a little further. He'd find a hiding place near the trail and keep a lookout for Garrison. They'd find the buried Frenchman's gold together and leave the stolen money in its place. Then they would still ride away rich and with no one chasing them.

The morning air was beginning to warm, but the searing heat would come later. Ike was riding into an area of large rock formations, Gambel oak and fir trees scattered among them. The trail led past an enormous boulder, a smaller, table-sized rock with a flat surface sitting in front of it. As the mare limped past the boulder, Ike heard an ominous rattle. Coiled on top of the flat rock, just a few feet from the horse, was a rattlesnake newly wakened from its sleep. The sound of the rattle startled the blue dun, causing it to rear up on its hind legs. With a terror-stricken whinny the mare took off racing down the trail.

"You stupid son of a bitch lying horse!" Ike shouted. Now aware this was no lame horse, he held onto the reins for dear life. He pulled back on them with all his strength but the mare would not slow down. Ike was afraid he'd be bounced from the saddle, the horse and the saddlebags full of money running all the way back to Stovepipe. The mare was rampaging over ground covered with sagebrush and greasewood, heading toward a long rock formation shaped like a band shell.

Ike couldn't see until too late the oncoming rush of holes in the ground hidden among scrub brush. It was a prairie dog town. "Oh shit!" he cried. The holes were everywhere. He didn't know what to do. A hoof found one of the deep holes. The mare was sent crashing down to the ground with a loud snap, and a piercing cry of pain. Ike's mind seized up, but his natural reflexes took over. As the mare fell headfirst, Ike withdrew his boots from the stirrups. Dropping the reins, he pushed down on the horse's neck and vaulted over its lowered head. Instead of tucking his head in to land on his back, he landed on one foot as he hit the ground, his momentum sending him tumbling from the mare. He stopped a few feet away, lying on his back and waiting for the world stop spinning. After the world stabilized, he pushed himself up into a sitting position. His hat hung between his shoulders, held by the leather strap.

His body had survived the fall, somewhat bruised but overall intact. He didn't think he'd broken any bones. He got up and began to run toward the fallen horse. The foot he'd landed on forced him back down to the ground. He had a twisted ankle. Not quite sprained, it still hurt to put weight on the foot. But he had to make it over to the saddlebags with the money. He forced himself onto his feet, focusing on putting one foot in front of the other. Now, *he* was the one limping in pain.

The mare lay on the ground, writhing in its own pain. The right foreleg was broken for real this time. Whinnying and snorting, it was trying vainly to get to its feet. Ike knew what to do. He had watched Uncle Roy dispatch a horse that had suffered a similar fate. He drew one of the revolvers from its holster and tried to aim it at the mare's head. The horse was flailing about, struggling with the agonizing pain and the effort to stand up. Ike placed the gun barrel directly against the side of its head and pulled the trigger.

With a brief cry of shock, the blue dun's head dropped to the ground and lay still. Ike told himself he was glad to have a reason to kill that stupid son of bitch horse, fooling him with that phony lame leg routine. But now he was on foot in a place he knew nothing about. Utes could come swarming down on him at any moment.

Ike then noticed the blue dun had fallen on its right side, trapping the Winchester and the water canteen underneath the carcass. Son of a bitch! He'd been so focused on staying ahead of the posse he'd never gotten the chance to try out the rifle. Now he'd never be able to use it!

It was then he saw one of the saddlebags with the money flattened underneath the weight of the dead horse. Ike was so mad he felt like putting another bullet into the mare's head. But he couldn't afford to waste any more ammunition. He holstered his gun and settled for kicking the mare's back. "You stupid son of a bitch horse! Look what you done to me! I'm glad you're dead!"

The truth was, he was not glad at all. This had greatly changed his plans. He now had to come up with a new plan, not just to remain free, but to stay alive. He wished he was as smart as his brother. Garrison had always made all the plans for both of them. What would Garrison think up in this spot? All Ike could come up with was to stay put and wait for his brother, who was sure to follow his trail and find him. Ike tested the ankle again by putting some weight on it. It was very sore, but he could walk on it. He just couldn't walk very far. There went looking for the Frenchmen's gold all by himself.

So far, he hadn't seen any Utes. Maybe they were still all asleep someplace far from here. Or maybe they were just keeping out of sight, watching him. Ike instinctively wrapped his hands around both guns. He had to get out of plain sight. He looked around for some concealed shelter. There was that big, long rock split in two a few feet away. Maybe he could hide there, but it was off the trail. Maybe there was a way to climb to the top of it. He should be able to see Garrison riding toward him. He'd fire his revolvers and Garrison would know where he was. But why hadn't he tracked him down yet? That's what Garrison did, find outlaws on the run.

For the first time since he had ridden away from the stagecoach, the thought entered Ike's mind: Garrison might not be following him. Maybe he never saw the note. Maybe Mr. Binghamton had put him in jail for being part of the robbery. What if Garrison wanted nothing to do with him because *he'd* become a road agent? Suddenly, Ike felt very alone.

OK, if that's the way things were, he'd take care of himself from now on. Ike looked again at the dead horse. The money in one saddlebag was sitting there, right on top. He thought that he should be happy with the $200,000 he could easily get to, but he didn't ride all this way just to settle for half. He had more than earned all of it.

Ike tried to pull the trapped saddlebag out from under the horse, but it wouldn't budge. He looked around for something to pry the mare's buttock off the ground but there was only the scrub brush. He yelled again in frustration and kicked the horse, hurting his injured ankle. "Son of a bitch!" he shouted as he hopped in pain on one leg.

He'd just have to settle for half, but how was he going to carry twenty bundles of money? He didn't have a knife, so he couldn't cut through leather to free the top saddlebag from the other one. The bundles would just have to be stuffed down his shirt, like he'd done with the food he stole. He got down on his knees, reached into the saddlebag and grabbed two bundles with one hand.

From the long rock formation behind him, Ike heard a grunt followed by a rifle shot. He whipped around, drawing his gun as he turned. He fired once at an Indian boy falling to the ground from behind a rock wall. The bullet hit the boy in the chest. A rifle dropped from his hands before his body flopped to the ground, The Indian boy lay still.

Ike froze, the money in one hand and his gun in the other. He stood up and hurriedly limped over to where the Indian boy lay. Kneeling over him, Ike was in shock. Open, sightless eyes gazed downward from the boy's face, blood spreading across his buckskin shirt. Ike's bullet had pierced the heart as the boy fell.

Ike kept staring at the lifeless body. God, this was just a kid, younger than him. He had never killed a boy before. Engulfed in shock and remorse, he barely heard the sounds of horses behind him. He whirled around and saw a line of six mounted Indian warriors, their bows and arrows pointed directly at him. These had to be the Utes that Duke had talked about. Ike was paralyzed by fright. His lifelong fear of an Indian attack had been realized. "Son of a bitch," he said under his breath.

He managed to rise up from the ground, slowly backing away until he was up against the rock wall. He began to lift his revolver. Maybe he could kill at least two of the Utes and scare off the others.

A bundle of money began to slip from his hand. Reaching down to try to grab it, he heard a blood-curdling war cry. A stabbing pain shot through his left arm as an arrow embedded itself in his shoulder. Ike screamed. Another arrow drove itself deep into his chest. More war cries, and four more arrows buried themselves into his upper body. Ike slid slowly down the wall to a sitting position, one bundle of money still in his hand, a gun held loosely in the other hand. That was how he died.

Chief Spotted Wolf and the other warriors slowly walked their horses up to where Ike's body was slumped against the rock wall. Spotted Wolf dismounted and stood close to Ike, making sure he was dead. He then walked over to Left Arrow, knelt down and gently picked up his son. Cradling the body in his arms, he started on foot toward Bear Mountain. His son's spirit was floating just above the body. He had to return Left Arrow to the mountain to perform the death ceremonies so that his son's spirit would know how reach the afterlife.

Left Arrow's older brother kicked his horse over to where the Henry rifle lay on the ground and leaned down to pick it up. He then rode back to where his father's horse stood, gathered up the reins, and moved his horse to within a few feet of his father to follow behind as he walked. One of Left Arrow's cousins rode behind the two men. The other cousin rode around to the back of the rock to retrieve Left Arrow's pinto pony and then fell in line behind the others. Spotted Wolf's two brothers joined in at the end of the funereal procession, riding one behind the other.

Even though it was a bullet from the white man's gun that killed Left Arrow, Spotted Wolf blamed himself for his son's death. He had given him the rifle and had left him alone. He had known his son had a curious nature, one that had gotten him into trouble before. He should have kept his son with him, protected him from all dangers his curiosity could lead him into.

I should have…I should have. That one thought kept replaying itself in Spotted Wolf's mind. He finally managed to wipe it away along with all conscious thought. He kept his eyes locked on his destination. It was almost twenty miles back to Bear Mountain. Spotted Wolf would walk all the way on foot, carrying his son back home to the village. It was his self-imposed penance. The muscles in his arms would tire, the pain would follow, searing pain so intense it would feel as if his arms would tear themselves from his body. He would withstand the pain. He would work to turn his body into unfeeling stone as he walked. He would not let his son fall from his arms. He would bring Left Arrow home.

The mounted hunting party rode in a single line behind their chief and his fallen son. Not one of them spoke.

CHAPTER 33

Yulin Temple was not happy. He had overslept, waking up just as the sun crested the horizon. He was getting old, he thought. These long rides were a lot harder on his body than they used to be.

As back at the jail, he had to awaken Garrison who had finally fallen asleep an hour before. Garrison was even less happy. With this late start, there was very little chance they would overtake Ike wherever he had camped for the night—if he had had the sense to stop for the night. It could take them that much longer to find him.

The camp was packed up and the horses saddled within ten minutes. With riding through the hills stealing time they couldn't afford to lose, Garrison wished they had made a dry camp closer to the gunrunner's trail. Ike was slipping from his grasp, and it made him feel uneasy.

When they were back on the trail, he was relieved to see the distinctive tracks of the blue dun mare—three shod hoofs with one unshod. Ike had kept to the trail after all. The tracks were fresh enough, no more than a few hours old. This meant they were closing in on him. But Garrison was also worried. While he knew Ike had Gilroy's canteen and most likely filled it at the creek yesterday, he feared for the condition of the mare. They were a long way from that creek, and with the Rio de los Pinos hidden behind those hills, Ike wouldn't come across another source of water if he stuck to the trail. Forced to race down toward New Mexico Territory under sweltering daytime temperatures, the horse might suffer heat stroke—and with a whole damn river running parallel to the trail less than a couple of miles away.

Shortly after crossing the state border, Garrison and Yulin found where the blue dun mare had wandered off toward the Rio San Antonio.

"What's Ike up to now?" asked Garrison. "

"The Rio San Antonio's over that way," said Yulin. "Maybe your brother did something smart for once and camped out at the river overnight."

"He may still be over there. I'm going to find out." Garrison turned his horse to head toward the river.

Yulin, who had kept his horse along the trail, stopped and called out, "Hold up, Garrison. I found some tracks here. Ike returned to the trail. Come take a look."

Garrison quickly reined up, looking at Yulin in confusion and amazement. He rode the sorrel over to where Yulin had stopped. Yes, these were the blue dun's tracks coming back from the river.

Yulin said, "Since your brother doesn't know this country, I'm betting his horse led him to the river last night. Ike was somehow able to find his way back here." He nodded toward the hoofprints. "Those tracks are no more than a couple of hours old. We're getting closer. He's not that far ahead of us."

"I hope you're right. All I know is Ike has a couple of horses to thank for keeping him alive."

Yulin looked at him quizzically but was in no mood to get into it further. He set the bay into a gallop down the trail. Garrison rode past and took the lead.

They rode on through the morning, occasionally but frustratingly slowing their horses to a trot in order to avoid tiring them out before they reached Ike. As they rode, they saw off to the west a sight they had never seen before, one that confused them both. It was a column of six mounted Indians, two of the Indians leading riderless horses. One of the horses was a pinto pony. A seventh Indian walked ahead of the others. Yulin couldn't tell for sure from that distance, but the one on foot might have been carrying something in his arms. The group was traveling in the opposite direction toward Bear Mountain. They had to be Utes from Spotted Wolf's band. But why was that one guy walking? Indians warriors never walked when they could ride.

Acting on intuition, Yulin kicked the bay into a flat-out gallop. Garrison not yet knowing why, allowed Yulin to pass him. A sense of foreboding descended upon him as he looked back at the Utes. Leaning forward in the saddle, he dug his heels into the sorrel and shook the reins, sending the horse sprinting past the bay as the men raced towards Tres Piedras. Whatever they were riding into, Garrison intended to get there first.

Garrison and Yulin followed the tracks down the trail until they saw a little ways off buzzards circling in the sky over a specific area. Garrison's heart sank as he felt twinges of queasiness and apprehension over what he was about to find. The blue dun mare's tracks led to where the buzzards were circling. Garrison kept his horse at a full gallop, Yulin following right behind. The trail led them past the rock where the rattlesnake had spooked the blue dun, sending it into that final run.

When they reined up, they saw a few of the vultures feeding on the mare. Garrison took off riding toward them, then stopped when he saw the prairie dog holes. Setting a course wide around them, he kicked the sorrel back into a gallop, waving his hat and yelling to scare them away. He didn't want to look for Ike just yet.

The winged carnivores rose to rejoin the others still circling overhead. Yulin glanced up as he rode behind Garrison. He'd seen too many of those ugly bastards in his time.

Looking toward the band shell rock, they saw Ike's body slumped upright against the base of the rock wall, about twenty feet away from the dead mare. Luckily, the vultures had chosen the larger carcass of the dead horse to feed upon, leaving Ike's body alone. With the sorrel still in motion, Garrison jumped to the ground and rushed over to his brother.

Yulin reined up, staying on his horse to survey the scene. Looking at what was left of the blue dun, he saw where the right foreleg—the one without a horseshoe—had snapped from the prairie dog hole. Well sir, it looked like ol' Sam wasn't getting Lucy back. The canteen was staying put, too.

He gazed over at Ike's body. It appeared to him the Utes had left their arrows embedded in the kid as a warning to other white trespassers to stay off their land. He visually surveyed the area to piece together what had happened. A few yards off to the side of the prairie dog town, traces of wagon wheel tracks circled in front of that band shell rock. In front of it was a blackened fire pit. Yulin realized this was where the gunrunners came to sell their wares to the Utes and the Jicarilla Apaches. Ike had had no idea what he was riding into, thought Yulin. The kid had indeed followed the wrong trail.

After slowly dismounting from the bay, he walked over to stand behind Garrison, who had fallen to his knees in front of Ike's body. Yulin heard him choking off his grief.

"Ike," Garrison whispered, angrily. He waved a fist in impotent rage. "Oh, Ike," the whisper, gentler now, acknowledging defeat. He unclenched his fist and let it fall. His rage spent, he reached out and brushed his hand across his brother's hair and caressed his cheek.

For the first time in his life, Garrison Fleck cried. He cried for all the wasted years when he was rarely home with Ike, and he cried for all the years he would never have with him. He grinned sardonically; he was the one who made plans, the one who knew everything. That's what Ike had always bragged about, wasn't it? Well, he had thought up this great plan and now Ike was dead. Duke and Gully were both dead. That was all he knew.

He wanted to embrace Ike, to hold his brother tightly to him but he had a grisly job to do first. He lifted Ike's hat by the crown and laid it on the ground next to him. Grasping Ike's shoulders, Garrison delicately laid him on his back. He pulled the bundle of silver certificates from Ike's hand and tossed it next to the other one on the ground. The revolver was not in as tight of a grip. Garrison easily took the gun from Ike's hand and slowly pushed it into the empty holster. He took his knife out of its sheath and set to work digging the arrows out of Ike's body.

Yulin stared at Ike. Seeing the kid's face this close, he realized it didn't look like his memory of Weed at all. How could he have ever thought it did? OK, there was the hangover. But the two boys had had the same blond hair and Weed would've been the same age as Ike had he lived. Suddenly, there it

was: *had he lived*. At some level, Weed and Ike had become tangled together in
his mind. It sounded crazy, Yulin thought, but maybe trying to prevent Ike's
death had been like a second chance at keeping Weed from dying. Or maybe
after a lifetime of ending lives he had wanted to save one, for once. He didn't
know for sure.

But he now realized that Ike's life had never been his to save; the kid had
doomed himself from the start. Yulin was realizing a lot of things now. Back at
the river, Garrison had forced him to confront the truth; Weed was gone and
beyond saving. So was Lillian. It was time to finally let them go and move on
with his life. He glanced over at Garrison. The man was entitled to grieve but
let him bury his guilt along with his brother and move on as well. Living with
ghosts makes a man just as dead.

Yulin examined Ike more closely. He counted the number of arrows
embedded in the body. Why so many when one well-aimed arrow would have
killed him outright? Why the hell would Ute warriors make such an example of
one lone rider? He hoped to have time to find answers to these questions.
There was no way of knowing if the Utes would return.

Yulin again surveyed the scene around him. Long ago he had become
adept at reading sign. Usually if you pieced enough of them together, they told
a story. He wanted to know the story behind what had happened here, why Ike
had been so brutally murdered.

He saw the tracks of six unshod horses assembled near where his own
horse stood. Two sets of a man's large moccasin prints led from the horses
over to the band shell rock and back again. The first set led to fresh
bloodstains in the dirt to the side of the rock wall. There, he saw vague outlines
of what might have been a small body—a child's body, perhaps. He crouched
down for a closer look. The body had fallen to the ground facing away from
the wall. Yulin stood up and followed the tracks. The owner of the moccasin
prints had stooped to gather up the child and then walked back to the horses.
No, he continued walking past them, still carrying the child.

Returning to where the body had lain, he saw scuff marks and some
scattered pebbles. The child could have tripped over those pebbles and fallen,
right there where the blood stains were. A pair of child's moccasin prints led
through the passageway and out behind the band shell rock. Finding where an
Indian pony had stood, he saw the tracks of those same unshod horses a few
feet away. All the horses had been ridden around to the front of the rock.

He nudged the brim of his hat upwards with his finger, his mind working
to figure out the story of what had occurred. He remembered that Ute
procession heading toward Bear Mountain, the warrior on foot carrying
something in his arms. Why would the others follow behind *him* unless…?

Then it hit him. That kid from the teepee years ago. He might be old
enough to ride with the men now. Then he knew for sure. The Ute on foot in
front of the others was Spotted Wolf, walking back toward the mountain with

his son's body in his arms. Those two riderless horses—one of them had been a pony. His son's pony.

Yulin walked back through the passageway and stood near Garrison. He knew if he checked Ike's revolver, there would be at least two empty cartridges in the cylinder. Ike had killed the blue dun out of necessity. And then he had shot and killed Chief Spotted Wolf's son—probably after the boy tripped and fell. The arrows sticking out of Ike's body were not a warning, but a summary execution for a murderer. What terror must have filled the last seconds of the kid's life, facing the Utes with their drawn arrows pointed at him. There was no reason to tell Garrison what the story was here. Yulin hoped Garrison would never feel the need to ask.

Garrison had finished his grisly, agonizing work. He felt trapped inside another nightmare, but this time the nightmare was real. Still on his knees, he clutched Ike's body to his. He slowly moved back into a sitting position, and cradled Ike's head in his lap. He lovingly stroked Ike's hair, stroking it the way he had back at the Crossing, sitting by the fire with Uncle Roy all those years ago.

This was the moment he had always feared, but at the same time knew would someday come. Ike's fate was sealed the day he first held a gun. His bad decision to take that money from the stage had led to irreversible consequences. Garrison reflected on all the death that had permeated his life, death that had robbed him of everyone he had ever loved. Was this some great universal plan, or just random, catastrophic events happening one after another? It didn't matter; Ike was dead either way.

A strong resolve welled up inside him as he gently laid Ike back on the ground and got to his feet, the front of his shirt covered in blood. He walked over to the sorrel and led it to where Ike lay. "I'll be damned if I'll leave my brother out here alone," he said. He untied the bedroll from behind the saddle and carried it along with the ropes over to Ike's body, dropping them on the ground. He tied the two ropes together.

He spread the blanket out. Lifting Ike's body off the ground, he felt something in a back pocket of the jeans. After laying Ike down on the blanket, Garrison reached into the pocket and pulled out the deerskin map. He unfolded it and stared at the expert craftsmanship. So, this was Duke's map. There had been a crude copy of it on Hank Bellum—the one Conley had given to him. Yes, he would pay Conley a visit back in Pueblo.

Garrison folded the map and returned it to the jeans pocket. It belonged to Ike now. He picked up Ike's hat and placed it on his brother's head, gently laying the chinstrap against his neck. He took one last look at Ike's face, memorizing every feature. Ike could have been asleep. Garrison felt his tears welling up again, but he held them back. He had another job to finish first.

He extended Ike's hands and feet. After wrapping the blanket around Ike like a shroud, Garrison picked him up and stood alongside the sorrel mare. Yulin walked over to hold the bridle, gentling the horse by rubbing its snout. Garrison slung Ike's body over the saddle and looped one end of the rope around Ike's wrists. He ran it under the mare's belly and looped the other end around Ike's ankles, taking up the slack and tying off the rope. Satisfied that the body was tightly secured to the saddle, Garrison walked over to where the two bundles of silver certificates lay on the ground. He picked them up and stuffed them inside one of his saddlebags.

Yulin had gone back to the bay, taken his rope from the saddle and begun to uncoil it. He planned to use his horse to lift the blue dun's dead carcass to free the trapped saddlebag underneath. Maybe the Winchester was still usable, too.

Garrison saw what Yulin intended to do. "Hold off, Yulin," he said, "leave Gilroy's horse be. Binghamton can fetch his own damn money."

Yulin looked at Garrison, standing defiantly in that bloodied shirt. He coiled the rope and placed it back on the pommel. The stock on the Winchester was probably busted anyway.

It was nearing midday. Yulin was sure they'd never make the Colorado border before dark. He suddenly noticed six Ute warriors sitting their horses about two hundred yards away, watching. He decided not to say anything to Garrison.

"If you're all set, we better go," said Yulin. "We've got six hours before sunset. I want to bed down where I can be sure I'll wake up in the morning. You gonna walk the whole way?"

"Yes," said Garrison, "I'm going to lead my brother to safety." He took the sorrel's reins in one hand and started walking the trail. It was twenty-five miles back to the border.

Yulin mounted the bay and fell in behind Garrison. He rode with one hand holding the reins, the other hand resting on his thigh near the shotgun. He turned his head slightly to look at the Utes. The Indians were moving too, riding parallel to the trail while maintaining their distance. Slowly, he moved his right hand to the holster, slipping the thong from the hammer on the Schofield. He carefully moved his hand back near the shotgun.

The sun burned white hot upon their heads as they made their way across the Taos Plateau. Sweat ran down Yulin's face. There was a scarf in his shirt pocket, but he never touched it. He knew Garrison had to be wilting under the desert heat, but the man never betrayed any trace of fatigue or thirst. This Garrison Fleck had stamina he had rarely seen in other men. The detective was not someone Yulin would ever want to have on his trail.

The warriors kept their distance, allowing Yulin the momentary distraction of gazing around him. Heat shimmers rose from the desert floor in all directions. Across the hazy miles to the east, he could see the dormant volcano that was Ute Mountain, mirrored by Bear Mountain to the west.

Looking up, he saw the cloudless cobalt blue sky that always inspired awe in him. High above, a red-tailed hawk glided in lazy circles, riding across the air currents as it searched below for food. A palette of earthen desert colors of reds, oranges, and tans infused the mountains and rock formations. A strong, warm breeze picked up from the southeast, filling him with a longing for something he could not define. No, that wasn't true, he knew exactly what it was. It was no longer whiskey; those days were over and done. He was tired of riding the trail alone. He wanted a life with Reva. He hoped she would be waiting for him when he returned.

Garrison's pace never flagged as he led the sorrel carrying Ike's body, keeping his eyes glued on the trail ahead. Yulin occasionally glanced at their Ute escort, still two hundred yards off to their side. Eight hours passed but Garrison never stopped to rest. The sun had already set, but at 8,000 feet up on the Plateau, its reddish orange glow remained visible above the peaks of the Tusas Mountains.

There was a chill in the night air, yet neither man put on his coat. An hour later, moonlight had replaced the sun's faded glow. The blues, purples and blacks of the night sky surrounded the infinite pinpoints of light from the stars. Somewhere they passed the invisible line that marked the Colorado border. Yulin again turned his eyes toward their mounted escort. In the luminescent twilight, he could see the Utes were gone.

CHAPTER 34

Garrison Fleck and Yulin Temple were standing on the boardwalk in front of Ben Aldenburg's funeral parlor. It had been two days since the men arrived back in town. The undertaker and his assistant had finished loading Ike's casket onto a buckboard wagon Garrison had rented from Gomez. Garrison's saddle and gear were already in the wagon bed. The two undertakers laid a canvas tarpaulin over the casket and tied it to the wagon with ropes to hold the casket in place.

 Hitched to the wagon was the black gelding along with a gentle but sturdy chestnut mare. Together, they had the strength and stamina to pull the buckboard over La Veta Pass to El Moro. The bench seat, positioned over the flatbed, would enable Garrison to keep an eye on the tarpaulin-covered casket beneath him. This would be his last journey alone with Ike. He could look down and talk to him, even pretend Ike was sitting next to him on the bench seat. The irony of it all struck him like a cruel joke. He finally had time to spend with his brother, it was just a little too late.

 The heat wave had finally broken. A cold front now settled over the region with the promise of snow in the mountains, but not enough to slow the journey. The cold weather would help preserve Ike's body, packed in ice inside the casket. At the El Moro railroad station, the casket would be loaded into a freight car with Garrison watching over it all the way to Denver. He had wired money ahead to a livery stable to have a horse and wagon waiting when the train arrived. From the station, he would shepherd his brother the final leg of the journey back to the ranch in Boulder.

 Aldenburg and his assistant stepped onto the boardwalk. "We got 'er fastened down good and tight, Mr. Fleck. That box won't be slidin' around none when you make your way over the Sanger Crista range."

 Garrison inwardly flinched at the word "box", as if Ike was just mere cargo now. "I appreciate the extra work you men put in," he said, handing the undertaker his fee plus an extra silver dollar. They shook hands and then Aldenburg and his assistant walked back inside the funeral parlor. Garrison stepped down into the street and walked up to the buckboard. He pulled on the ropes, checking their tautness and the strength of the knots although he knew they were fine. His hand caressed the tarpaulin just above where Ike's head was resting. Yulin stepped down from the boardwalk to stand next to him.

"We got a ranch in a pocket canyon northwest of Boulder," Garrison said. "There's a stand of box elders overlooking a creek that runs through our land. Pretty, little spot. It's where we buried Uncle Roy. Ike will feel right proud lying next to his uncle. He'll always have— "

Garrison choked up, the words almost refusing to budge from his throat. "He'll always have family to look after him. And Uncle Roy was the best there was. Better 'n' me."

Yulin didn't know what to say. The best he could come up with was, "Think Binghamton will get upset about you leaving his money back there in the Territory?"

"I don't give a damn about him or his money anymore. I'm done with all of it. All I'm thinking about is getting Ike home." As was his habit, Garrison sought distraction from unpleasant thoughts by changing the subject. "Gomez said he'd ride out to El Moro to retrieve his buckboard and the mare when he gets around to it."

"Yeah, he will," said Yulin, just trying to make conversation. "You planning on catching the train at Uptop to take you over to Walsenburg?"

Garrison lowered his head towards the wooden casket. "No. Heading straight out to El Moro. I want it to be just me and Ike for a while."

Yulin was quiet for a moment, trying to find the right words to say next. "I'm sorry it ended this way, Garrison."

Garrison paused, still trying to suppress his emotions. "Yeah, well, that's how it happens sometimes. I think I knew it was always going to end this way, finding Ike…dead. That's what my dream was telling me, Yulin, all that time." He glared into the distance. "Ike did something stupid and paid the price. Hell, If I'd caught him first I might've shot him myself."

Yulin took the makin's out of his shirt pocket and began to roll a cigarette. He handed the finished cigarette to Garrison and lit it for him. Garrison took a drag.

"I did wire Binghamton telling him where he could find his money," said Garrison. "Felt I owed him that much. He can send Tate Mallory after it."

Yulin rolled a cigarette for himself and lit it. Deciding not to blow a smoke ring this time, he simply exhaled the smoke. "What about that station agent in Pueblo?"

"Conley? I'd love to put a bullet through his skull right now," Garrison snapped. A tangible darkness, like a menacing storm cloud, descended upon his face. Then just like a cloud, it seemed to move on. When he spoke again, the anger appeared to have moved on as well. But inwardly, it consumed him almost as much as the grief. He chose to conceal it from Yulin. "But he's not my problem anymore."

He stood there for a moment. "Ike always wanted to go see Deadwood, see the chair Hickok was shot dead in, like it was a damn shrine or something." He took another drag on the cigarette. "Ike was all the family I had left. Now I got no one." There was a distant look in his misted eyes. "I'm twenty-seven years old and never been all alone before. It's strange, you know?"

Yulin took a drag from his cigarette. "Yeah, I know." Reva flashed into his mind. As much as he wanted to see her, he had avoided it since coming back to town. But she had made no attempts to see him, either. Yeah, that's the way it happens sometimes, he thought. Reva...

Garrison looked at him. "Does it ever get better?"

Yulin took one last drag, then dropped the cigarette to the ground and crushed it with his boot. "I'm the wrong man to ask. I don't know what 'better' is. But I've been told that if you want it to, yeah...it can get better. Just might take a helluva long time."

"I guess." Garrison paused. "I was thinking. After I take Ike back to Boulder and, uh, lay him to rest, I might head out to Deadwood myself. I think Ike would want me to."

Yulin had nothing to say.

Garrison tossed his cigarette away. He looked as if something was pressing on his mind. He reached into his coat pocket and pulled out an overstuffed white envelope. He looked at it for a moment, then held it out to Yulin. "There's a $20,000 reward for capturing Ike. "

Yulin took the envelope and opened the gummed flap. Inside were the two $10,000 bundles Ike had taken from the saddlebag. "The reward's a thousand dollars," said Yulin. "But I'm not the one who brought Ike back here." He closed the envelope and handed it back.

Garrison placed his hand over Yulin's. "You read the poster wrong, Yulin. It was twenty thousand. And it doesn't matter who brought him back. Goddamn it, man. Ike had to die for *something*, and not just because he made a stupid choice. It has to bring some good to somebody else, the second chance Ike was hoping for."

Second chance. Yulin was taken aback by his own words coming back at him. He looked into Garrison's eyes. Tears were glistening in the late morning sun.

"Take it, Yulin. Take it and marry that girl and get the hell away from here," Garrison said. "Take her further out west and start a new life. Start a new family." Garrison's eyes pleaded with him. "Yulin, for God's sake, take it," he said in quiet desperation. He released Yulin's hand.

Yulin held onto the envelope. His mind echoed back to when he had forced Emmett to take the money from the sale of their herd, along with sole ownership of the ranch. He glanced at the envelope and looked again at Garrison's face. "OK, I'll think on it. You never can tell. I just might." He smiled and stuffed the envelope in his coat pocket.

Garrison returned the smile and extended his hand. Yulin grasped it warmly. They shook hands firmly, acknowledging the deep bond they had forged between them. Garrison withdrew his hand and walked over to the wagon. He climbed up onto the seat, sat down and grabbed the reins. "You joked about it with Reva but why not do it for real? Someone who fell into some money could do right well in California. If he had the right woman, he could do twice as good—specially in San Francisco. I hear they have good sourdough there, too." He grinned.

"Like I said, I'll think on it. I'm going to give a lot of things some thought. You take care, Garrison. Maybe we'll run into each other again someday."

"You never can tell. We just might," said Garrison.

Yulin turned his back and started to walk away when Garrison called to him, "Sure glad you had that scattergun when those Utes were following us."

Turning around, Yulin stared at him, dumbfounded.

Garrison smiled broadly. He shook the reins, clicked his tongue and with a "H'ya" started the horses moving forward.

Yulin gave a slight grin and patted the envelope inside his coat pocket. As Garrison drove off in the buckboard, Yulin walked in the opposite direction toward Reva's Café. Food, however, was not on his mind.

Chapter 35

Reva was already setting tables for dinner when he entered the café. She looked up, hesitated, then returned to her work.

Yulin walked up, took a stack of plates from her hands and set them down on the table. Reva stood there looking apprehensive. He lifted her head up and kissed her deeply, hungrily. She embraced him, almost throwing herself against his body as his arms encircled her.

"I was wrong, Reva," he said, holding her tightly to him. "I never stopped grieving for Lillian and Weed. It almost cost me the wife I'm going to have." He stepped back and gently took both of her hands in his. "Reva Delgado, will you marry me?"

Reva was silent and gazed downward. Her face wore a serious expression, yet there was a hint of mischief playing around the corners of her mouth. "No, Yulin. Reva Delgado won't marry you." Yulin stood there confused, letting her hands fall from his. A grin spread slowly across her lips. "But if you ask Eula Mae Sundstrom to marry you, she just might say yes," she said.

Yulin stared at her in confusion.

Eula laughed nervously. "It's my real name, silly. I'm not really from Argentina."

"I figured that from the beginning," said Yulin. "I knew you were from someplace, just not goddamn Argentina." His expression shifted from agitation back to warmth and tenderness. He gazed at Eula's beauty, smiling as he caressed her face. "It's like meeting you for the first time all over again."

She grinned, coyly. "You hiding any secret identity I should know about?"

"Do you really think I could make up a name like Yulin Temple?" he asked.

They laughed gently at each other. Yulin grasped her hands again and drew her close. "Eula Mae Sundstrom, will you marry me?"

"Of course I will, Yulin Temple!" They embraced each other tightly, exultant in their love. Eula began to giggle against his chest.

"What's that about?" asked Yulin.

"It just occurred to me," said Eula. "Yulin and Eula Temple. People will joke about our names."

Yulin grinned. "Let them joke. It doesn't matter. Long as I can still call you Reva in bed."

"Oh, maybe sometimes. We'll see…" Eula said coquettishly. She flashed a sly smile, her lips slightly parted in a way that always made him feel weak inside. "Does your fiancée get a kiss?"

"How's this?" asked Yulin, pulling her to him again. He kissed her deeply, passionately.

When their lips parted, Eula smiled. "Mmmm, it'll do…for now."

She took the pins out of her hair, gently shaking her head as the honey-blonde tresses fell to her shoulders. Yulin lovingly studied her beautiful Swedish face, slowly gliding his fingertips across her cheek, then into the softness of her hair. He gazed into her blue eyes. They kissed again, just as passionately, both knowing this time it would do forever.

****

After Eula accepted Yulin's marriage proposal he told her about the money Garrison had given him. They both agreed that it was better to wait a few weeks before enacting plans to depart Stovepipe for California. Still calling herself Reva, she offered to sell her café back to Chet Carson, who proved to be an eager buyer. It wasn't until after the deal closed and the money securely in her handbag that Carson learned of Rita's true identity. He then realized she had bought and sold the property illegally, using a false name. He threatened to sue her in court for fraud but one look from Yulin silenced him.

Four weeks later, the newlyweds were seated in a horse-drawn freight wagon loaned to them by Armando Gomez. The wagon was loaded with everything they could pack in the wagon bed, including Eula's sourdough starter. Yulin had sold his bay gelding to Gomez, who would ride behind them to the new Alamosa train station. From Alamosa, the newlyweds would begin their long journey to San Francisco and their new life.

Mayor Chet Carson, the town council and the townspeople gathered around the wagon to say good-bye. Phipps said, "Where you headed to, Sheriff and Mrs. Temple?"

Yulin smiled. "I hear they need a new sheriff in Carson City…Nevada."

Everyone looked at Carson and laughed. The mayor awkwardly joined in, his eyes shooting bullets through the ex-sheriff's skull.

Eula folded her arms around Yulin's arm and snuggled against him. Yulin whistled and shook the reins. The wagon pulled out, starting the Temples' journey to their future, at last freed from the past. For the present, their destination was California. But the future would decide that. And whatever the future had in store for them, Yulin and Eula Temple would meet it together.

ACKNOWLEDGMENTS

I would like to thank my son Kyle who helped inspire the Ike Fleck character, and my daughter Courtney who suggested a change that inspired the Gully Walton character. My love and appreciation to Aunt Trudy Boltuch who kept me motivated to finish and publish the book while she was still around to read it.

A sheepish thank you goes to Mitch Metcalf who spent decades telling me what a great writer I was and should write a book. It took decades for me to believe he was right.

My heartfelt thanks goes to thank Thaddeus Cooper and Kevin B. Kreitman for serving as mentors and guides through the self-publishing process and put in the work to help convert my manuscript into an actual book.

I'd also like to thank Richard Ferrell and Glenn Gilbert for reading later drafts of the book and giving me much needed feedback. Thanks also to Susan Osada for being a reliable reader and commenter on my "book page" on Facebook. Thanks also to Eileen Rogers, Margaret Rinearson, Christine Steichmann, and Tom Thompson for their encouragement while I was writing the book.

Made in the USA
Coppell, TX
18 December 2020